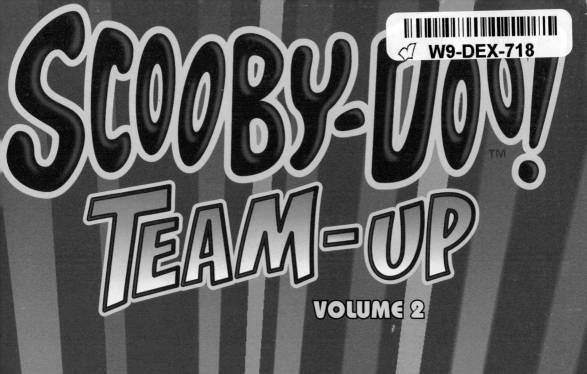

SCOOBY-DOO! TEAM-UP

VOLUME 2

Sholly Fisch Writer **Dario Brizuela** **Scott Jeralds** Artists
Franco Riesco **Wendy Broome** Colorists
Saida Temofonte Letterer **Dario Brizuela** with **Franco Riesco** Cover Artists

Superman Created by **Jerry Siegel** and **Joe Shuster**
By special arrangement with the **Jerry Siegel family**
Batman created by **Bob Kane**
Harley Quinn created by **Paul Dini** and **Bruce Timm**

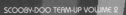

SCOOBY-DOO TEAM-UP VOLUME 2

Published by DC Comics. Compilation Copyright © 2015
Hanna-Barbera. All Rights Reserved.

Originally published online as SCOOBY-DOO TEAM-UP Digital
Chapters 13-24 Copyright © 2015 Hanna-Barbera. All Rights
Reserved.

Copyright © Hanna-Barbera SCOOBY-DOO, THE FLINTSTONES,
THE JETSONS, JONNY QUEST, SECRET SQUIRREL and all related
characters and elements are ™ & © Hanna-Barbera (s15)

Copyright © DC Comics SUPERMAN, BATGIRL, CATWOMAN,
HARLEY QUINN, POISON IVY and all related characters and
elements are ™ & © DC COMICS (s15)

The stories, characters and incidents featured in this publica-
tion are entirely fictional. DC Comics does not read or accept
unsolicited ideas, stories or artwork.

DC Comics, 4000 Warner Blvd., Burbank, CA 91522
A Warner Bros. Entertainment Company.
Printed by RR Donnelley, Salem, VA, USA. 10/9/15.
First Printing.
ISBN: 978-1-4012-5859-7

Library of Congress Cataloging-in-Publication Data

Fisch, Sholly.
Scooby-Doo team-up. Volume 2 / Sholly Fisch, Dario Brizuela.
pages cm
ISBN 978-1-4012-5859-7 (paperback)
1. Graphic novels. I. Brizuela, Dario, illustrator. II. Title.
PZ7.7.F57Sbo 2015
741.5'973—dc23
2015012138

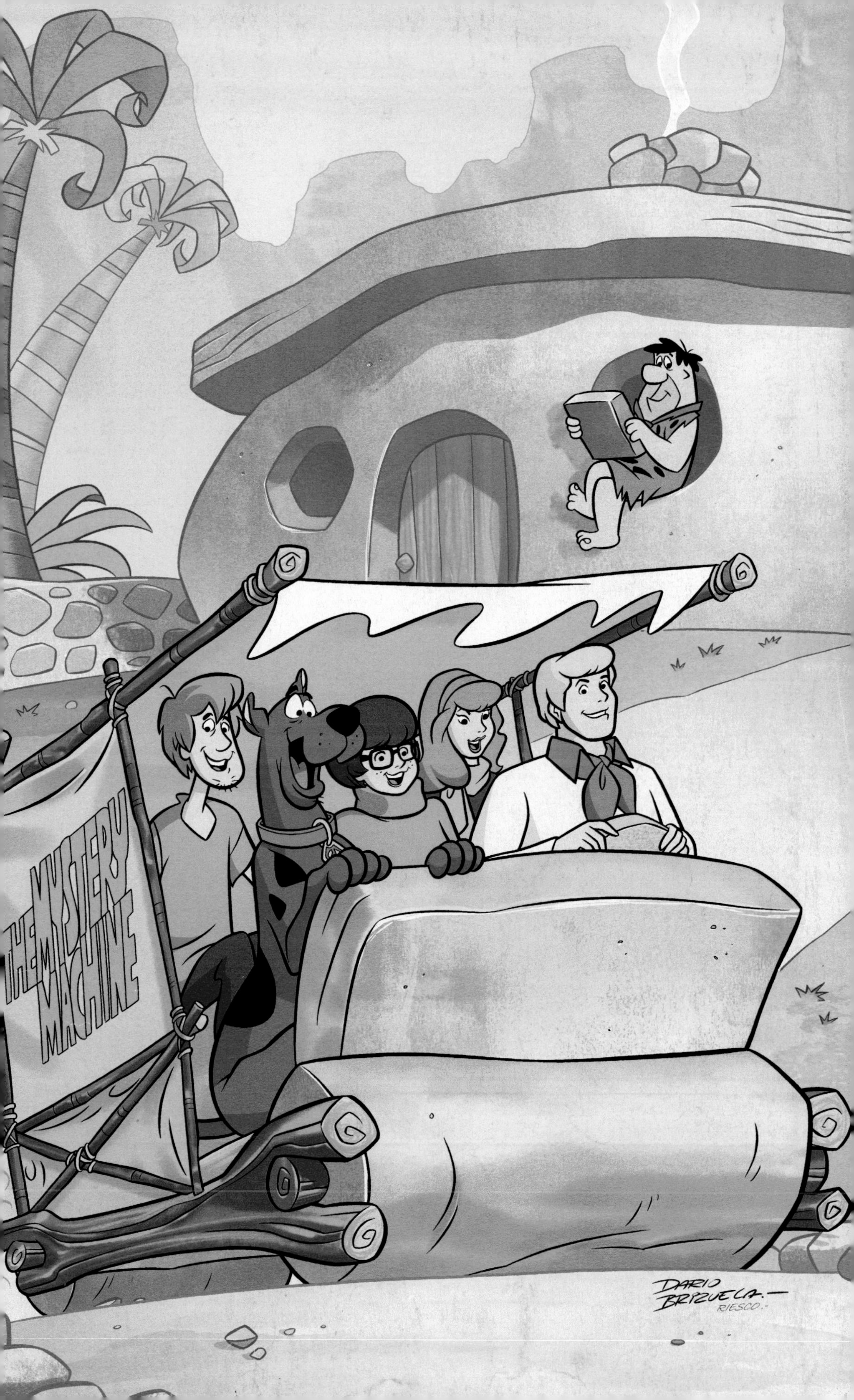
THE MYSTERY MACHINE
DARIO BRIZUELA
RIESCO

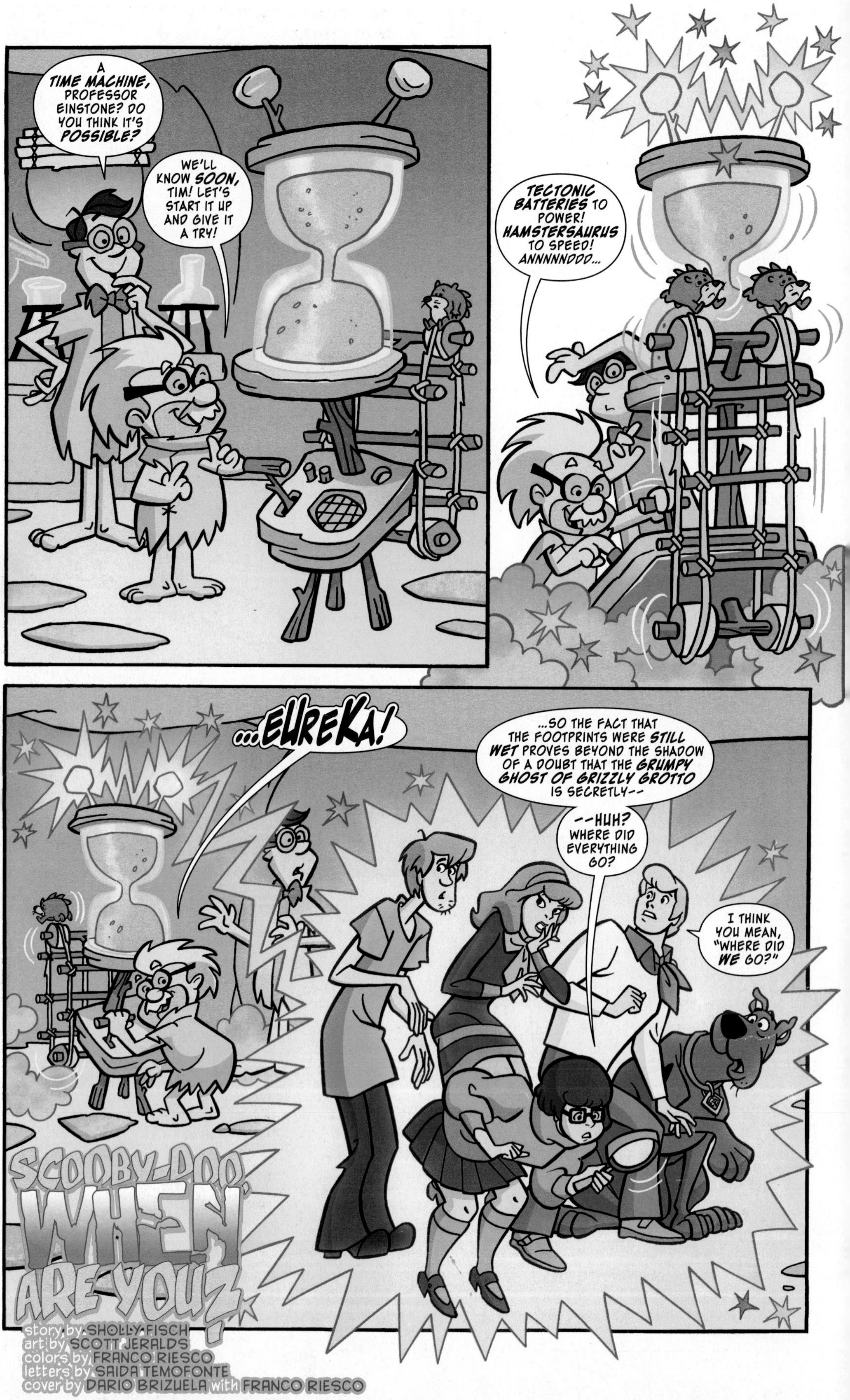

A TIME MACHINE, PROFESSOR EINSTONE? DO YOU THINK IT'S POSSIBLE?
WE'LL KNOW SOON, TIM! LET'S START IT UP AND GIVE IT A TRY!
TECTONIC BATTERIES TO POWER! HAMSTERSAURUS TO SPEED! ANNNNNDDD...
...EUREKA!
...SO THE FACT THAT THE FOOTPRINTS WERE STILL WET PROVES BEYOND THE SHADOW OF A DOUBT THAT THE GRUMPY GHOST OF GRIZZLY GROTTO IS SECRETLY--
--HUH? WHERE DID EVERYTHING GO?
I THINK YOU MEAN, "WHERE DID WE GO?"
SCOOBY-DOO, WHEN ARE YOU?
story by: SHOLLY FISCH
art by: SCOTT JERALDS
colors by: FRANCO RIESCO
letters by: SAIDA TEMOFONTE
cover by DARIO BRIZUELA with FRANCO RIESCO

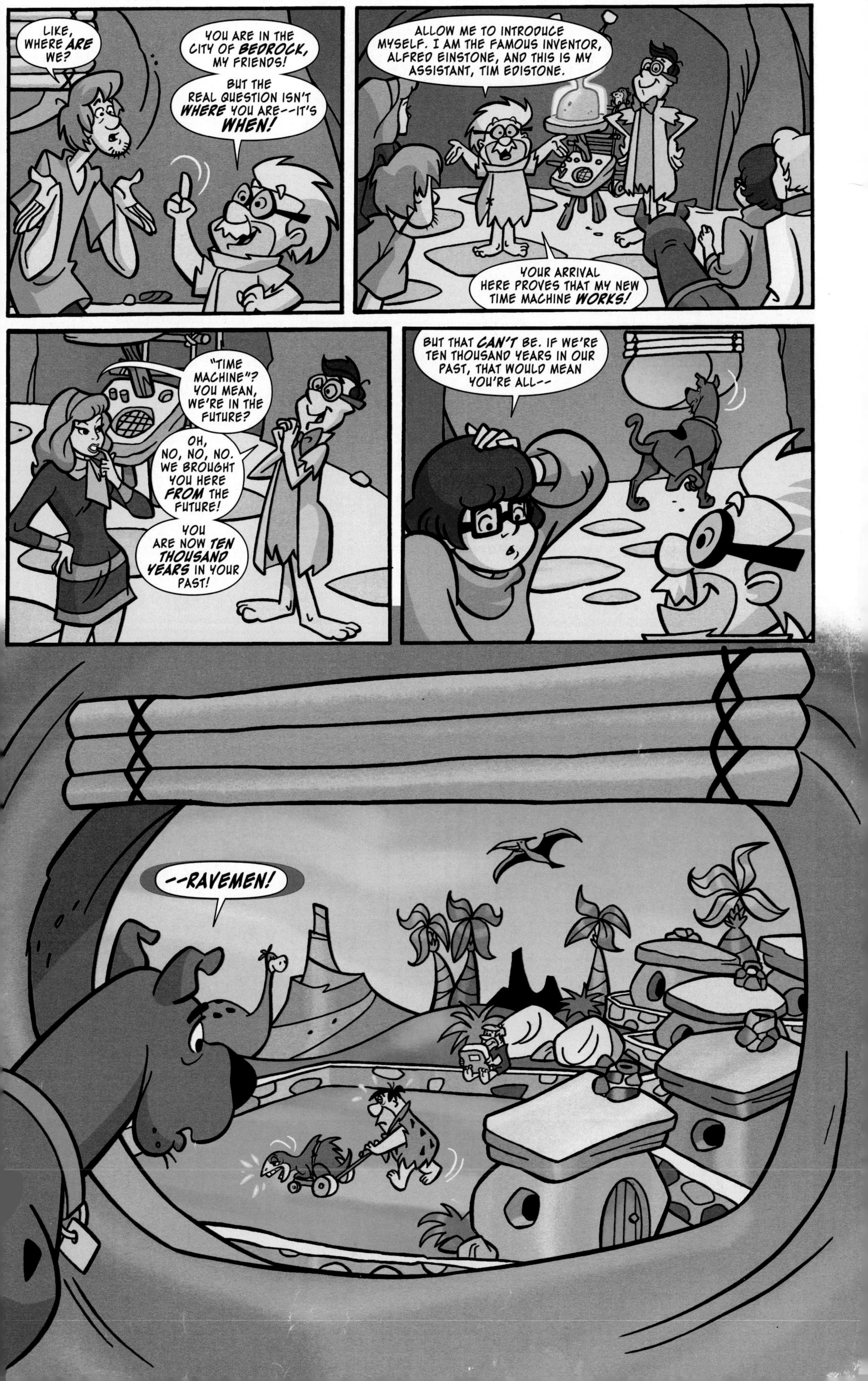

LIKE, WHERE ARE WE?
YOU ARE IN THE CITY OF BEDROCK, MY FRIENDS!
BUT THE REAL QUESTION ISN'T WHERE YOU ARE--IT'S WHEN!
ALLOW ME TO INTRODUCE MYSELF. I AM THE FAMOUS INVENTOR, ALFRED EINSTONE, AND THIS IS MY ASSISTANT, TIM EDISTONE.
YOUR ARRIVAL HERE PROVES THAT MY NEW TIME MACHINE WORKS!
"TIME MACHINE"? YOU MEAN, WE'RE IN THE FUTURE?
OH, NO, NO, NO. WE BROUGHT YOU HERE FROM THE FUTURE!
YOU ARE NOW TEN THOUSAND YEARS IN YOUR PAST!
BUT THAT CAN'T BE. IF WE'RE TEN THOUSAND YEARS IN OUR PAST, THAT WOULD MEAN YOU'RE ALL--
--RAVEMEN!

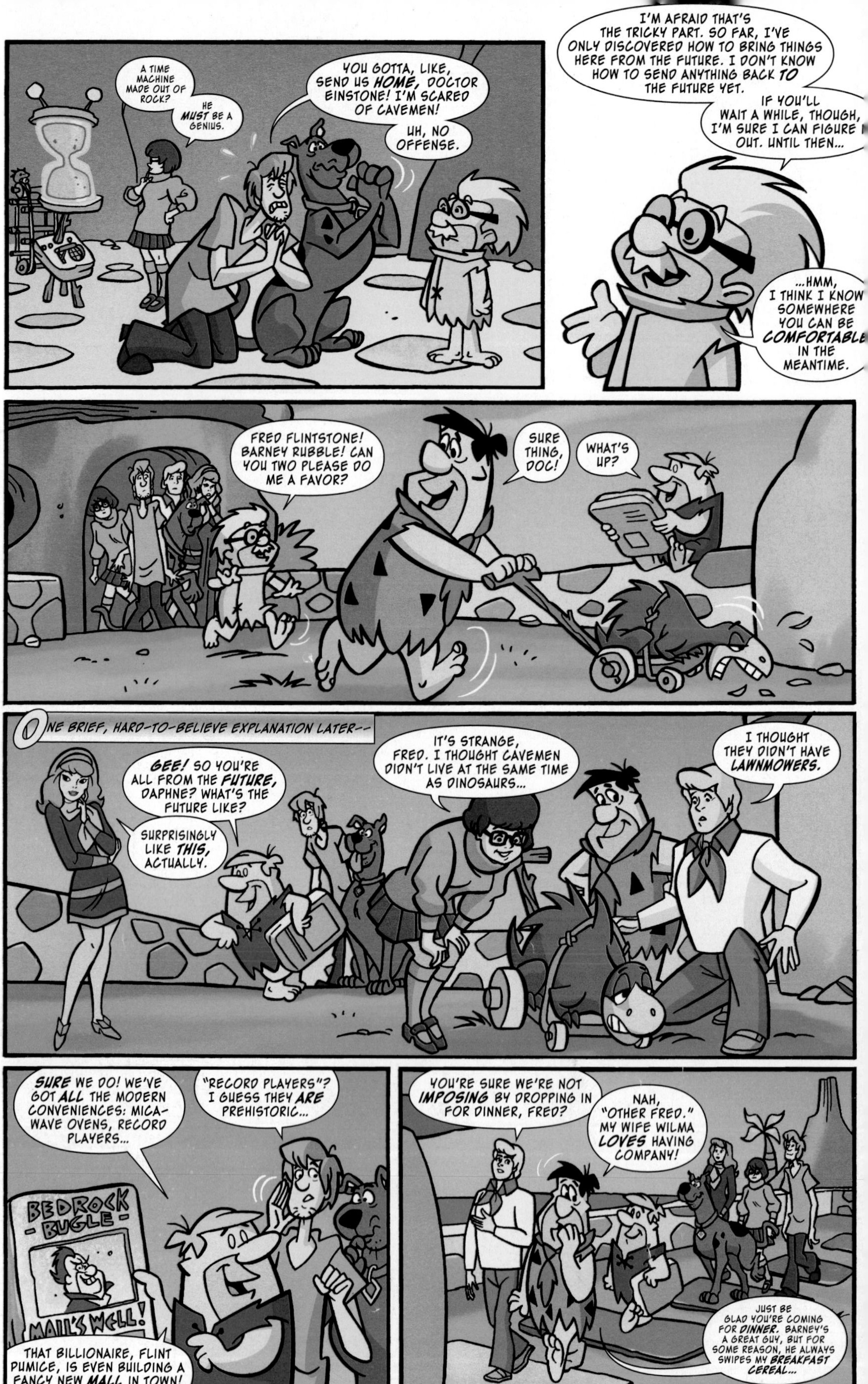
A TIME MACHINE MADE OUT OF ROCK?
HE *MUST* BE A GENIUS.
YOU GOTTA, LIKE, SEND US *HOME,* DOCTOR EINSTONE! I'M SCARED OF CAVEMEN!
UH, NO OFFENSE.
I'M AFRAID THAT'S THE TRICKY PART. SO FAR, I'VE ONLY DISCOVERED HOW TO BRING THINGS HERE FROM THE FUTURE. I DON'T KNOW HOW TO SEND ANYTHING BACK *TO* THE FUTURE YET.
IF YOU'LL WAIT A WHILE, THOUGH, I'M SURE I CAN FIGURE I OUT. UNTIL THEN...
...HMM, I THINK I KNOW SOMEWHERE YOU CAN BE *COMFORTABLE* IN THE MEANTIME.
FRED FLINTSTONE! BARNEY RUBBLE! CAN YOU TWO PLEASE DO ME A FAVOR?
SURE THING, DOC!
WHAT'S UP?
ONE BRIEF, HARD-TO-BELIEVE EXPLANATION LATER--
GEE! SO YOU'RE ALL FROM THE *FUTURE,* DAPHNE? WHAT'S THE FUTURE LIKE?
SURPRISINGLY LIKE *THIS,* ACTUALLY.
IT'S STRANGE, FRED. I THOUGHT CAVEMEN DIDN'T LIVE AT THE SAME TIME AS DINOSAURS...
I THOUGHT THEY DIDN'T HAVE *LAWNMOWERS.*
SURE WE DO! WE'VE GOT *ALL* THE MODERN CONVENIENCES: MICA-WAVE OVENS, RECORD PLAYERS...
"RECORD PLAYERS"? I GUESS THEY *ARE* PREHISTORIC...
BEDROCK BUGLE
MALL'S WELL!
THAT BILLIONAIRE, FLINT PUMICE, IS EVEN BUILDING A FANCY NEW *MALL* IN TOWN!
YOU'RE SURE WE'RE NOT *IMPOSING* BY DROPPING IN FOR DINNER, FRED?
NAH, "OTHER FRED." MY WIFE WILMA *LOVES* HAVING COMPANY!
JUST BE GLAD YOU'RE COMING FOR *DINNER.* BARNEY'S A GREAT GUY, BUT FOR SOME REASON, HE ALWAYS SWIPES MY *BREAKFAST CEREAL...*

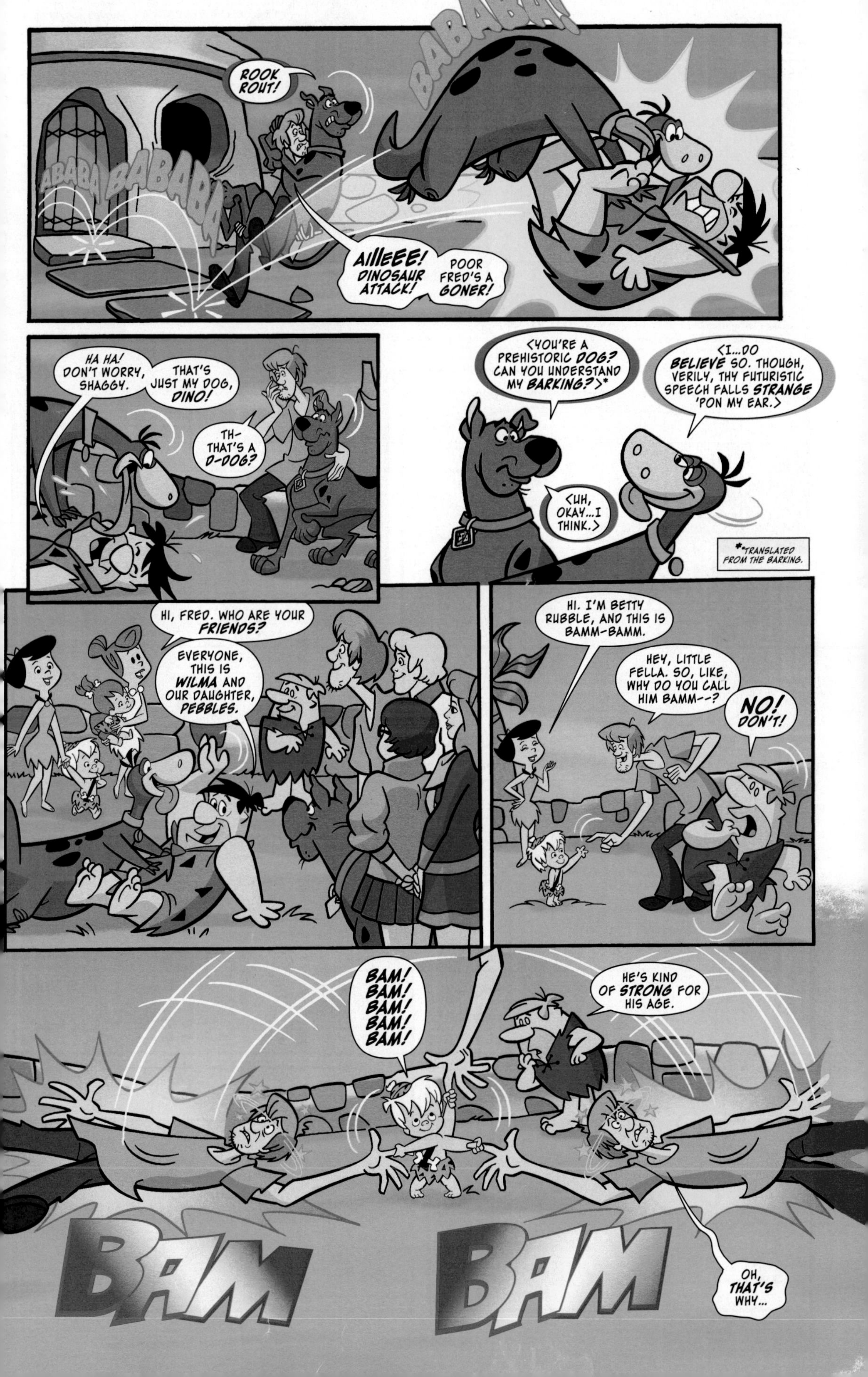
BABABA!
ROOK ROUT!
ABABA BABABA BABABA
AIIEEE! DINOSAUR ATTACK!
POOR FRED'S A GONER!
HA HA! DON'T WORRY, SHAGGY.
THAT'S JUST MY DOG, DINO!
TH-THAT'S A D-DOG?
<YOU'RE A PREHISTORIC DOG? CAN YOU UNDERSTAND MY BARKING?>*
<I...DO BELIEVE SO. THOUGH, VERILY, THY FUTURISTIC SPEECH FALLS STRANGE 'PON MY EAR.>
<UH, OKAY...I THINK.>
*TRANSLATED FROM THE BARKING.
HI, FRED. WHO ARE YOUR FRIENDS?
EVERYONE, THIS IS WILMA AND OUR DAUGHTER, PEBBLES.
HI. I'M BETTY RUBBLE, AND THIS IS BAMM-BAMM.
HEY, LITTLE FELLA. SO, LIKE, WHY DO YOU CALL HIM BAMM--?
NO! DON'T!
BAM! BAM! BAM! BAM! BAM!
HE'S KIND OF STRONG FOR HIS AGE.
BAM BAM
OH, THAT'S WHY...

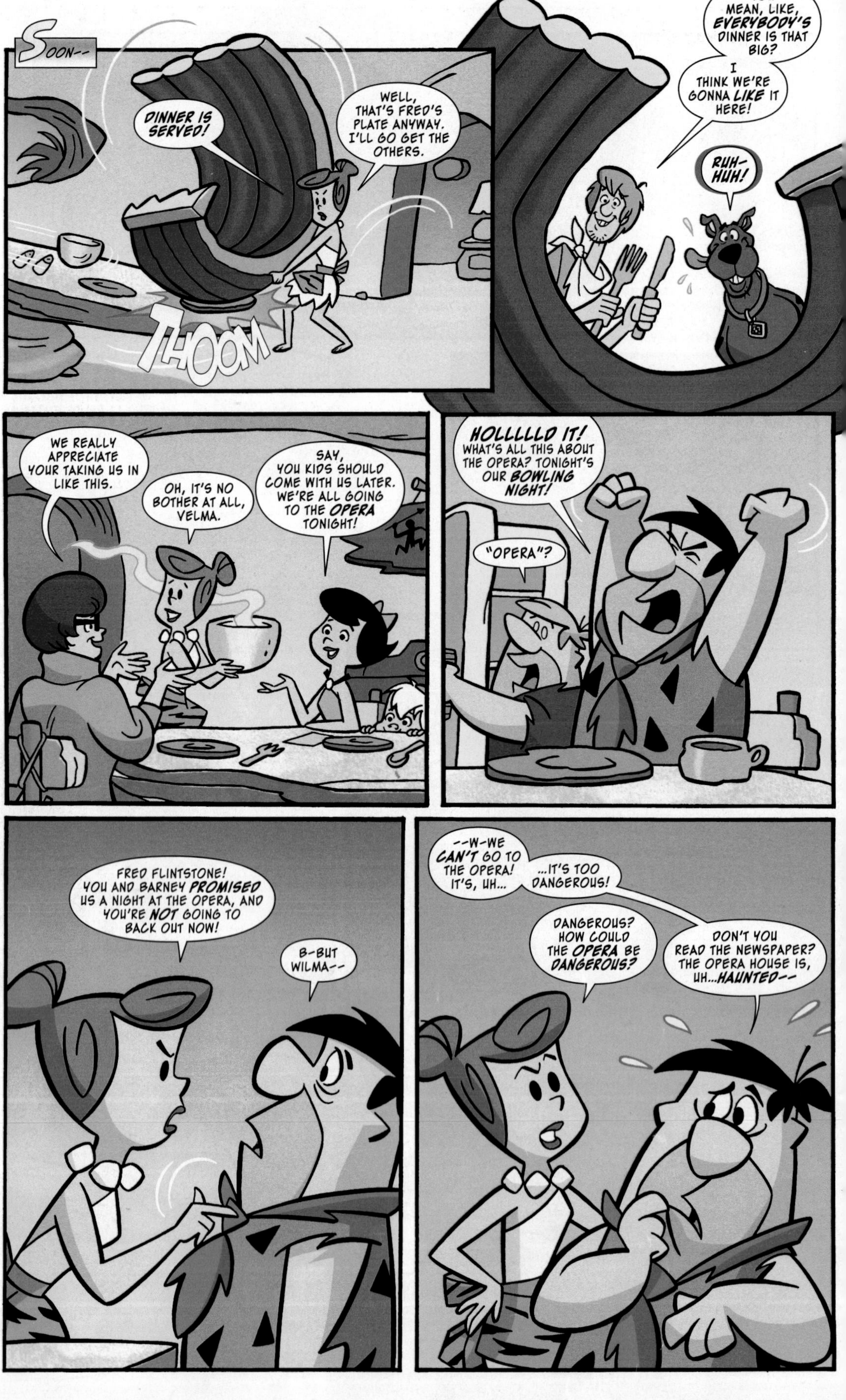
SOON--
DINNER IS SERVED!
THOOM
WELL, THAT'S FRED'S PLATE ANYWAY. I'LL GO GET THE OTHERS.
YOU MEAN, LIKE, EVERYBODY'S DINNER IS THAT BIG?
I THINK WE'RE GONNA LIKE IT HERE!
RUH-HUH!
WE REALLY APPRECIATE YOUR TAKING US IN LIKE THIS.
OH, IT'S NO BOTHER AT ALL, VELMA.
SAY, YOU KIDS SHOULD COME WITH US LATER. WE'RE ALL GOING TO THE OPERA TONIGHT!
HOLLLLLD IT! WHAT'S ALL THIS ABOUT THE OPERA? TONIGHT'S OUR BOWLING NIGHT!
"OPERA"?
FRED FLINTSTONE! YOU AND BARNEY PROMISED US A NIGHT AT THE OPERA, AND YOU'RE NOT GOING TO BACK OUT NOW!
B-BUT WILMA--
--W-WE CAN'T GO TO THE OPERA! IT'S, UH...
...IT'S TOO DANGEROUS!
DANGEROUS? HOW COULD THE OPERA BE DANGEROUS?
DON'T YOU READ THE NEWSPAPER? THE OPERA HOUSE IS, UH...HAUNTED--

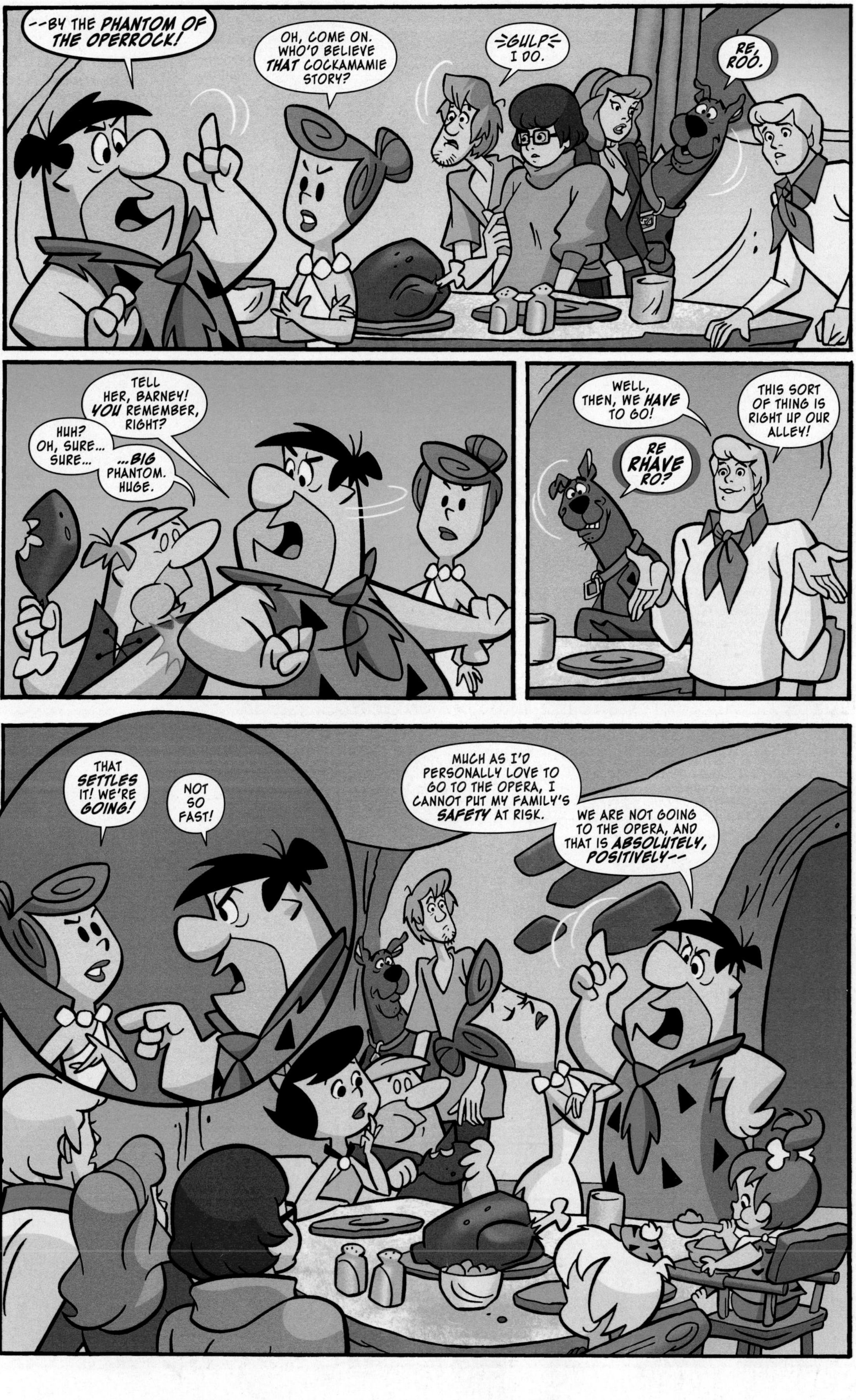
--BY THE PHANTOM OF THE OPERROCK!
OH, COME ON. WHO'D BELIEVE THAT COCKAMAMIE STORY?
GULP I DO.
RE, ROO.
TELL HER, BARNEY! YOU REMEMBER, RIGHT?
HUH? OH, SURE... SURE...
...BIG PHANTOM. HUGE.
WELL, THEN, WE HAVE TO GO!
THIS SORT OF THING IS RIGHT UP OUR ALLEY!
RE RHAVE RO?
THAT SETTLES IT! WE'RE GOING!
NOT SO FAST!
MUCH AS I'D PERSONALLY LOVE TO GO TO THE OPERA, I CANNOT PUT MY FAMILY'S SAFETY AT RISK.
WE ARE NOT GOING TO THE OPERA, AND THAT IS ABSOLUTELY, POSITIVELY--

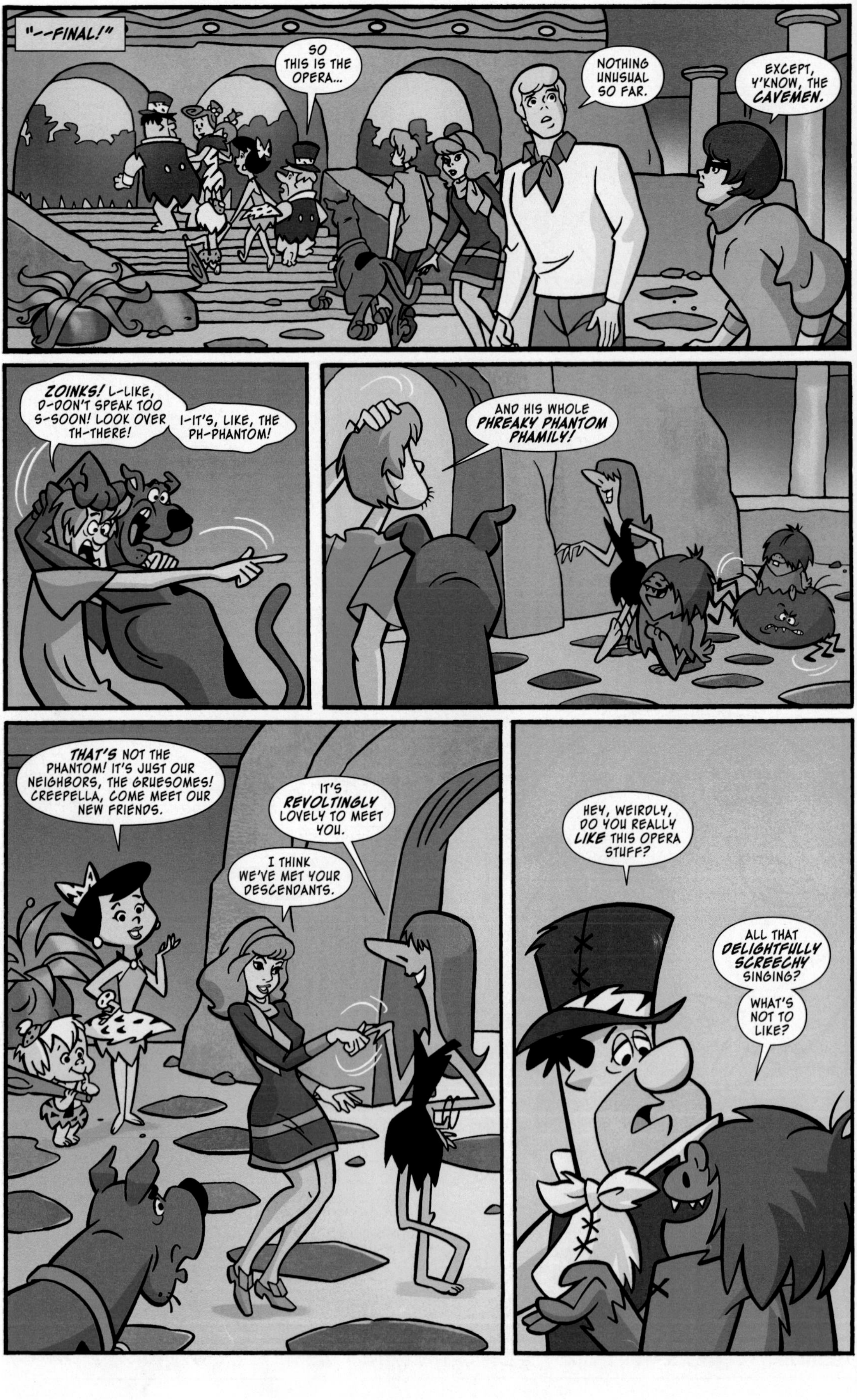
"--FINAL!"
SO THIS IS THE OPERA...
NOTHING UNUSUAL SO FAR.
EXCEPT, Y'KNOW, THE CAVEMEN.
ZOINKS! L-LIKE, D-DON'T SPEAK TOO S-SOON! LOOK OVER TH-THERE!
I-IT'S, LIKE, THE PH-PHANTOM!
AND HIS WHOLE PHREAKY PHANTOM PHAMILY!
THAT'S NOT THE PHANTOM! IT'S JUST OUR NEIGHBORS, THE GRUESOMES! CREEPELLA, COME MEET OUR NEW FRIENDS.
IT'S REVOLTINGLY LOVELY TO MEET YOU.
I THINK WE'VE MET YOUR DESCENDANTS.
HEY, WEIRDLY, DO YOU REALLY LIKE THIS OPERA STUFF?
ALL THAT DELIGHTFULLY SCREECHY SINGING?
WHAT'S NOT TO LIKE?

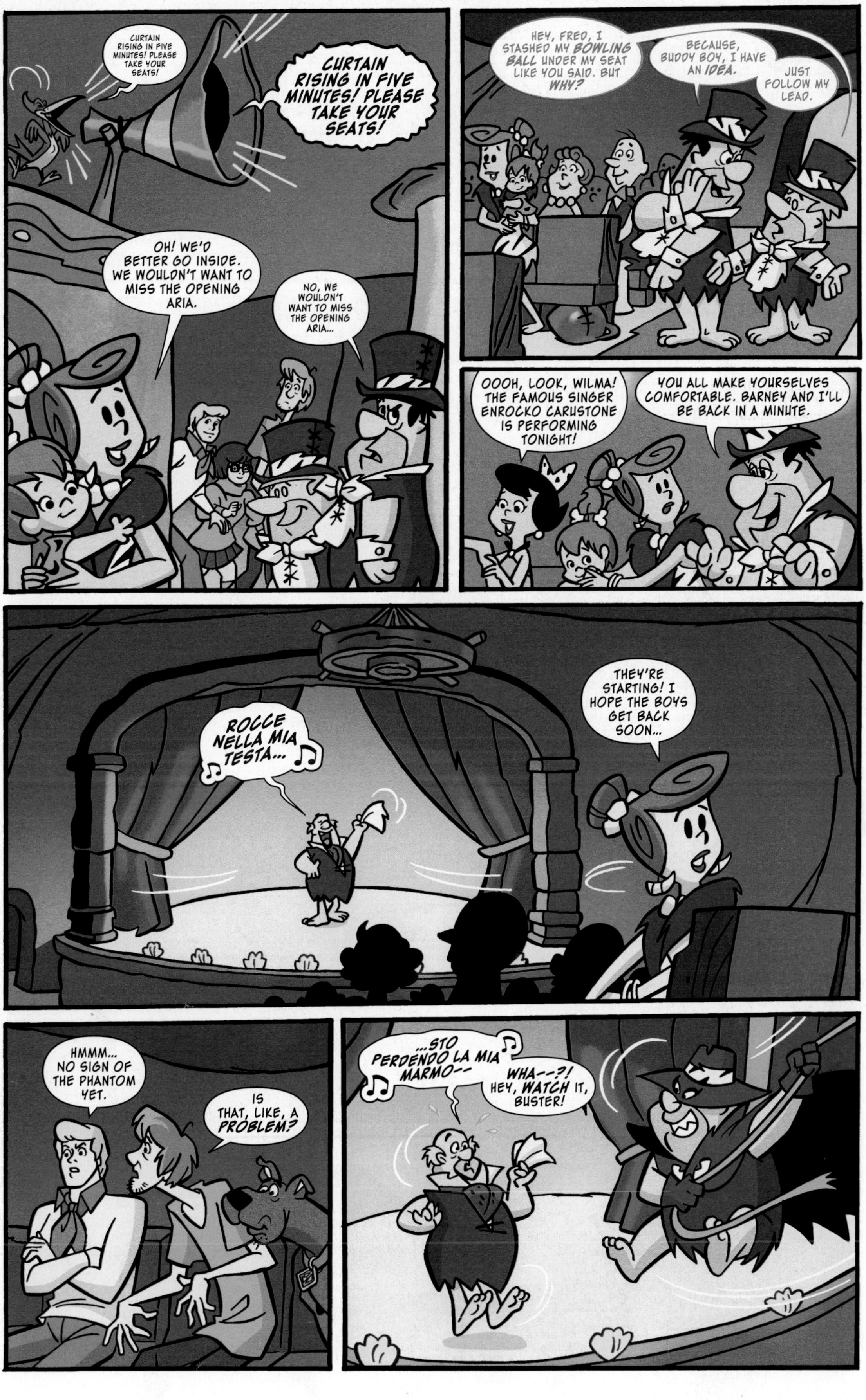
CURTAIN RISING IN FIVE MINUTES! PLEASE TAKE YOUR SEATS!
CURTAIN RISING IN FIVE MINUTES! PLEASE TAKE YOUR SEATS!
OH! WE'D BETTER GO INSIDE. WE WOULDN'T WANT TO MISS THE OPENING ARIA.
NO, WE WOULDN'T WANT TO MISS THE OPENING ARIA...
HEY, FRED, I STASHED MY BOWLING BALL UNDER MY SEAT LIKE YOU SAID. BUT WHY?
BECAUSE, BUDDY BOY, I HAVE AN IDEA.
JUST FOLLOW MY LEAD.
OOOH, LOOK, WILMA! THE FAMOUS SINGER ENROCKO CARUSTONE IS PERFORMING TONIGHT!
YOU ALL MAKE YOURSELVES COMFORTABLE. BARNEY AND I'LL BE BACK IN A MINUTE.
ROCCE NELLA MIA TESTA...
THEY'RE STARTING! I HOPE THE BOYS GET BACK SOON...
HMMM... NO SIGN OF THE PHANTOM YET.
IS THAT, LIKE, A PROBLEM?
...STO PERDENDO LA MIA MARMO--
WHA--?! HEY, WATCH IT, BUSTER!

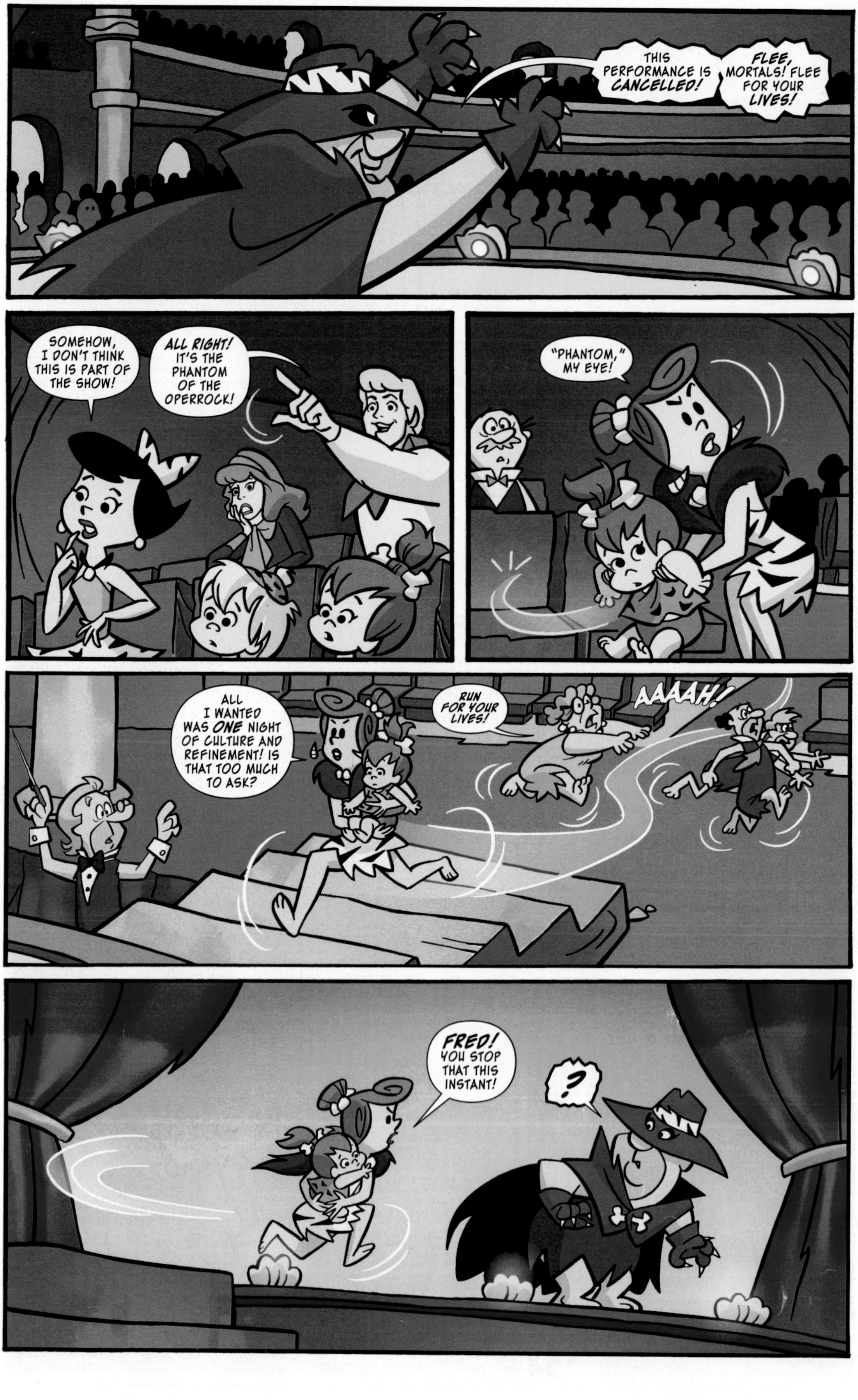

THIS PERFORMANCE IS CANCELLED!
FLEE, MORTALS! FLEE FOR YOUR LIVES!
SOMEHOW, I DON'T THINK THIS IS PART OF THE SHOW!
ALL RIGHT! IT'S THE PHANTOM OF THE OPERROCK!
"PHANTOM," MY EYE!
ALL I WANTED WAS ONE NIGHT OF CULTURE AND REFINEMENT! IS THAT TOO MUCH TO ASK?
RUN FOR YOUR LIVES!
AAAAH!
FRED! YOU STOP THAT THIS INSTANT!
?

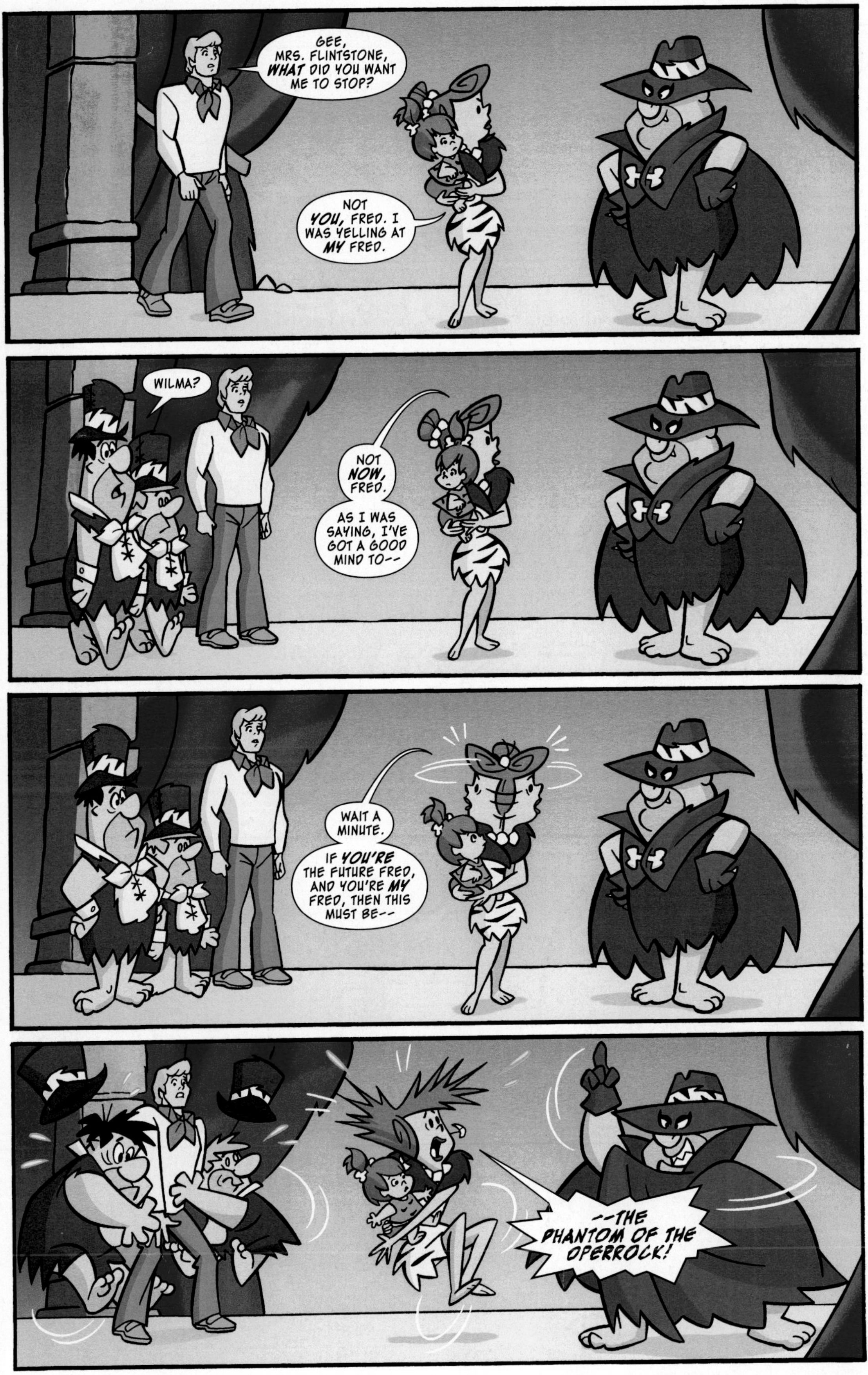
GEE, MRS. FLINTSTONE, WHAT DID YOU WANT ME TO STOP?
NOT YOU, FRED. I WAS YELLING AT MY FRED.
WILMA?
NOT NOW, FRED.
AS I WAS SAYING, I'VE GOT A GOOD MIND TO--
WAIT A MINUTE.
IF YOU'RE THE FUTURE FRED, AND YOU'RE MY FRED, THEN THIS MUST BE--
--THE PHANTOM OF THE OPERROCK!

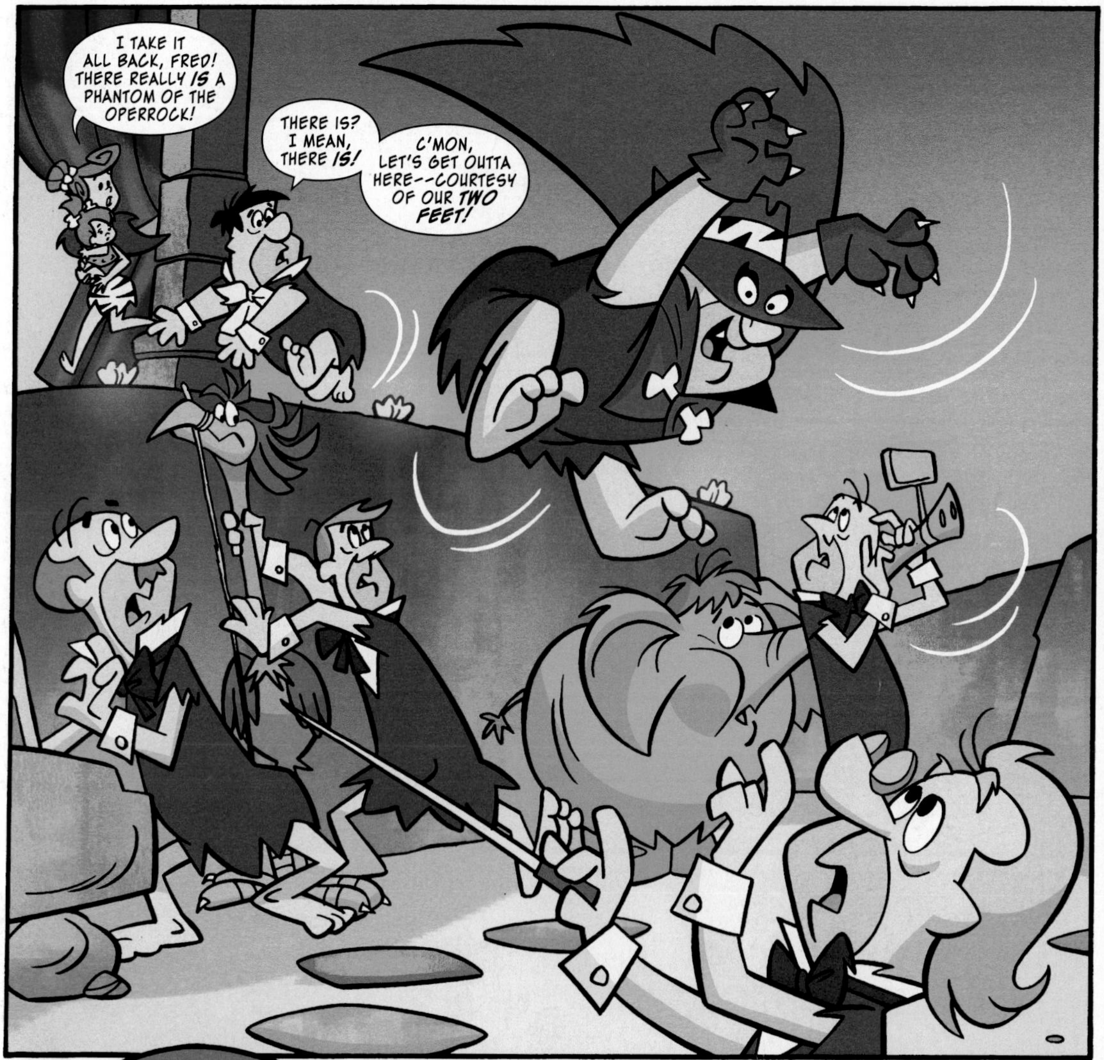
I TAKE IT ALL BACK, FRED! THERE REALLY IS A PHANTOM OF THE OPERROCK!
THERE IS? I MEAN, THERE IS!
C'MON, LET'S GET OUTTA HERE--COURTESY OF OUR TWO FEET!

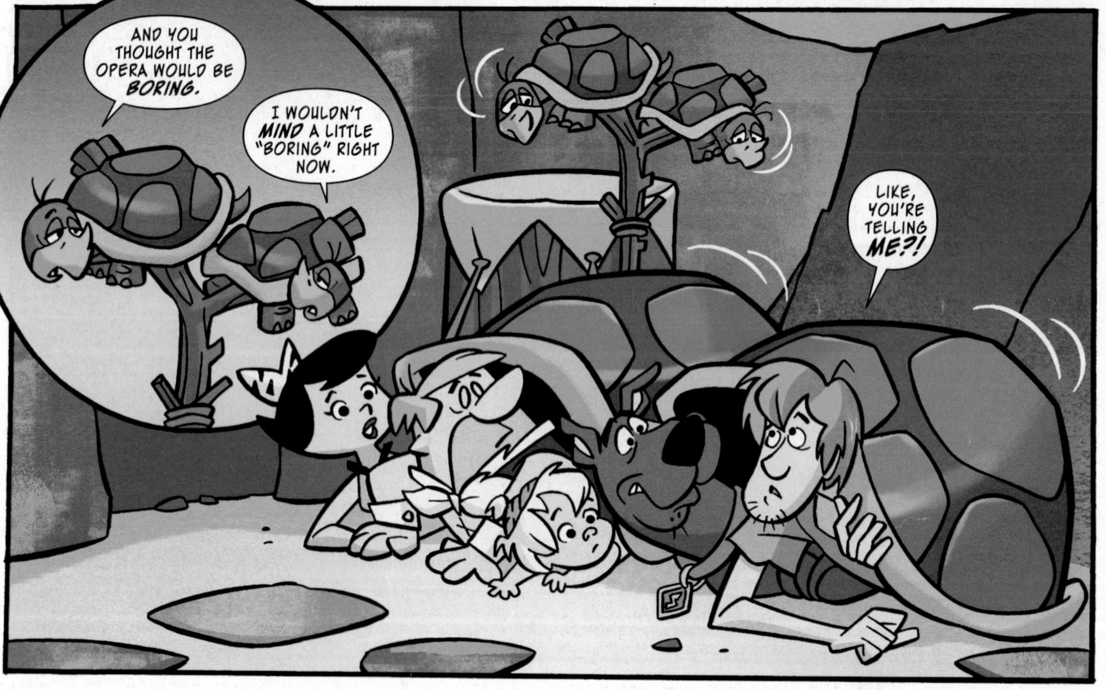
AND YOU THOUGHT THE OPERA WOULD BE BORING.
I WOULDN'T MIND A LITTLE "BORING" RIGHT NOW.
LIKE, YOU'RE TELLING ME?!

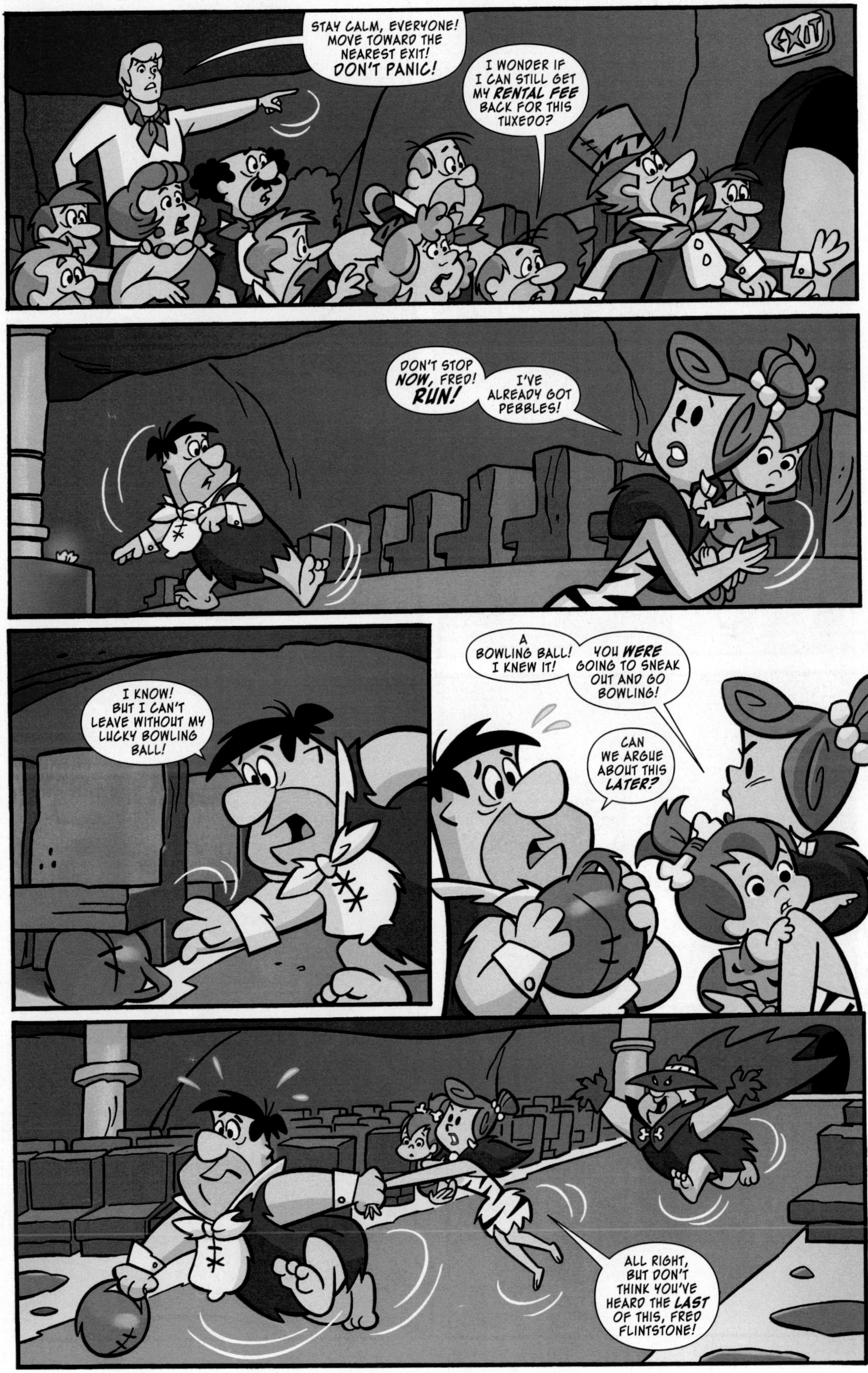
STAY CALM, EVERYONE! MOVE TOWARD THE NEAREST EXIT! DON'T PANIC!
I WONDER IF I CAN STILL GET MY RENTAL FEE BACK FOR THIS TUXEDO?
EXIT
DON'T STOP NOW, FRED! RUN!
I'VE ALREADY GOT PEBBLES!
I KNOW! BUT I CAN'T LEAVE WITHOUT MY LUCKY BOWLING BALL!
A BOWLING BALL! I KNEW IT!
YOU WERE GOING TO SNEAK OUT AND GO BOWLING!
CAN WE ARGUE ABOUT THIS LATER?
ALL RIGHT, BUT DON'T THINK YOU'VE HEARD THE LAST OF THIS, FRED FLINTSTONE!

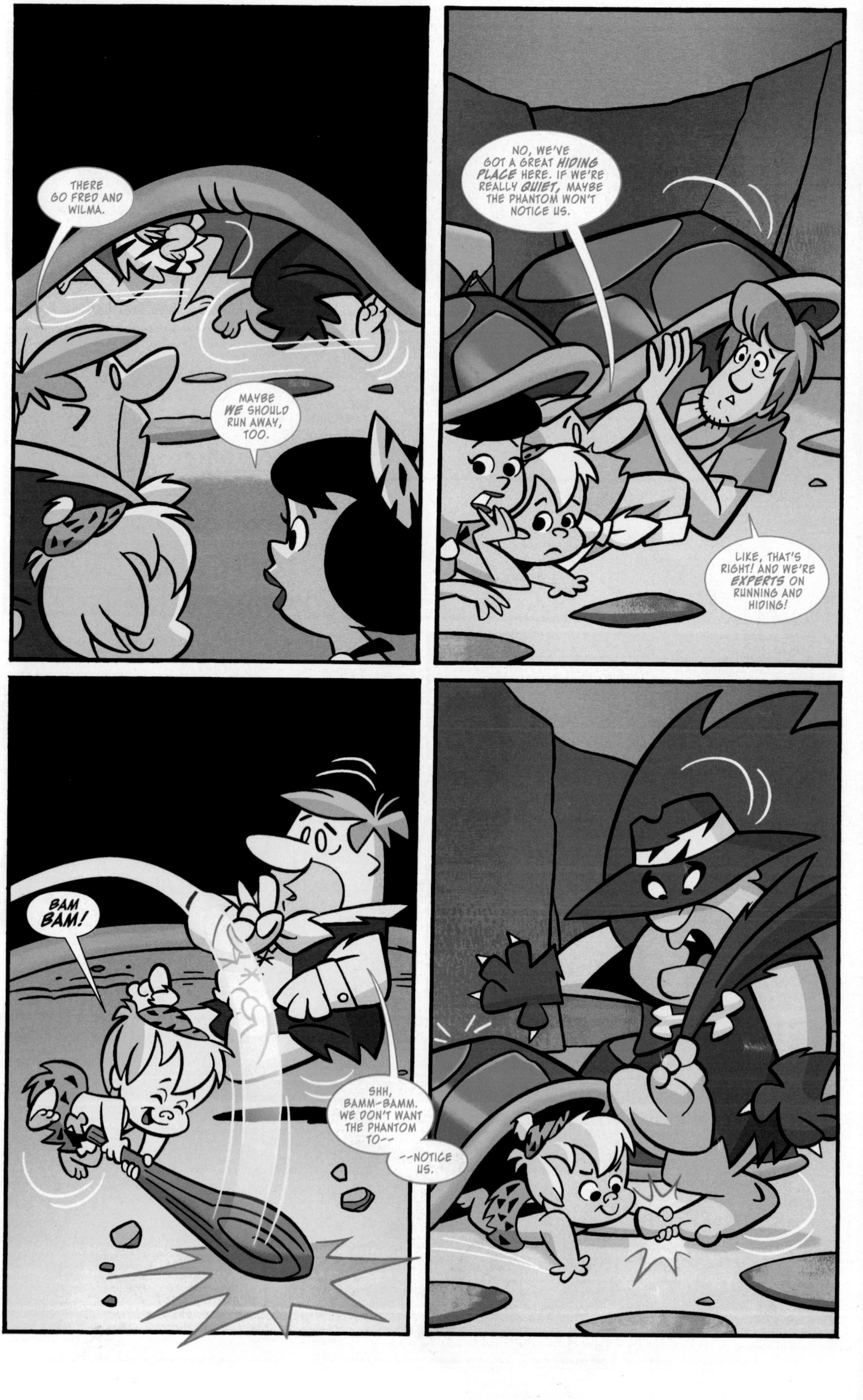
THERE GO FRED AND WILMA.
MAYBE WE SHOULD RUN AWAY, TOO.
NO, WE'VE GOT A GREAT HIDING PLACE HERE. IF WE'RE REALLY QUIET, MAYBE THE PHANTOM WON'T NOTICE US.
LIKE, THAT'S RIGHT! AND WE'RE EXPERTS ON RUNNING AND HIDING!
BAM BAM!
SHH, BAMM-BAMM. WE DON'T WANT THE PHANTOM TO--
--NOTICE US.

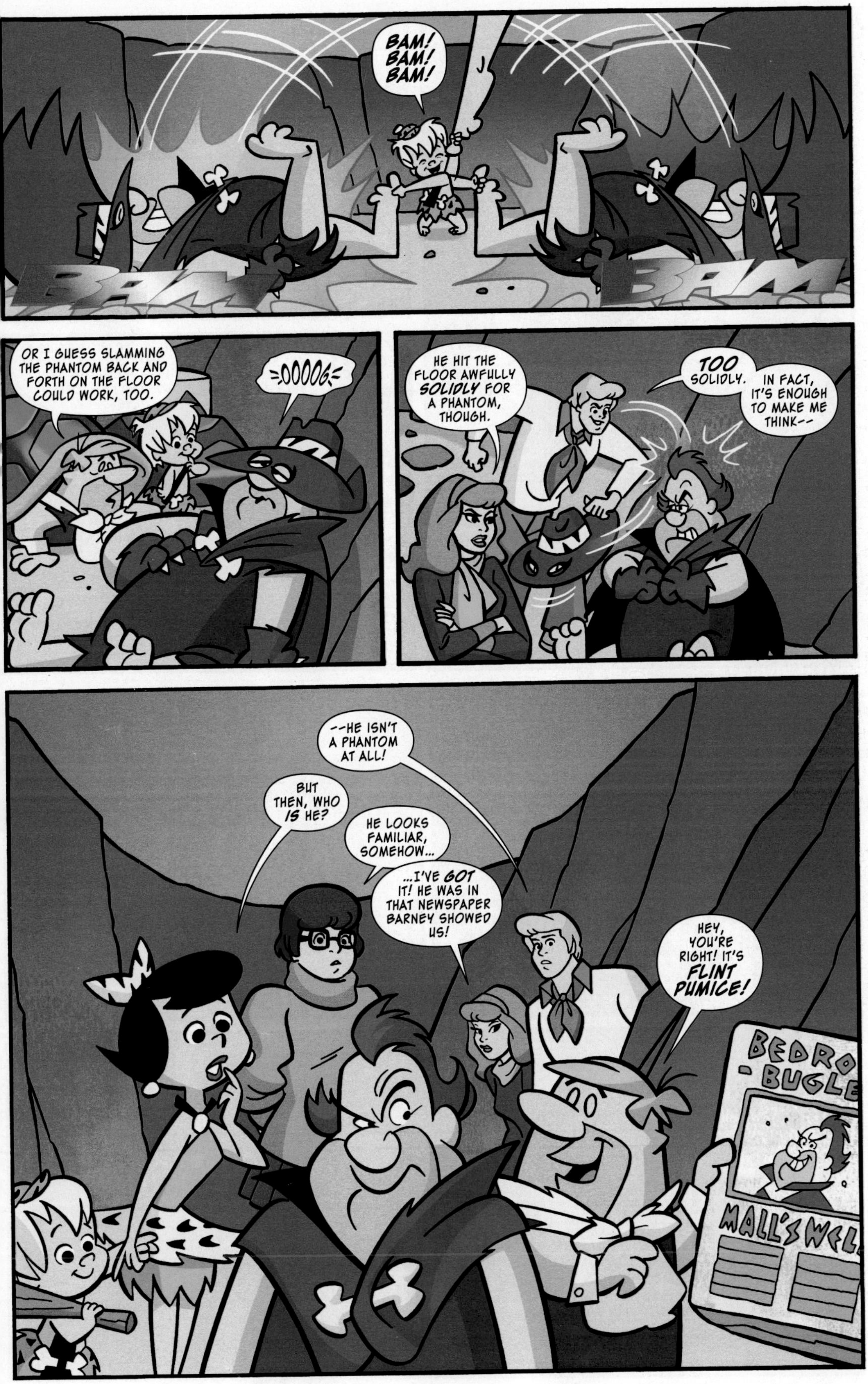
BAM! BAM! BAM!
BAM
BAM
OR I GUESS SLAMMING THE PHANTOM BACK AND FORTH ON THE FLOOR COULD WORK, TOO.
OOOOG
HE HIT THE FLOOR AWFULLY SOLIDLY FOR A PHANTOM, THOUGH.
TOO SOLIDLY.
IN FACT, IT'S ENOUGH TO MAKE ME THINK--
--HE ISN'T A PHANTOM AT ALL!
BUT THEN, WHO IS HE?
HE LOOKS FAMILIAR, SOMEHOW...
...I'VE GOT IT! HE WAS IN THAT NEWSPAPER BARNEY SHOWED US!
HEY, YOU'RE RIGHT! IT'S FLINT PUMICE!
BEDRO BUGLE
MALL'S WEL

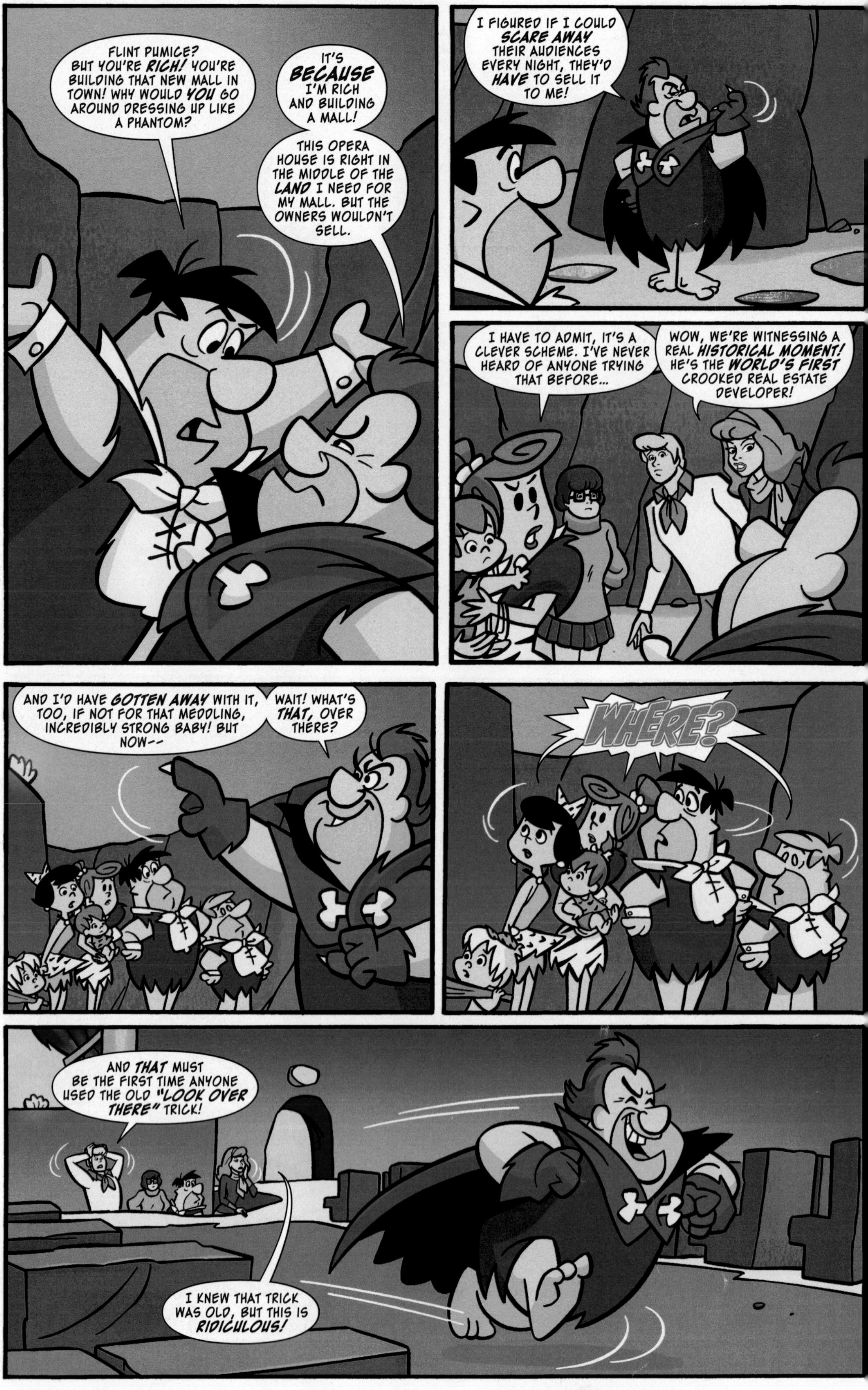
FLINT PUMICE? BUT YOU'RE RICH! YOU'RE BUILDING THAT NEW MALL IN TOWN! WHY WOULD YOU GO AROUND DRESSING UP LIKE A PHANTOM?
IT'S BECAUSE I'M RICH AND BUILDING A MALL!
THIS OPERA HOUSE IS RIGHT IN THE MIDDLE OF THE LAND I NEED FOR MY MALL. BUT THE OWNERS WOULDN'T SELL.
I FIGURED IF I COULD SCARE AWAY THEIR AUDIENCES EVERY NIGHT, THEY'D HAVE TO SELL IT TO ME!
I HAVE TO ADMIT, IT'S A CLEVER SCHEME. I'VE NEVER HEARD OF ANYONE TRYING THAT BEFORE...
WOW, WE'RE WITNESSING A REAL HISTORICAL MOMENT! HE'S THE WORLD'S FIRST CROOKED REAL ESTATE DEVELOPER!
AND I'D HAVE GOTTEN AWAY WITH IT, TOO, IF NOT FOR THAT MEDDLING, INCREDIBLY STRONG BABY! BUT NOW--
WAIT! WHAT'S THAT, OVER THERE?
WHERE?
AND THAT MUST BE THE FIRST TIME ANYONE USED THE OLD "LOOK OVER THERE" TRICK!
I KNEW THAT TRICK WAS OLD, BUT THIS IS RIDICULOUS!

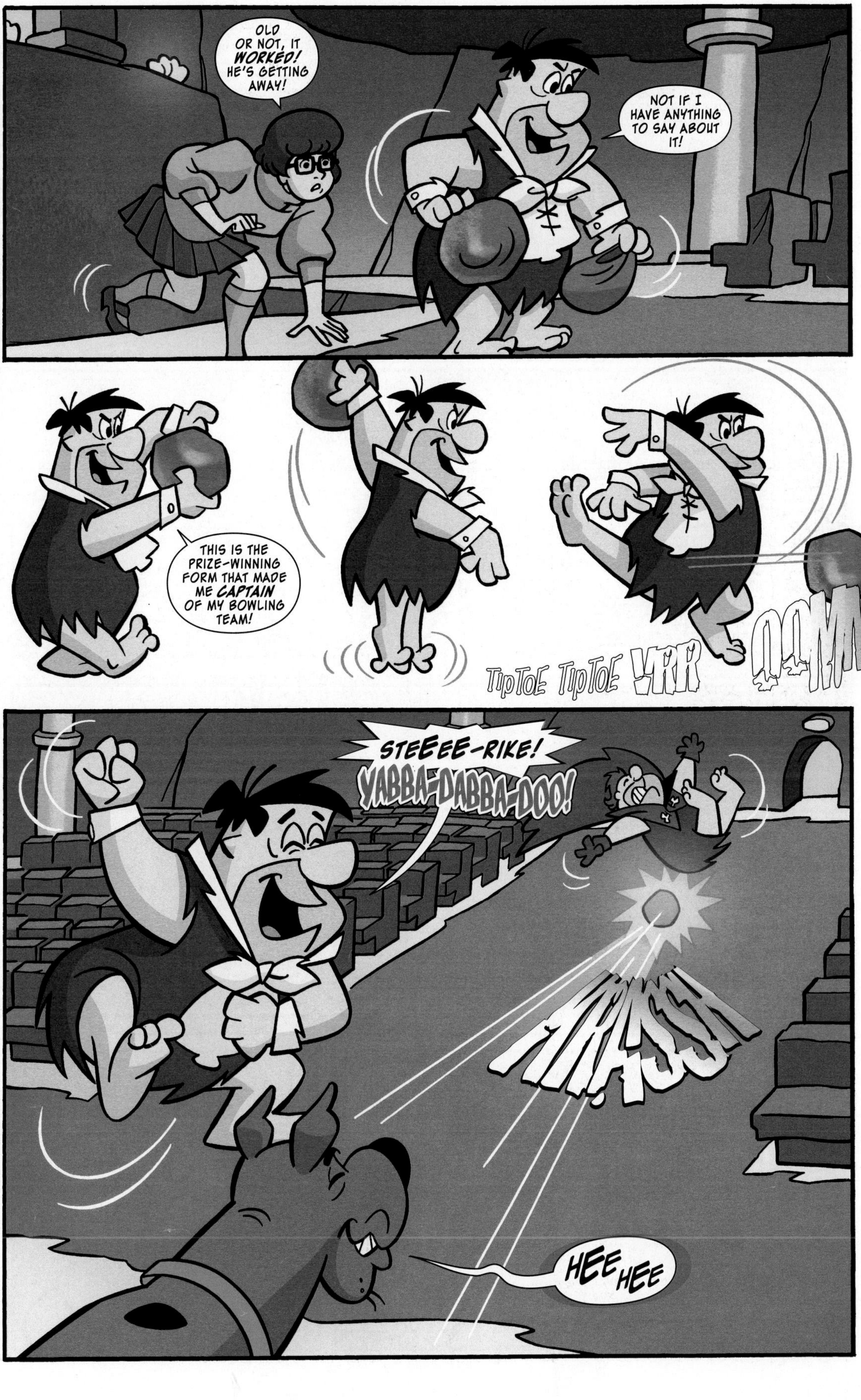
OLD OR NOT, IT WORKED! HE'S GETTING AWAY!
NOT IF I HAVE ANYTHING TO SAY ABOUT IT!
THIS IS THE PRIZE-WINNING FORM THAT MADE ME CAPTAIN OF MY BOWLING TEAM!
TIPTOE TIPTOE VRR
OOMM
STEEEE-RIKE! YABBA-DABBA-DOO!
THASSH
HEE HEE

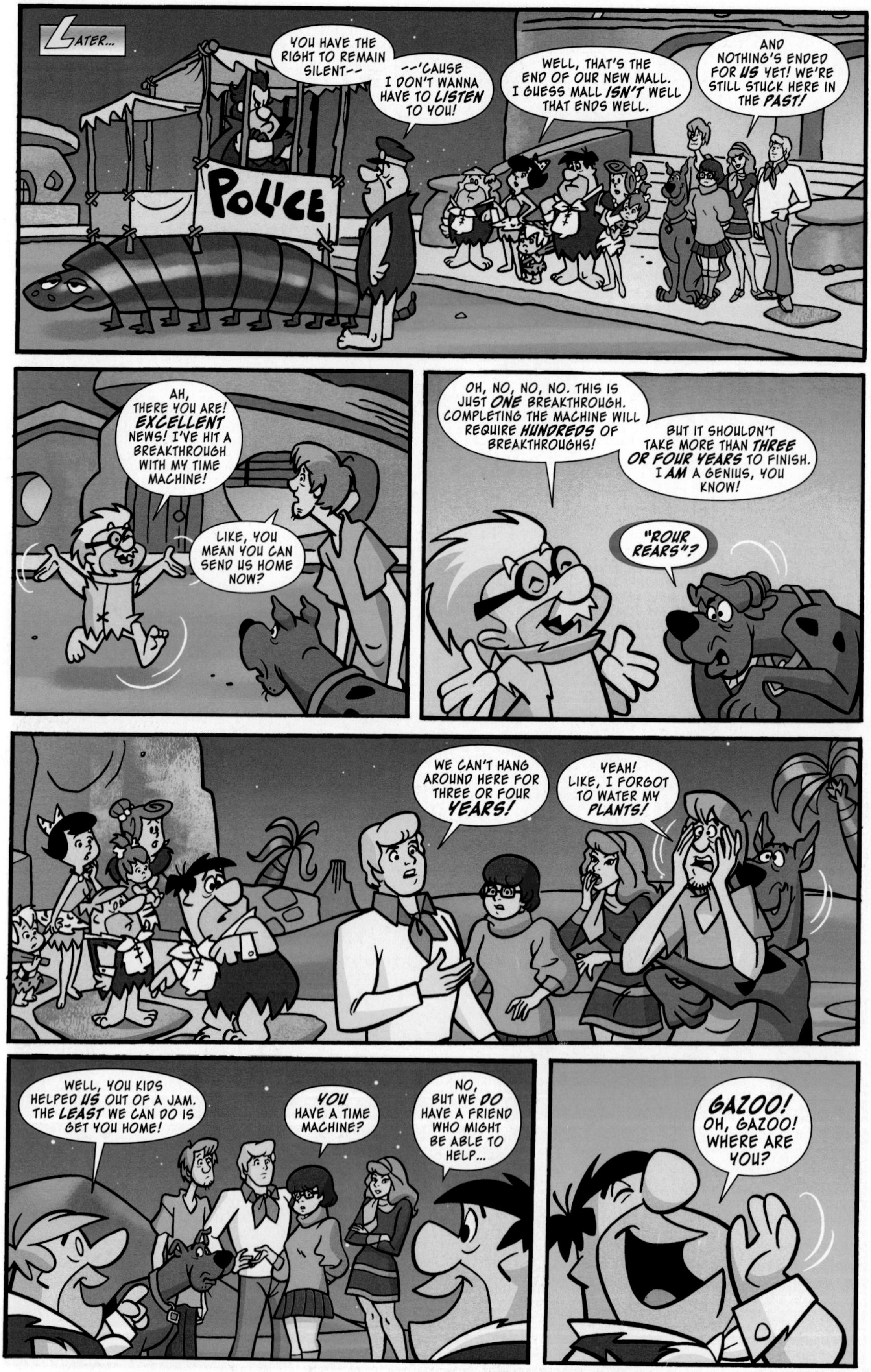
LATER...
YOU HAVE THE RIGHT TO REMAIN SILENT--
--'CAUSE I DON'T WANNA HAVE TO LISTEN TO YOU!
POLICE
WELL, THAT'S THE END OF OUR NEW MALL. I GUESS MALL ISN'T WELL THAT ENDS WELL.
AND NOTHING'S ENDED FOR US YET! WE'RE STILL STUCK HERE IN THE PAST!
AH, THERE YOU ARE! EXCELLENT NEWS! I'VE HIT A BREAKTHROUGH WITH MY TIME MACHINE!
LIKE, YOU MEAN YOU CAN SEND US HOME NOW?
OH, NO, NO, NO. THIS IS JUST ONE BREAKTHROUGH. COMPLETING THE MACHINE WILL REQUIRE HUNDREDS OF BREAKTHROUGHS!
BUT IT SHOULDN'T TAKE MORE THAN THREE OR FOUR YEARS TO FINISH. I AM A GENIUS, YOU KNOW!
"ROUR REARS"?
WE CAN'T HANG AROUND HERE FOR THREE OR FOUR YEARS!
YEAH! LIKE, I FORGOT TO WATER MY PLANTS!
WELL, YOU KIDS HELPED US OUT OF A JAM. THE LEAST WE CAN DO IS GET YOU HOME!
YOU HAVE A TIME MACHINE?
NO, BUT WE DO HAVE A FRIEND WHO MIGHT BE ABLE TO HELP...
GAZOO! OH, GAZOO! WHERE ARE YOU?

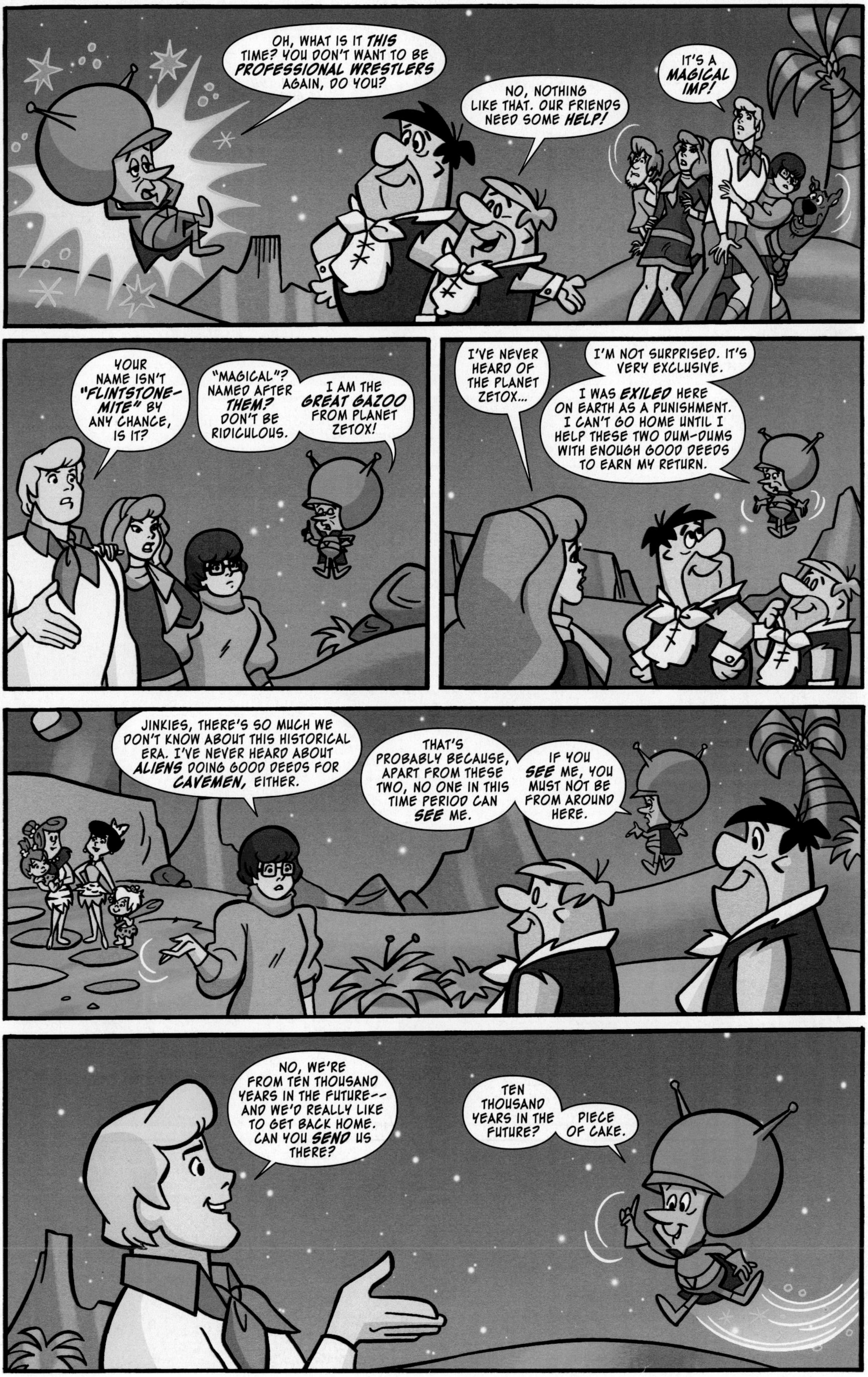
OH, WHAT IS IT THIS TIME? YOU DON'T WANT TO BE PROFESSIONAL WRESTLERS AGAIN, DO YOU?
NO, NOTHING LIKE THAT. OUR FRIENDS NEED SOME HELP!
IT'S A MAGICAL IMP!
YOUR NAME ISN'T "FLINTSTONE-MITE" BY ANY CHANCE, IS IT?
"MAGICAL"? NAMED AFTER THEM? DON'T BE RIDICULOUS.
I AM THE GREAT GAZOO FROM PLANET ZETOX!
I'VE NEVER HEARD OF THE PLANET ZETOX...
I'M NOT SURPRISED. IT'S VERY EXCLUSIVE.
I WAS EXILED HERE ON EARTH AS A PUNISHMENT. I CAN'T GO HOME UNTIL I HELP THESE TWO DUM-DUMS WITH ENOUGH GOOD DEEDS TO EARN MY RETURN.
JINKIES, THERE'S SO MUCH WE DON'T KNOW ABOUT THIS HISTORICAL ERA. I'VE NEVER HEARD ABOUT ALIENS DOING GOOD DEEDS FOR CAVEMEN, EITHER.
THAT'S PROBABLY BECAUSE, APART FROM THESE TWO, NO ONE IN THIS TIME PERIOD CAN SEE ME.
IF YOU SEE ME, YOU MUST NOT BE FROM AROUND HERE.
NO, WE'RE FROM TEN THOUSAND YEARS IN THE FUTURE--AND WE'D REALLY LIKE TO GET BACK HOME. CAN YOU SEND US THERE?
TEN THOUSAND YEARS IN THE FUTURE?
PIECE OF CAKE.

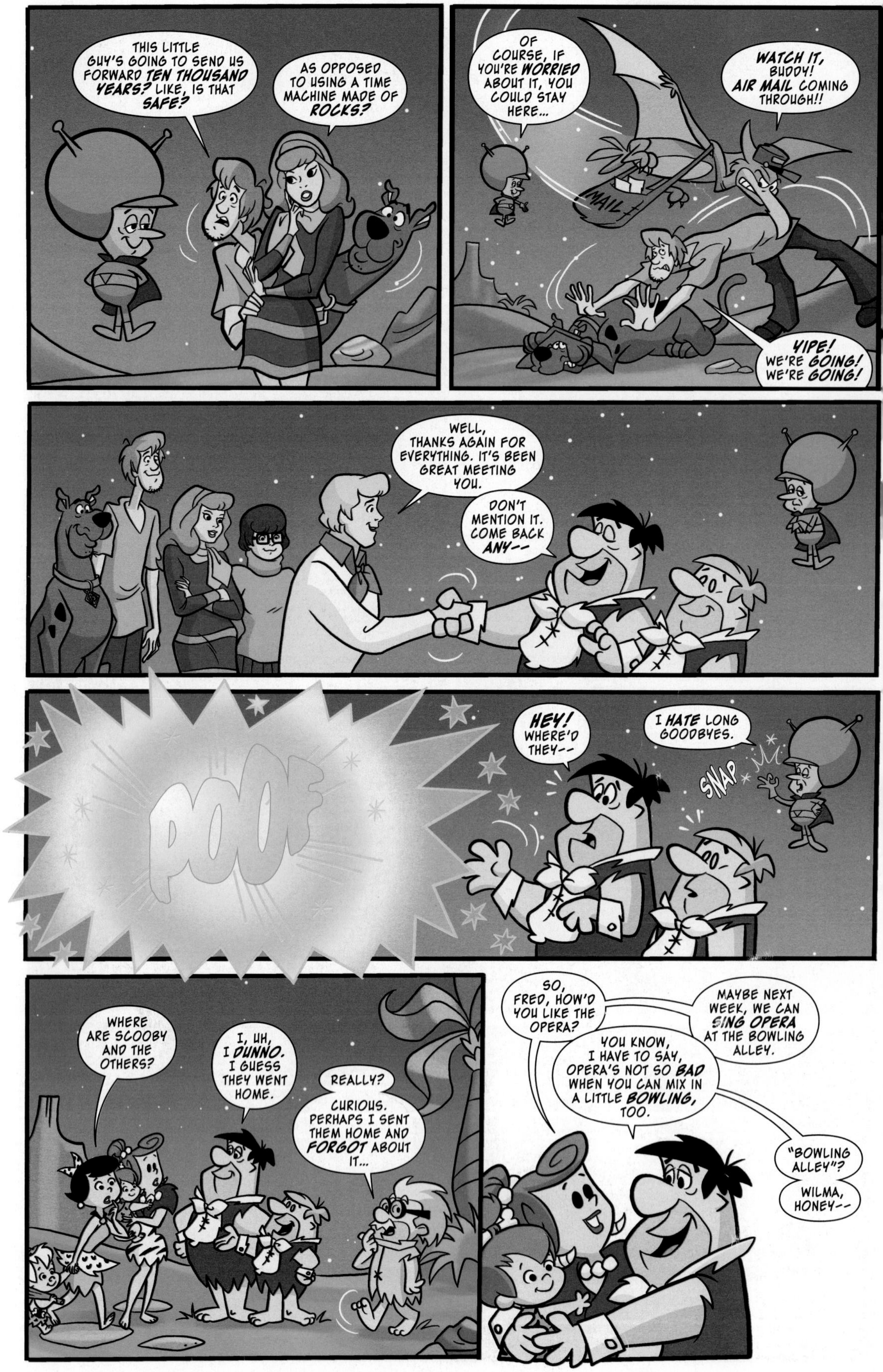

THIS LITTLE GUY'S GOING TO SEND US FORWARD TEN THOUSAND YEARS? LIKE, IS THAT SAFE?
AS OPPOSED TO USING A TIME MACHINE MADE OF ROCKS?
OF COURSE, IF YOU'RE WORRIED ABOUT IT, YOU COULD STAY HERE...
WATCH IT, BUDDY! AIR MAIL COMING THROUGH!!
MAIL
YIPE! WE'RE GOING! WE'RE GOING!
WELL, THANKS AGAIN FOR EVERYTHING. IT'S BEEN GREAT MEETING YOU.
DON'T MENTION IT. COME BACK ANY--
POOF
HEY! WHERE'D THEY--
I HATE LONG GOODBYES.
SNAP
WHERE ARE SCOOBY AND THE OTHERS?
I, UH, I DUNNO. I GUESS THEY WENT HOME.
REALLY?
CURIOUS. PERHAPS I SENT THEM HOME AND FORGOT ABOUT IT...
SO, FRED, HOW'D YOU LIKE THE OPERA?
MAYBE NEXT WEEK, WE CAN SING OPERA AT THE BOWLING ALLEY.
YOU KNOW, I HAVE TO SAY, OPERA'S NOT SO BAD WHEN YOU CAN MIX IN A LITTLE BOWLING, TOO.
"BOWLING ALLEY"?
WILMA, HONEY--

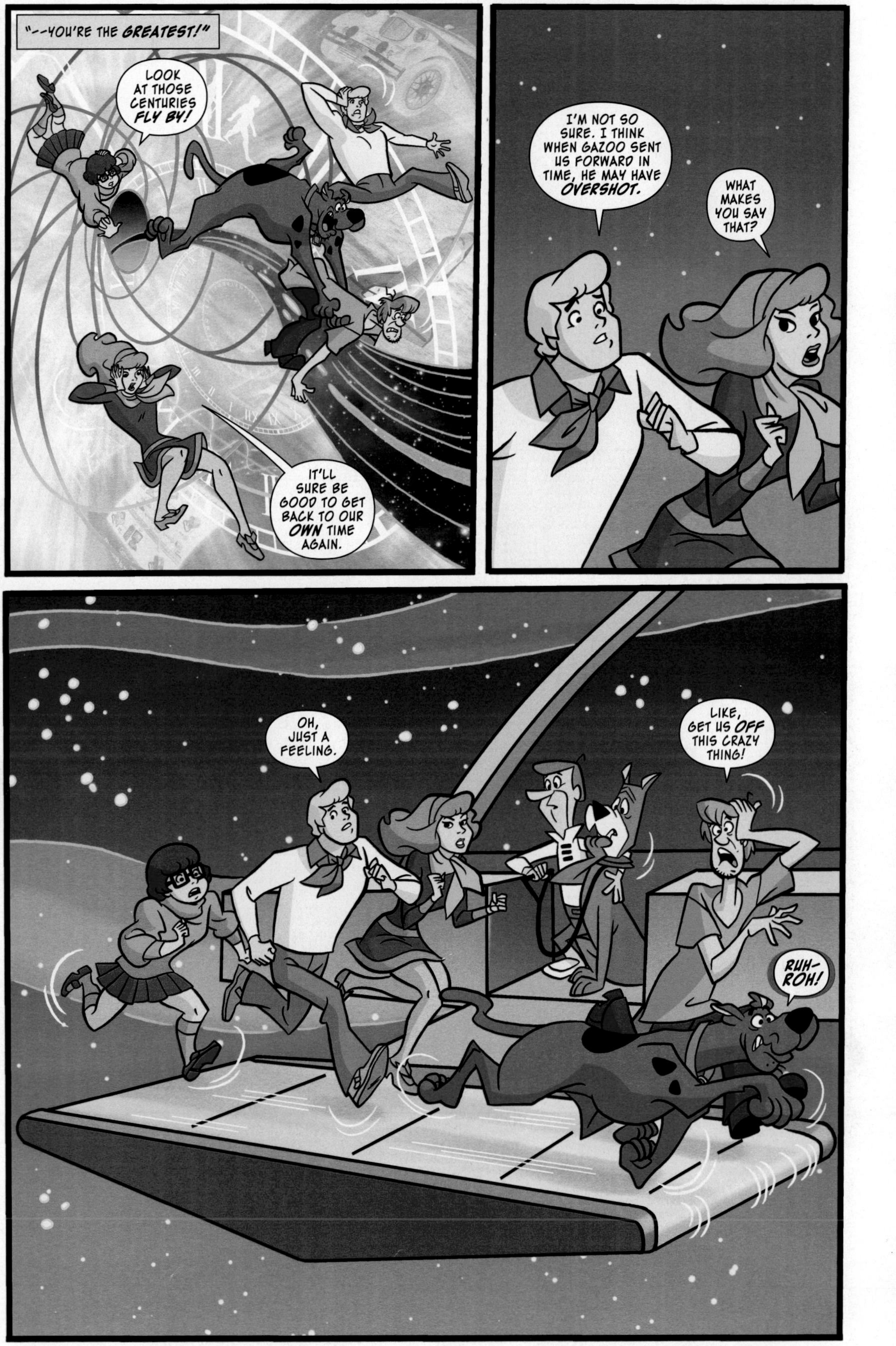
"--YOU'RE THE GREATEST!"
LOOK AT THOSE CENTURIES FLY BY!
IT'LL SURE BE GOOD TO GET BACK TO OUR OWN TIME AGAIN.
I'M NOT SO SURE. I THINK WHEN GAZOO SENT US FORWARD IN TIME, HE MAY HAVE OVERSHOT.
WHAT MAKES YOU SAY THAT?
OH, JUST A FEELING.
LIKE, GET US OFF THIS CRAZY THING!
RUH-ROH!

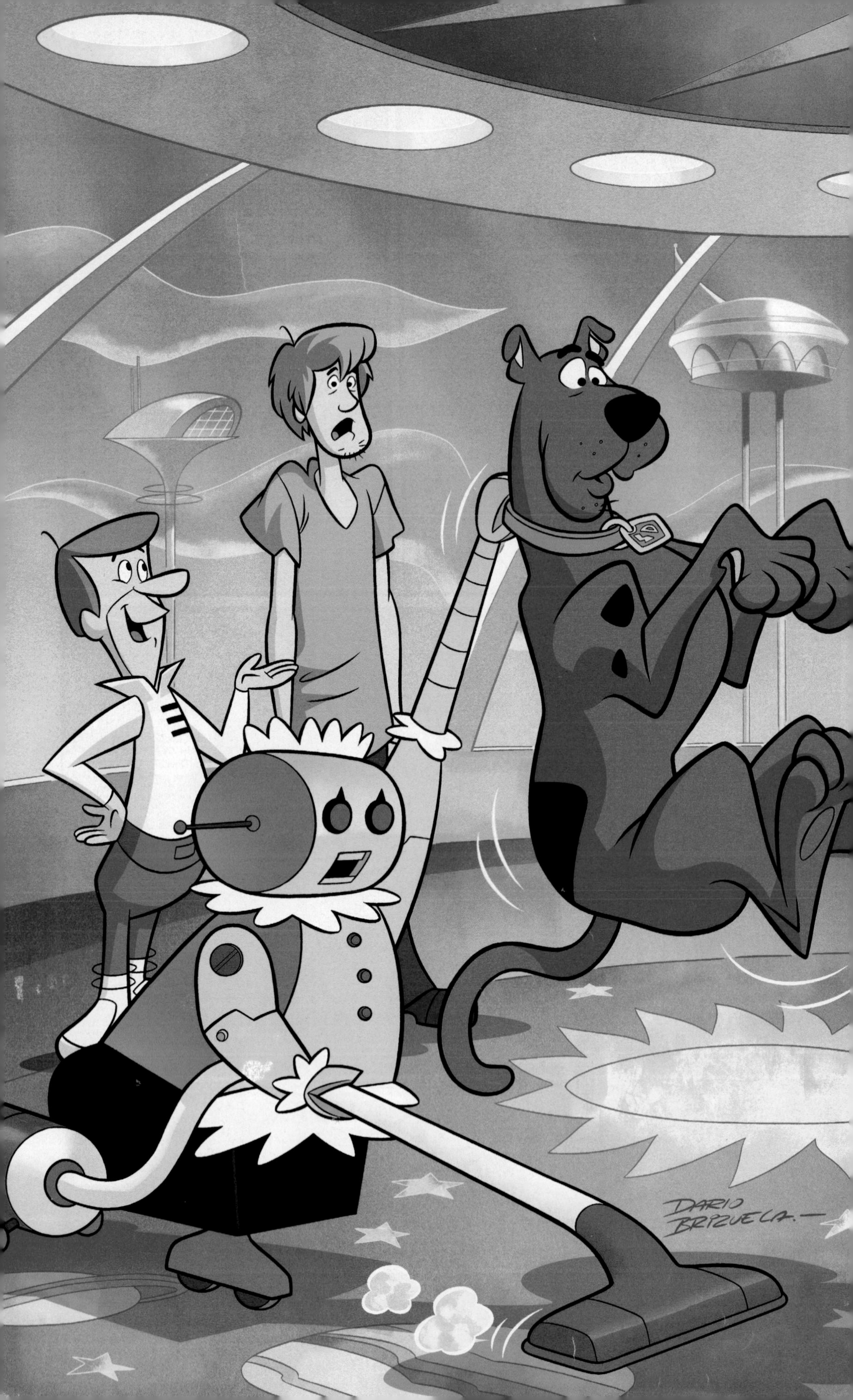
DARIO
BRIZUELA

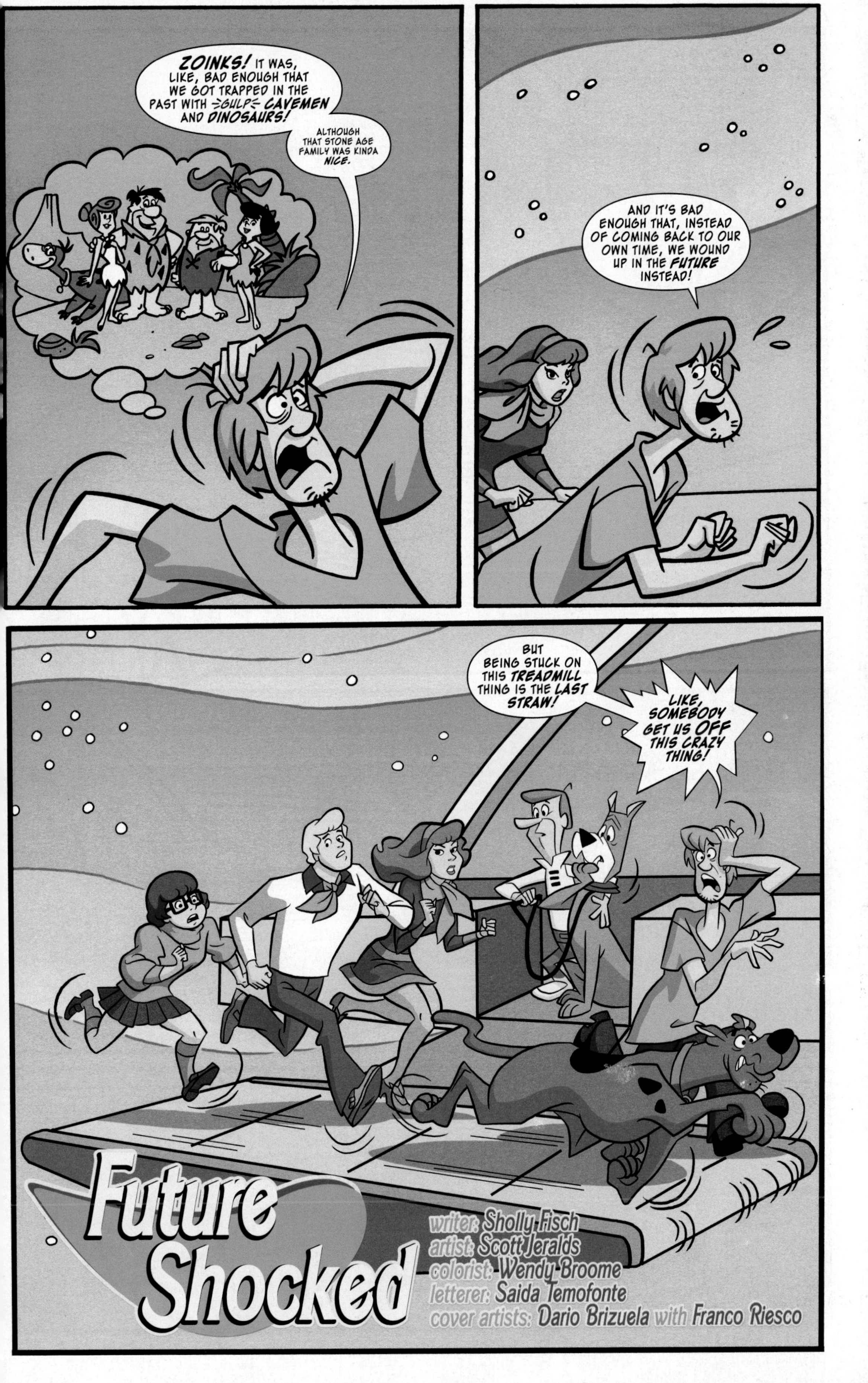
ZOINKS! IT WAS, LIKE, BAD ENOUGH THAT WE GOT TRAPPED IN THE PAST WITH =GULP= CAVEMEN AND DINOSAURS!
ALTHOUGH THAT STONE AGE FAMILY WAS KINDA NICE.
AND IT'S BAD ENOUGH THAT, INSTEAD OF COMING BACK TO OUR OWN TIME, WE WOUND UP IN THE FUTURE INSTEAD!
BUT BEING STUCK ON THIS TREADMILL THING IS THE LAST STRAW!
LIKE, SOMEBODY GET US OFF THIS CRAZY THING!
Future Shocked
writer: Sholly Fisch
artist: Scott Jeralds
colorist: Wendy Broome
letterer: Saida Temofonte
cover artists: Dario Brizuela with Franco Riesco

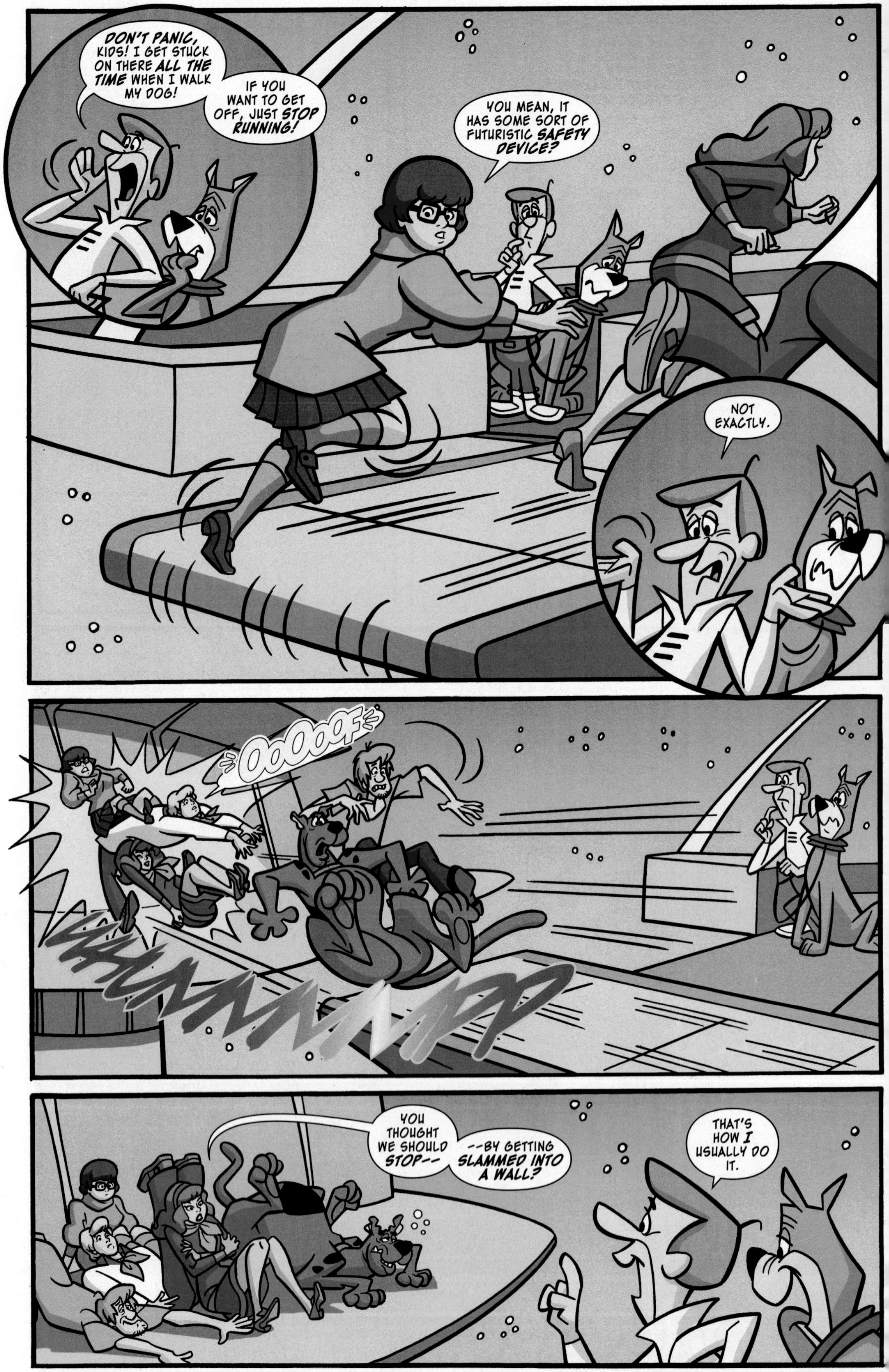

DON'T PANIC, KIDS! I GET STUCK ON THERE ALL THE TIME WHEN I WALK MY DOG!
IF YOU WANT TO GET OFF, JUST STOP RUNNING!
YOU MEAN, IT HAS SOME SORT OF FUTURISTIC SAFETY DEVICE?
NOT EXACTLY.
OoOooF
WHAMMMMP
YOU THOUGHT WE SHOULD STOP--
--BY GETTING SLAMMED INTO A WALL?
THAT'S HOW I USUALLY DO IT.

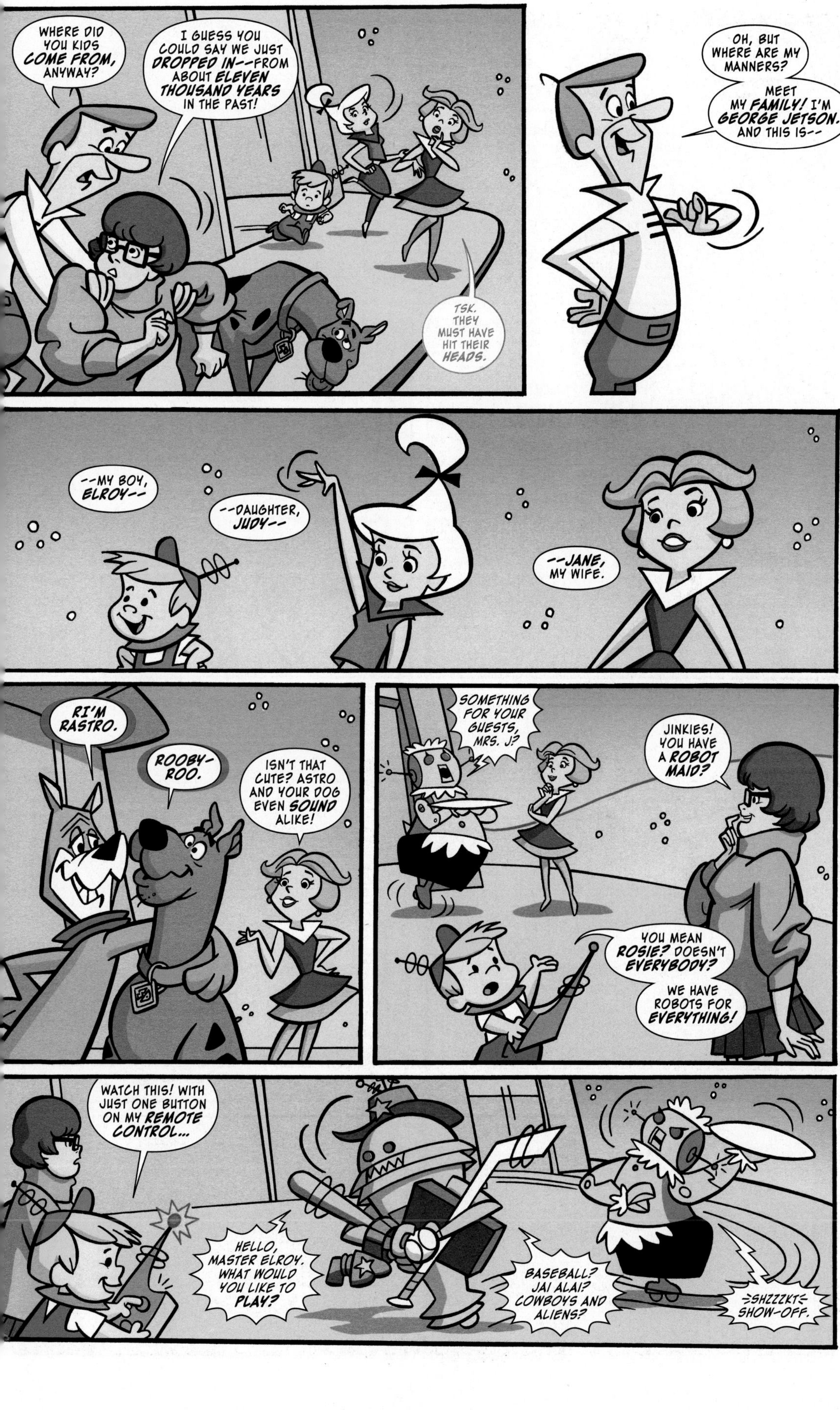
WHERE DID YOU KIDS COME FROM, ANYWAY?
I GUESS YOU COULD SAY WE JUST DROPPED IN--FROM ABOUT ELEVEN THOUSAND YEARS IN THE PAST!
TSK. THEY MUST HAVE HIT THEIR HEADS.
OH, BUT WHERE ARE MY MANNERS?
MEET MY FAMILY! I'M GEORGE JETSON. AND THIS IS--
--MY BOY, ELROY--
--DAUGHTER, JUDY--
--JANE, MY WIFE.
RI'M RASTRO.
ROOBY-ROO.
ISN'T THAT CUTE? ASTRO AND YOUR DOG EVEN SOUND ALIKE!
SOMETHING FOR YOUR GUESTS, MRS. J?
JINKIES! YOU HAVE A ROBOT MAID?
YOU MEAN ROSIE? DOESN'T EVERYBODY?
WE HAVE ROBOTS FOR EVERYTHING!
WATCH THIS! WITH JUST ONE BUTTON ON MY REMOTE CONTROL...
HELLO, MASTER ELROY. WHAT WOULD YOU LIKE TO PLAY?
BASEBALL? JAI ALAI? COWBOYS AND ALIENS?
=SHZZZKT= SHOW-OFF.

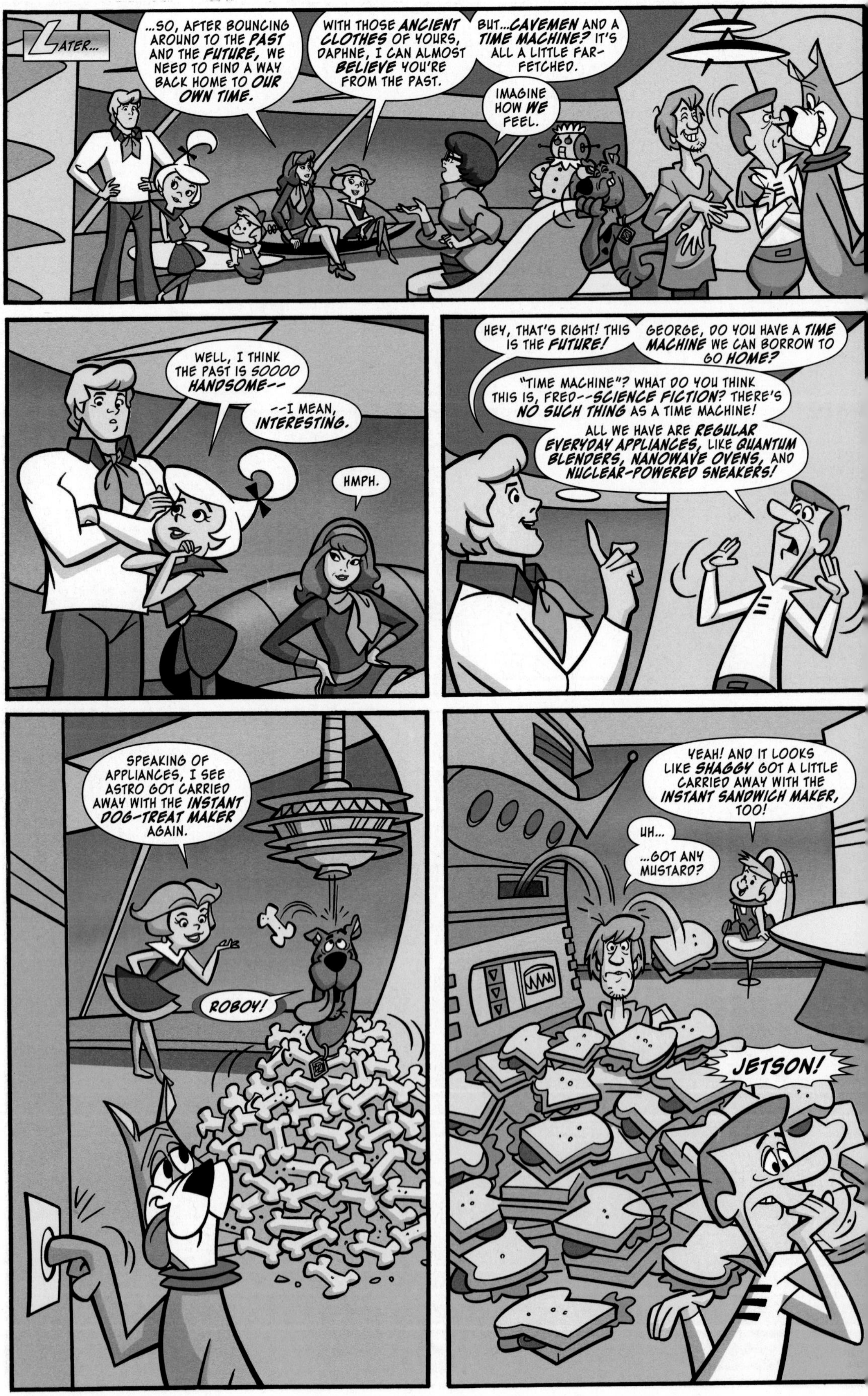
LATER...
...SO, AFTER BOUNCING AROUND TO THE PAST AND THE FUTURE, WE NEED TO FIND A WAY BACK HOME TO OUR OWN TIME.
WITH THOSE ANCIENT CLOTHES OF YOURS, DAPHNE, I CAN ALMOST BELIEVE YOU'RE FROM THE PAST.
BUT...CAVEMEN AND A TIME MACHINE? IT'S ALL A LITTLE FAR-FETCHED.
IMAGINE HOW WE FEEL.
WELL, I THINK THE PAST IS SOOOO HANDSOME--
--I MEAN, INTERESTING.
HMPH.
HEY, THAT'S RIGHT! THIS IS THE FUTURE!
GEORGE, DO YOU HAVE A TIME MACHINE WE CAN BORROW TO GO HOME?
"TIME MACHINE"? WHAT DO YOU THINK THIS IS, FRED--SCIENCE FICTION? THERE'S NO SUCH THING AS A TIME MACHINE!
ALL WE HAVE ARE REGULAR EVERYDAY APPLIANCES, LIKE QUANTUM BLENDERS, NANOWAVE OVENS, AND NUCLEAR-POWERED SNEAKERS!
SPEAKING OF APPLIANCES, I SEE ASTRO GOT CARRIED AWAY WITH THE INSTANT DOG-TREAT MAKER AGAIN.
ROBOY!
YEAH! AND IT LOOKS LIKE SHAGGY GOT A LITTLE CARRIED AWAY WITH THE INSTANT SANDWICH MAKER, TOO!
UH...
...GOT ANY MUSTARD?
JETSON!

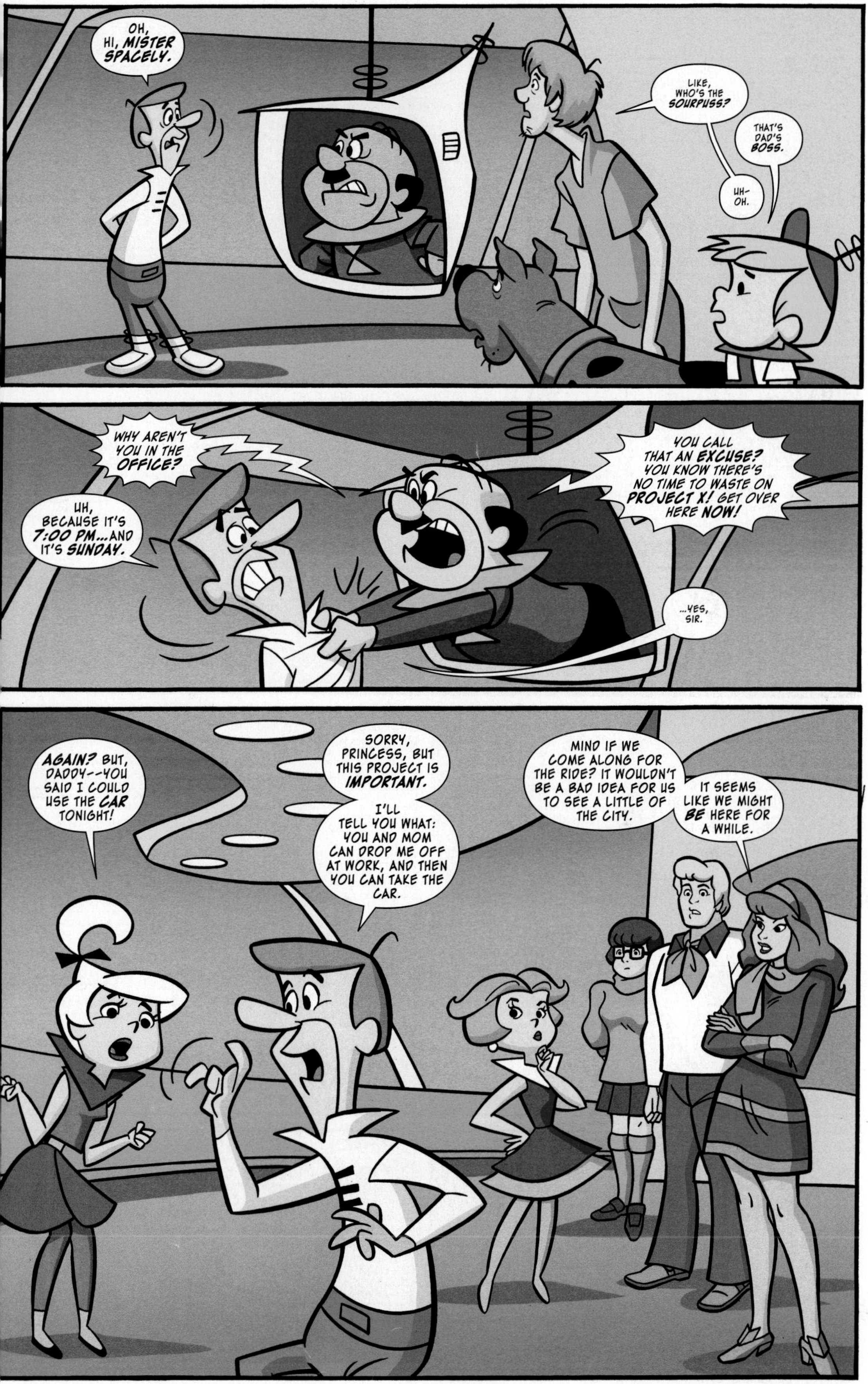
OH, HI, MISTER SPACELY.
LIKE, WHO'S THE SOURPUSS?
THAT'S DAD'S BOSS.
UH-OH.
WHY AREN'T YOU IN THE OFFICE?
UH, BECAUSE IT'S 7:00 PM...AND IT'S SUNDAY.
YOU CALL THAT AN EXCUSE? YOU KNOW THERE'S NO TIME TO WASTE ON PROJECT X! GET OVER HERE NOW!
...YES, SIR.
AGAIN? BUT, DADDY--YOU SAID I COULD USE THE CAR TONIGHT!
SORRY, PRINCESS, BUT THIS PROJECT IS IMPORTANT.
I'LL TELL YOU WHAT: YOU AND MOM CAN DROP ME OFF AT WORK, AND THEN YOU CAN TAKE THE CAR.
MIND IF WE COME ALONG FOR THE RIDE? IT WOULDN'T BE A BAD IDEA FOR US TO SEE A LITTLE OF THE CITY.
IT SEEMS LIKE WE MIGHT BE HERE FOR A WHILE.

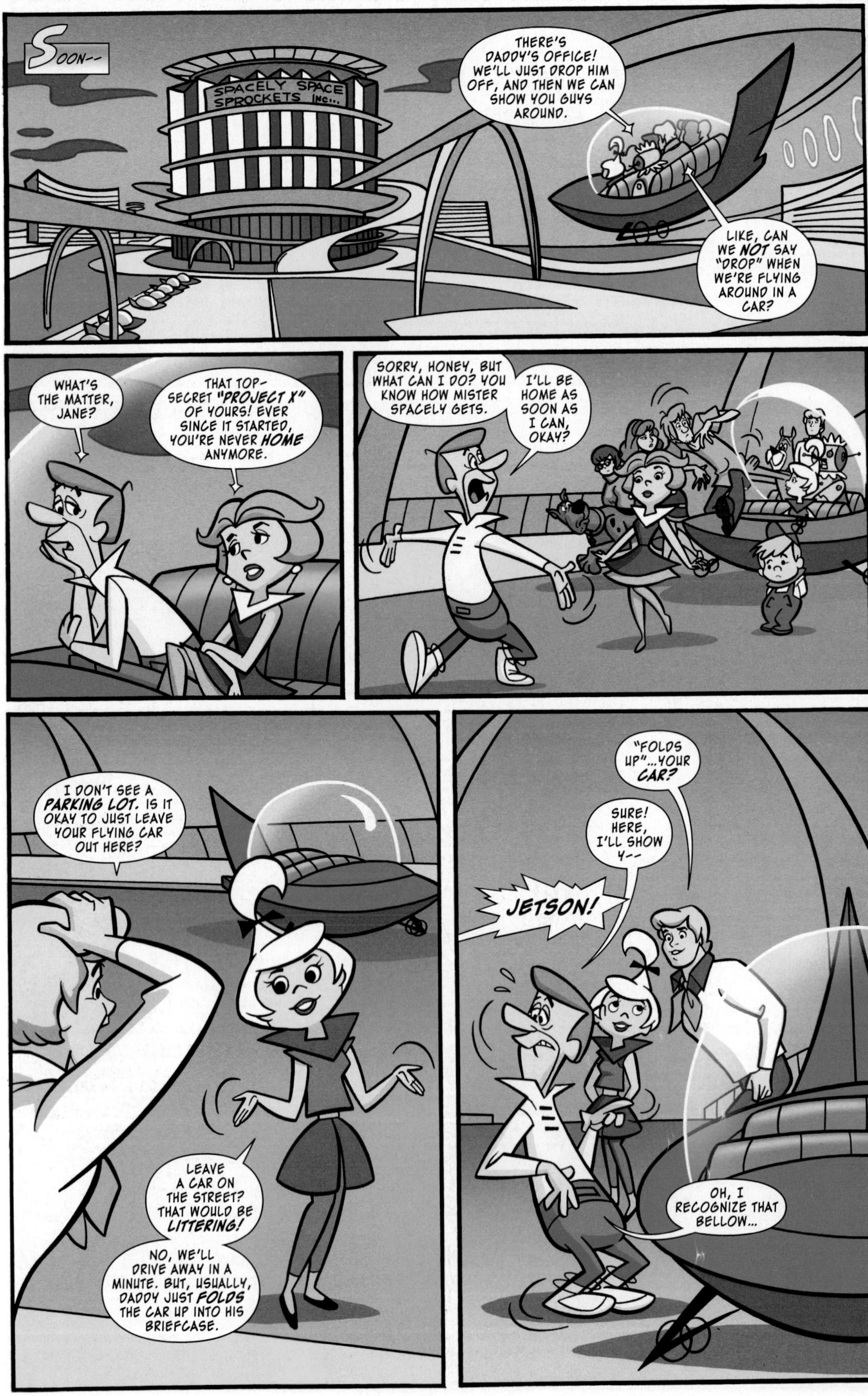
SOON--
SPACELY SPACE SPROCKETS INC...
THERE'S DADDY'S OFFICE! WE'LL JUST DROP HIM OFF, AND THEN WE CAN SHOW YOU GUYS AROUND.
LIKE, CAN WE NOT SAY "DROP" WHEN WE'RE FLYING AROUND IN A CAR?
WHAT'S THE MATTER, JANE?
THAT TOP-SECRET "PROJECT X" OF YOURS! EVER SINCE IT STARTED, YOU'RE NEVER HOME ANYMORE.
SORRY, HONEY, BUT WHAT CAN I DO? YOU KNOW HOW MISTER SPACELY GETS.
I'LL BE HOME AS SOON AS I CAN, OKAY?
I DON'T SEE A PARKING LOT. IS IT OKAY TO JUST LEAVE YOUR FLYING CAR OUT HERE?
LEAVE A CAR ON THE STREET? THAT WOULD BE LITTERING!
NO, WE'LL DRIVE AWAY IN A MINUTE. BUT, USUALLY, DADDY JUST FOLDS THE CAR UP INTO HIS BRIEFCASE.
"FOLDS UP"...YOUR CAR?
SURE! HERE, I'LL SHOW Y--
JETSON!
OH, I RECOGNIZE THAT BELLOW...

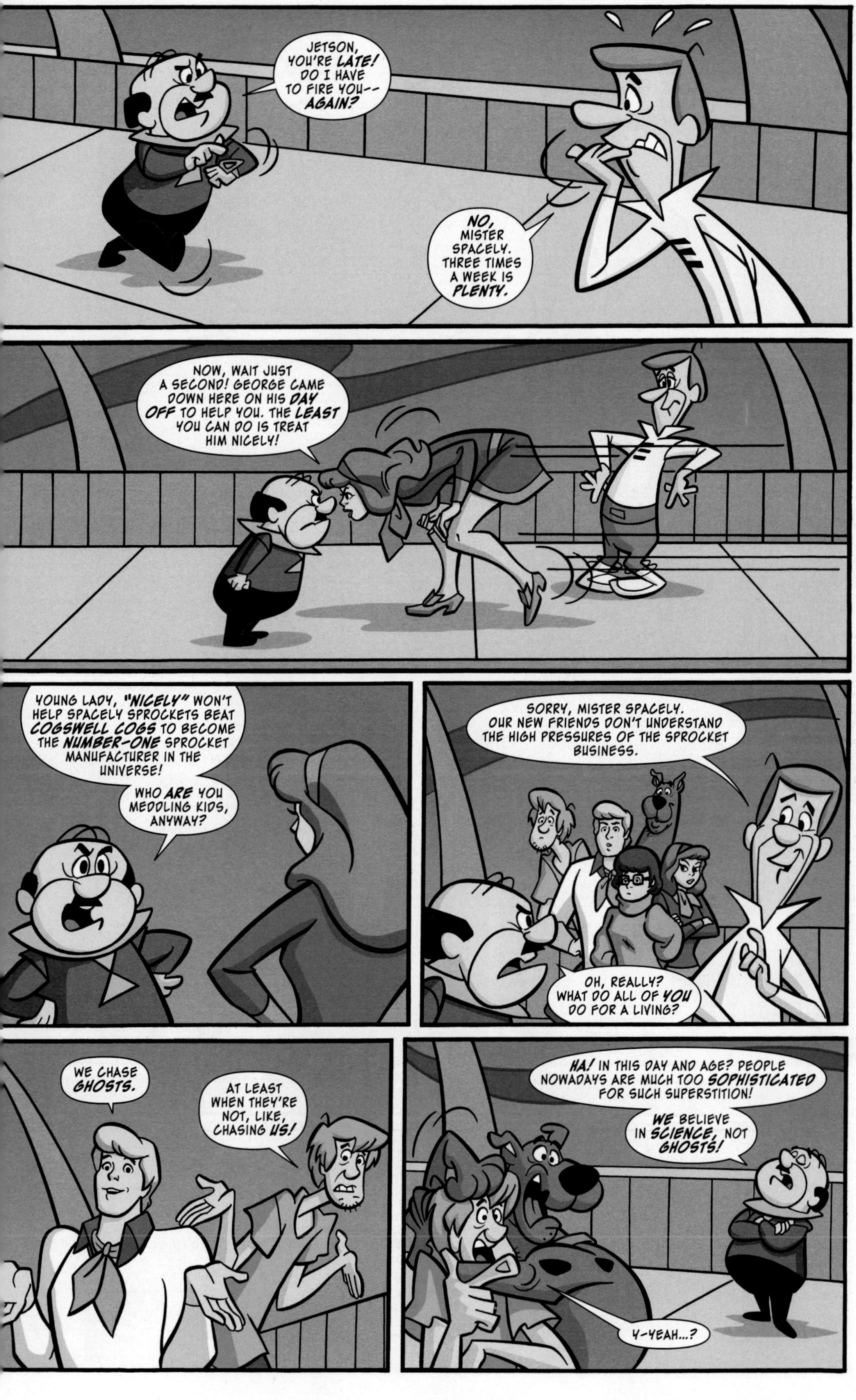
JETSON, YOU'RE LATE! DO I HAVE TO FIRE YOU-- AGAIN?
NO, MISTER SPACELY. THREE TIMES A WEEK IS PLENTY.
NOW, WAIT JUST A SECOND! GEORGE CAME DOWN HERE ON HIS DAY OFF TO HELP YOU. THE LEAST YOU CAN DO IS TREAT HIM NICELY!
YOUNG LADY, "NICELY" WON'T HELP SPACELY SPROCKETS BEAT COGSWELL COGS TO BECOME THE NUMBER-ONE SPROCKET MANUFACTURER IN THE UNIVERSE!
WHO ARE YOU MEDDLING KIDS, ANYWAY?
SORRY, MISTER SPACELY. OUR NEW FRIENDS DON'T UNDERSTAND THE HIGH PRESSURES OF THE SPROCKET BUSINESS.
OH, REALLY? WHAT DO ALL OF YOU DO FOR A LIVING?
WE CHASE GHOSTS.
AT LEAST WHEN THEY'RE NOT, LIKE, CHASING US!
HA! IN THIS DAY AND AGE? PEOPLE NOWADAYS ARE MUCH TOO SOPHISTICATED FOR SUCH SUPERSTITION!
WE BELIEVE IN SCIENCE, NOT GHOSTS!
Y-YEAH...?

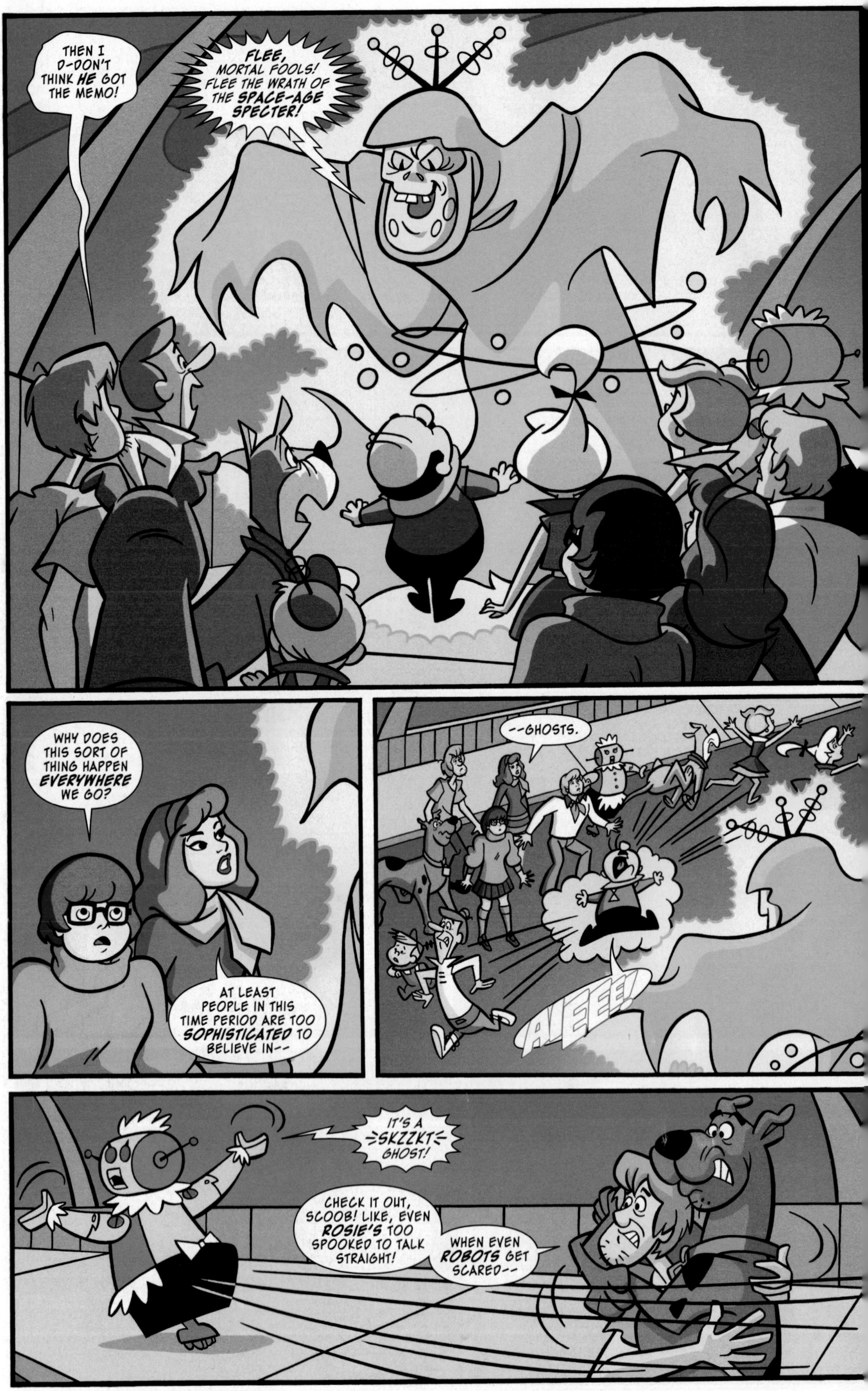
THEN I D-DON'T THINK HE GOT THE MEMO!
FLEE, MORTAL FOOLS! FLEE THE WRATH OF THE SPACE-AGE SPECTER!
WHY DOES THIS SORT OF THING HAPPEN EVERYWHERE WE GO?
AT LEAST PEOPLE IN THIS TIME PERIOD ARE TOO SOPHISTICATED TO BELIEVE IN--
--GHOSTS.
AIEEE!
IT'S A =SKZZKT= GHOST!
CHECK IT OUT, SCOOB! LIKE, EVEN ROSIE'S TOO SPOOKED TO TALK STRAIGHT!
WHEN EVEN ROBOTS GET SCARED--

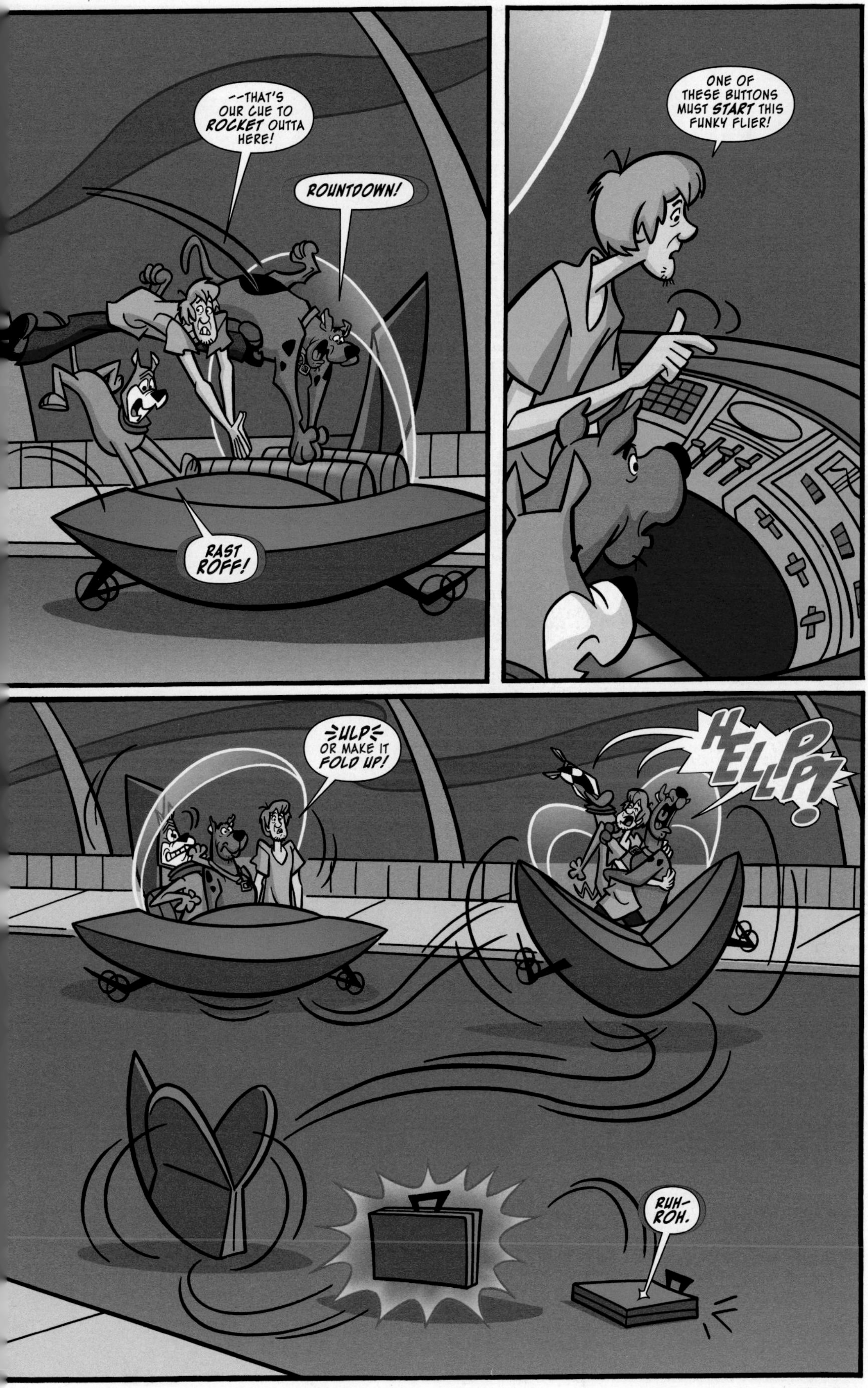
--THAT'S OUR CUE TO ROCKET OUTTA HERE!
ROUNTDOWN!
RAST ROFF!
ONE OF THESE BUTTONS MUST START THIS FUNKY FLIER!
ULP OR MAKE IT FOLD UP!
HELLP!
RUH-ROH.

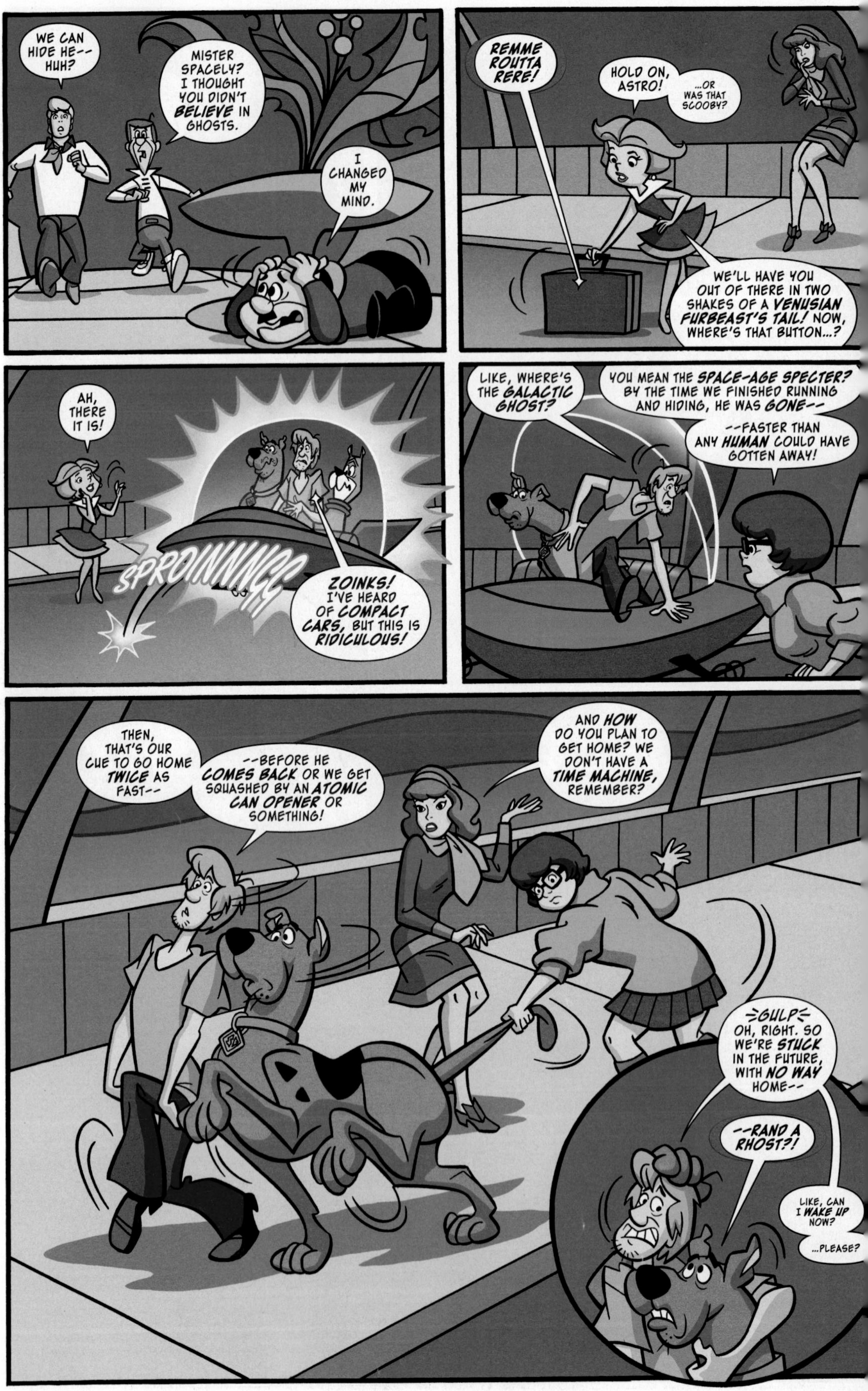
WE CAN HIDE HE-- HUH?
MISTER SPACELY? I THOUGHT YOU DIDN'T BELIEVE IN GHOSTS.
I CHANGED MY MIND.
REMME ROUTTA RERE!
HOLD ON, ASTRO!
...OR WAS THAT SCOOBY?
WE'LL HAVE YOU OUT OF THERE IN TWO SHAKES OF A VENUSIAN FURBEAST'S TAIL! NOW, WHERE'S THAT BUTTON...?
AH, THERE IT IS!
SPROINNNG
ZOINKS! I'VE HEARD OF COMPACT CARS, BUT THIS IS RIDICULOUS!
LIKE, WHERE'S THE GALACTIC GHOST?
YOU MEAN THE SPACE-AGE SPECTER? BY THE TIME WE FINISHED RUNNING AND HIDING, HE WAS GONE--
--FASTER THAN ANY HUMAN COULD HAVE GOTTEN AWAY!
THEN, THAT'S OUR CUE TO GO HOME TWICE AS FAST--
--BEFORE HE COMES BACK OR WE GET SQUASHED BY AN ATOMIC CAN OPENER OR SOMETHING!
AND HOW DO YOU PLAN TO GET HOME? WE DON'T HAVE A TIME MACHINE, REMEMBER?
=GULP= OH, RIGHT. SO WE'RE STUCK IN THE FUTURE, WITH NO WAY HOME--
--RAND A RHOST?!
LIKE, CAN I WAKE UP NOW?
...PLEASE?

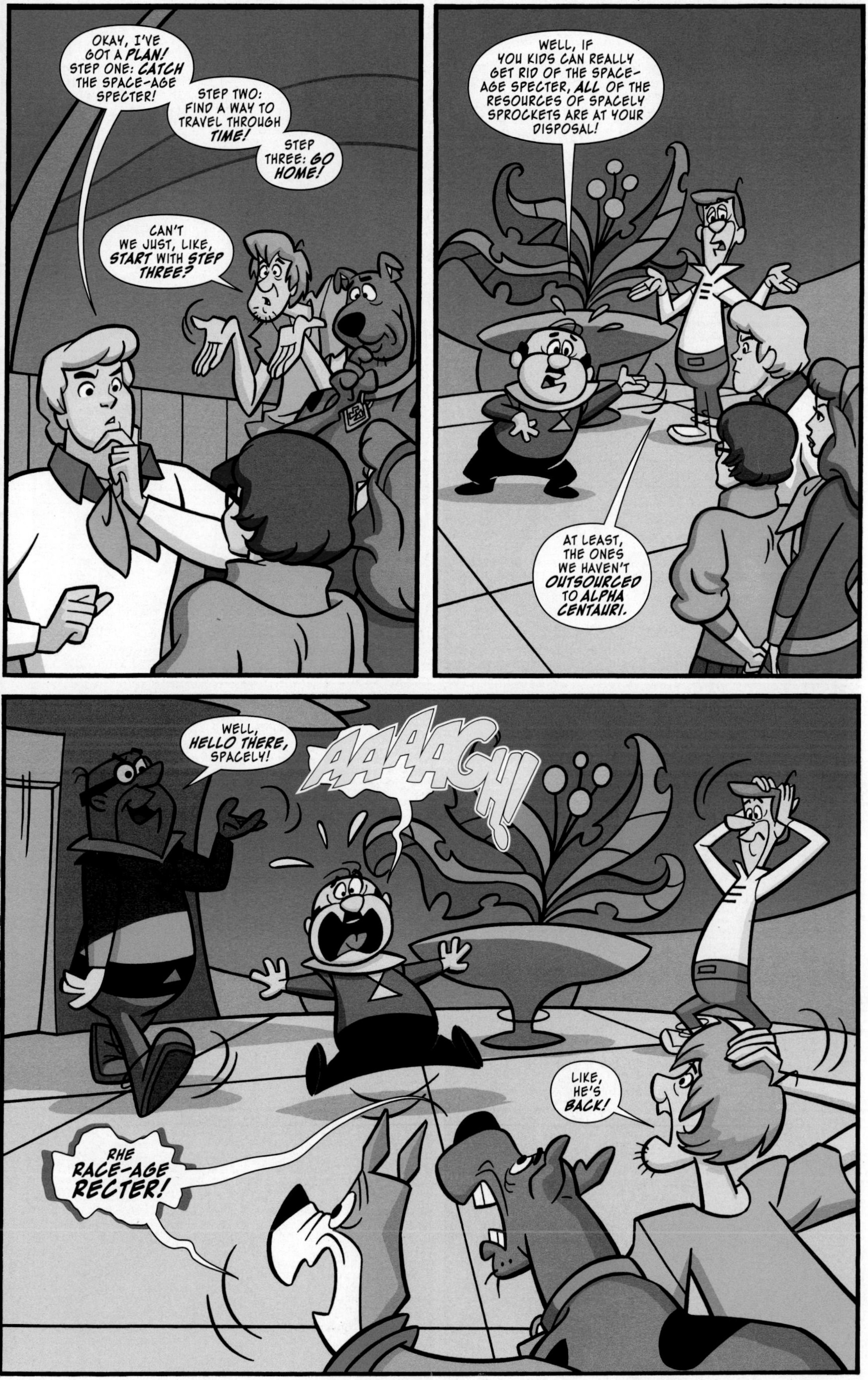
OKAY, I'VE GOT A PLAN! STEP ONE: CATCH THE SPACE-AGE SPECTER!
STEP TWO: FIND A WAY TO TRAVEL THROUGH TIME!
STEP THREE: GO HOME!
CAN'T WE JUST, LIKE, START WITH STEP THREE?
WELL, IF YOU KIDS CAN REALLY GET RID OF THE SPACE-AGE SPECTER, ALL OF THE RESOURCES OF SPACELY SPROCKETS ARE AT YOUR DISPOSAL!
AT LEAST, THE ONES WE HAVEN'T OUTSOURCED TO ALPHA CENTAURI.
WELL, HELLO THERE, SPACELY!
AAAAGH!
LIKE, HE'S BACK!
RHE RACE-AGE RECTER!

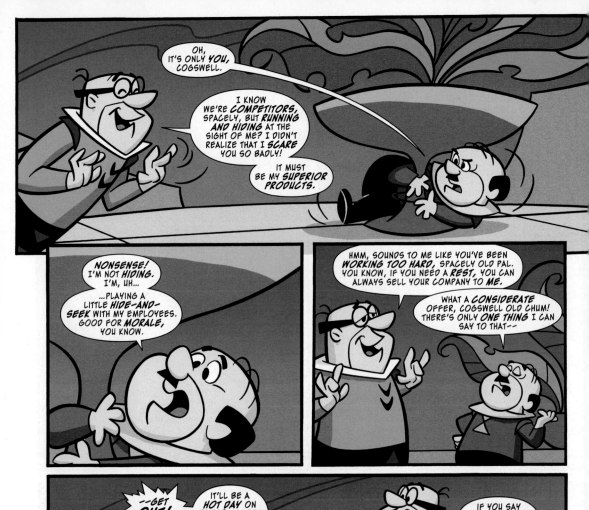

OH, IT'S ONLY *YOU*, COGSWELL.

I KNOW WE'RE *COMPETITORS*, SPACELY, BUT *RUNNING AND HIDING* AT THE SIGHT OF ME? I DIDN'T REALIZE THAT I *SCARE* YOU SO BADLY!

IT MUST BE MY *SUPERIOR* PRODUCTS.

NONSENSE! I'M NOT *HIDING*. I'M, UH...

...PLAYING A LITTLE *HIDE-AND-SEEK* WITH MY EMPLOYEES. GOOD FOR *MORALE*, YOU KNOW.

HMM, SOUNDS TO ME LIKE YOU'VE BEEN *WORKING TOO HARD*, SPACELY OLD PAL. YOU KNOW, IF YOU NEED A *REST*, YOU CAN ALWAYS SELL YOUR COMPANY TO *ME*.

WHAT A *CONSIDERATE* OFFER, COGSWELL OLD CHUM! THERE'S ONLY *ONE THING* I CAN SAY TO THAT--

--GET *OUT!*

IT'LL BE A *HOT DAY* ON *PLUTO* BEFORE I EVER SELL MY COMPANY TO YOU!

IF YOU SAY SO, OLD BUDDY. I'LL BE *SEEING* YOU!

WHO'S THAT?

MISTER COGSWELL? HE'S THE OWNER OF *COGSWELL'S COGS*--MISTER SPACELY'S BIGGEST *RIVAL*.

THAT'S NOT *ALL* HE IS.

NO?

HE'S ALSO A *SUSPECT!*

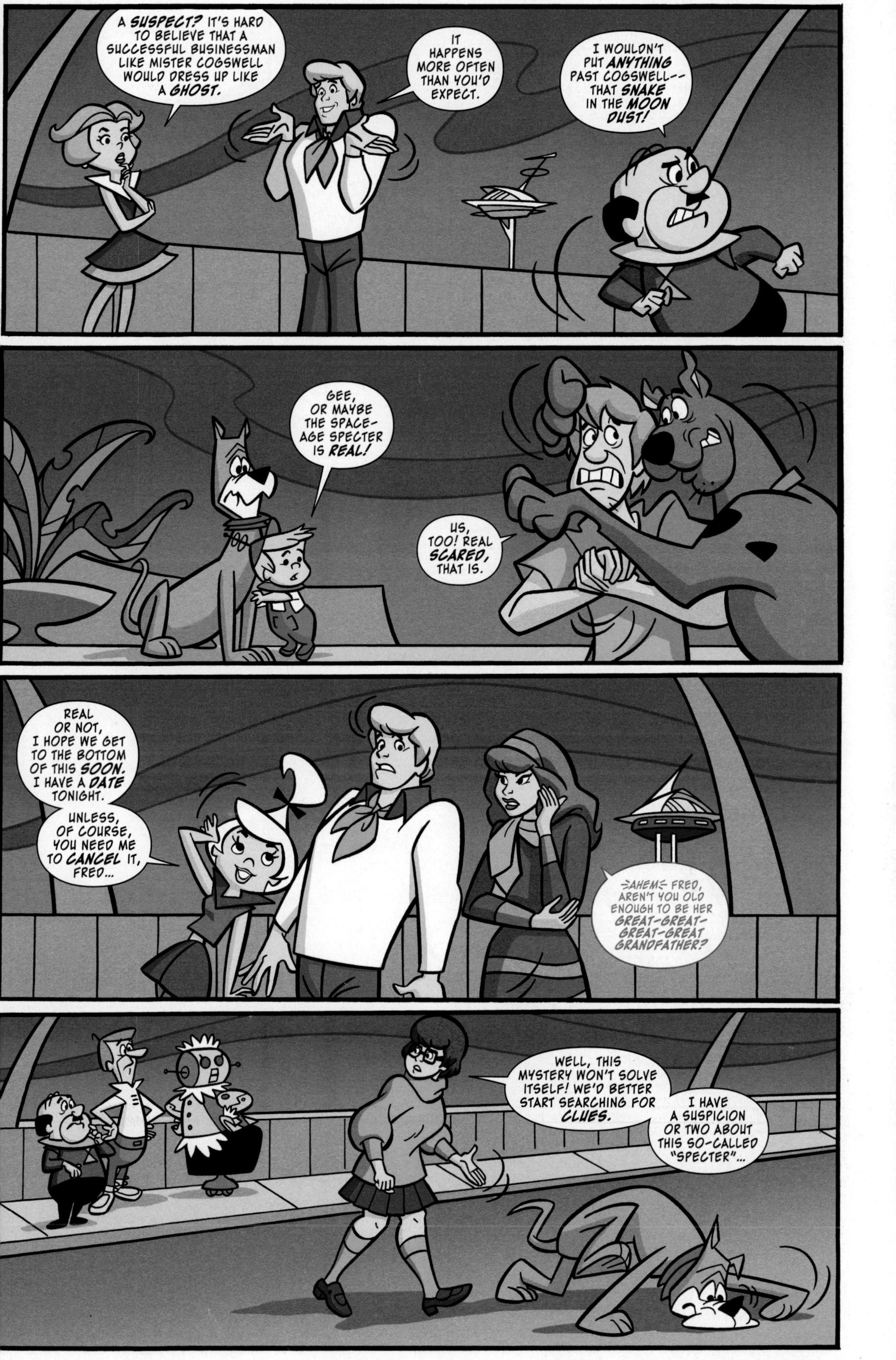
A SUSPECT? IT'S HARD TO BELIEVE THAT A SUCCESSFUL BUSINESSMAN LIKE MISTER COGSWELL WOULD DRESS UP LIKE A GHOST.
IT HAPPENS MORE OFTEN THAN YOU'D EXPECT.
I WOULDN'T PUT ANYTHING PAST COGSWELL-- THAT SNAKE IN THE MOON DUST!
GEE, OR MAYBE THE SPACE-AGE SPECTER IS REAL!
US, TOO! REAL SCARED, THAT IS.
REAL OR NOT, I HOPE WE GET TO THE BOTTOM OF THIS SOON. I HAVE A DATE TONIGHT.
UNLESS, OF COURSE, YOU NEED ME TO CANCEL IT, FRED...
=AHEM= FRED, AREN'T YOU OLD ENOUGH TO BE HER GREAT-GREAT-GREAT-GREAT GRANDFATHER?
WELL, THIS MYSTERY WON'T SOLVE ITSELF! WE'D BETTER START SEARCHING FOR CLUES.
I HAVE A SUSPICION OR TWO ABOUT THIS SO-CALLED "SPECTER"...

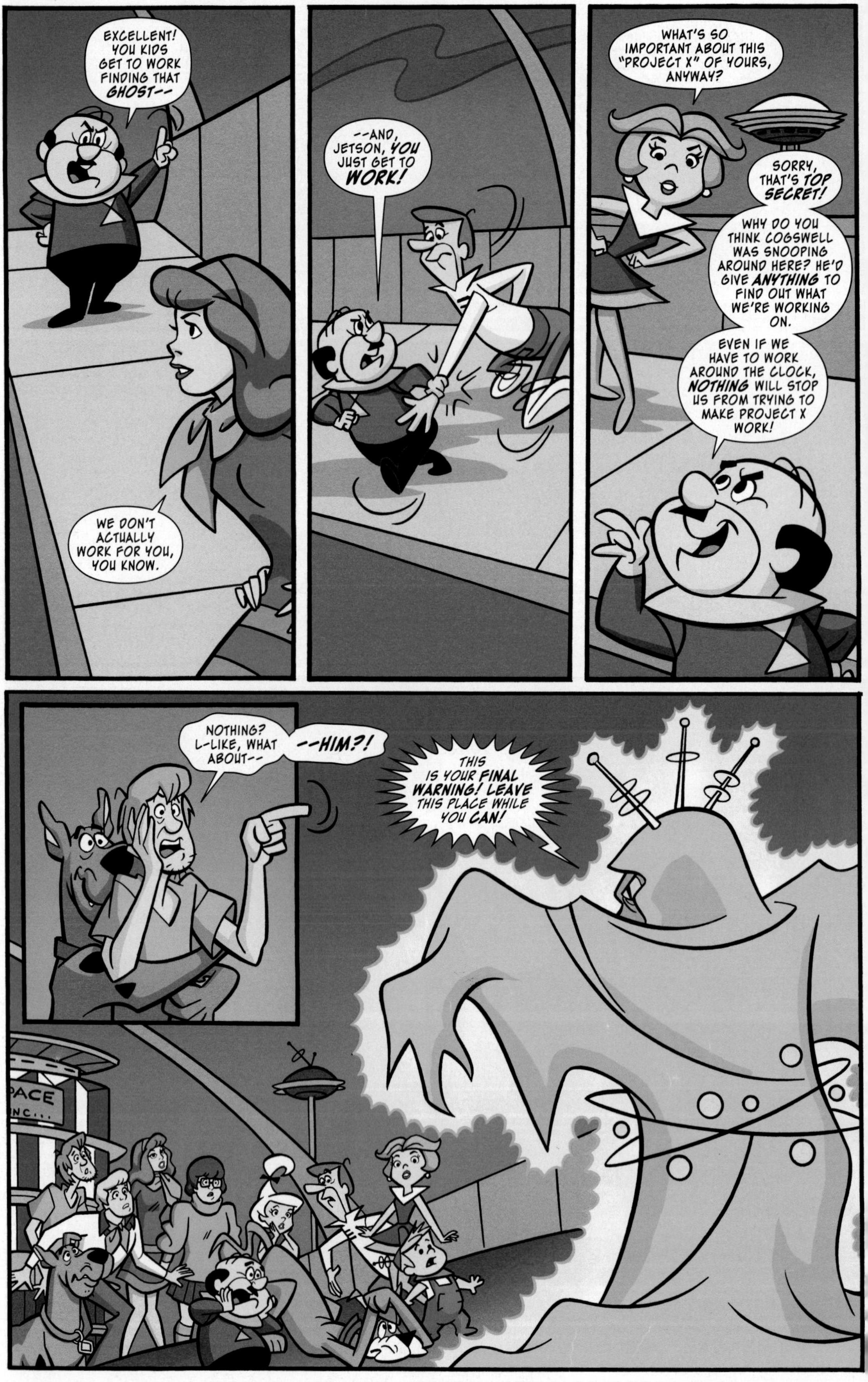
EXCELLENT! YOU KIDS GET TO WORK FINDING THAT *GHOST*--
WE DON'T ACTUALLY WORK FOR YOU, YOU KNOW.
--AND, JETSON, *YOU* JUST GET TO *WORK!*
WHAT'S SO IMPORTANT ABOUT THIS "PROJECT X" OF YOURS, ANYWAY?
SORRY, THAT'S *TOP SECRET!*
WHY DO YOU THINK COGSWELL WAS SNOOPING AROUND HERE? HE'D GIVE *ANYTHING* TO FIND OUT WHAT WE'RE WORKING ON.
EVEN IF WE HAVE TO WORK AROUND THE CLOCK, *NOTHING* WILL STOP US FROM TRYING TO MAKE PROJECT X WORK!
NOTHING? L-LIKE, WHAT ABOUT--
--*HIM?!*
THIS IS YOUR **FINAL WARNING! LEAVE** THIS PLACE WHILE YOU **CAN!**

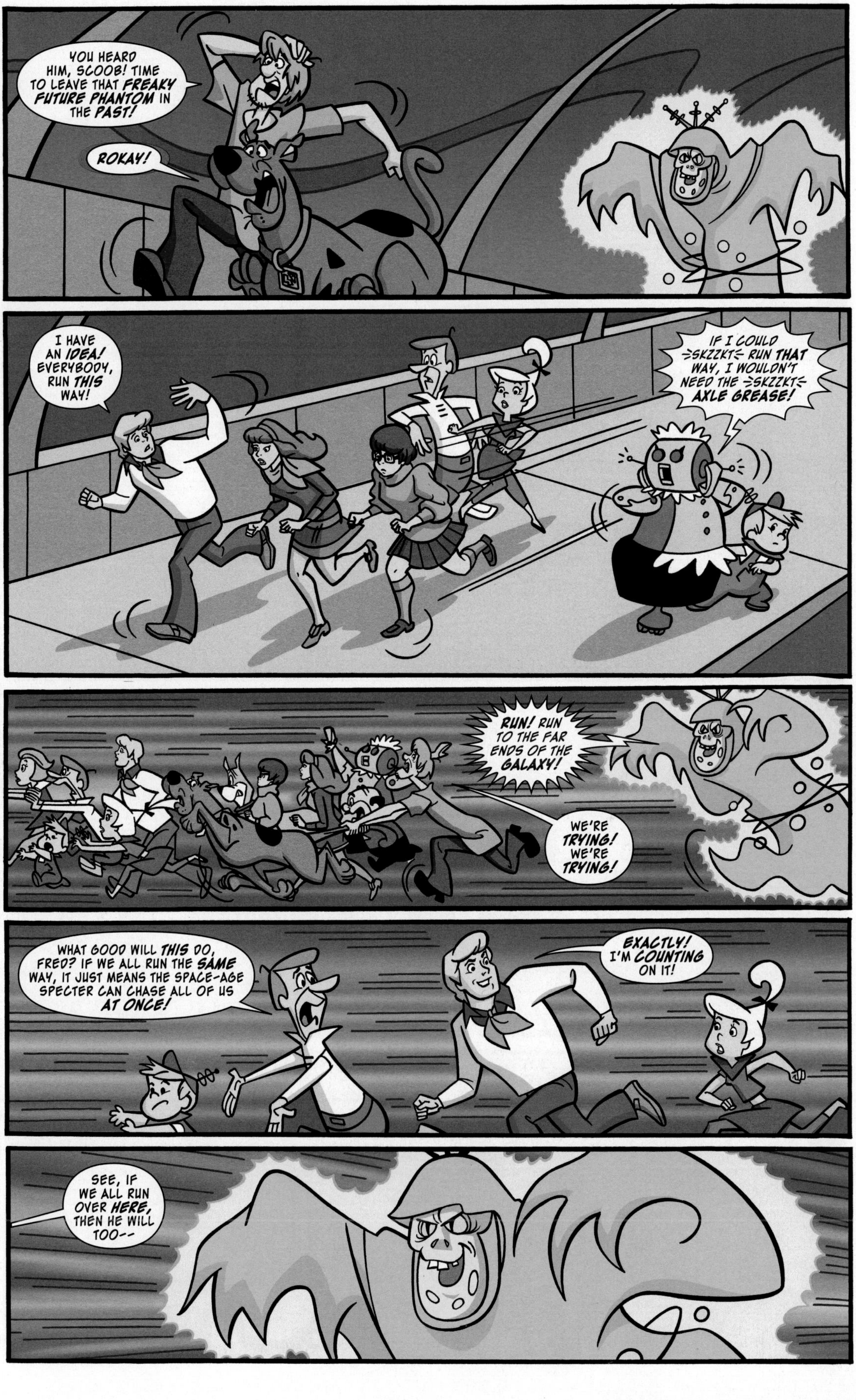
YOU HEARD HIM, SCOOB! TIME TO LEAVE THAT FREAKY FUTURE PHANTOM IN THE PAST!
ROKAY!
I HAVE AN IDEA! EVERYBODY, RUN THIS WAY!
IF I COULD =SKZZKT= RUN THAT WAY, I WOULDN'T NEED THE =SKZZKT= AXLE GREASE!
RUN! RUN TO THE FAR ENDS OF THE GALAXY!
WE'RE TRYING! WE'RE TRYING!
WHAT GOOD WILL THIS DO, FRED? IF WE ALL RUN THE SAME WAY, IT JUST MEANS THE SPACE-AGE SPECTER CAN CHASE ALL OF US AT ONCE!
EXACTLY! I'M COUNTING ON IT!
SEE, IF WE ALL RUN OVER HERE, THEN HE WILL TOO--

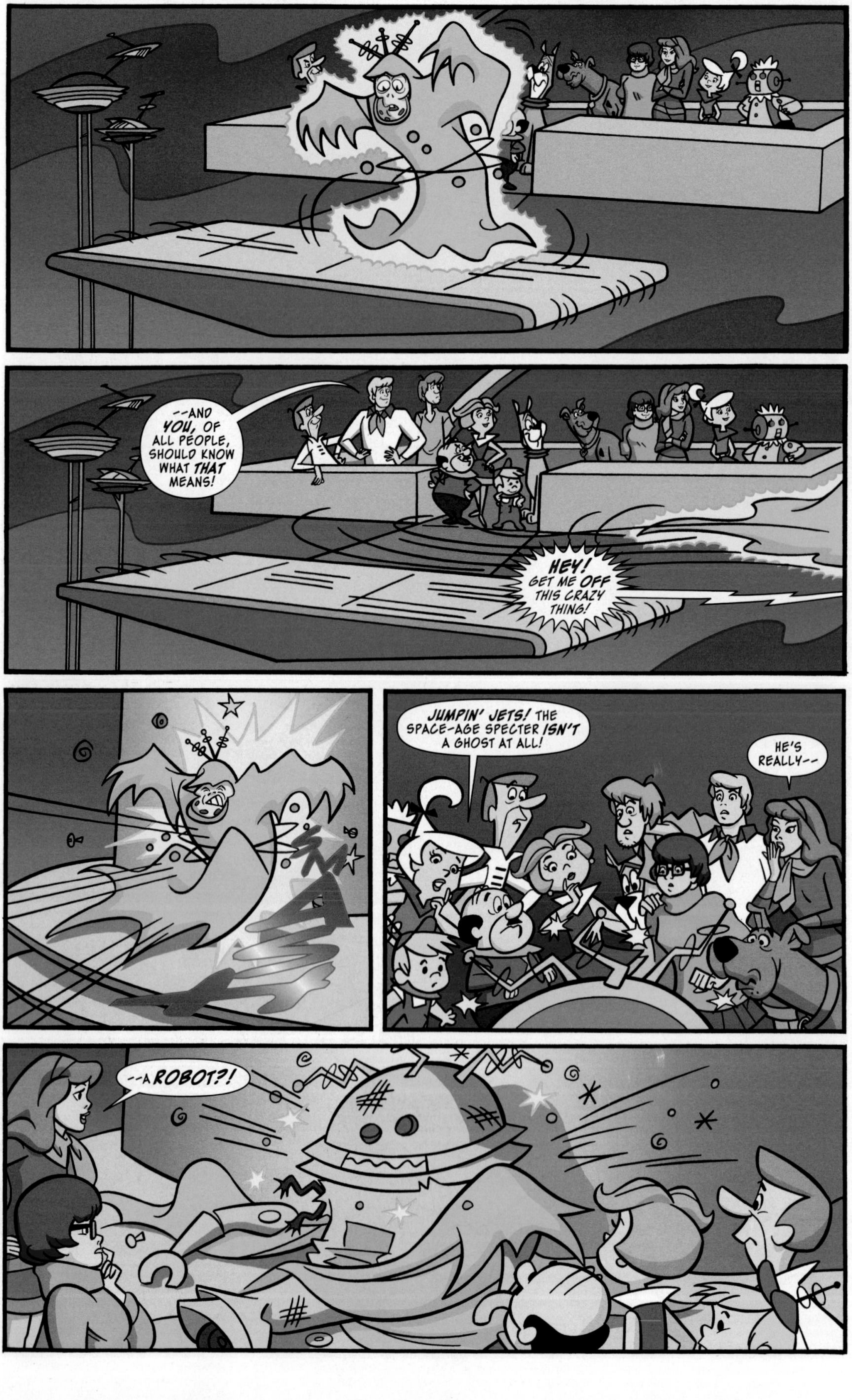
--AND YOU, OF ALL PEOPLE, SHOULD KNOW WHAT THAT MEANS!
HEY! GET ME OFF THIS CRAZY THING!
JUMPIN' JETS! THE SPACE-AGE SPECTER ISN'T A GHOST AT ALL!
HE'S REALLY--
--A ROBOT?!

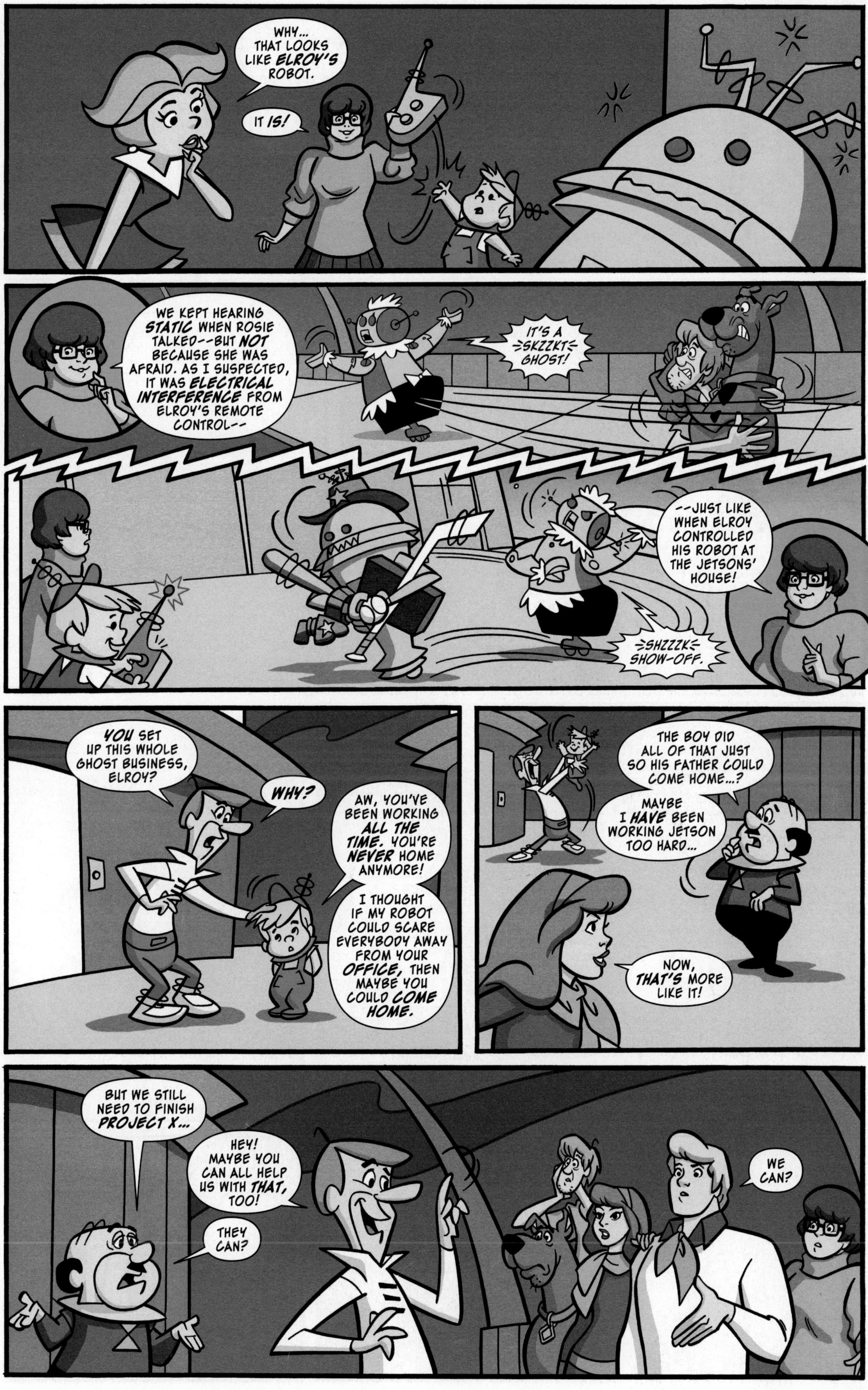

WHY... THAT LOOKS LIKE ELROY'S ROBOT.
IT IS!
WE KEPT HEARING STATIC WHEN ROSIE TALKED--BUT NOT BECAUSE SHE WAS AFRAID. AS I SUSPECTED, IT WAS ELECTRICAL INTERFERENCE FROM ELROY'S REMOTE CONTROL--
IT'S A SKZZKT GHOST!
--JUST LIKE WHEN ELROY CONTROLLED HIS ROBOT AT THE JETSONS' HOUSE!
SHZZZK SHOW-OFF.
YOU SET UP THIS WHOLE GHOST BUSINESS, ELROY?
WHY?
AW, YOU'VE BEEN WORKING ALL THE TIME. YOU'RE NEVER HOME ANYMORE!
I THOUGHT IF MY ROBOT COULD SCARE EVERYBODY AWAY FROM YOUR OFFICE, THEN MAYBE YOU COULD COME HOME.
THE BOY DID ALL OF THAT JUST SO HIS FATHER COULD COME HOME...?
MAYBE I HAVE BEEN WORKING JETSON TOO HARD...
NOW, THAT'S MORE LIKE IT!
BUT WE STILL NEED TO FINISH PROJECT X...
HEY! MAYBE YOU CAN ALL HELP US WITH THAT, TOO!
THEY CAN?
WE CAN?

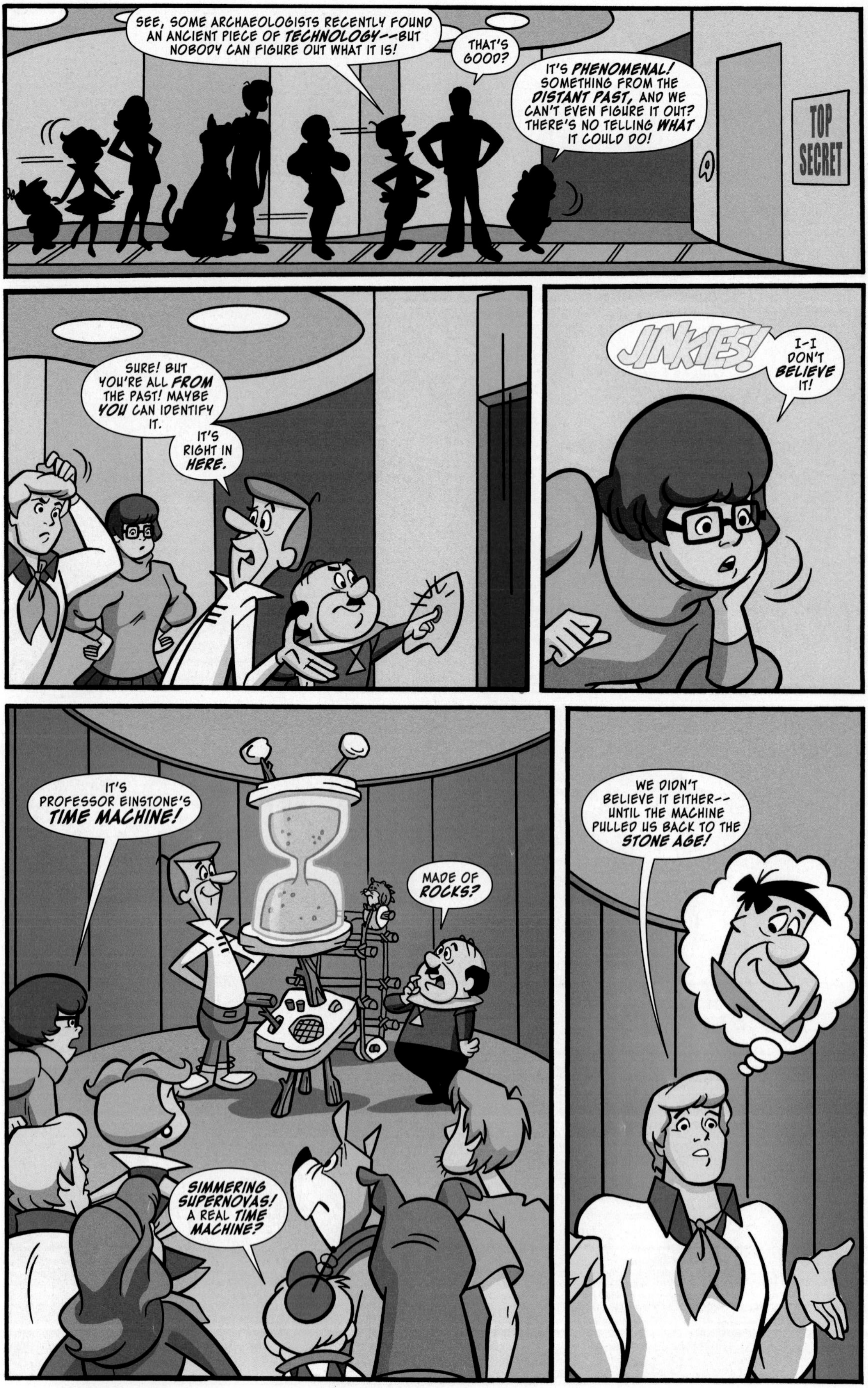
SEE, SOME ARCHAEOLOGISTS RECENTLY FOUND AN ANCIENT PIECE OF TECHNOLOGY--BUT NOBODY CAN FIGURE OUT WHAT IT IS!
THAT'S GOOD?
IT'S PHENOMENAL! SOMETHING FROM THE DISTANT PAST, AND WE CAN'T EVEN FIGURE IT OUT? THERE'S NO TELLING WHAT IT COULD DO!
TOP SECRET
SURE! BUT YOU'RE ALL FROM THE PAST! MAYBE YOU CAN IDENTIFY IT.
IT'S RIGHT IN HERE.
JINKIES!
I-I DON'T BELIEVE IT!
IT'S PROFESSOR EINSTONE'S TIME MACHINE!
MADE OF ROCKS?
SIMMERING SUPERNOVAS! A REAL TIME MACHINE?
WE DIDN'T BELIEVE IT EITHER--UNTIL THE MACHINE PULLED US BACK TO THE STONE AGE!

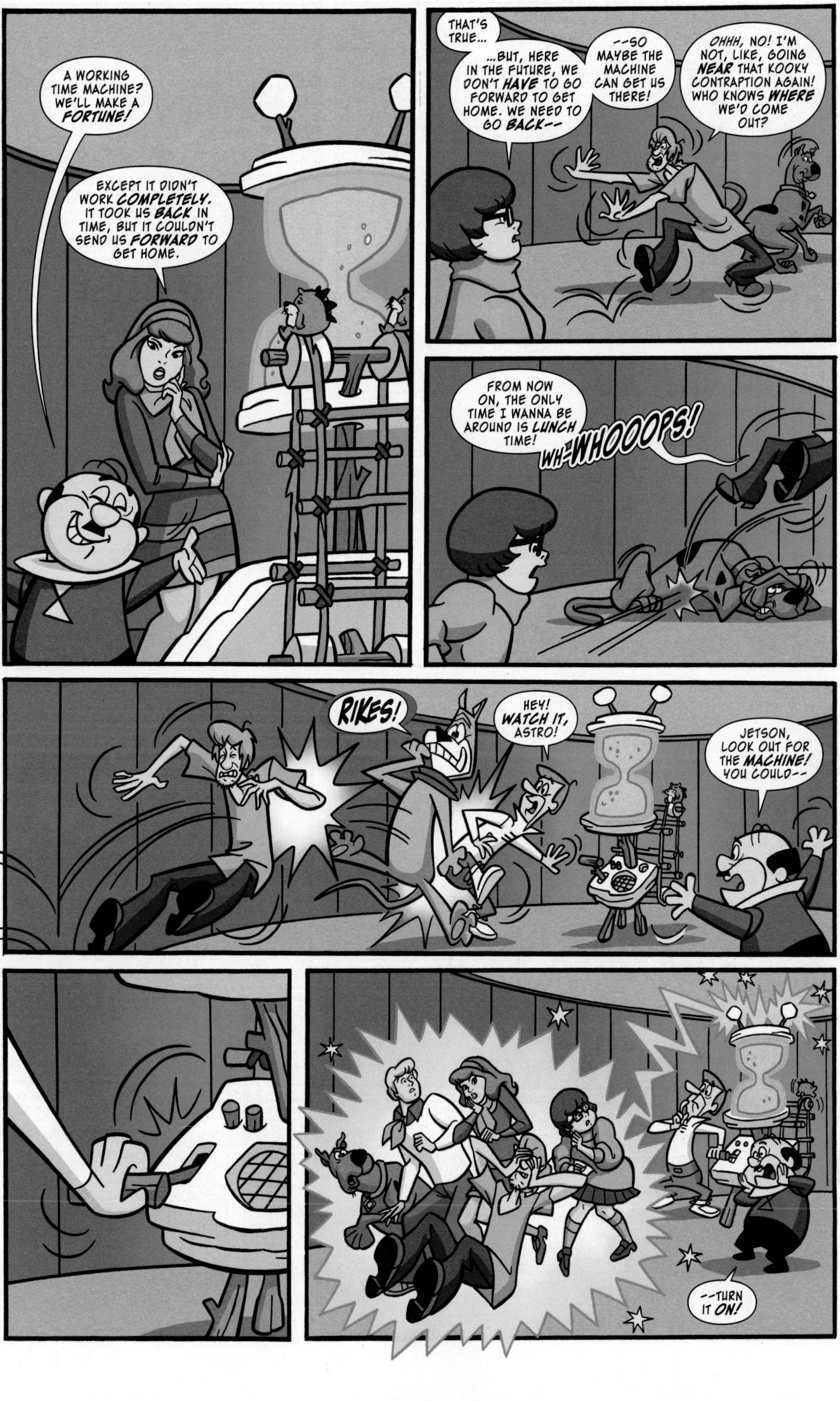
A WORKING TIME MACHINE? WE'LL MAKE A FORTUNE!
EXCEPT IT DIDN'T WORK COMPLETELY. IT TOOK US BACK IN TIME, BUT IT COULDN'T SEND US FORWARD TO GET HOME.
THAT'S TRUE...
...BUT, HERE IN THE FUTURE, WE DON'T HAVE TO GO FORWARD TO GET HOME. WE NEED TO GO BACK--
--SO MAYBE THE MACHINE CAN GET US THERE!
OHHH, NO! I'M NOT, LIKE, GOING NEAR THAT KOOKY CONTRAPTION AGAIN! WHO KNOWS WHERE WE'D COME OUT?
FROM NOW ON, THE ONLY TIME I WANNA BE AROUND IS LUNCH TIME!
WH-WHOOOOPS!
RIKES!
HEY! WATCH IT, ASTRO!
JETSON, LOOK OUT FOR THE MACHINE! YOU COULD--
--TURN IT ON!

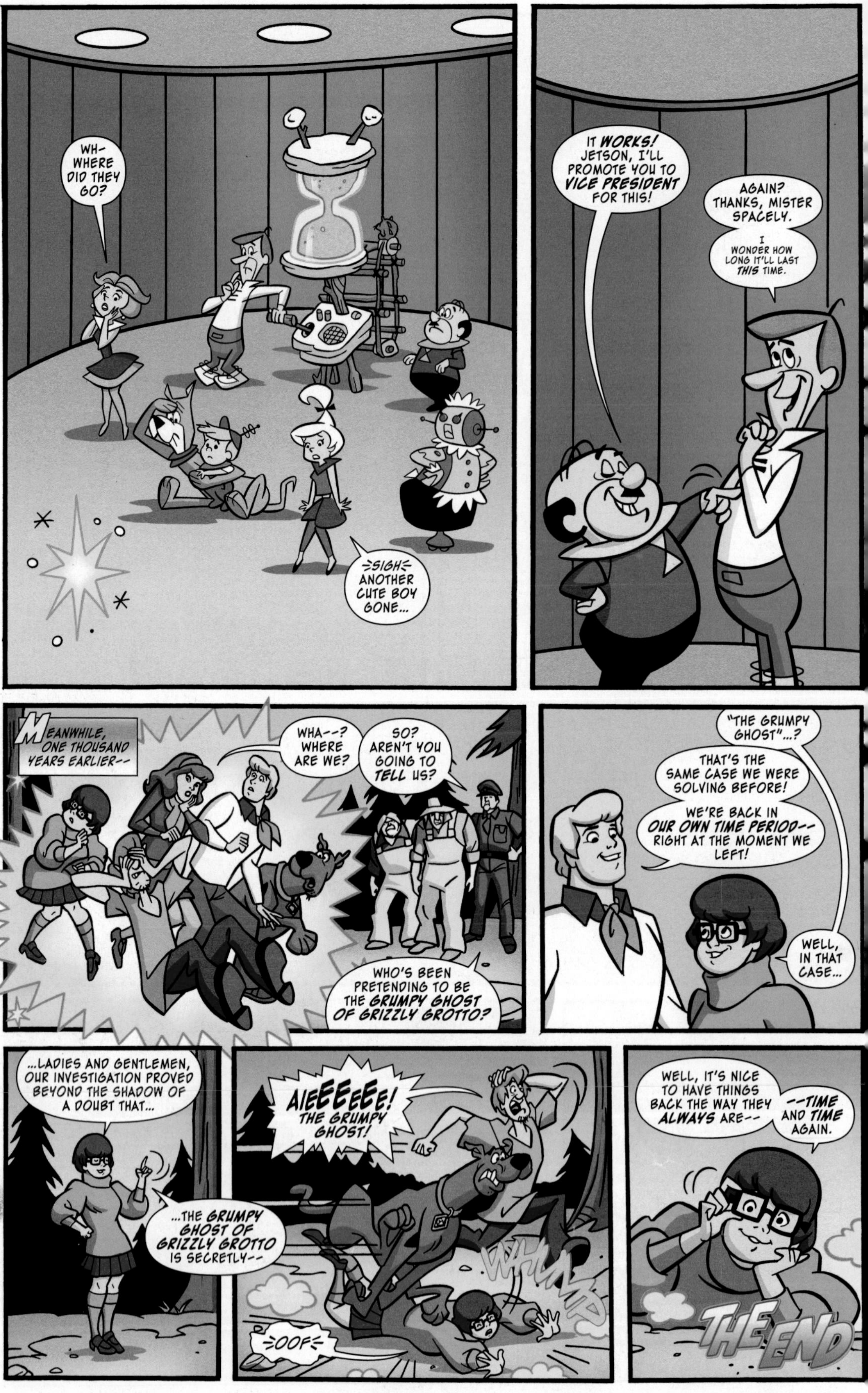

WH-WHERE DID THEY GO?
=SIGH= ANOTHER CUTE BOY GONE...
IT WORKS! JETSON, I'LL PROMOTE YOU TO VICE PRESIDENT FOR THIS!
AGAIN? THANKS, MISTER SPACELY.
I WONDER HOW LONG IT'LL LAST THIS TIME.
MEANWHILE, ONE THOUSAND YEARS EARLIER--
WHA--? WHERE ARE WE?
SO? AREN'T YOU GOING TO TELL US?
WHO'S BEEN PRETENDING TO BE THE GRUMPY GHOST OF GRIZZLY GROTTO?
"THE GRUMPY GHOST"...?
THAT'S THE SAME CASE WE WERE SOLVING BEFORE!
WE'RE BACK IN OUR OWN TIME PERIOD--RIGHT AT THE MOMENT WE LEFT!
WELL, IN THAT CASE...
...LADIES AND GENTLEMEN, OUR INVESTIGATION PROVED BEYOND THE SHADOW OF A DOUBT THAT...
...THE GRUMPY GHOST OF GRIZZLY GROTTO IS SECRETLY--
AIEEEEEE! THE GRUMPY GHOST!
WHUMP
=OOF=
WELL, IT'S NICE TO HAVE THINGS BACK THE WAY THEY ALWAYS ARE--
--TIME AND TIME AGAIN.
THE END

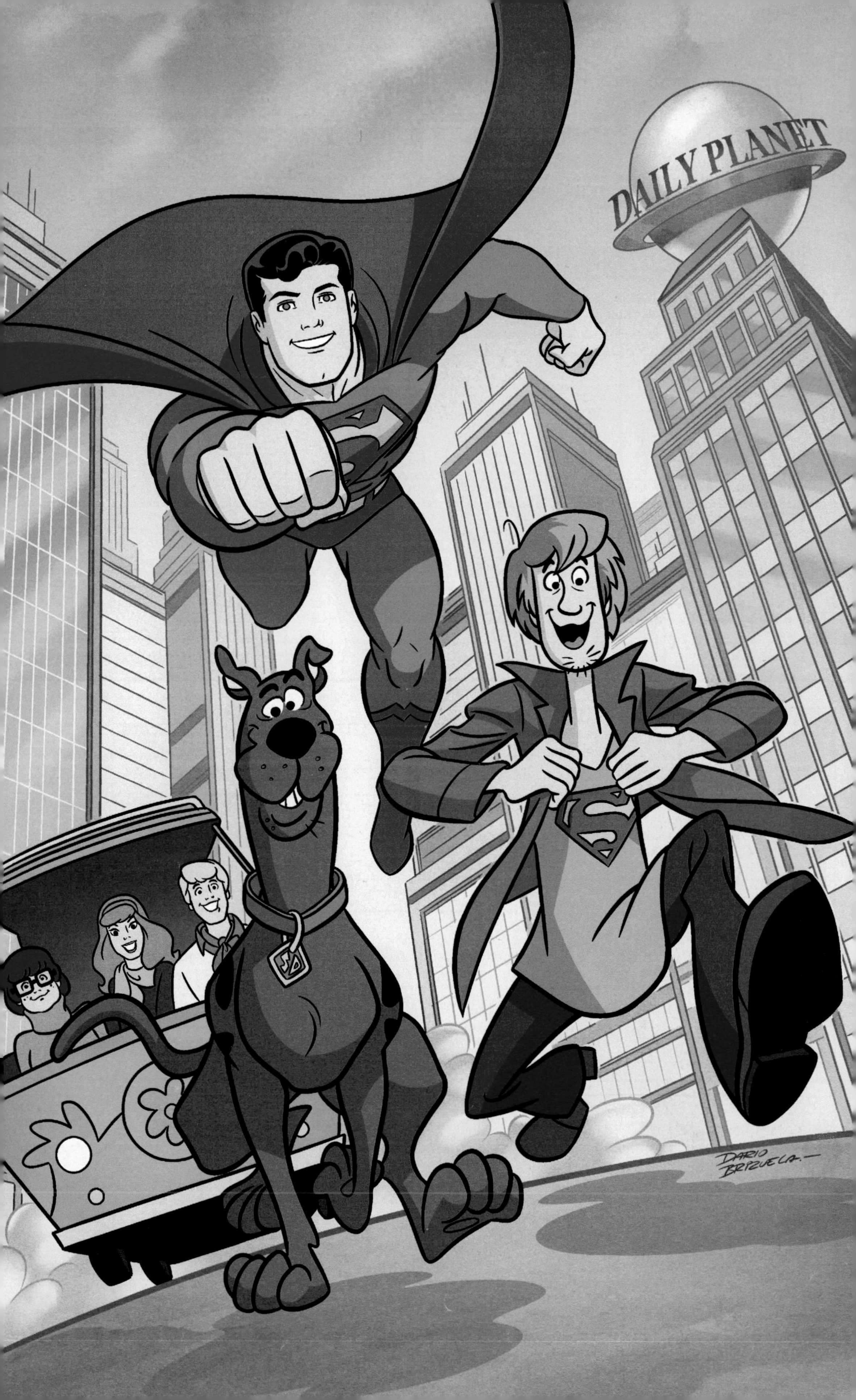
DAILY PLANET
DARIO BRIZUELA

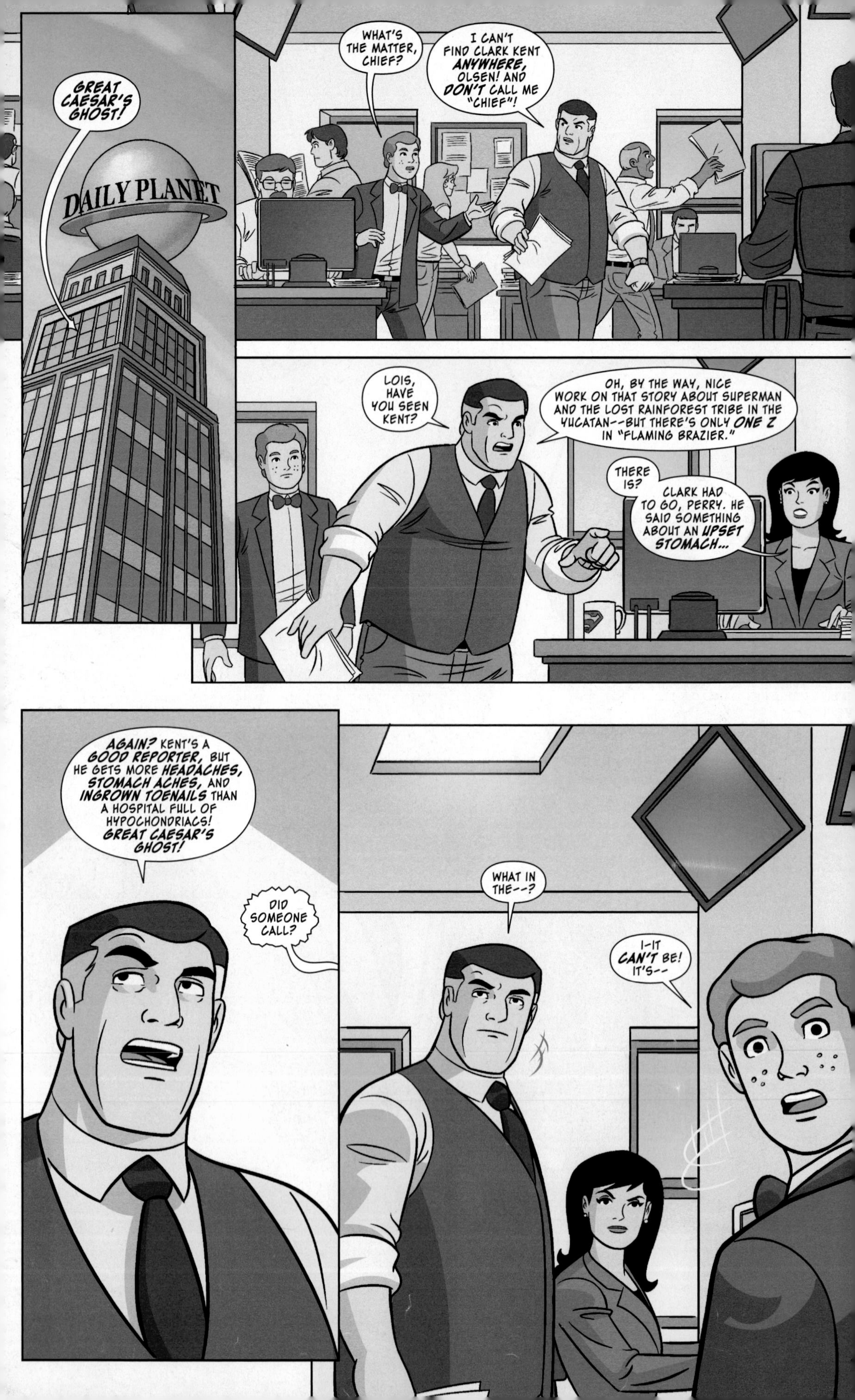
GREAT CAESAR'S GHOST!
DAILY PLANET
WHAT'S THE MATTER, CHIEF?
I CAN'T FIND CLARK KENT ANYWHERE, OLSEN! AND DON'T CALL ME "CHIEF"!
LOIS, HAVE YOU SEEN KENT?
OH, BY THE WAY, NICE WORK ON THAT STORY ABOUT SUPERMAN AND THE LOST RAINFOREST TRIBE IN THE YUCATAN--BUT THERE'S ONLY ONE Z IN "FLAMING BRAZIER."
THERE IS?
CLARK HAD TO GO, PERRY. HE SAID SOMETHING ABOUT AN UPSET STOMACH...
AGAIN? KENT'S A GOOD REPORTER, BUT HE GETS MORE HEADACHES, STOMACH ACHES, AND INGROWN TOENAILS THAN A HOSPITAL FULL OF HYPOCHONDRIACS! GREAT CAESAR'S GHOST!
DID SOMEONE CALL?
WHAT IN THE--?
I-IT CAN'T BE! IT'S--

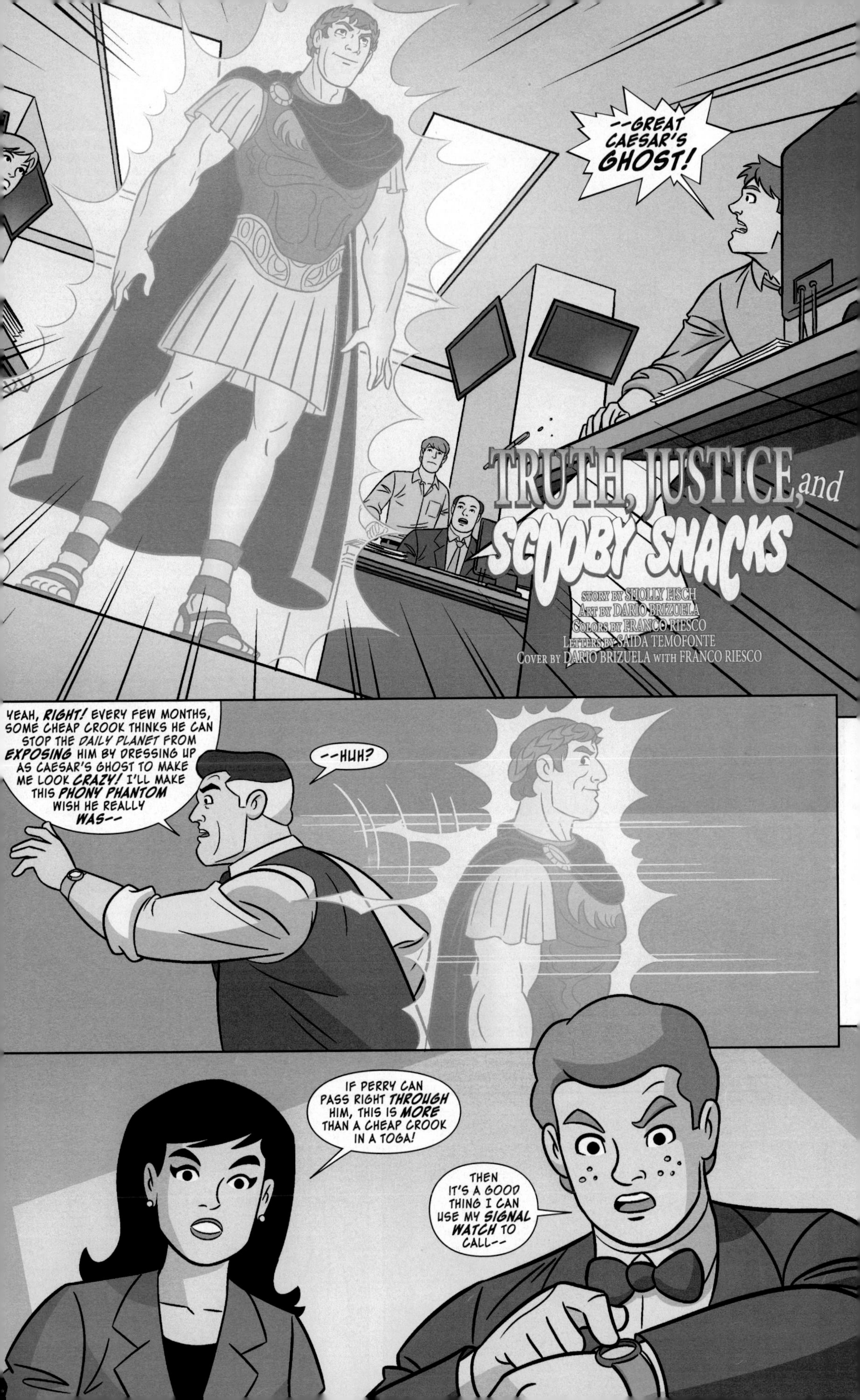
--GREAT CAESAR'S GHOST!
TRUTH, JUSTICE, and SCOOBY SNACKS
STORY BY SHOLLY FISCH
ART BY DARIO BRIZUELA
COLORS BY FRANCO RIESCO
LETTERS BY SAIDA TEMOFONTE
COVER BY DARIO BRIZUELA WITH FRANCO RIESCO
YEAH, RIGHT! EVERY FEW MONTHS, SOME CHEAP CROOK THINKS HE CAN STOP THE DAILY PLANET FROM EXPOSING HIM BY DRESSING UP AS CAESAR'S GHOST TO MAKE ME LOOK CRAZY! I'LL MAKE THIS PHONY PHANTOM WISH HE REALLY WAS--
--HUH?
IF PERRY CAN PASS RIGHT THROUGH HIM, THIS IS MORE THAN A CHEAP CROOK IN A TOGA!
THEN IT'S A GOOD THING I CAN USE MY SIGNAL WATCH TO CALL--

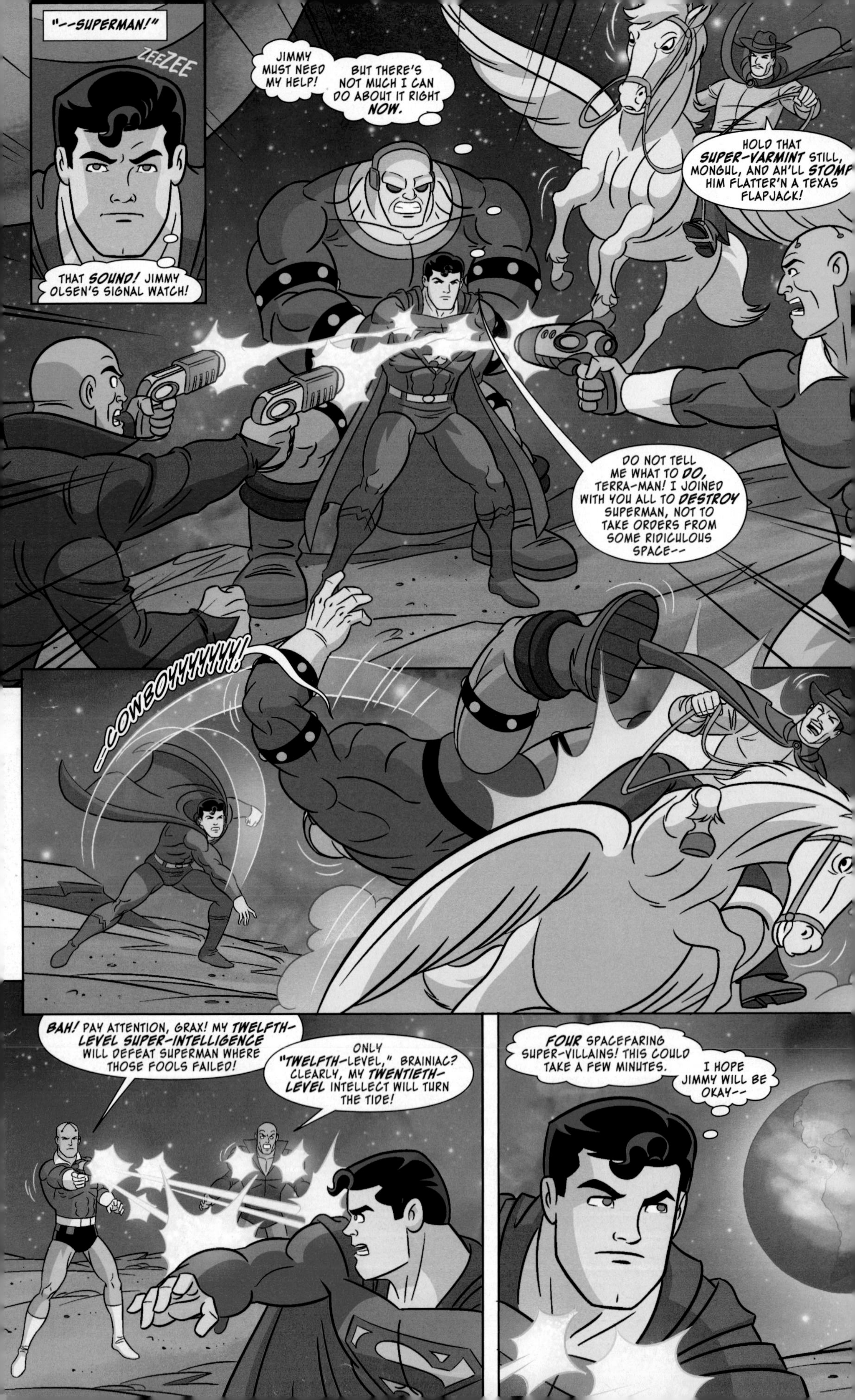
"--SUPERMAN!"
ZEEZEE
THAT SOUND! JIMMY OLSEN'S SIGNAL WATCH!
JIMMY MUST NEED MY HELP!
BUT THERE'S NOT MUCH I CAN DO ABOUT IT RIGHT NOW.
HOLD THAT SUPER-VARMINT STILL, MONGUL, AND AH'LL STOMP HIM FLATTER'N A TEXAS FLAPJACK!
DO NOT TELL ME WHAT TO DO, TERRA-MAN! I JOINED WITH YOU ALL TO DESTROY SUPERMAN, NOT TO TAKE ORDERS FROM SOME RIDICULOUS SPACE--
--COWBOYYYYYY!!
BAH! PAY ATTENTION, GRAX! MY TWELFTH-LEVEL SUPER-INTELLIGENCE WILL DEFEAT SUPERMAN WHERE THOSE FOOLS FAILED!
ONLY "TWELFTH-LEVEL," BRAINIAC? CLEARLY, MY TWENTIETH-LEVEL INTELLECT WILL TURN THE TIDE!
FOUR SPACEFARING SUPER-VILLAINS! THIS COULD TAKE A FEW MINUTES.
I HOPE JIMMY WILL BE OKAY--

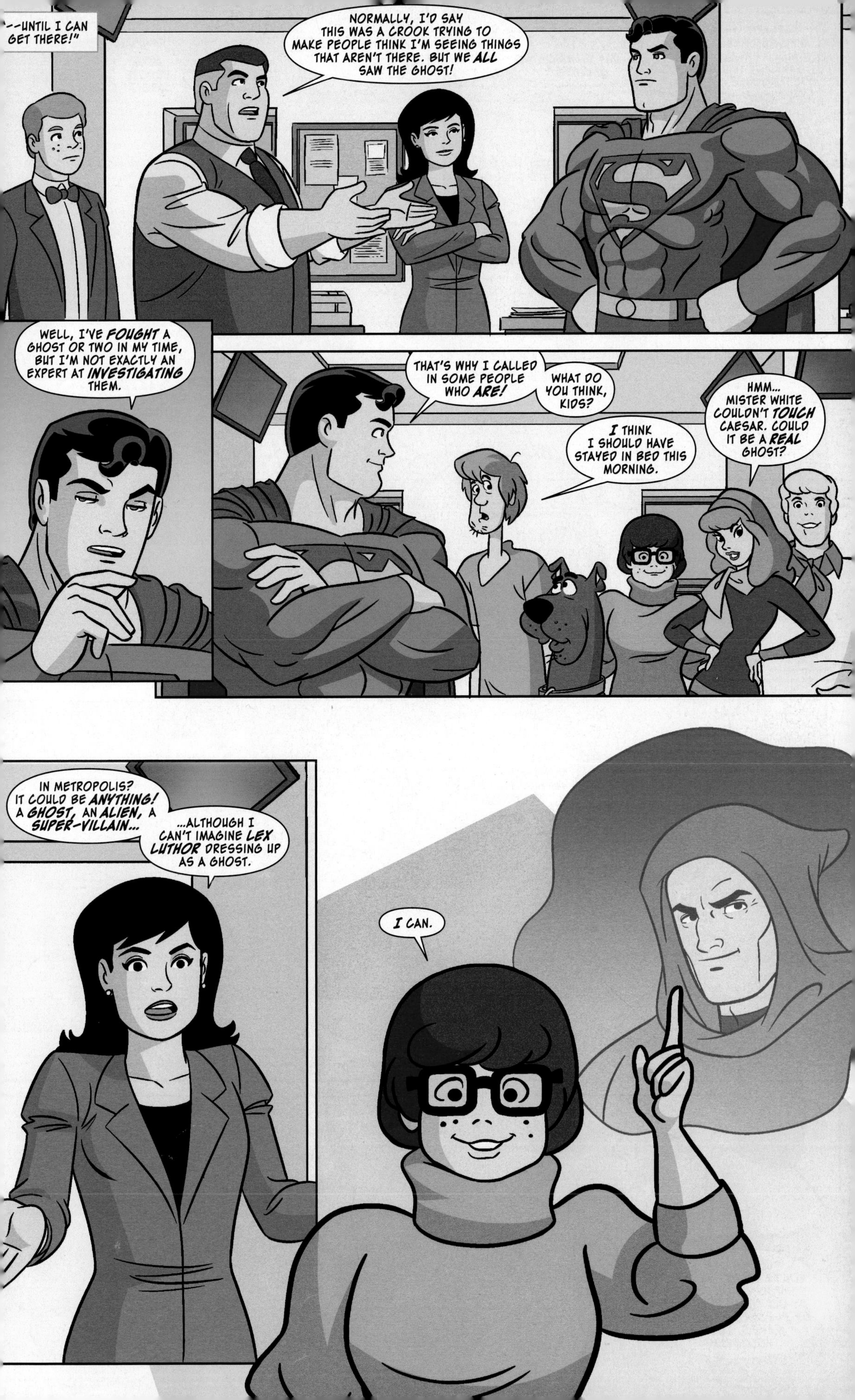

--UNTIL I CAN GET THERE!"
NORMALLY, I'D SAY THIS WAS A CROOK TRYING TO MAKE PEOPLE THINK I'M SEEING THINGS THAT AREN'T THERE. BUT WE ALL SAW THE GHOST!
WELL, I'VE FOUGHT A GHOST OR TWO IN MY TIME, BUT I'M NOT EXACTLY AN EXPERT AT INVESTIGATING THEM.
THAT'S WHY I CALLED IN SOME PEOPLE WHO ARE!
WHAT DO YOU THINK, KIDS?
I THINK I SHOULD HAVE STAYED IN BED THIS MORNING.
HMM... MISTER WHITE COULDN'T TOUCH CAESAR. COULD IT BE A REAL GHOST?
IN METROPOLIS? IT COULD BE ANYTHING! A GHOST, AN ALIEN, A SUPER-VILLAIN...
...ALTHOUGH I CAN'T IMAGINE LEX LUTHOR DRESSING UP AS A GHOST.
I CAN.

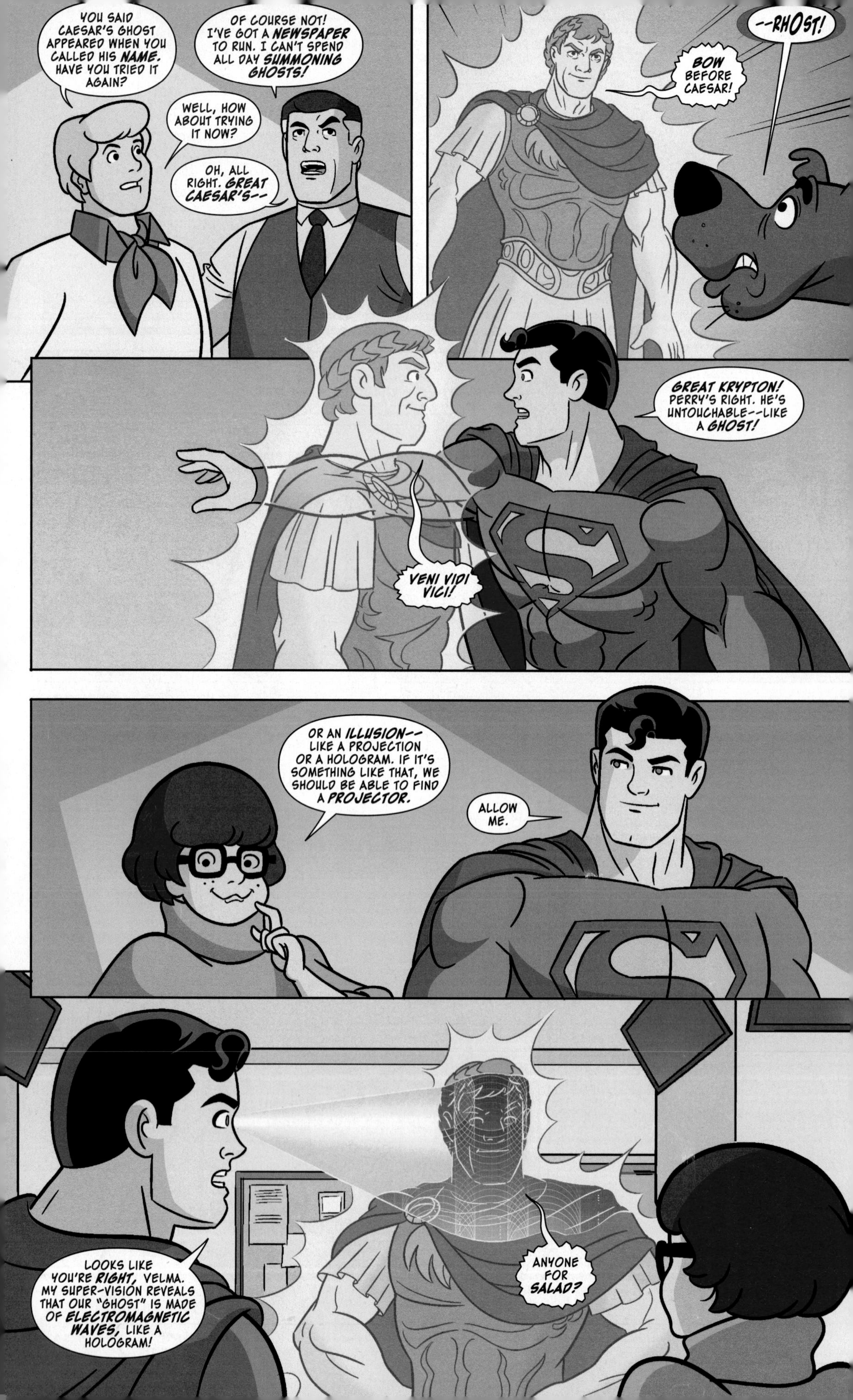
YOU SAID CAESAR'S GHOST APPEARED WHEN YOU CALLED HIS NAME. HAVE YOU TRIED IT AGAIN?
OF COURSE NOT! I'VE GOT A NEWSPAPER TO RUN. I CAN'T SPEND ALL DAY SUMMONING GHOSTS!
WELL, HOW ABOUT TRYING IT NOW?
OH, ALL RIGHT. GREAT CAESAR'S--
--RHOST!
BOW BEFORE CAESAR!
GREAT KRYPTON! PERRY'S RIGHT. HE'S UNTOUCHABLE--LIKE A GHOST!
VENI VIDI VICI!
OR AN ILLUSION--LIKE A PROJECTION OR A HOLOGRAM. IF IT'S SOMETHING LIKE THAT, WE SHOULD BE ABLE TO FIND A PROJECTOR.
ALLOW ME.
LOOKS LIKE YOU'RE RIGHT, VELMA. MY SUPER-VISION REVEALS THAT OUR "GHOST" IS MADE OF ELECTROMAGNETIC WAVES, LIKE A HOLOGRAM!
ANYONE FOR SALAD?

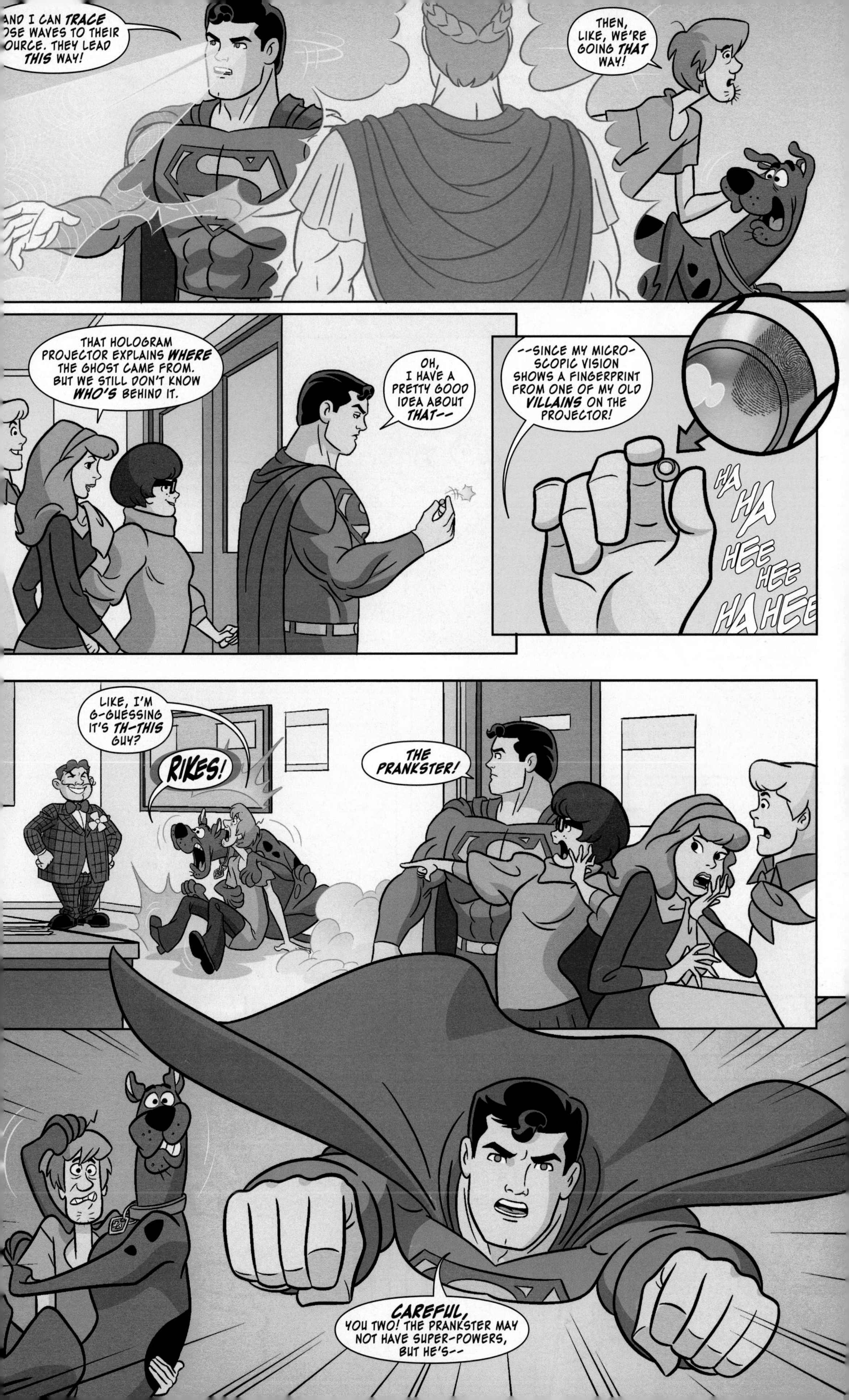

AND I CAN TRACE
OSE WAVES TO THEIR
OURCE. THEY LEAD
THIS WAY!
THEN, LIKE, WE'RE GOING THAT WAY!
THAT HOLOGRAM PROJECTOR EXPLAINS WHERE THE GHOST CAME FROM. BUT WE STILL DON'T KNOW WHO'S BEHIND IT.
OH, I HAVE A PRETTY GOOD IDEA ABOUT THAT--
--SINCE MY MICRO-SCOPIC VISION SHOWS A FINGERPRINT FROM ONE OF MY OLD VILLAINS ON THE PROJECTOR!
HA HA HEE HEE HA HEE
LIKE, I'M G-GUESSING IT'S TH-THIS GUY?
RIKES!
THE PRANKSTER!
CAREFUL, YOU TWO! THE PRANKSTER MAY NOT HAVE SUPER-POWERS, BUT HE'S--

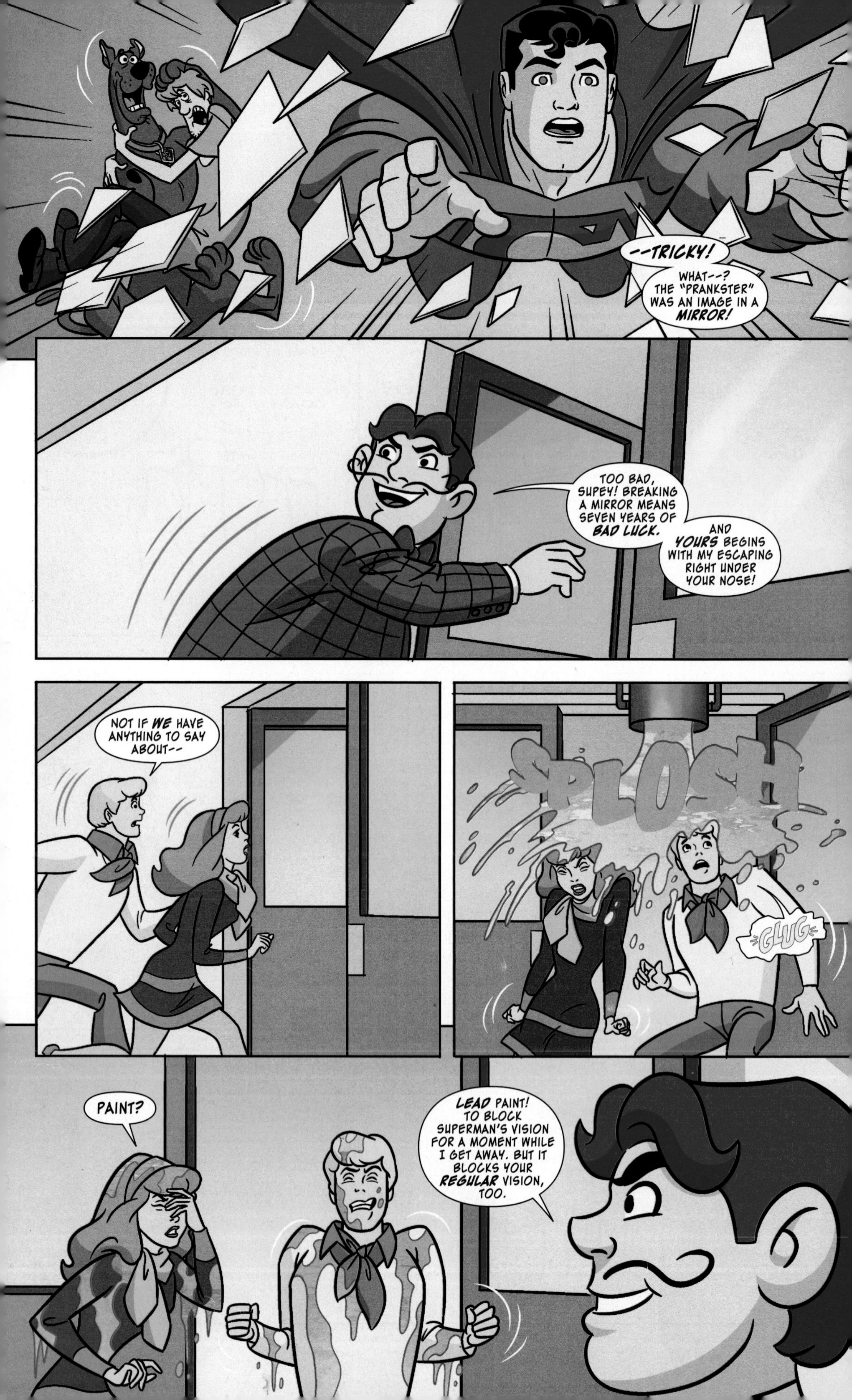
--TRICKY!
WHAT--? THE "PRANKSTER" WAS AN IMAGE IN A MIRROR!
TOO BAD, SUPEY! BREAKING A MIRROR MEANS SEVEN YEARS OF BAD LUCK.
AND YOURS BEGINS WITH MY ESCAPING RIGHT UNDER YOUR NOSE!
NOT IF WE HAVE ANYTHING TO SAY ABOUT--
SPLOSH
GLUG
PAINT?
LEAD PAINT! TO BLOCK SUPERMAN'S VISION FOR A MOMENT WHILE I GET AWAY. BUT IT BLOCKS YOUR REGULAR VISION, TOO.

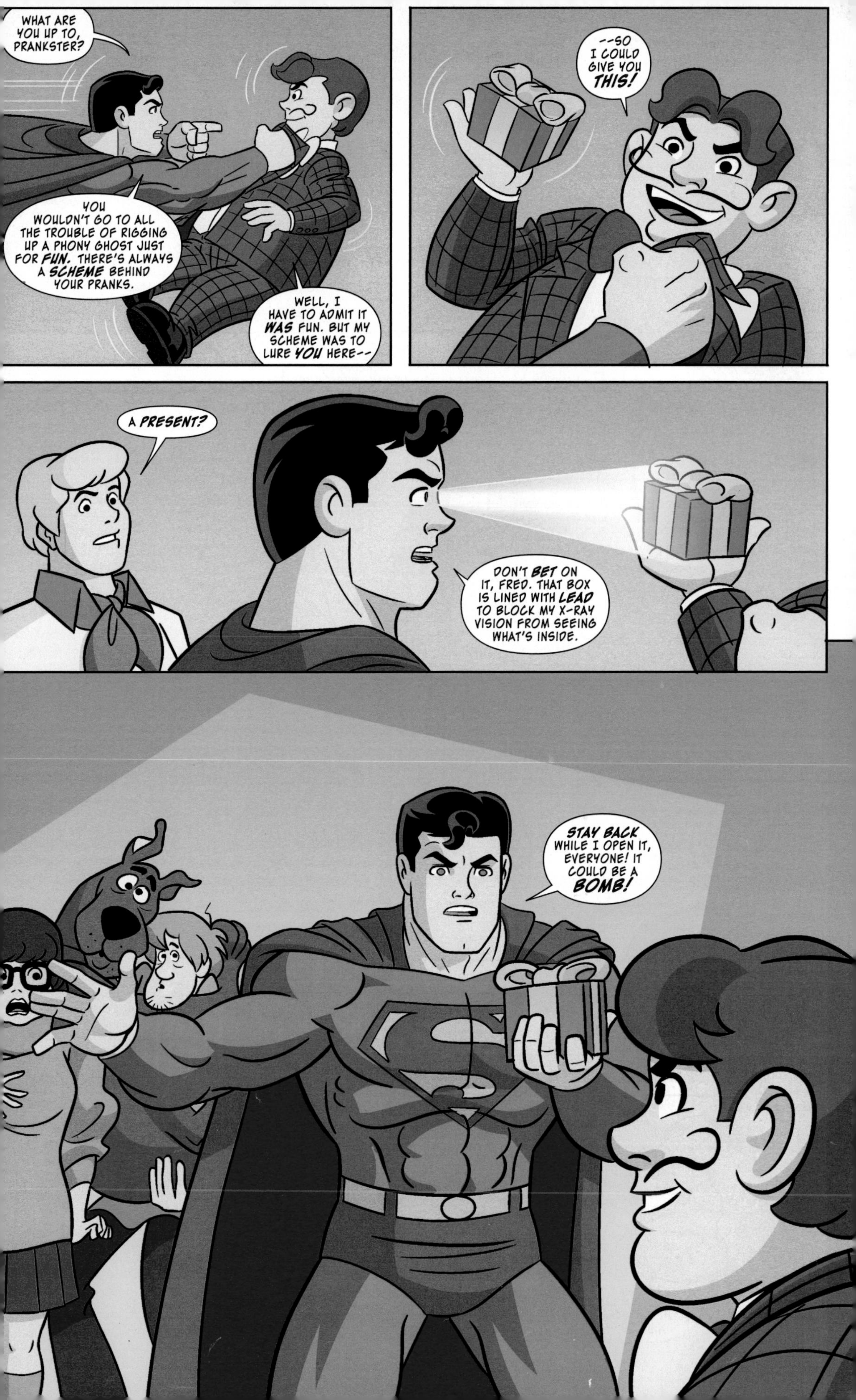
WHAT ARE YOU UP TO, PRANKSTER?
YOU WOULDN'T GO TO ALL THE TROUBLE OF RIGGING UP A PHONY GHOST JUST FOR FUN. THERE'S ALWAYS A SCHEME BEHIND YOUR PRANKS.
WELL, I HAVE TO ADMIT IT WAS FUN. BUT MY SCHEME WAS TO LURE YOU HERE--
--SO I COULD GIVE YOU THIS!
A PRESENT?
DON'T BET ON IT, FRED. THAT BOX IS LINED WITH LEAD TO BLOCK MY X-RAY VISION FROM SEEING WHAT'S INSIDE.
STAY BACK WHILE I OPEN IT, EVERYONE! IT COULD BE A BOMB!

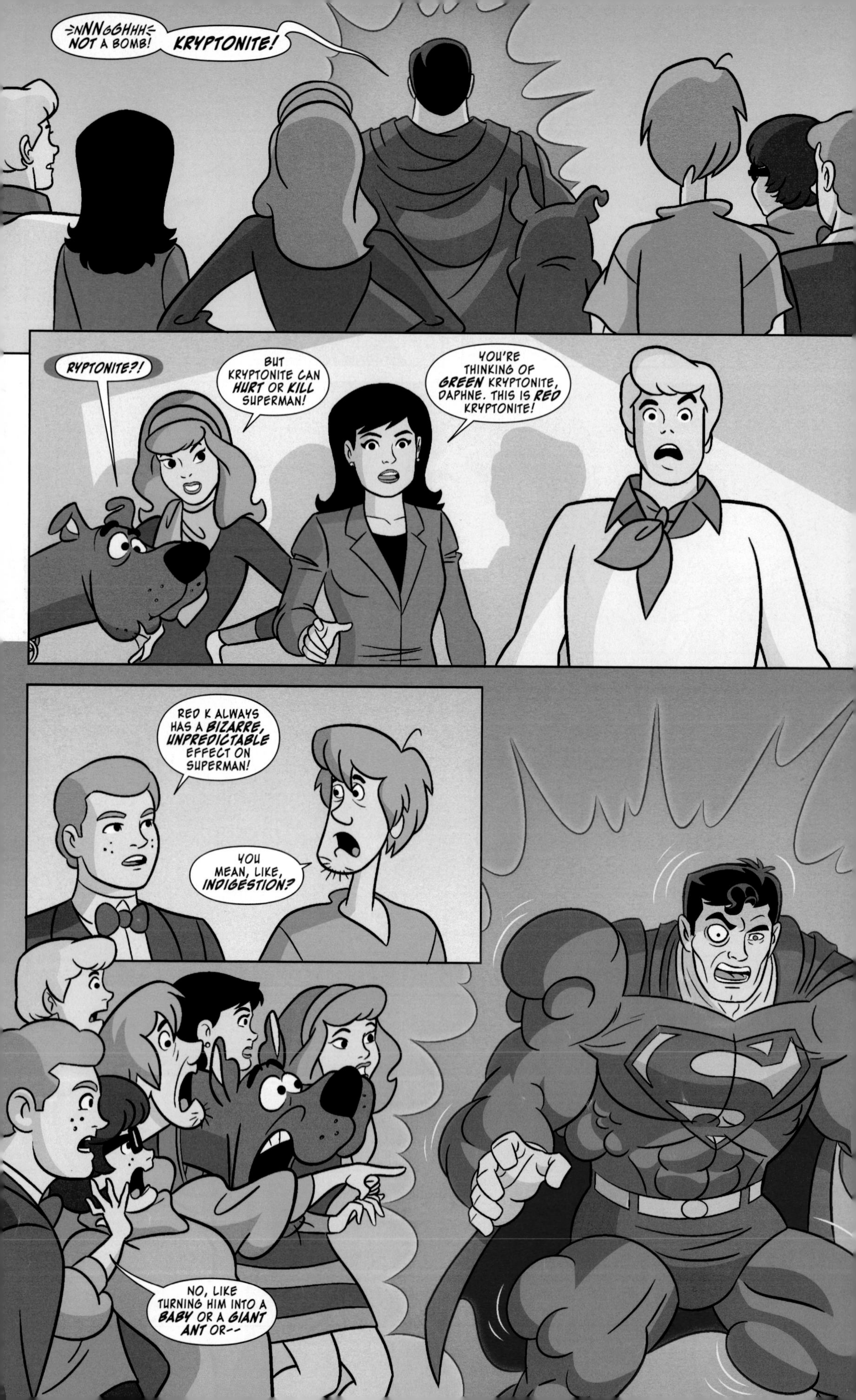

NNNGGHHH NOT A BOMB!
KRYPTONITE!
RYPTONITE?!
BUT KRYPTONITE CAN HURT OR KILL SUPERMAN!
YOU'RE THINKING OF GREEN KRYPTONITE, DAPHNE. THIS IS RED KRYPTONITE!
RED K ALWAYS HAS A BIZARRE, UNPREDICTABLE EFFECT ON SUPERMAN!
YOU MEAN, LIKE, INDIGESTION?
NO, LIKE TURNING HIM INTO A BABY OR A GIANT ANT OR--

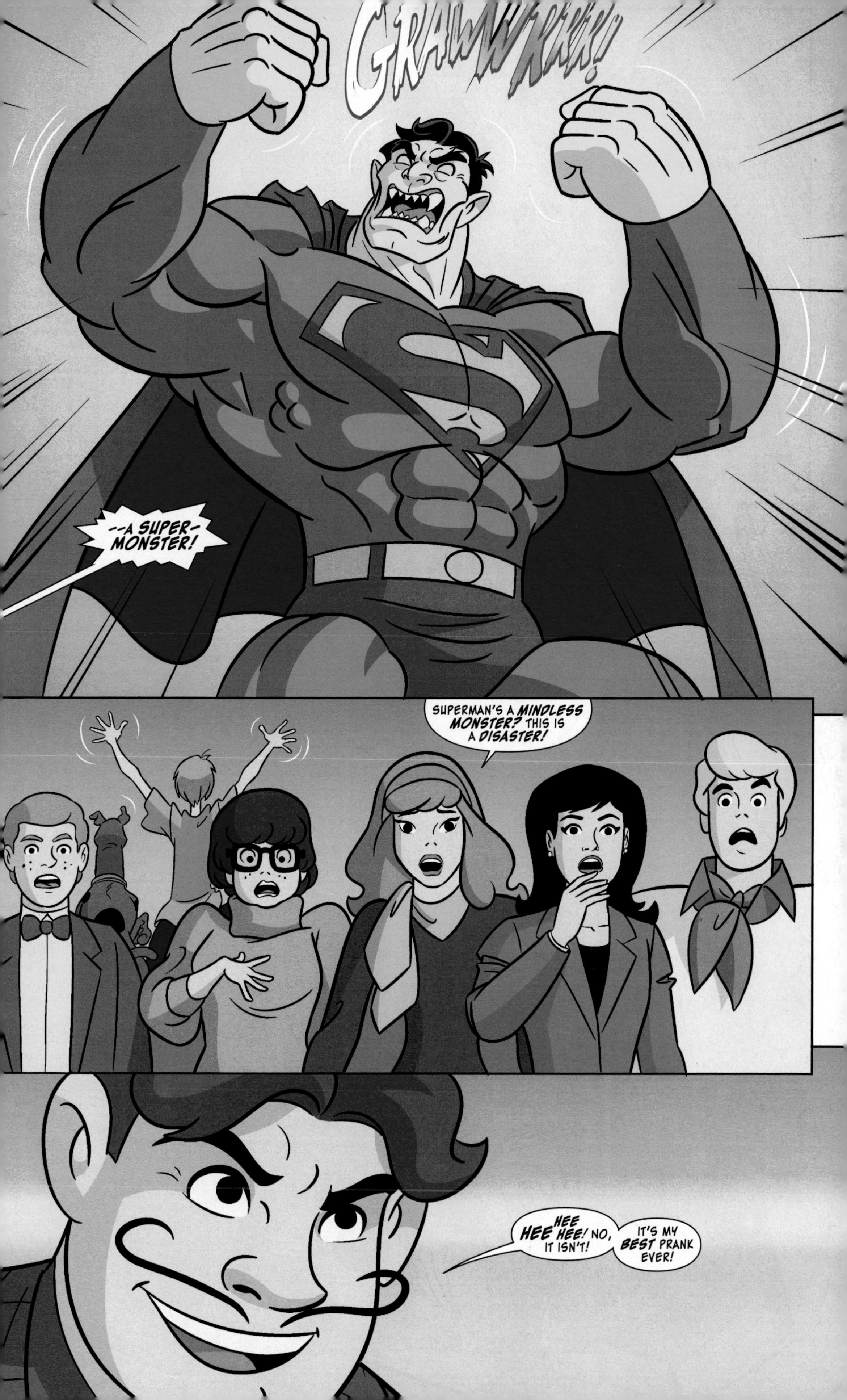
GRAWWKKK!
--A SUPER-MONSTER!
SUPERMAN'S A MINDLESS MONSTER? THIS IS A DISASTER!
HEE HEE HEE! NO, IT ISN'T!
IT'S MY BEST PRANK EVER!

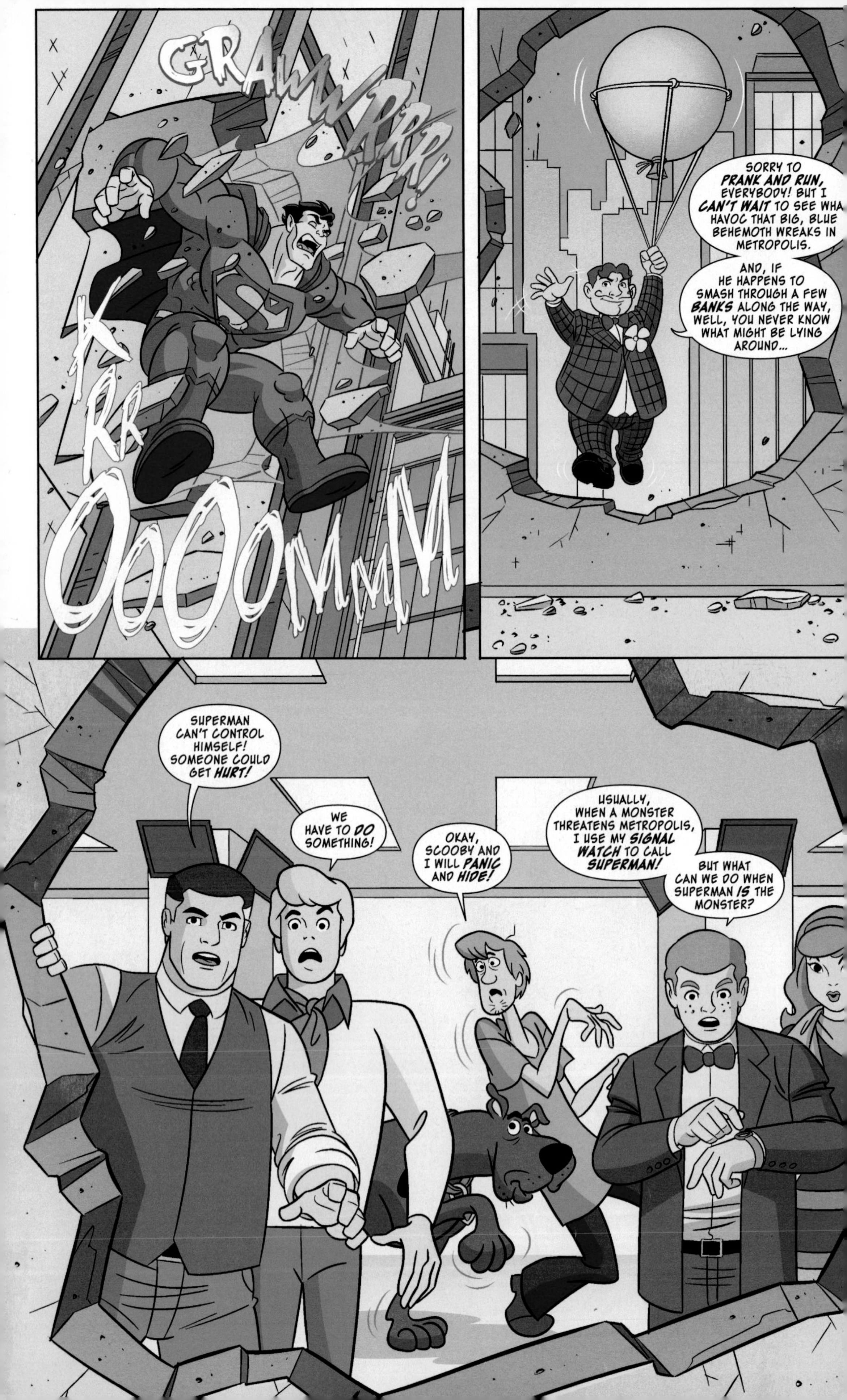
GRAWWRRR!
KRRROOOOMMMM
SORRY TO PRANK AND RUN, EVERYBODY! BUT I CAN'T WAIT TO SEE WHA HAVOC THAT BIG, BLUE BEHEMOTH WREAKS IN METROPOLIS.
AND, IF HE HAPPENS TO SMASH THROUGH A FEW BANKS ALONG THE WAY, WELL, YOU NEVER KNOW WHAT MIGHT BE LYING AROUND...
SUPERMAN CAN'T CONTROL HIMSELF! SOMEONE COULD GET HURT!
WE HAVE TO DO SOMETHING!
OKAY, SCOOBY AND I WILL PANIC AND HIDE!
USUALLY, WHEN A MONSTER THREATENS METROPOLIS, I USE MY SIGNAL WATCH TO CALL SUPERMAN!
BUT WHAT CAN WE DO WHEN SUPERMAN IS THE MONSTER?

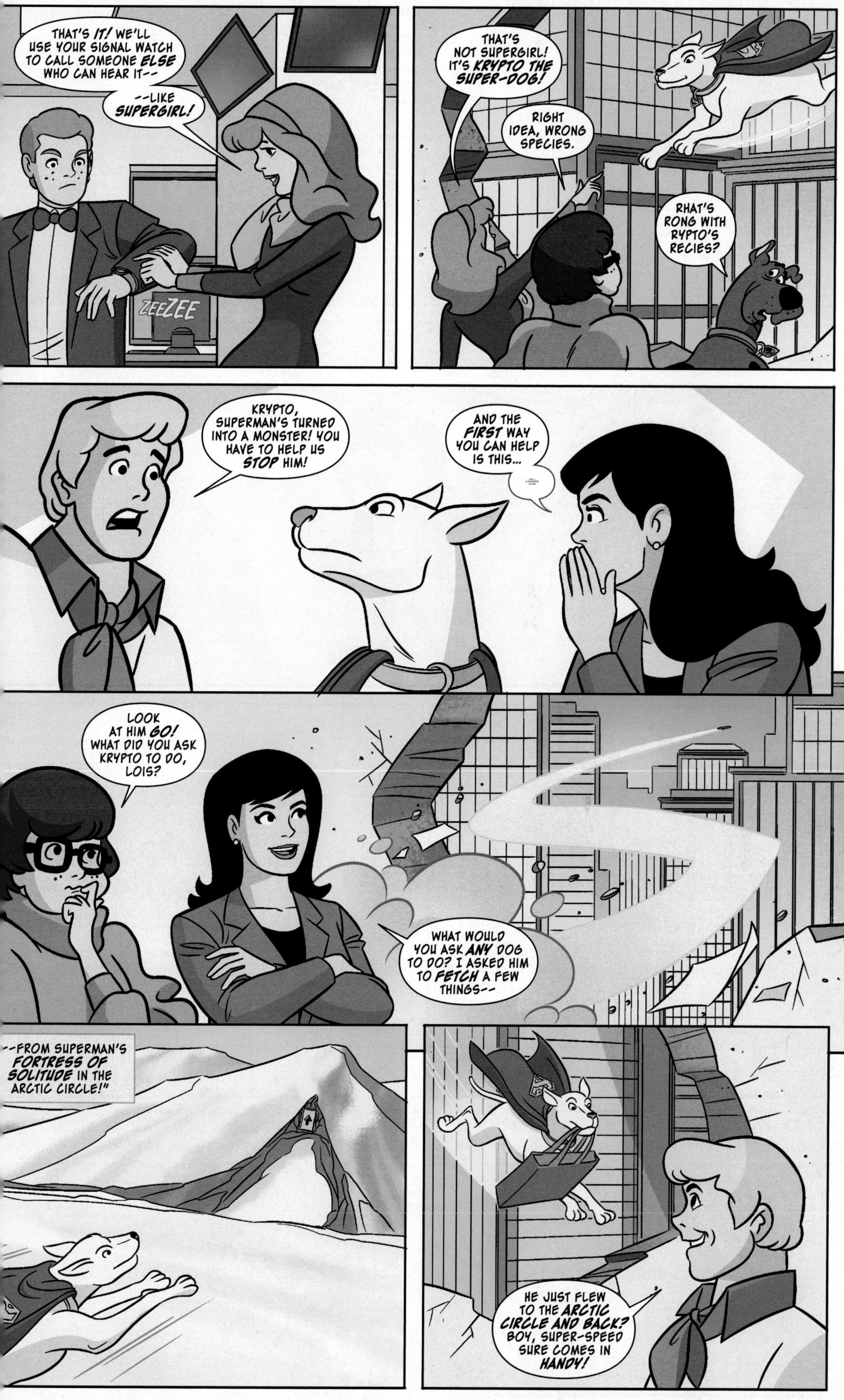
THAT'S IT! WE'LL USE YOUR SIGNAL WATCH TO CALL SOMEONE ELSE WHO CAN HEAR IT--
--LIKE SUPERGIRL!
ZEEZEE
THAT'S NOT SUPERGIRL! IT'S KRYPTO THE SUPER-DOG!
RIGHT IDEA, WRONG SPECIES.
RHAT'S RONG WITH RYPTO'S RECIES?
KRYPTO, SUPERMAN'S TURNED INTO A MONSTER! YOU HAVE TO HELP US STOP HIM!
AND THE FIRST WAY YOU CAN HELP IS THIS...
LOOK AT HIM GO! WHAT DID YOU ASK KRYPTO TO DO, LOIS?
WHAT WOULD YOU ASK ANY DOG TO DO? I ASKED HIM TO FETCH A FEW THINGS--
--FROM SUPERMAN'S FORTRESS OF SOLITUDE IN THE ARCTIC CIRCLE!"
HE JUST FLEW TO THE ARCTIC CIRCLE AND BACK? BOY, SUPER-SPEED SURE COMES IN HANDY!

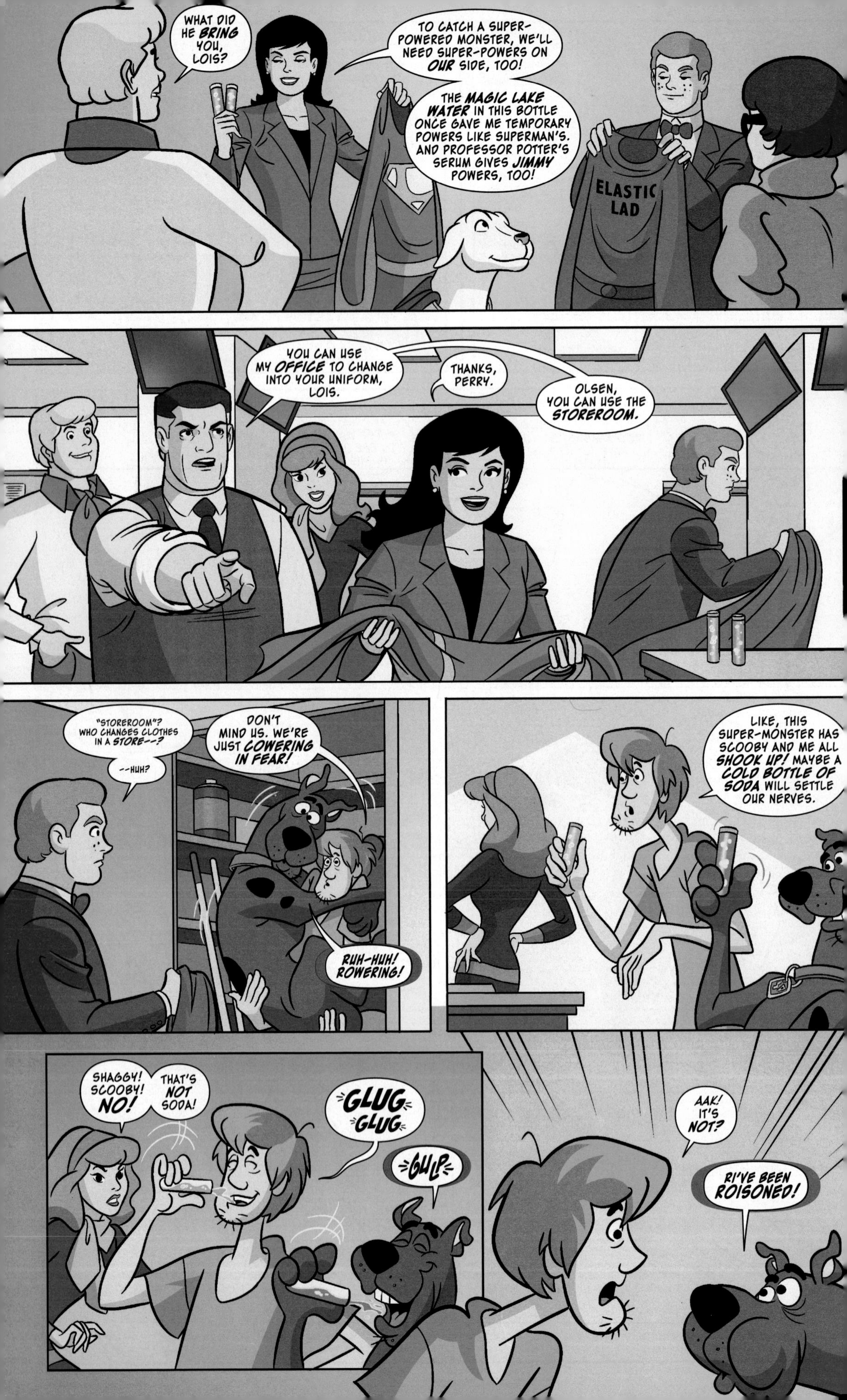
WHAT DID HE BRING YOU, LOIS?
TO CATCH A SUPER-POWERED MONSTER, WE'LL NEED SUPER-POWERS ON OUR SIDE, TOO!
THE MAGIC LAKE WATER IN THIS BOTTLE ONCE GAVE ME TEMPORARY POWERS LIKE SUPERMAN'S. AND PROFESSOR POTTER'S SERUM GIVES JIMMY POWERS, TOO!
ELASTIC LAD
YOU CAN USE MY OFFICE TO CHANGE INTO YOUR UNIFORM, LOIS.
THANKS, PERRY.
OLSEN, YOU CAN USE THE STOREROOM.
"STOREROOM"? WHO CHANGES CLOTHES IN A STORE--?
--HUH?
DON'T MIND US. WE'RE JUST COWERING IN FEAR!
RUH-HUH! ROWERING!
LIKE, THIS SUPER-MONSTER HAS SCOOBY AND ME ALL SHOOK UP! MAYBE A COLD BOTTLE OF SODA WILL SETTLE OUR NERVES.
SHAGGY! SCOOBY! NO!
THAT'S NOT SODA!
GLUG GLUG
GULP
AAK! IT'S NOT?
RI'VE BEEN ROISONED!

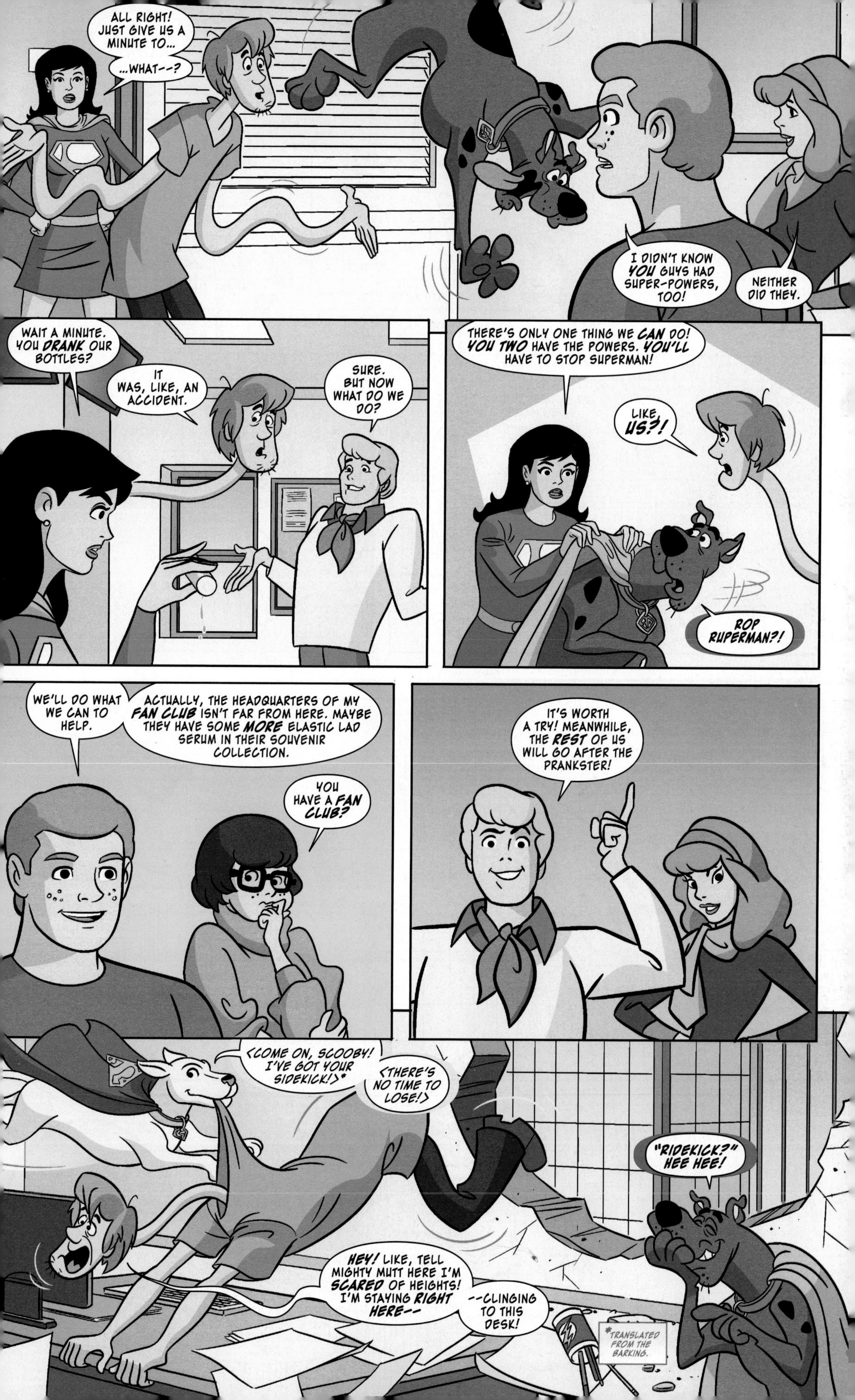
ALL RIGHT! JUST GIVE US A MINUTE TO...
...WHAT--?
I DIDN'T KNOW YOU GUYS HAD SUPER-POWERS, TOO!
NEITHER DID THEY.
WAIT A MINUTE. YOU DRANK OUR BOTTLES?
IT WAS, LIKE, AN ACCIDENT.
SURE. BUT NOW WHAT DO WE DO?
THERE'S ONLY ONE THING WE CAN DO! YOU TWO HAVE THE POWERS. YOU'LL HAVE TO STOP SUPERMAN!
LIKE, US?!
ROP RUPERMAN?!
WE'LL DO WHAT WE CAN TO HELP.
ACTUALLY, THE HEADQUARTERS OF MY FAN CLUB ISN'T FAR FROM HERE. MAYBE THEY HAVE SOME MORE ELASTIC LAD SERUM IN THEIR SOUVENIR COLLECTION.
YOU HAVE A FAN CLUB?
IT'S WORTH A TRY! MEANWHILE, THE REST OF US WILL GO AFTER THE PRANKSTER!
<COME ON, SCOOBY! I'VE GOT YOUR SIDEKICK!>*
<THERE'S NO TIME TO LOSE!>
"RIDEKICK?" HEE HEE!
HEY! LIKE, TELL MIGHTY MUTT HERE I'M SCARED OF HEIGHTS! I'M STAYING RIGHT HERE--
--CLINGING TO THIS DESK!
*TRANSLATED FROM THE BARKING.

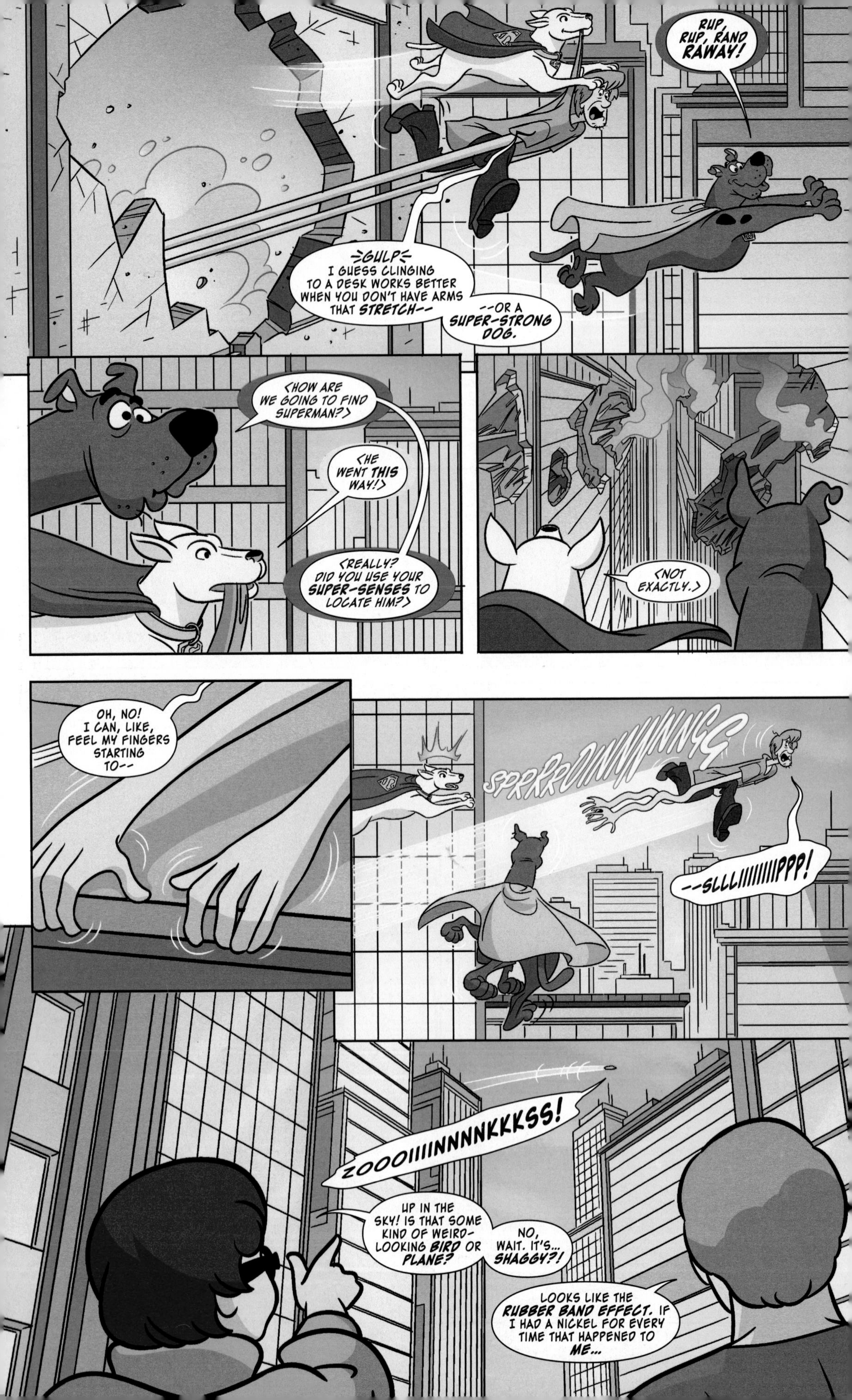
RUP, RUP, RAND RAWAY!
=GULP= I GUESS CLINGING TO A DESK WORKS BETTER WHEN YOU DON'T HAVE ARMS THAT STRETCH--
--OR A SUPER-STRONG DOG.
<HOW ARE WE GOING TO FIND SUPERMAN?>
<HE WENT THIS WAY!>
<REALLY? DID YOU USE YOUR SUPER-SENSES TO LOCATE HIM?>
<NOT EXACTLY.>
OH, NO! I CAN, LIKE, FEEL MY FINGERS STARTING TO--
SPRRROINNNNNNGG
--SLLLIIIIIIIIPPP!
ZOOOIIIIINNNNKKKSS!
UP IN THE SKY! IS THAT SOME KIND OF WEIRD-LOOKING BIRD OR PLANE?
NO, WAIT. IT'S... SHAGGY?!
LOOKS LIKE THE RUBBER BAND EFFECT. IF I HAD A NICKEL FOR EVERY TIME THAT HAPPENED TO ME...

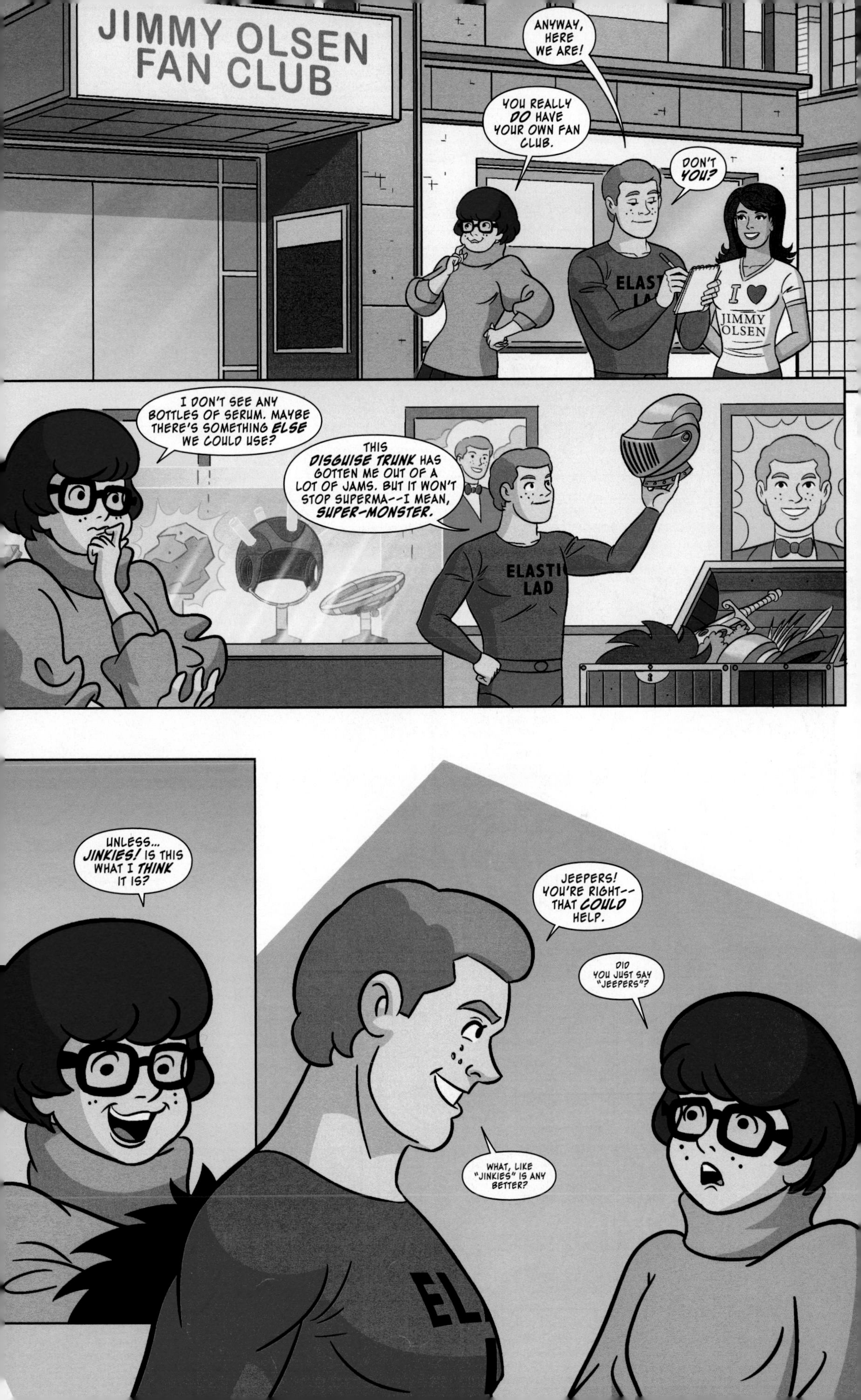
JIMMY OLSEN FAN CLUB
YOU REALLY DO HAVE YOUR OWN FAN CLUB.
ANYWAY, HERE WE ARE!
DON'T YOU?
ELASTIC LAD
I ♥ JIMMY OLSEN
I DON'T SEE ANY BOTTLES OF SERUM. MAYBE THERE'S SOMETHING ELSE WE COULD USE?
THIS DISGUISE TRUNK HAS GOTTEN ME OUT OF A LOT OF JAMS. BUT IT WON'T STOP SUPERMA--I MEAN, SUPER-MONSTER.
ELASTIC LAD
UNLESS... JINKIES! IS THIS WHAT I THINK IT IS?
JEEPERS! YOU'RE RIGHT-- THAT COULD HELP.
DID YOU JUST SAY "JEEPERS"?
WHAT, LIKE "JINKIES" IS ANY BETTER?

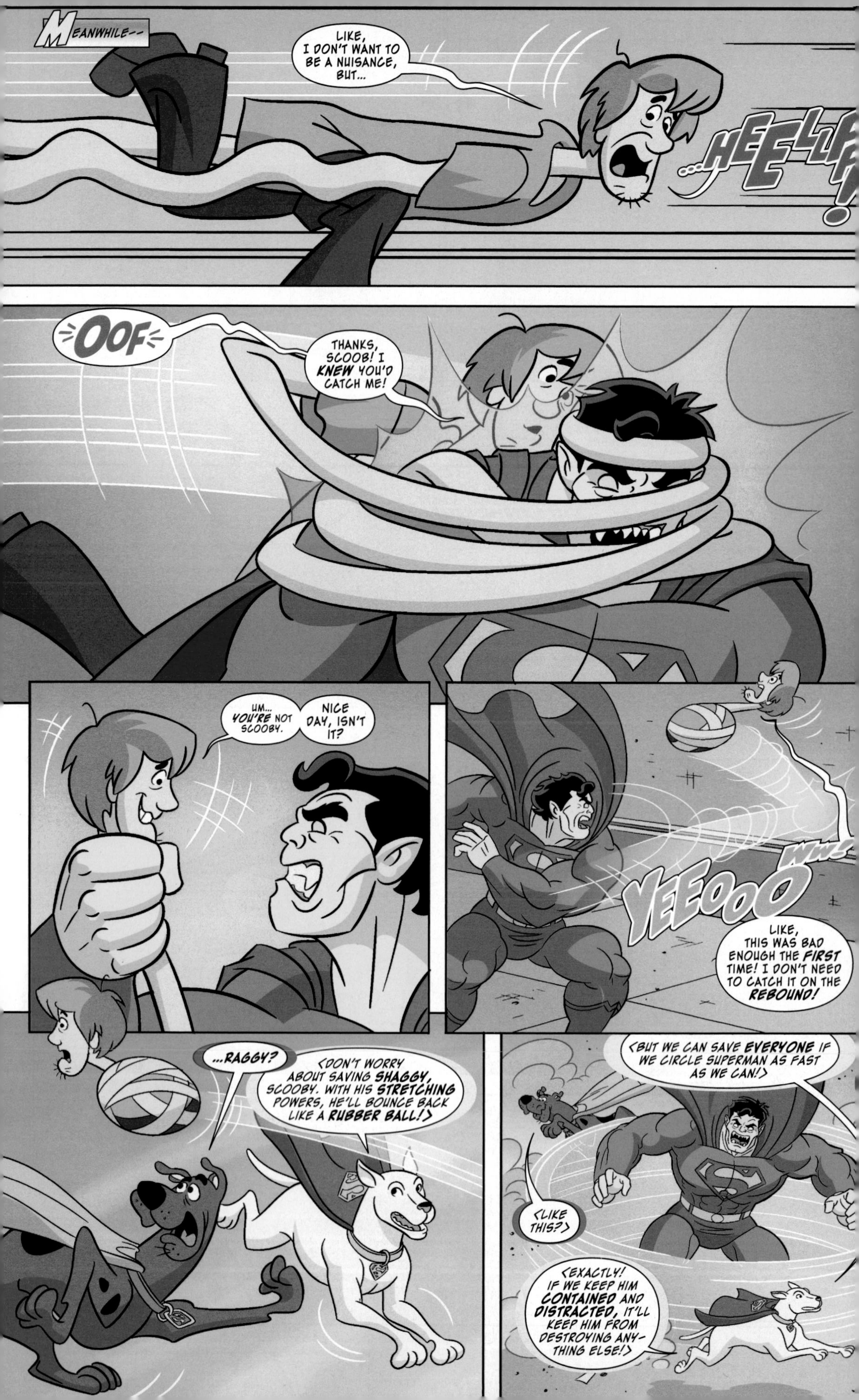
MEANWHILE--
LIKE, I DON'T WANT TO BE A NUISANCE, BUT...
...HEELLLP!
OOF
THANKS, SCOOB! I KNEW YOU'D CATCH ME!
UM... YOU'RE NOT SCOOBY.
NICE DAY, ISN'T IT?
YEEOOOWW!
LIKE, THIS WAS BAD ENOUGH THE FIRST TIME! I DON'T NEED TO CATCH IT ON THE REBOUND!
...RAGGY?
<DON'T WORRY ABOUT SAVING SHAGGY, SCOOBY. WITH HIS STRETCHING POWERS, HE'LL BOUNCE BACK LIKE A RUBBER BALL!>
<BUT WE CAN SAVE EVERYONE IF WE CIRCLE SUPERMAN AS FAST AS WE CAN!>
<LIKE THIS?>
<EXACTLY! IF WE KEEP HIM CONTAINED AND DISTRACTED, IT'LL KEEP HIM FROM DESTROYING ANYTHING ELSE!>

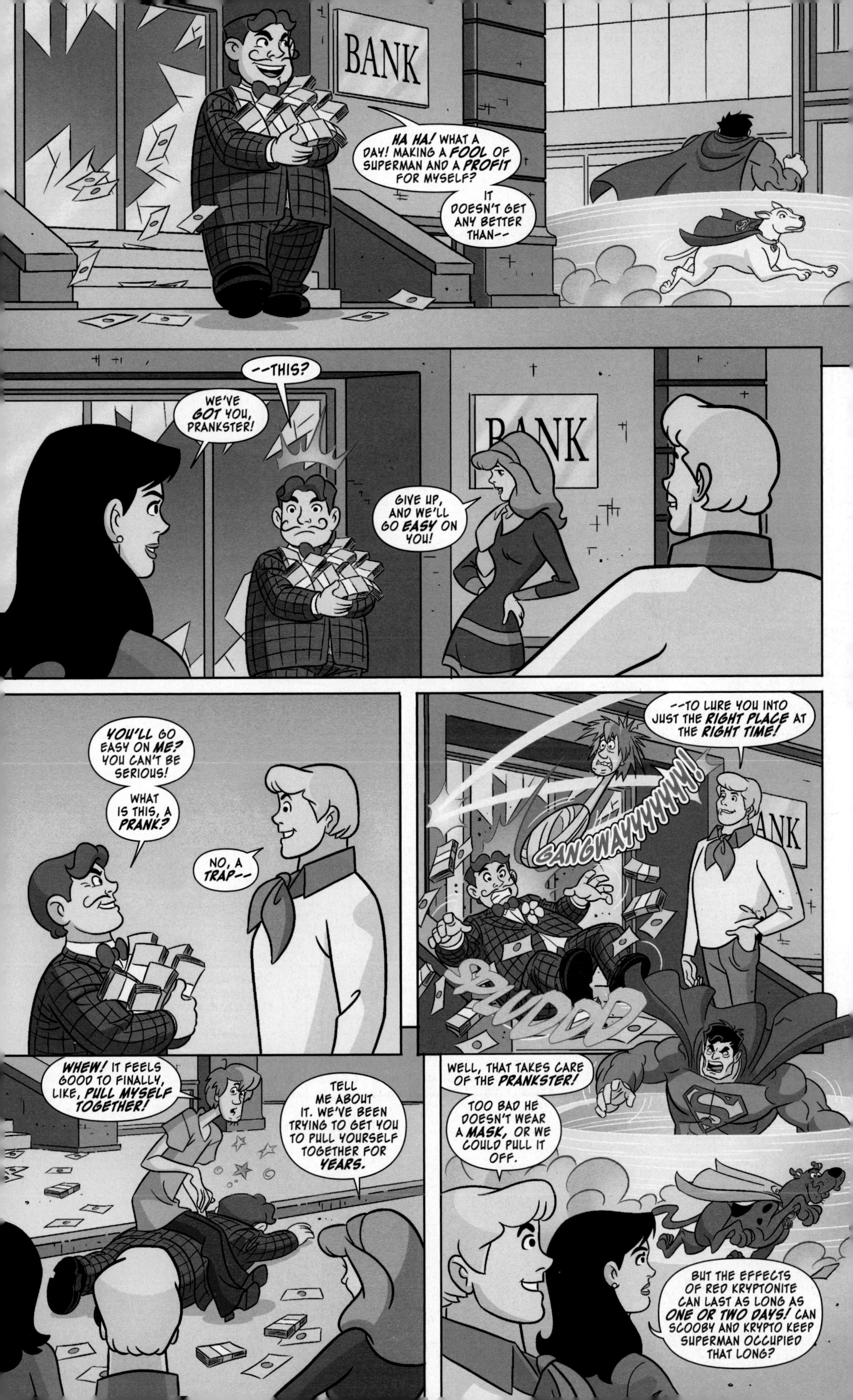
BANK
HA HA! WHAT A DAY! MAKING A FOOL OF SUPERMAN AND A PROFIT FOR MYSELF?
IT DOESN'T GET ANY BETTER THAN--
--THIS?
WE'VE GOT YOU, PRANKSTER!
BANK
GIVE UP, AND WE'LL GO EASY ON YOU!
YOU'LL GO EASY ON ME? YOU CAN'T BE SERIOUS!
WHAT IS THIS, A PRANK?
NO, A TRAP--
--TO LURE YOU INTO JUST THE RIGHT PLACE AT THE RIGHT TIME!
GANGWAYYYYYYY!
BLUDDD
WHEW! IT FEELS GOOD TO FINALLY, LIKE, PULL MYSELF TOGETHER!
TELL ME ABOUT IT. WE'VE BEEN TRYING TO GET YOU TO PULL YOURSELF TOGETHER FOR YEARS.
WELL, THAT TAKES CARE OF THE PRANKSTER!
TOO BAD HE DOESN'T WEAR A MASK, OR WE COULD PULL IT OFF.
BUT THE EFFECTS OF RED KRYPTONITE CAN LAST AS LONG AS ONE OR TWO DAYS! CAN SCOOBY AND KRYPTO KEEP SUPERMAN OCCUPIED THAT LONG?

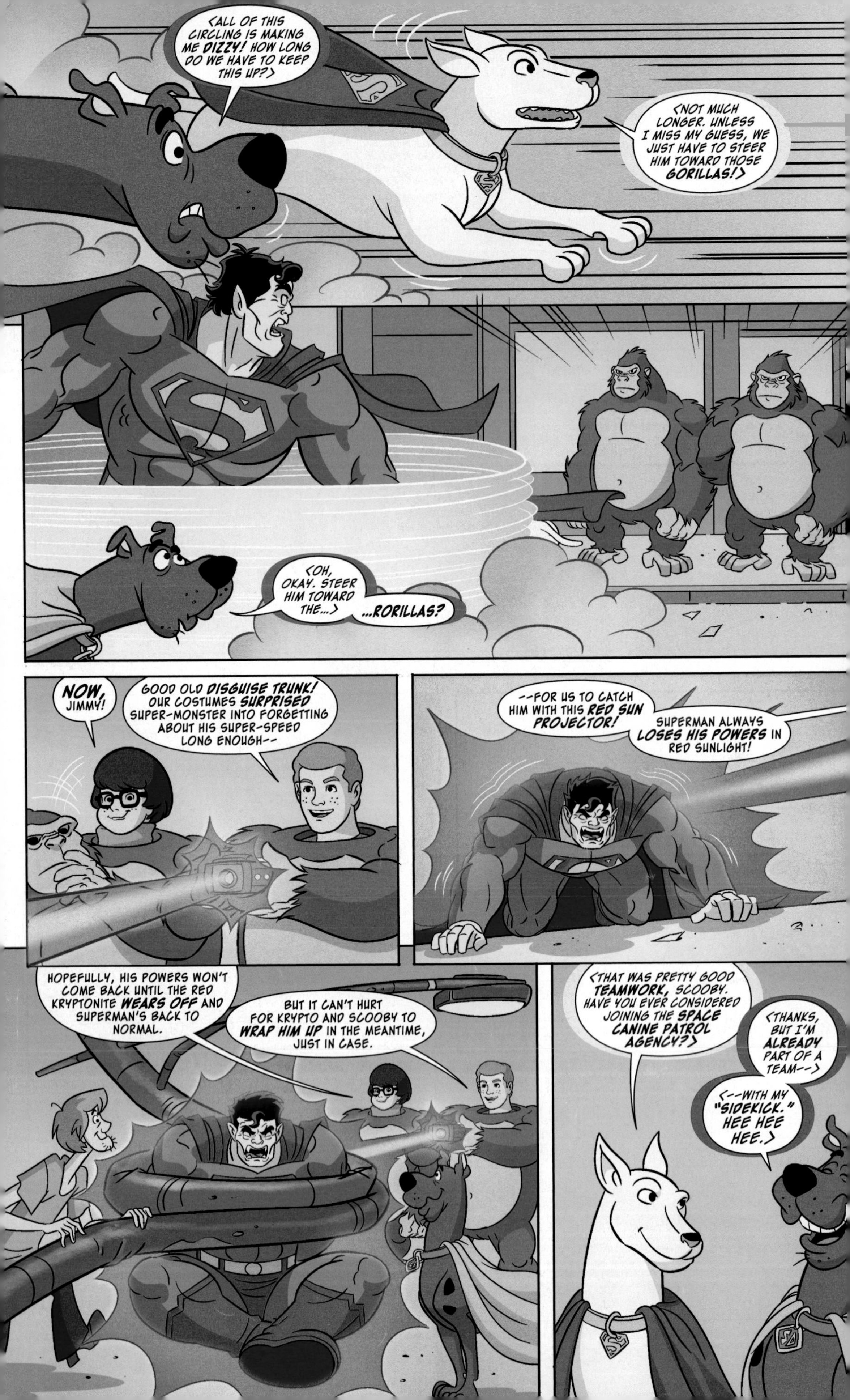

<ALL OF THIS CIRCLING IS MAKING ME DIZZY! HOW LONG DO WE HAVE TO KEEP THIS UP?>
<NOT MUCH LONGER. UNLESS I MISS MY GUESS, WE JUST HAVE TO STEER HIM TOWARD THOSE GORILLAS!>
<OH, OKAY. STEER HIM TOWARD THE...>
...RORILLAS?
NOW, JIMMY!
GOOD OLD DISGUISE TRUNK! OUR COSTUMES SURPRISED SUPER-MONSTER INTO FORGETTING ABOUT HIS SUPER-SPEED LONG ENOUGH--
--FOR US TO CATCH HIM WITH THIS RED SUN PROJECTOR!
SUPERMAN ALWAYS LOSES HIS POWERS IN RED SUNLIGHT!
HOPEFULLY, HIS POWERS WON'T COME BACK UNTIL THE RED KRYPTONITE WEARS OFF AND SUPERMAN'S BACK TO NORMAL.
BUT IT CAN'T HURT FOR KRYPTO AND SCOOBY TO WRAP HIM UP IN THE MEANTIME, JUST IN CASE.
<THAT WAS PRETTY GOOD TEAMWORK, SCOOBY. HAVE YOU EVER CONSIDERED JOINING THE SPACE CANINE PATROL AGENCY?>
<THANKS, BUT I'M ALREADY PART OF A TEAM-->
<--WITH MY "SIDEKICK." HEE HEE HEE.>

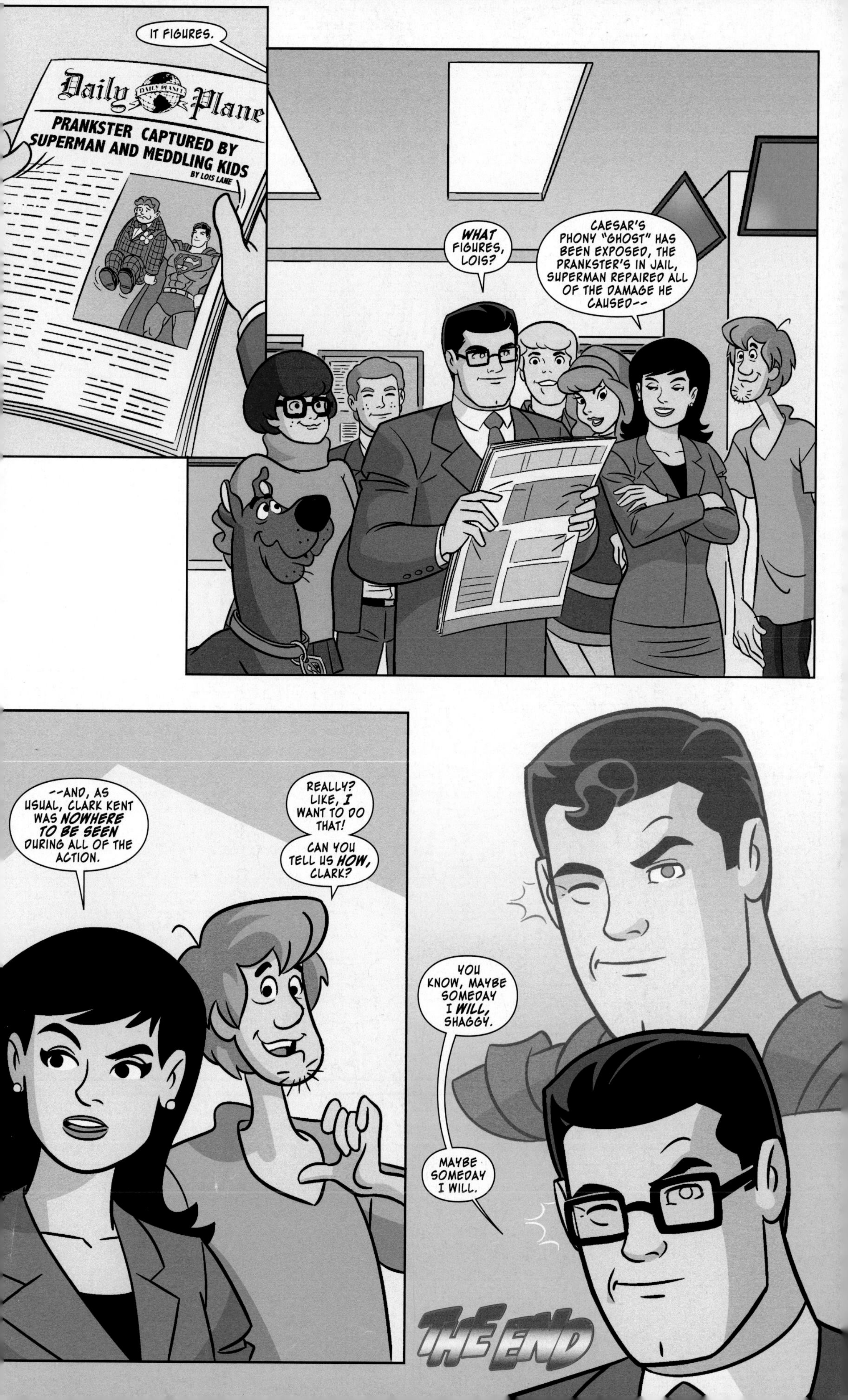
IT FIGURES.
Daily Planet
PRANKSTER CAPTURED BY SUPERMAN AND MEDDLING KIDS
BY LOIS LANE
WHAT FIGURES, LOIS?
CAESAR'S PHONY "GHOST" HAS BEEN EXPOSED, THE PRANKSTER'S IN JAIL, SUPERMAN REPAIRED ALL OF THE DAMAGE HE CAUSED--
--AND, AS USUAL, CLARK KENT WAS NOWHERE TO BE SEEN DURING ALL OF THE ACTION.
REALLY? LIKE, I WANT TO DO THAT!
CAN YOU TELL US HOW, CLARK?
YOU KNOW, MAYBE SOMEDAY I WILL, SHAGGY.
MAYBE SOMEDAY I WILL.
THE END

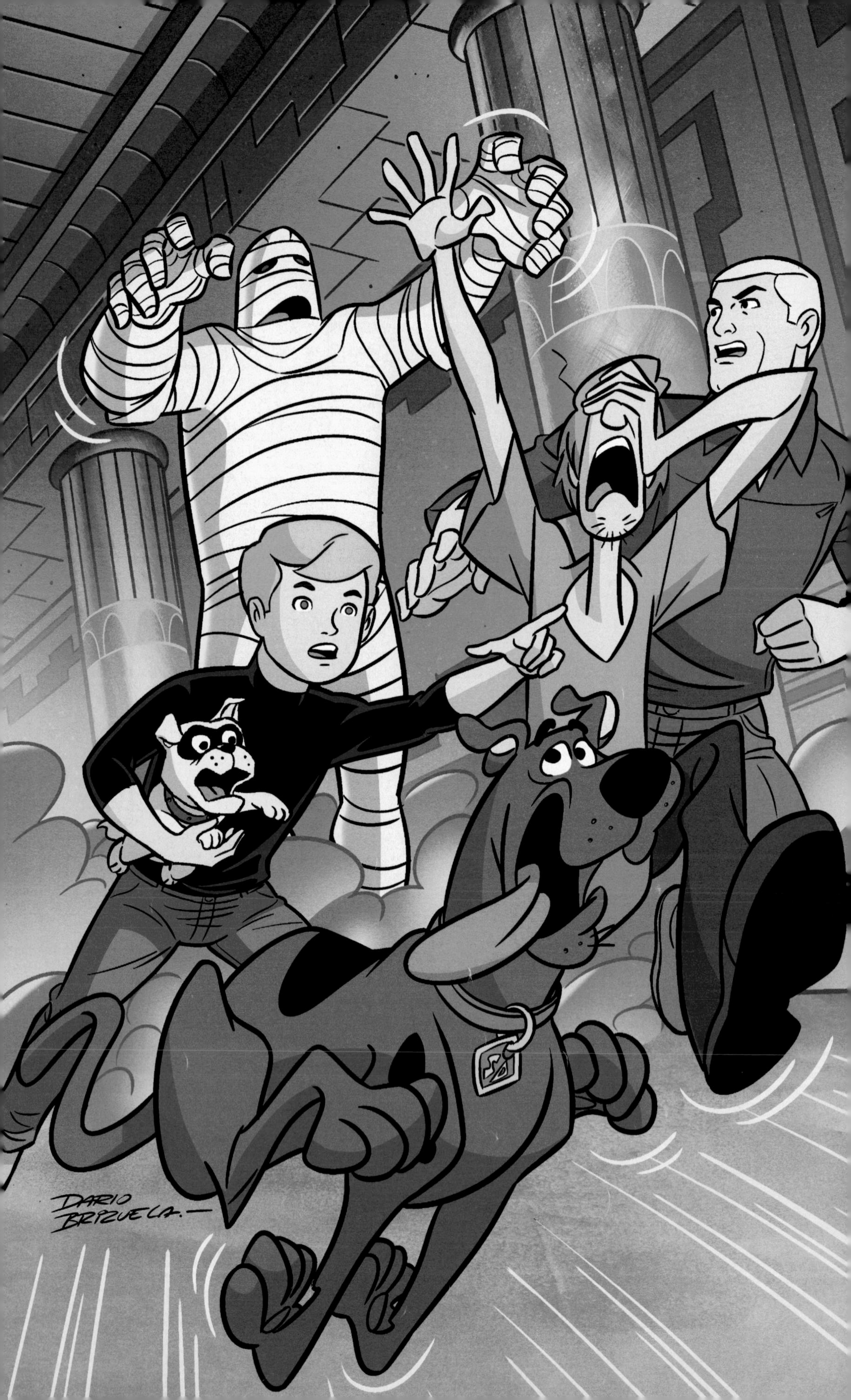
DARIO BRIZUELA

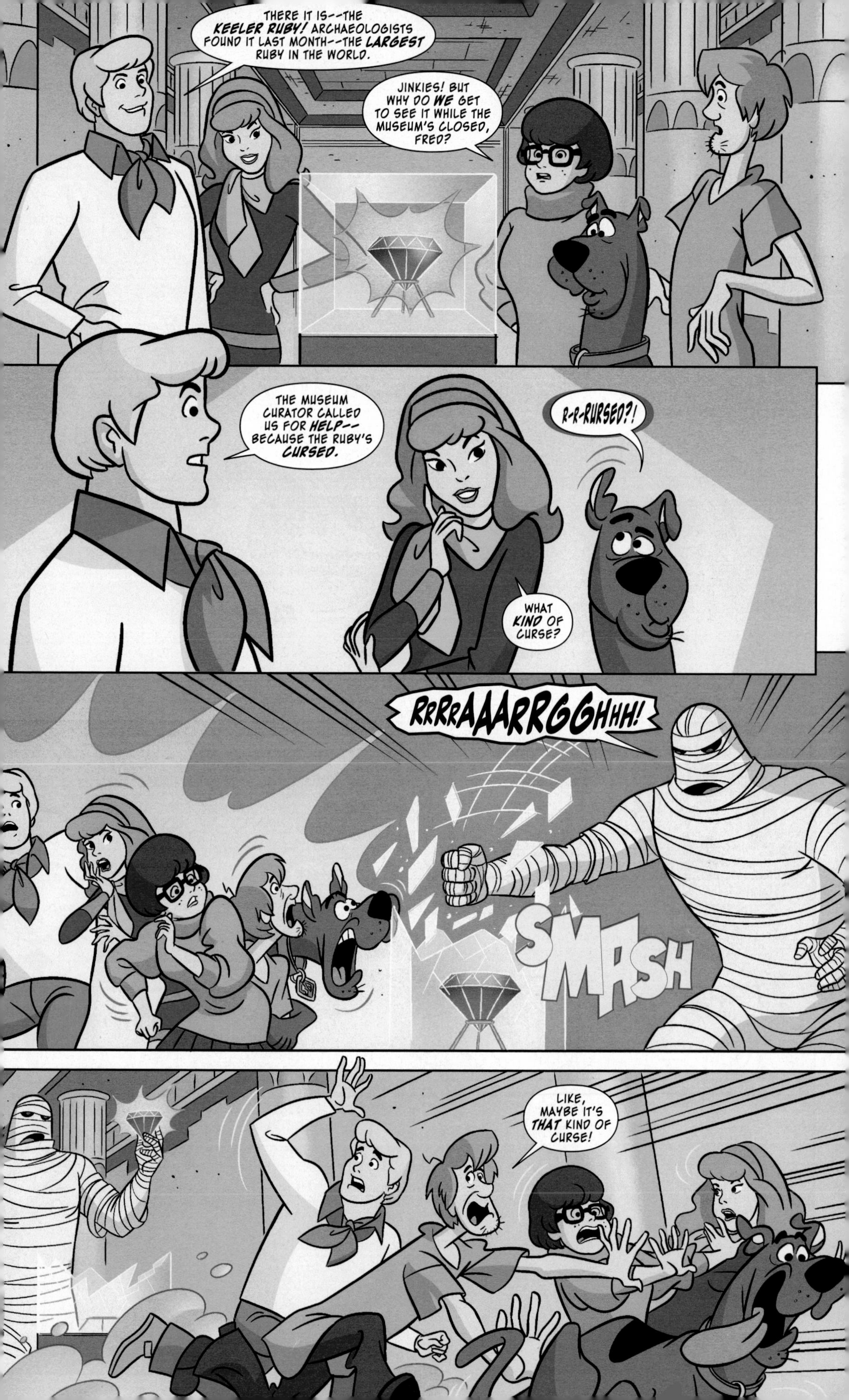
THERE IT IS--THE KEELER RUBY! ARCHAEOLOGISTS FOUND IT LAST MONTH--THE LARGEST RUBY IN THE WORLD.
JINKIES! BUT WHY DO WE GET TO SEE IT WHILE THE MUSEUM'S CLOSED, FRED?
THE MUSEUM CURATOR CALLED US FOR HELP--BECAUSE THE RUBY'S CURSED.
R-R-RURSED?!
WHAT KIND OF CURSE?
RRRRAAARRGGHHH!
SMASH
LIKE, MAYBE IT'S THAT KIND OF CURSE!

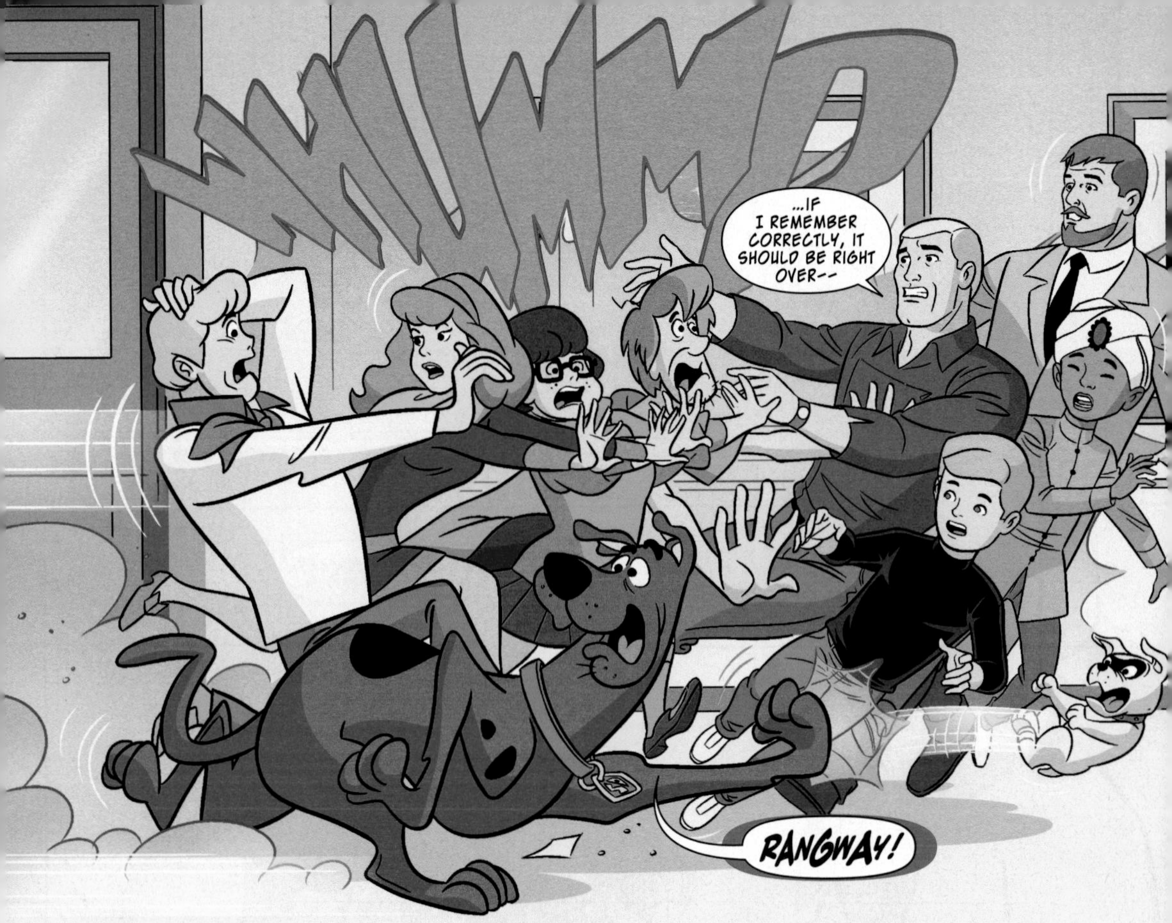
WHUMP
...IF I REMEMBER CORRECTLY, IT SHOULD BE RIGHT OVER--
RANGWAY!

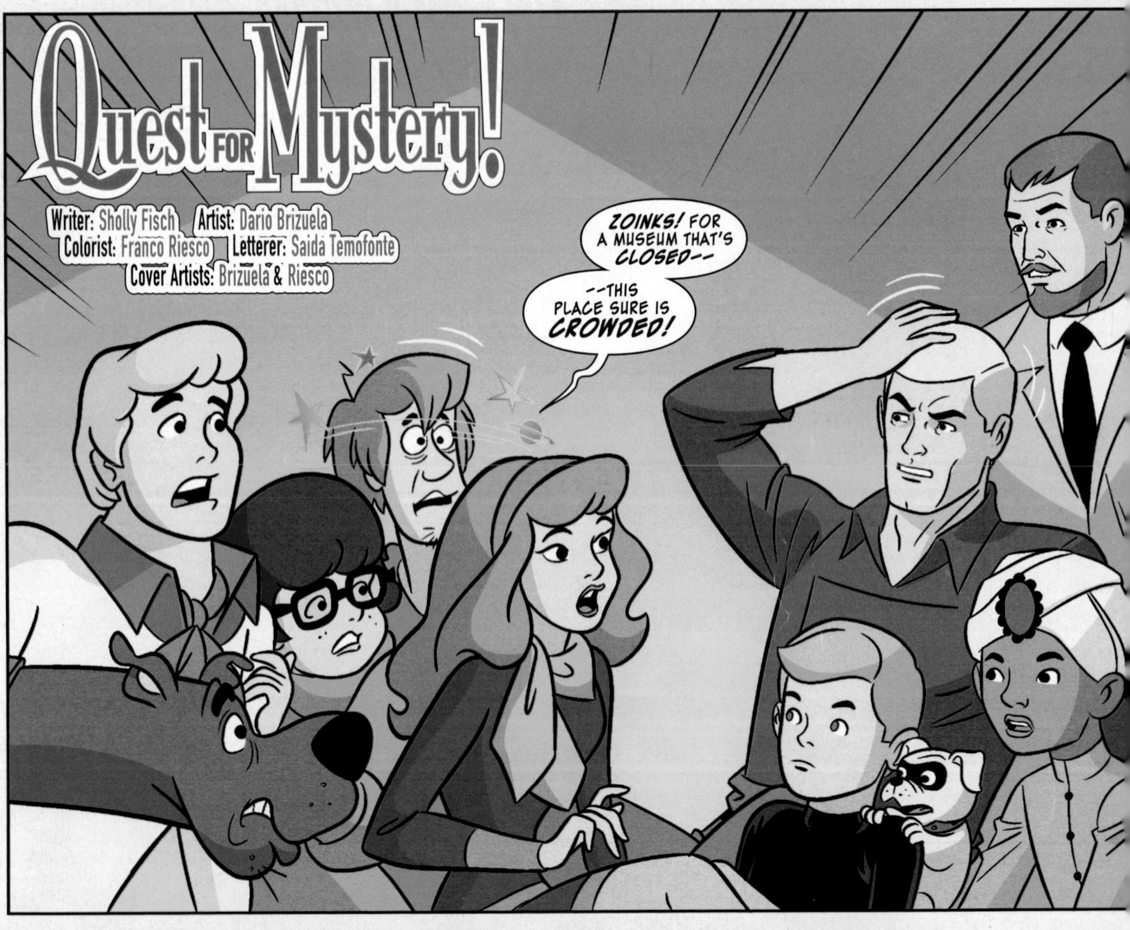
Quest FOR Mystery!
Writer: Sholly Fisch Artist: Dario Brizuela
Colorist: Franco Riesco Letterer: Saida Temofonte
Cover Artists: Brizuela & Riesco
ZOINKS! FOR A MUSEUM THAT'S CLOSED--
--THIS PLACE SURE IS CROWDED!

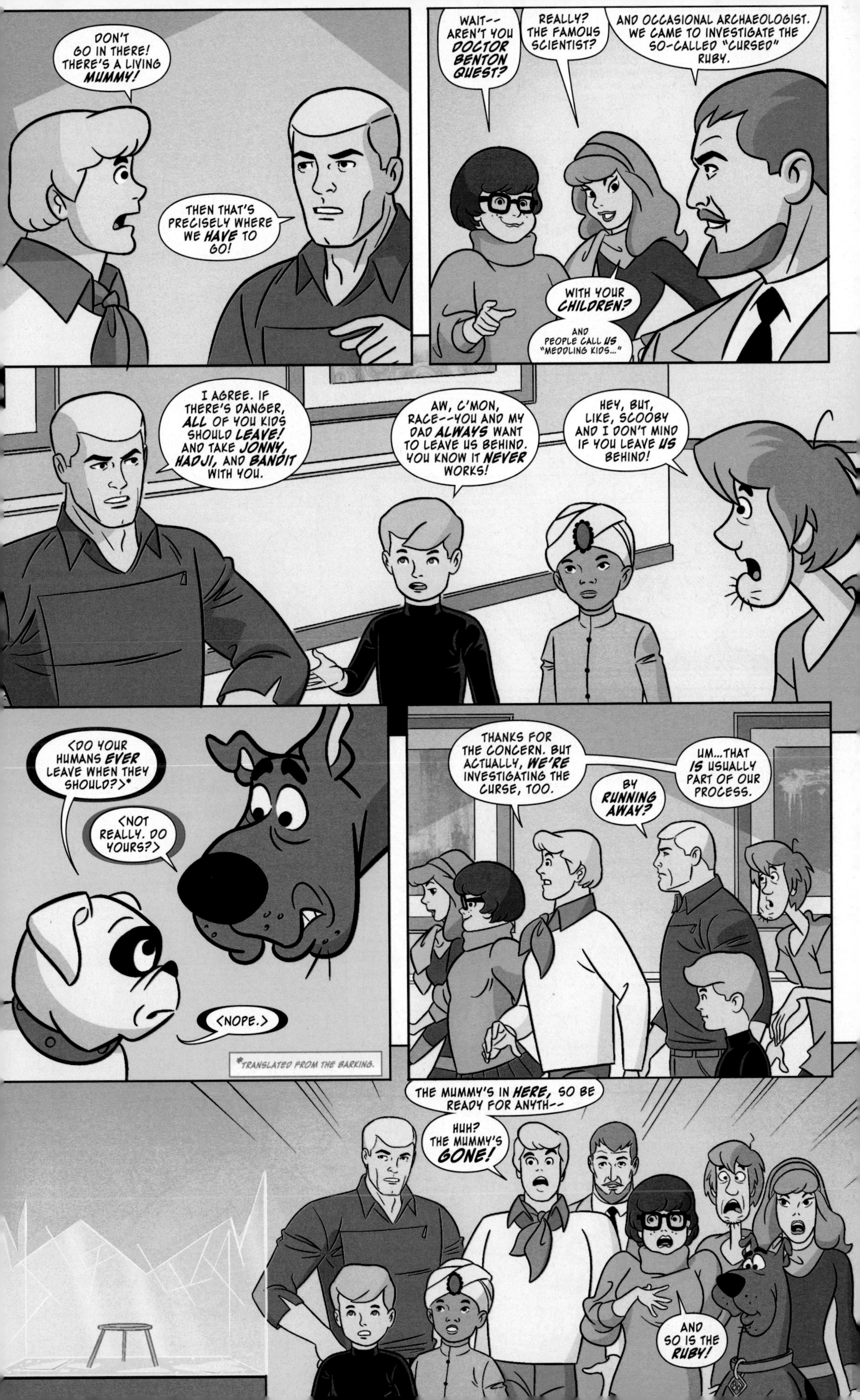
DON'T GO IN THERE! THERE'S A LIVING MUMMY!
THEN THAT'S PRECISELY WHERE WE HAVE TO GO!
WAIT-- AREN'T YOU DOCTOR BENTON QUEST?
REALLY? THE FAMOUS SCIENTIST?
AND OCCASIONAL ARCHAEOLOGIST. WE CAME TO INVESTIGATE THE SO-CALLED "CURSED" RUBY.
WITH YOUR CHILDREN?
AND PEOPLE CALL US "MEDDLING KIDS..."
I AGREE. IF THERE'S DANGER, ALL OF YOU KIDS SHOULD LEAVE! AND TAKE JONNY, HADJI, AND BANDIT WITH YOU.
AW, C'MON, RACE--YOU AND MY DAD ALWAYS WANT TO LEAVE US BEHIND. YOU KNOW IT NEVER WORKS!
HEY, BUT, LIKE, SCOOBY AND I DON'T MIND IF YOU LEAVE US BEHIND!
<DO YOUR HUMANS EVER LEAVE WHEN THEY SHOULD?>*
<NOT REALLY. DO YOURS?>
<NOPE.>
*TRANSLATED FROM THE BARKING.
THANKS FOR THE CONCERN. BUT ACTUALLY, WE'RE INVESTIGATING THE CURSE, TOO.
BY RUNNING AWAY?
UM...THAT IS USUALLY PART OF OUR PROCESS.
THE MUMMY'S IN HERE, SO BE READY FOR ANYTH--
HUH? THE MUMMY'S GONE!
AND SO IS THE RUBY!

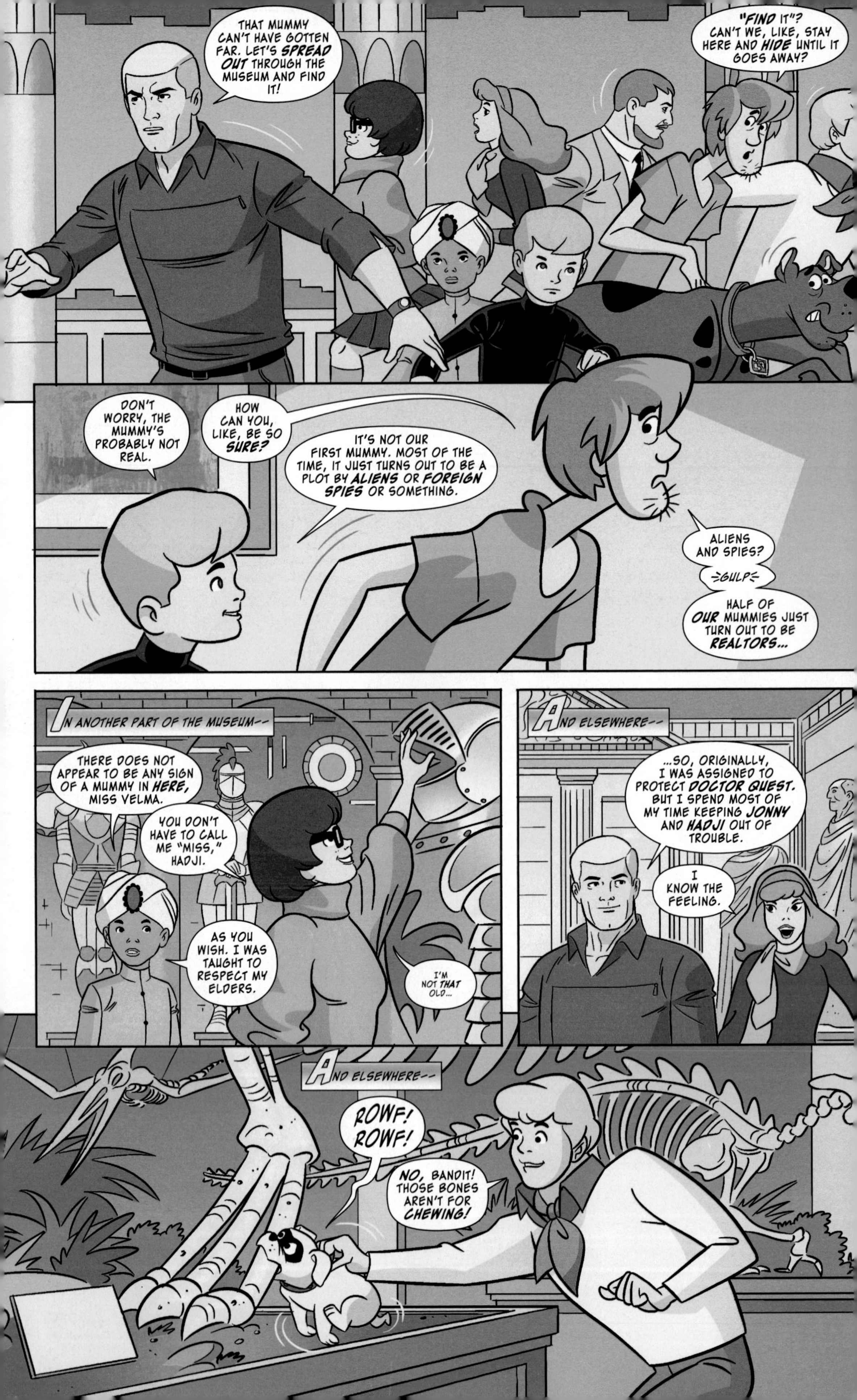
THAT MUMMY CAN'T HAVE GOTTEN FAR. LET'S SPREAD OUT THROUGH THE MUSEUM AND FIND IT!
"FIND IT"? CAN'T WE, LIKE, STAY HERE AND HIDE UNTIL IT GOES AWAY?
DON'T WORRY, THE MUMMY'S PROBABLY NOT REAL.
HOW CAN YOU, LIKE, BE SO SURE?
IT'S NOT OUR FIRST MUMMY. MOST OF THE TIME, IT JUST TURNS OUT TO BE A PLOT BY ALIENS OR FOREIGN SPIES OR SOMETHING.
ALIENS AND SPIES?
GULP
HALF OF OUR MUMMIES JUST TURN OUT TO BE REALTORS...
IN ANOTHER PART OF THE MUSEUM--
THERE DOES NOT APPEAR TO BE ANY SIGN OF A MUMMY IN HERE, MISS VELMA.
YOU DON'T HAVE TO CALL ME "MISS," HADJI.
AS YOU WISH. I WAS TAUGHT TO RESPECT MY ELDERS.
I'M NOT THAT OLD...
AND ELSEWHERE--
...SO, ORIGINALLY, I WAS ASSIGNED TO PROTECT DOCTOR QUEST. BUT I SPEND MOST OF MY TIME KEEPING JONNY AND HADJI OUT OF TROUBLE.
I KNOW THE FEELING.
AND ELSEWHERE--
ROWF! ROWF!
NO, BANDIT! THOSE BONES AREN'T FOR CHEWING!

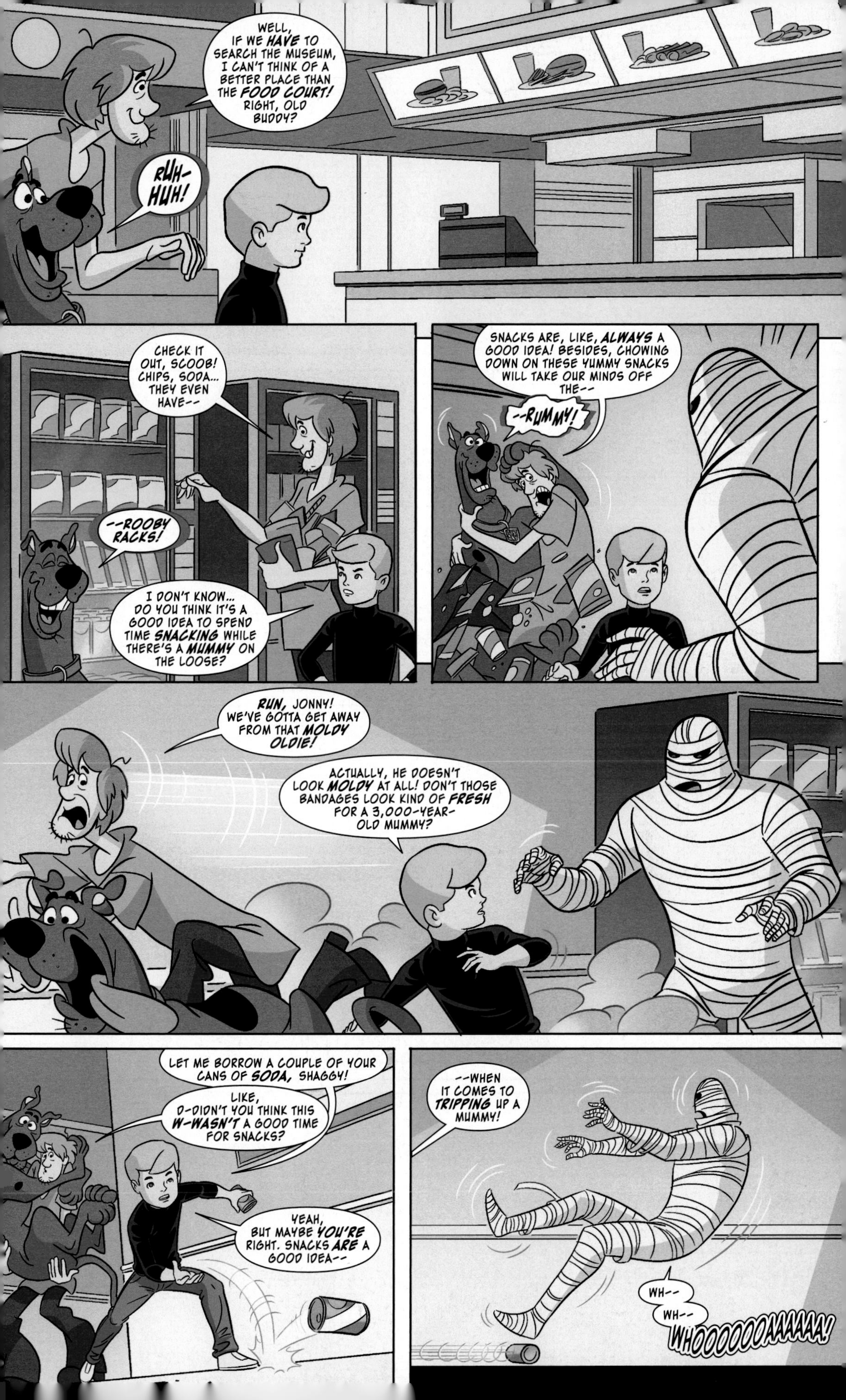
WELL, IF WE HAVE TO SEARCH THE MUSEUM, I CAN'T THINK OF A BETTER PLACE THAN THE FOOD COURT! RIGHT, OLD BUDDY?
RUH-HUH!
CHECK IT OUT, SCOOB! CHIPS, SODA... THEY EVEN HAVE--
--ROOBY RACKS!
I DON'T KNOW... DO YOU THINK IT'S A GOOD IDEA TO SPEND TIME SNACKING WHILE THERE'S A MUMMY ON THE LOOSE?
SNACKS ARE, LIKE, ALWAYS A GOOD IDEA! BESIDES, CHOWING DOWN ON THESE YUMMY SNACKS WILL TAKE OUR MINDS OFF THE--
--RUMMY!
RUN, JONNY! WE'VE GOTTA GET AWAY FROM THAT MOLDY OLDIE!
ACTUALLY, HE DOESN'T LOOK MOLDY AT ALL! DON'T THOSE BANDAGES LOOK KIND OF FRESH FOR A 3,000-YEAR-OLD MUMMY?
LET ME BORROW A COUPLE OF YOUR CANS OF SODA, SHAGGY!
LIKE, D-DIDN'T YOU THINK THIS W-WASN'T A GOOD TIME FOR SNACKS?
YEAH, BUT MAYBE YOU'RE RIGHT. SNACKS ARE A GOOD IDEA--
--WHEN IT COMES TO TRIPPING UP A MUMMY!
WH--
WH--
WHOOOOOOAAAAAA!

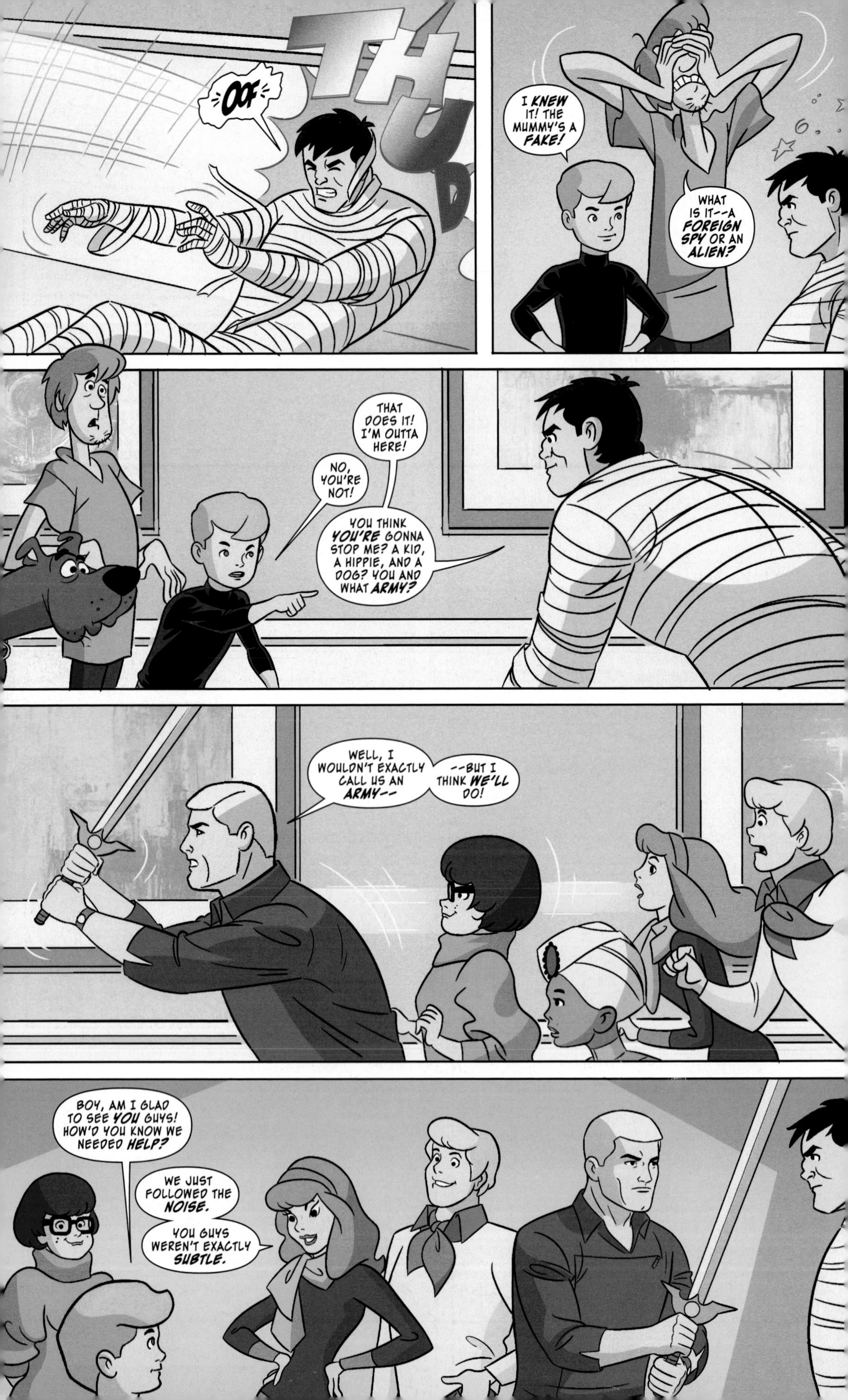
THUD
OOF
I KNEW IT! THE MUMMY'S A FAKE!
WHAT IS IT--A FOREIGN SPY OR AN ALIEN?
THAT DOES IT! I'M OUTTA HERE!
NO, YOU'RE NOT!
YOU THINK YOU'RE GONNA STOP ME? A KID, A HIPPIE, AND A DOG? YOU AND WHAT ARMY?
WELL, I WOULDN'T EXACTLY CALL US AN ARMY--
--BUT I THINK WE'LL DO!
BOY, AM I GLAD TO SEE YOU GUYS! HOW'D YOU KNOW WE NEEDED HELP?
WE JUST FOLLOWED THE NOISE.
YOU GUYS WEREN'T EXACTLY SUBTLE.

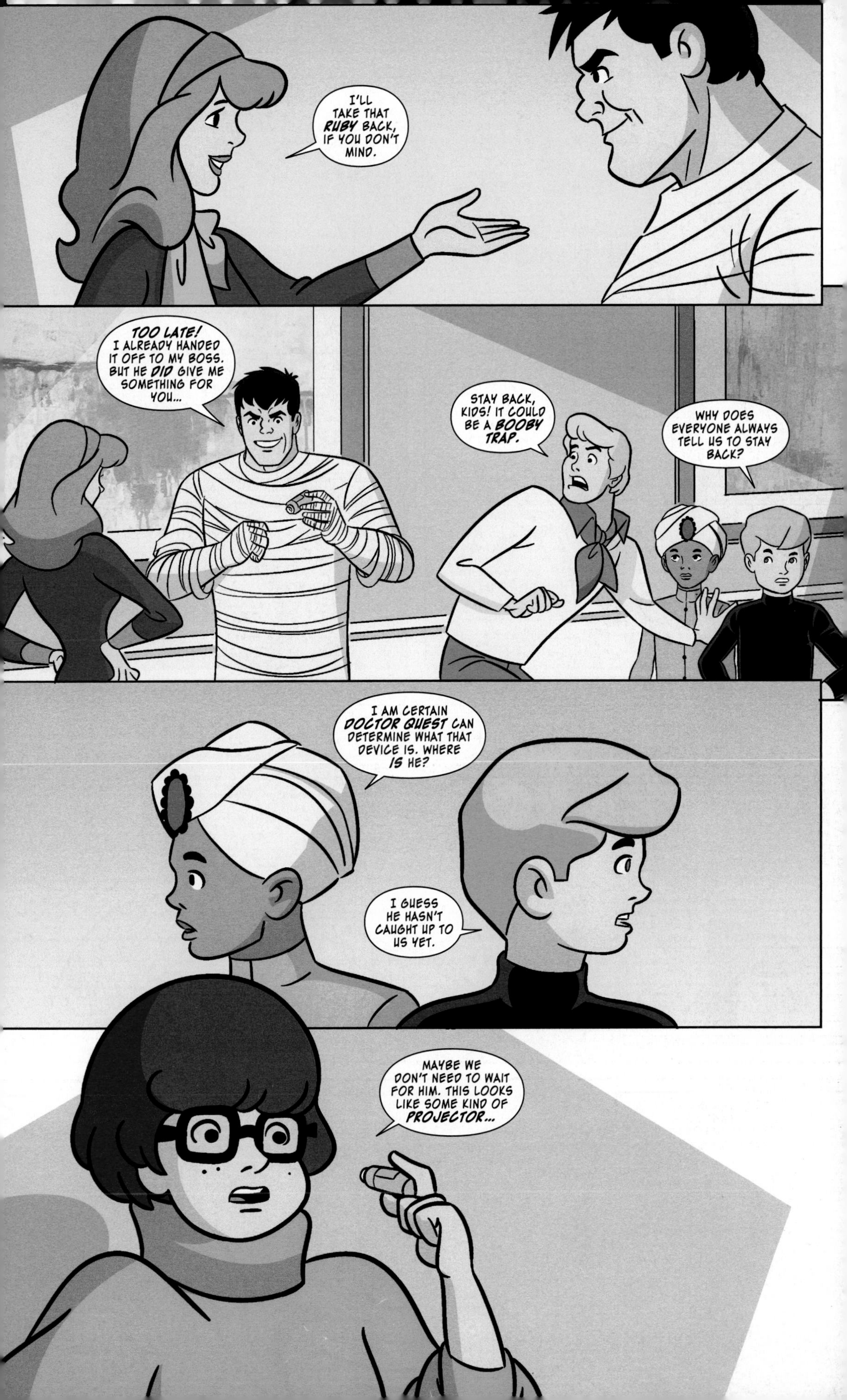
I'LL TAKE THAT RUBY BACK, IF YOU DON'T MIND.
TOO LATE! I ALREADY HANDED IT OFF TO MY BOSS. BUT HE DID GIVE ME SOMETHING FOR YOU...
STAY BACK, KIDS! IT COULD BE A BOOBY TRAP.
WHY DOES EVERYONE ALWAYS TELL US TO STAY BACK?
I AM CERTAIN DOCTOR QUEST CAN DETERMINE WHAT THAT DEVICE IS. WHERE IS HE?
I GUESS HE HASN'T CAUGHT UP TO US YET.
MAYBE WE DON'T NEED TO WAIT FOR HIM. THIS LOOKS LIKE SOME KIND OF PROJECTOR...

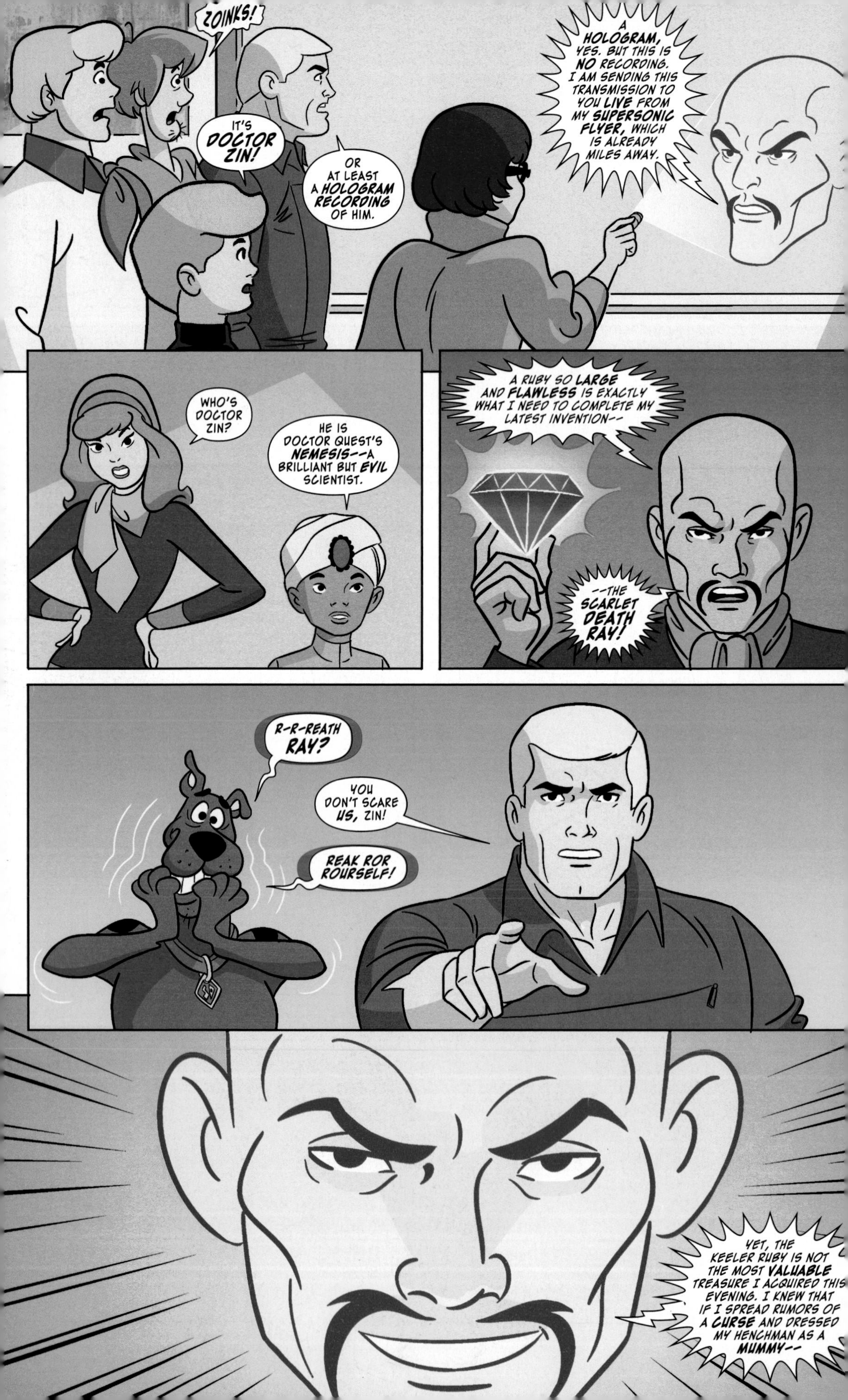
ZOINKS!
IT'S DOCTOR ZIN!
OR AT LEAST A HOLOGRAM RECORDING OF HIM.
A HOLOGRAM, YES. BUT THIS IS NO RECORDING. I AM SENDING THIS TRANSMISSION TO YOU LIVE FROM MY SUPERSONIC FLYER, WHICH IS ALREADY MILES AWAY.
WHO'S DOCTOR ZIN?
HE IS DOCTOR QUEST'S NEMESIS--A BRILLIANT BUT EVIL SCIENTIST.
A RUBY SO LARGE AND FLAWLESS IS EXACTLY WHAT I NEED TO COMPLETE MY LATEST INVENTION--
--THE SCARLET DEATH RAY!
R-R-REATH RAY?
YOU DON'T SCARE US, ZIN!
REAK ROR ROURSELF!
YET, THE KEELER RUBY IS NOT THE MOST VALUABLE TREASURE I ACQUIRED THIS EVENING. I KNEW THAT IF I SPREAD RUMORS OF A CURSE AND DRESSED MY HENCHMAN AS A MUMMY--

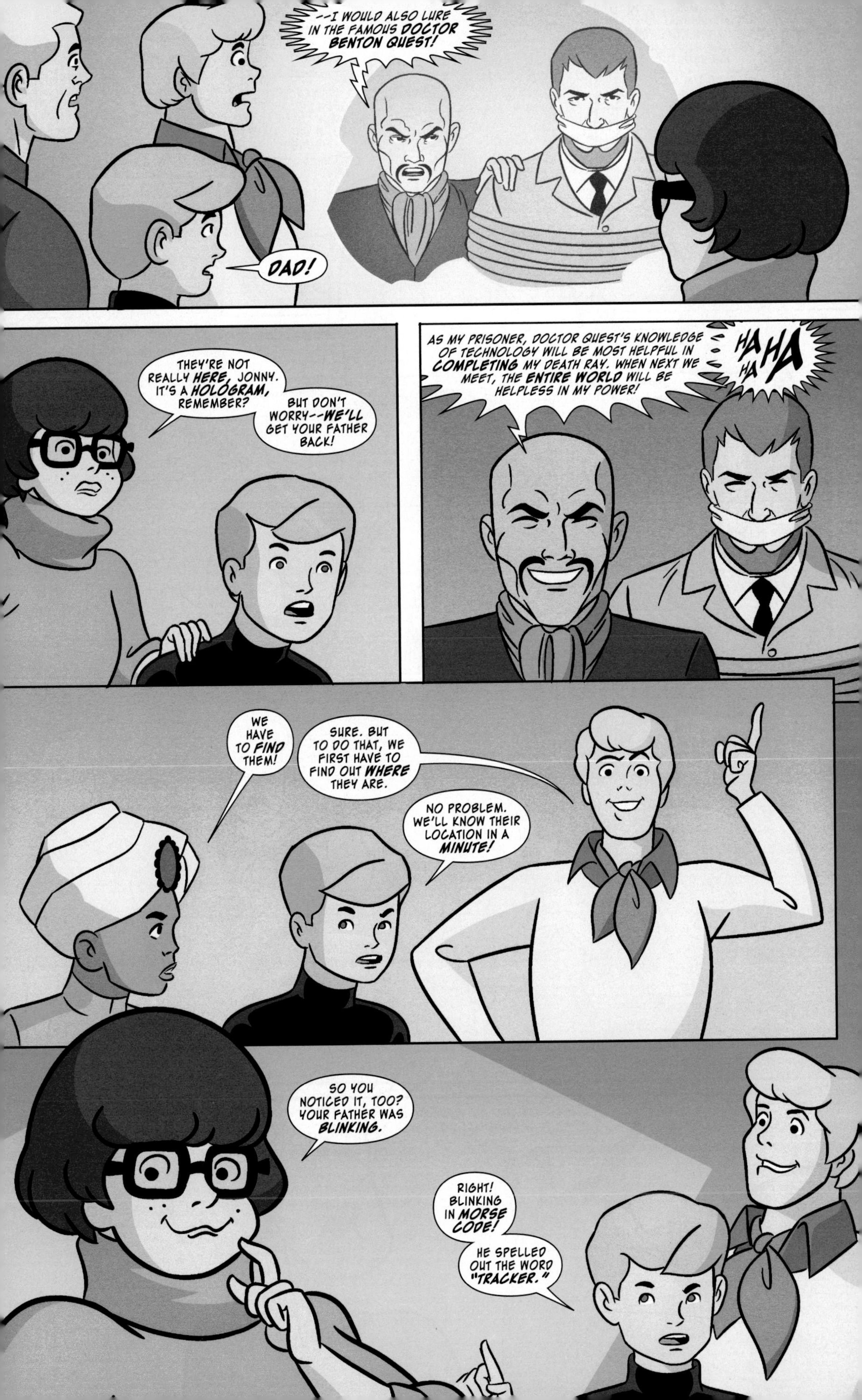
--I WOULD ALSO LURE IN THE FAMOUS DOCTOR BENTON QUEST!
DAD!
THEY'RE NOT REALLY HERE, JONNY. IT'S A HOLOGRAM, REMEMBER?
BUT DON'T WORRY--WE'LL GET YOUR FATHER BACK!
AS MY PRISONER, DOCTOR QUEST'S KNOWLEDGE OF TECHNOLOGY WILL BE MOST HELPFUL IN COMPLETING MY DEATH RAY. WHEN NEXT WE MEET, THE ENTIRE WORLD WILL BE HELPLESS IN MY POWER!
HA HA HA
WE HAVE TO FIND THEM!
SURE. BUT TO DO THAT, WE FIRST HAVE TO FIND OUT WHERE THEY ARE.
NO PROBLEM. WE'LL KNOW THEIR LOCATION IN A MINUTE!
SO YOU NOTICED IT, TOO? YOUR FATHER WAS BLINKING.
RIGHT! BLINKING IN MORSE CODE!
HE SPELLED OUT THE WORD "TRACKER."

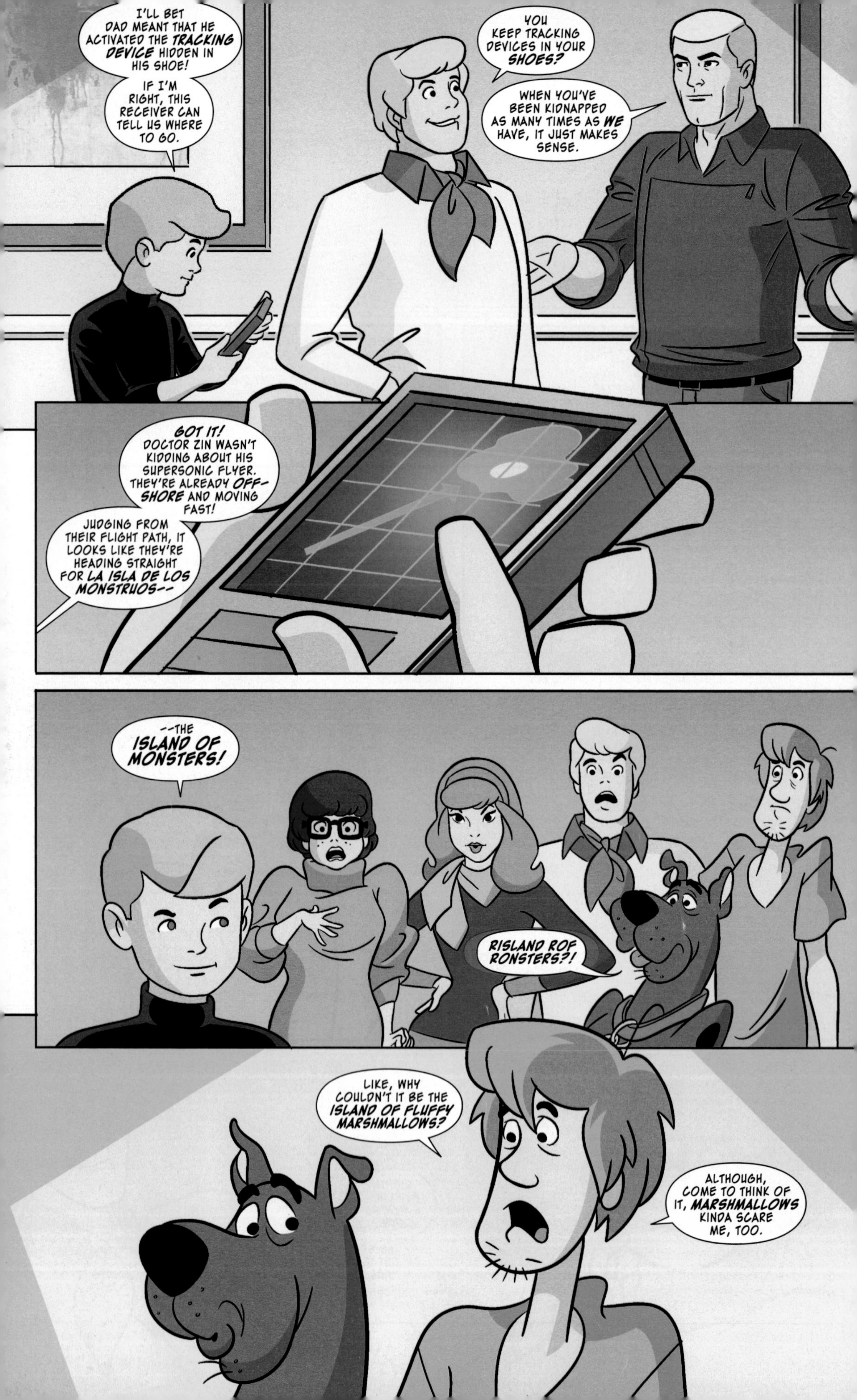
I'LL BET DAD MEANT THAT HE ACTIVATED THE TRACKING DEVICE HIDDEN IN HIS SHOE!
IF I'M RIGHT, THIS RECEIVER CAN TELL US WHERE TO GO.
YOU KEEP TRACKING DEVICES IN YOUR SHOES?
WHEN YOU'VE BEEN KIDNAPPED AS MANY TIMES AS WE HAVE, IT JUST MAKES SENSE.
GOT IT! DOCTOR ZIN WASN'T KIDDING ABOUT HIS SUPERSONIC FLYER. THEY'RE ALREADY OFF-SHORE AND MOVING FAST!
JUDGING FROM THEIR FLIGHT PATH, IT LOOKS LIKE THEY'RE HEADING STRAIGHT FOR LA ISLA DE LOS MONSTRUOS--
--THE ISLAND OF MONSTERS!
RISLAND ROF RONSTERS?!
LIKE, WHY COULDN'T IT BE THE ISLAND OF FLUFFY MARSHMALLOWS?
ALTHOUGH, COME TO THINK OF IT, MARSHMALLOWS KINDA SCARE ME, TOO.

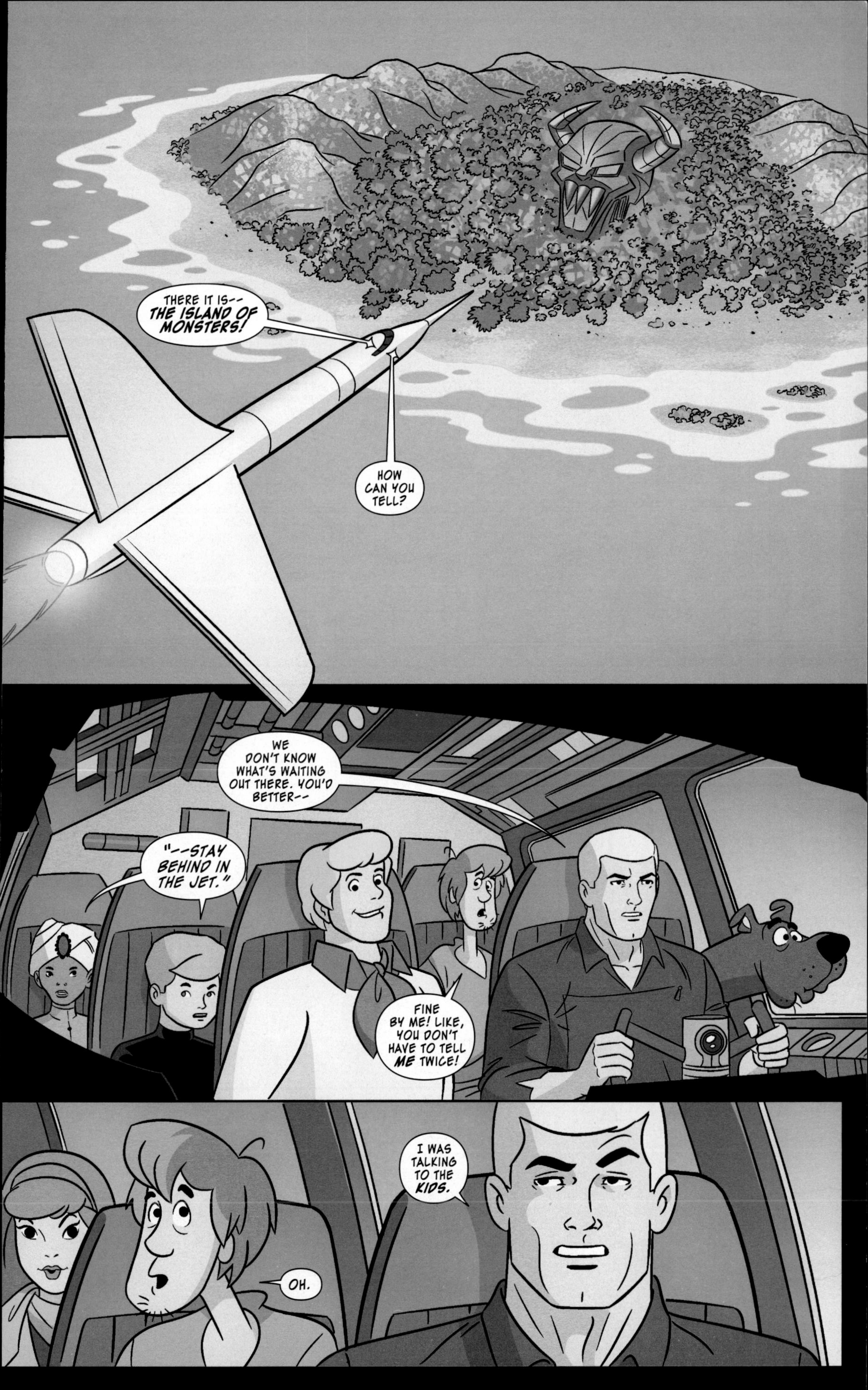
THERE IT IS-- THE ISLAND OF MONSTERS!
HOW CAN YOU TELL?
WE DON'T KNOW WHAT'S WAITING OUT THERE. YOU'D BETTER--
"--STAY BEHIND IN THE JET."
FINE BY ME! LIKE, YOU DON'T HAVE TO TELL ME TWICE!
I WAS TALKING TO THE KIDS.
OH.

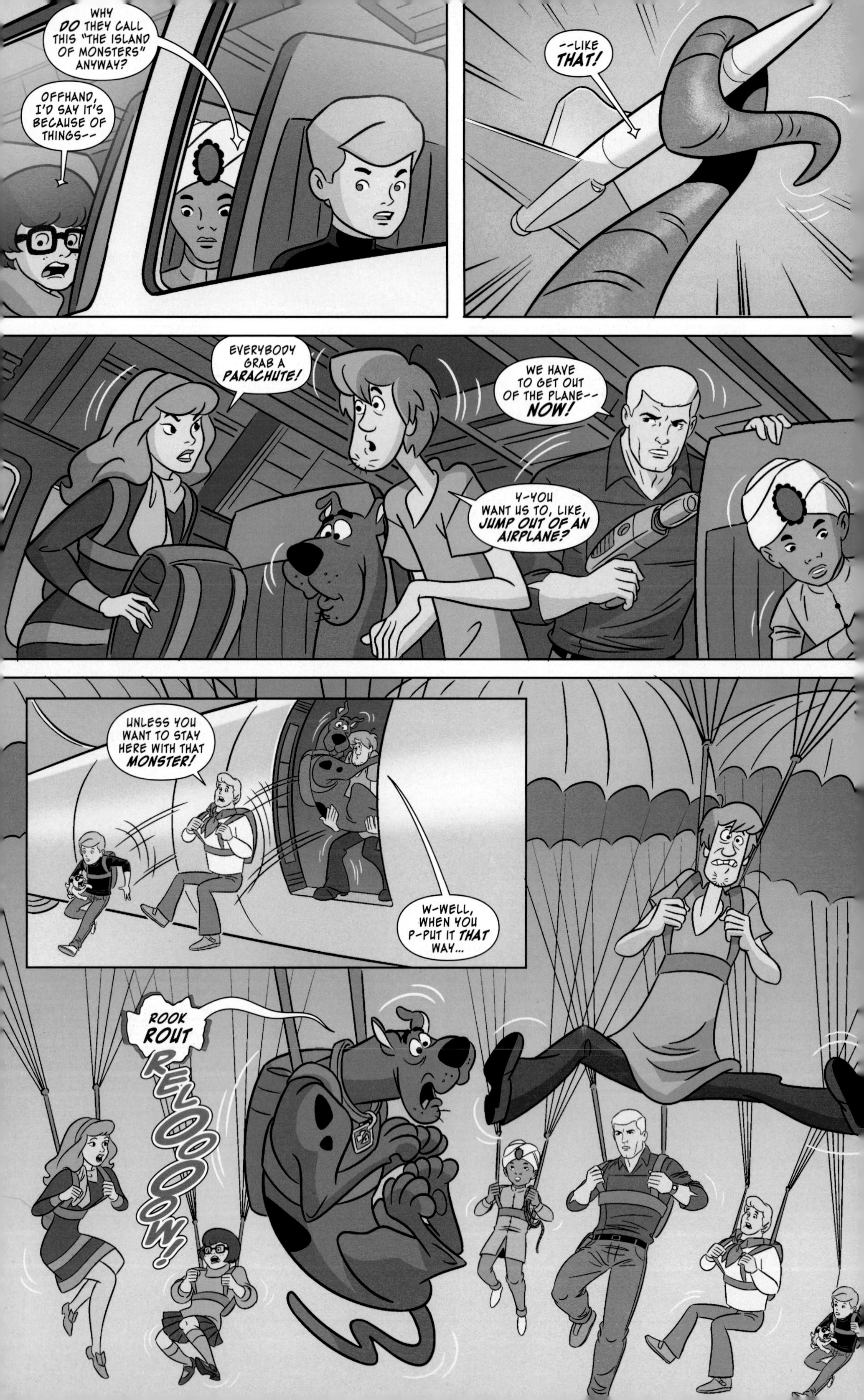
WHY DO THEY CALL THIS "THE ISLAND OF MONSTERS" ANYWAY?
OFFHAND, I'D SAY IT'S BECAUSE OF THINGS--
--LIKE THAT!
EVERYBODY GRAB A PARACHUTE!
WE HAVE TO GET OUT OF THE PLANE-- NOW!
Y-YOU WANT US TO, LIKE, JUMP OUT OF AN AIRPLANE?
UNLESS YOU WANT TO STAY HERE WITH THAT MONSTER!
W-WELL, WHEN YOU P-PUT IT THAT WAY...
ROOK ROUT
RELOOOOW!

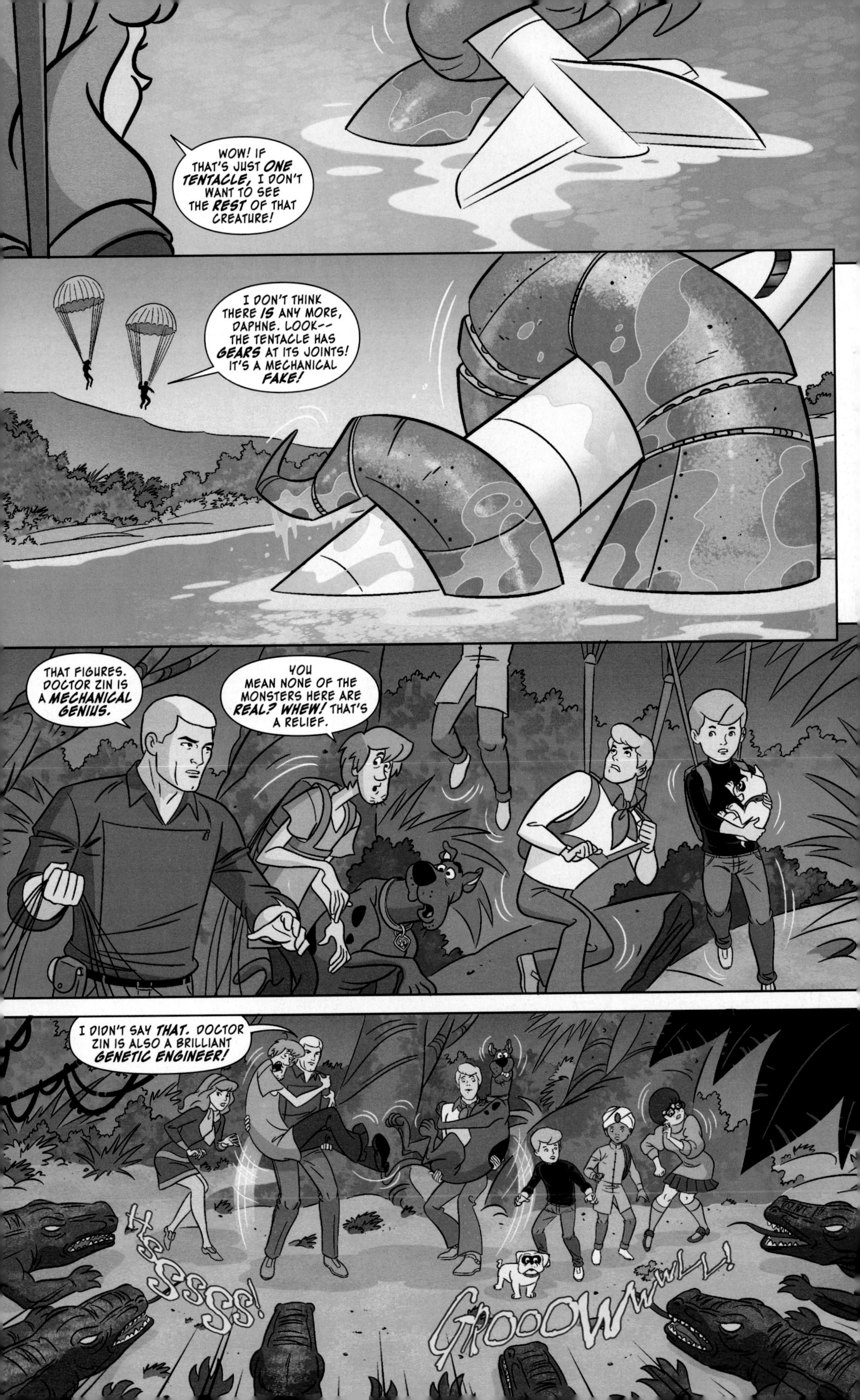
WOW! IF THAT'S JUST ONE TENTACLE, I DON'T WANT TO SEE THE REST OF THAT CREATURE!
I DON'T THINK THERE IS ANY MORE, DAPHNE. LOOK-- THE TENTACLE HAS GEARS AT ITS JOINTS! IT'S A MECHANICAL FAKE!
THAT FIGURES. DOCTOR ZIN IS A MECHANICAL GENIUS.
YOU MEAN NONE OF THE MONSTERS HERE ARE REAL? WHEW! THAT'S A RELIEF.
I DIDN'T SAY THAT. DOCTOR ZIN IS ALSO A BRILLIANT GENETIC ENGINEER!
HSSSSS!
GROOOWWLLL!

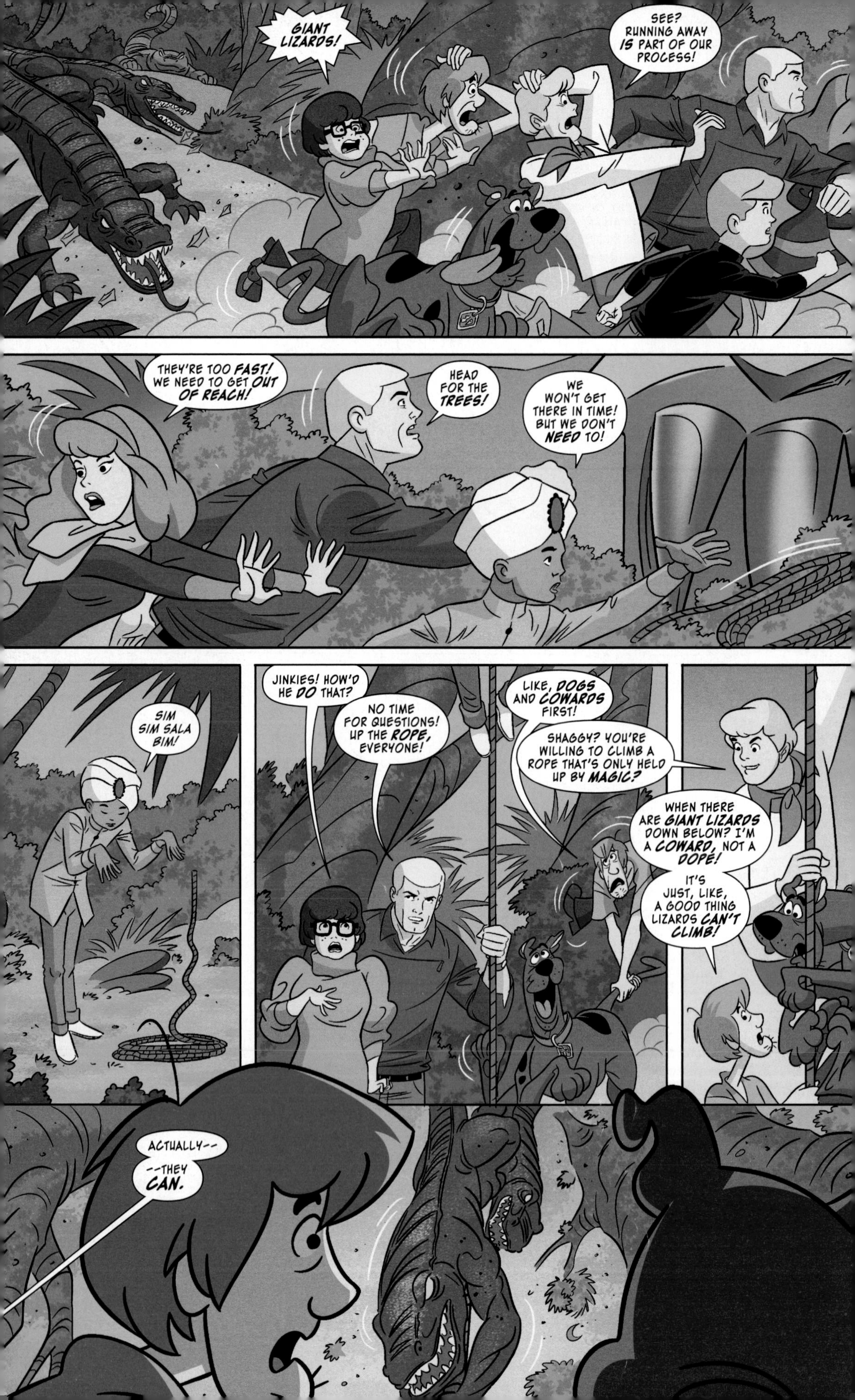
GIANT LIZARDS!
SEE? RUNNING AWAY IS PART OF OUR PROCESS!
THEY'RE TOO FAST! WE NEED TO GET OUT OF REACH!
HEAD FOR THE TREES!
WE WON'T GET THERE IN TIME! BUT WE DON'T NEED TO!
SIM SIM SALA BIM!
JINKIES! HOW'D HE DO THAT?
NO TIME FOR QUESTIONS! UP THE ROPE, EVERYONE!
LIKE, DOGS AND COWARDS FIRST!
SHAGGY? YOU'RE WILLING TO CLIMB A ROPE THAT'S ONLY HELD UP BY MAGIC?
WHEN THERE ARE GIANT LIZARDS DOWN BELOW? I'M A COWARD, NOT A DOPE!
IT'S JUST, LIKE, A GOOD THING LIZARDS CAN'T CLIMB!
ACTUALLY--
--THEY CAN.

REAPIN' RIZARDS!

RIMBIN' RIZARDS!

SCOOB! LIKE, DON'T LET GO OF THE ROPE!

RUH-ROH!

ROOK ROOOOWWWOUT!

HSSSSSSSS

'S BRAVE OF YOUR DOG TO ENDANGER HIMSELF TO KEEP THE LIZARDS AWAY FROM US.

SCOOBY? BRAVE?

NOW, LET'S SEE IF I CAN GET RID OF THEM FOR GOOD!

BY SHOOTING THOSE POOR ANIMALS?

NO, THIS IS DOCTOR QUEST'S SONIC BLASTER. IF I CAN FIND THE RIGHT FREQUENCY--

--I CAN USE ULTRASONIC WAVES TO DRIVE THOSE LIZARDS FAR AWAY!

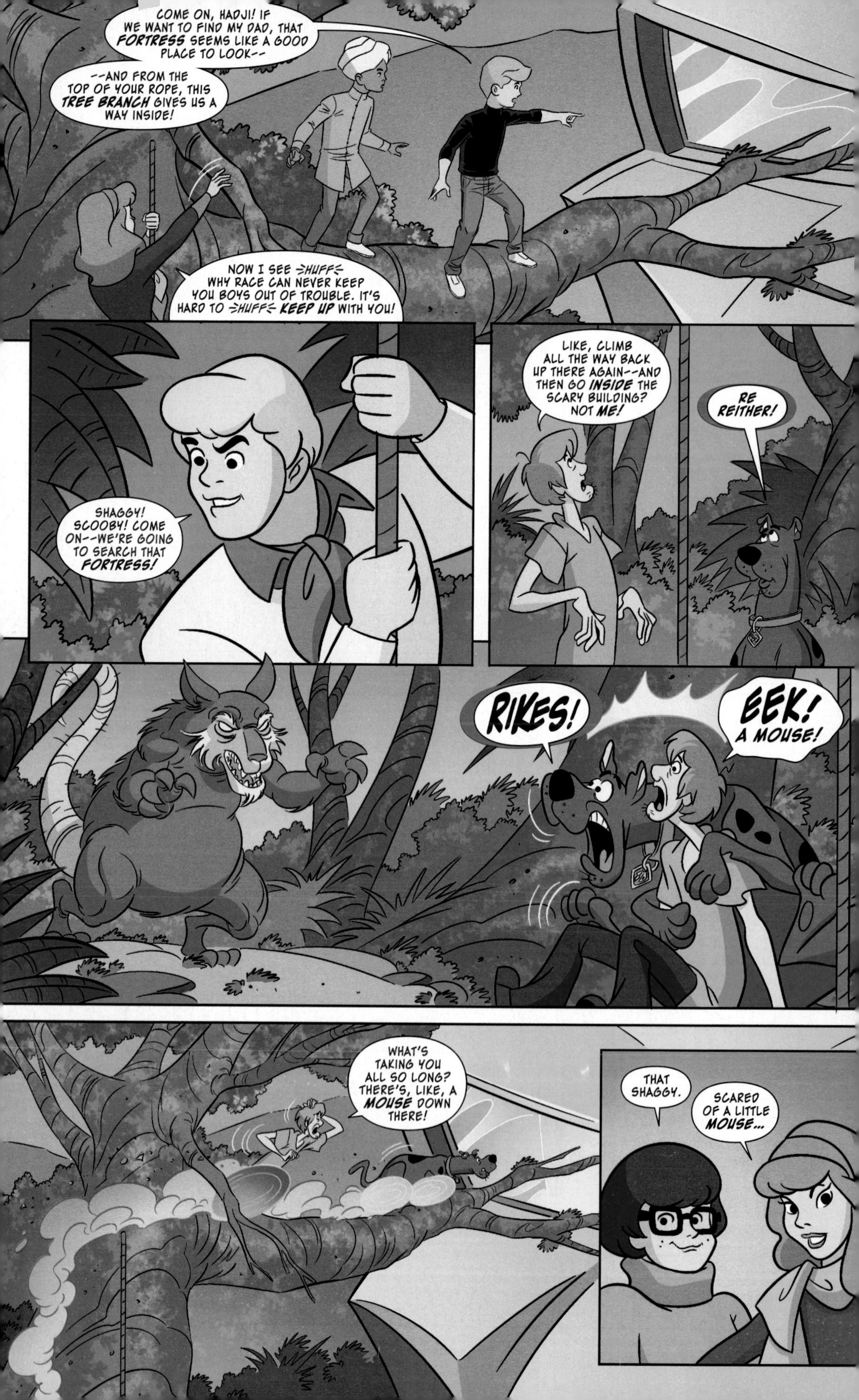
COME ON, HADJI! IF WE WANT TO FIND MY DAD, THAT FORTRESS SEEMS LIKE A GOOD PLACE TO LOOK--
--AND FROM THE TOP OF YOUR ROPE, THIS TREE BRANCH GIVES US A WAY INSIDE!
NOW I SEE =HUFF= WHY RACE CAN NEVER KEEP YOU BOYS OUT OF TROUBLE. IT'S HARD TO =HUFF= KEEP UP WITH YOU!
SHAGGY! SCOOBY! COME ON--WE'RE GOING TO SEARCH THAT FORTRESS!
LIKE, CLIMB ALL THE WAY BACK UP THERE AGAIN--AND THEN GO INSIDE THE SCARY BUILDING? NOT ME!
RE REITHER!
RIKES!
EEK! A MOUSE!
WHAT'S TAKING YOU ALL SO LONG? THERE'S, LIKE, A MOUSE DOWN THERE!
THAT SHAGGY.
SCARED OF A LITTLE MOUSE...

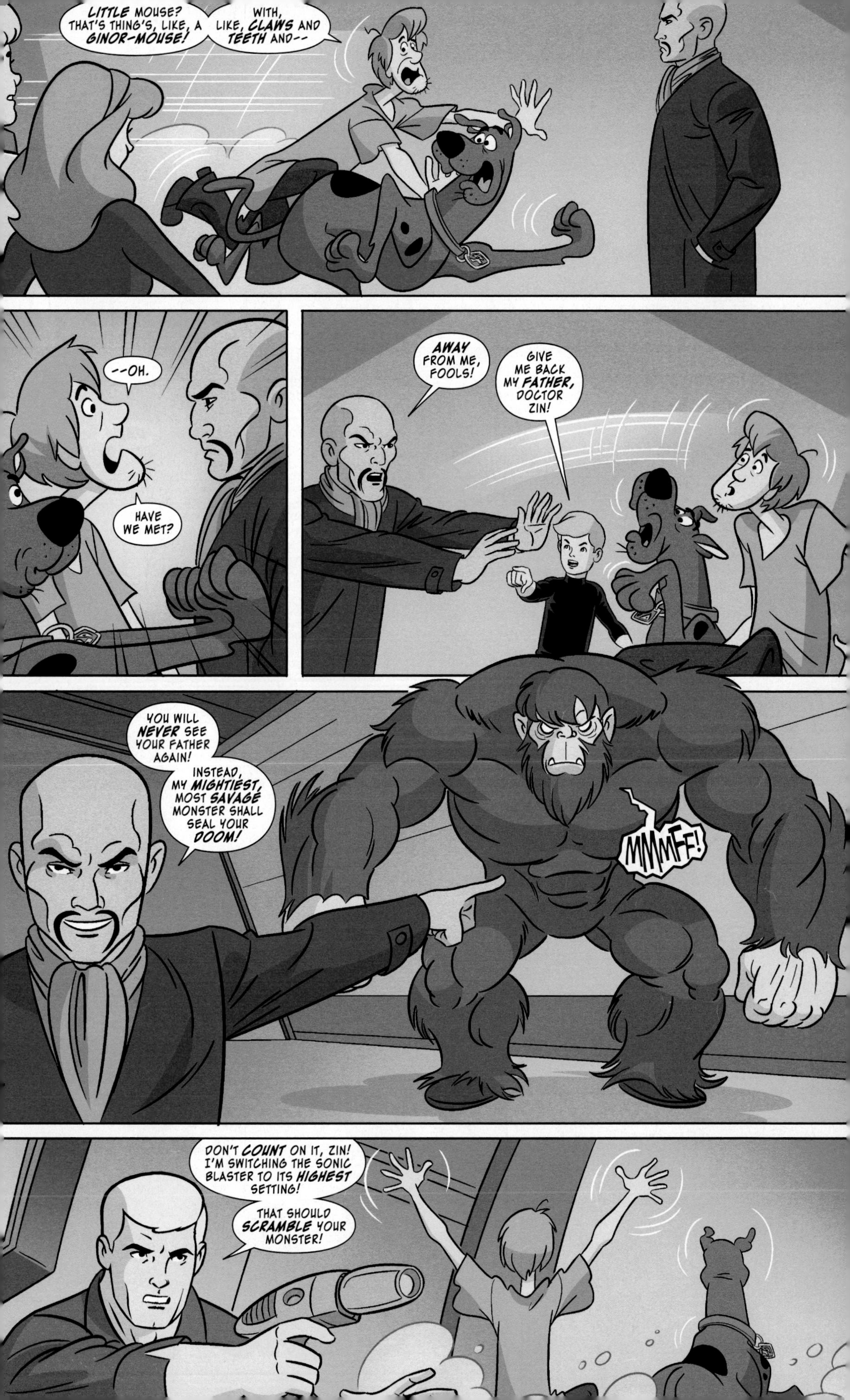
LITTLE MOUSE? THAT'S THING'S, LIKE, A GINOR-MOUSE!
WITH, LIKE, CLAWS AND TEETH AND--
--OH.
HAVE WE MET?
AWAY FROM ME, FOOLS!
GIVE ME BACK MY FATHER, DOCTOR ZIN!
YOU WILL NEVER SEE YOUR FATHER AGAIN!
INSTEAD, MY MIGHTIEST, MOST SAVAGE MONSTER SHALL SEAL YOUR DOOM!
MMMFF!
DON'T COUNT ON IT, ZIN! I'M SWITCHING THE SONIC BLASTER TO ITS HIGHEST SETTING!
THAT SHOULD SCRAMBLE YOUR MONSTER!

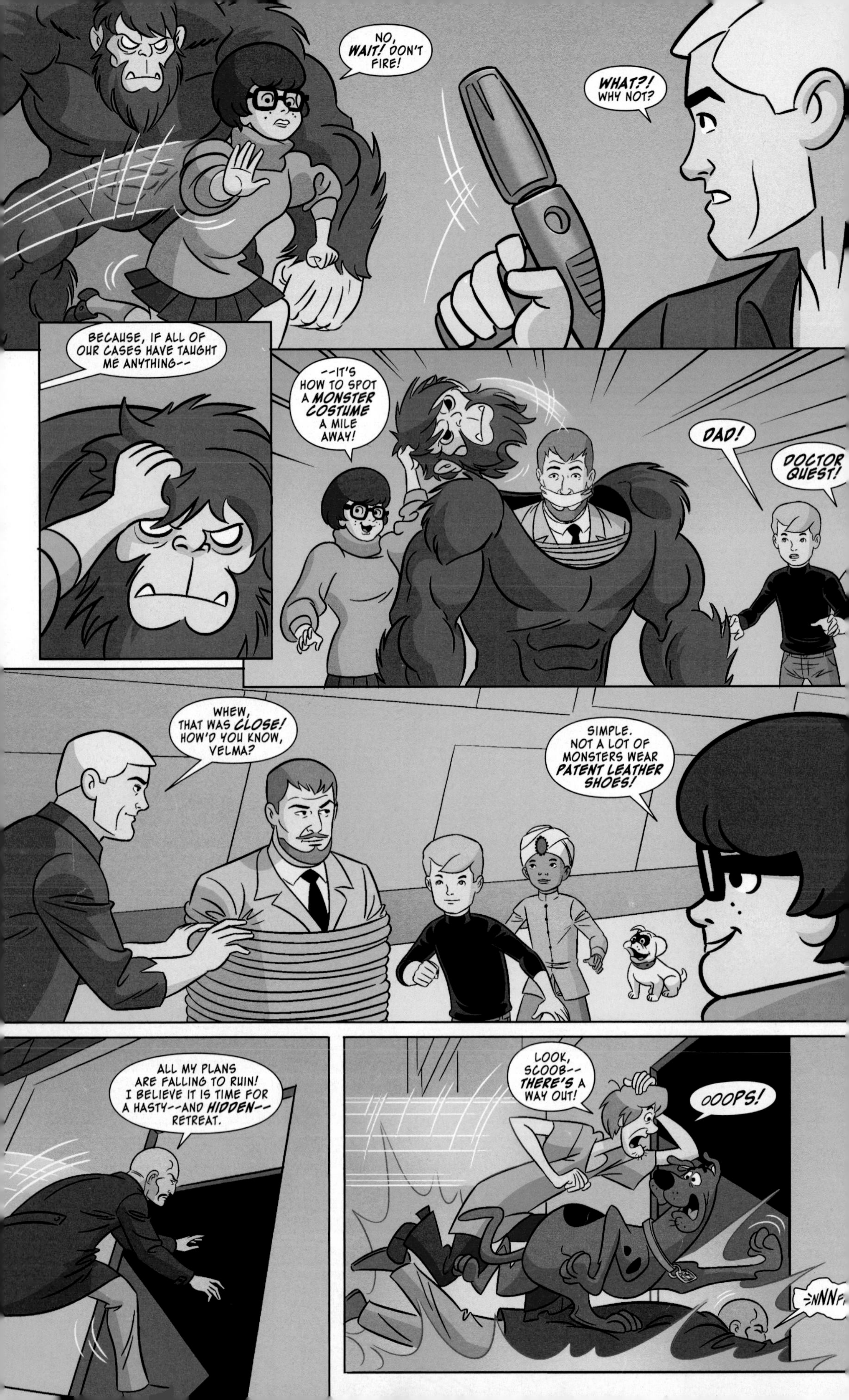
NO, WAIT! DON'T FIRE!
WHAT?! WHY NOT?
BECAUSE, IF ALL OF OUR CASES HAVE TAUGHT ME ANYTHING--
--IT'S HOW TO SPOT A MONSTER COSTUME A MILE AWAY!
DAD!
DOCTOR QUEST!
WHEW, THAT WAS CLOSE! HOW'D YOU KNOW, VELMA?
SIMPLE. NOT A LOT OF MONSTERS WEAR PATENT LEATHER SHOES!
ALL MY PLANS ARE FALLING TO RUIN! I BELIEVE IT IS TIME FOR A HASTY--AND HIDDEN--RETREAT.
LOOK, SCOOB--THERE'S A WAY OUT!
OOOPS!

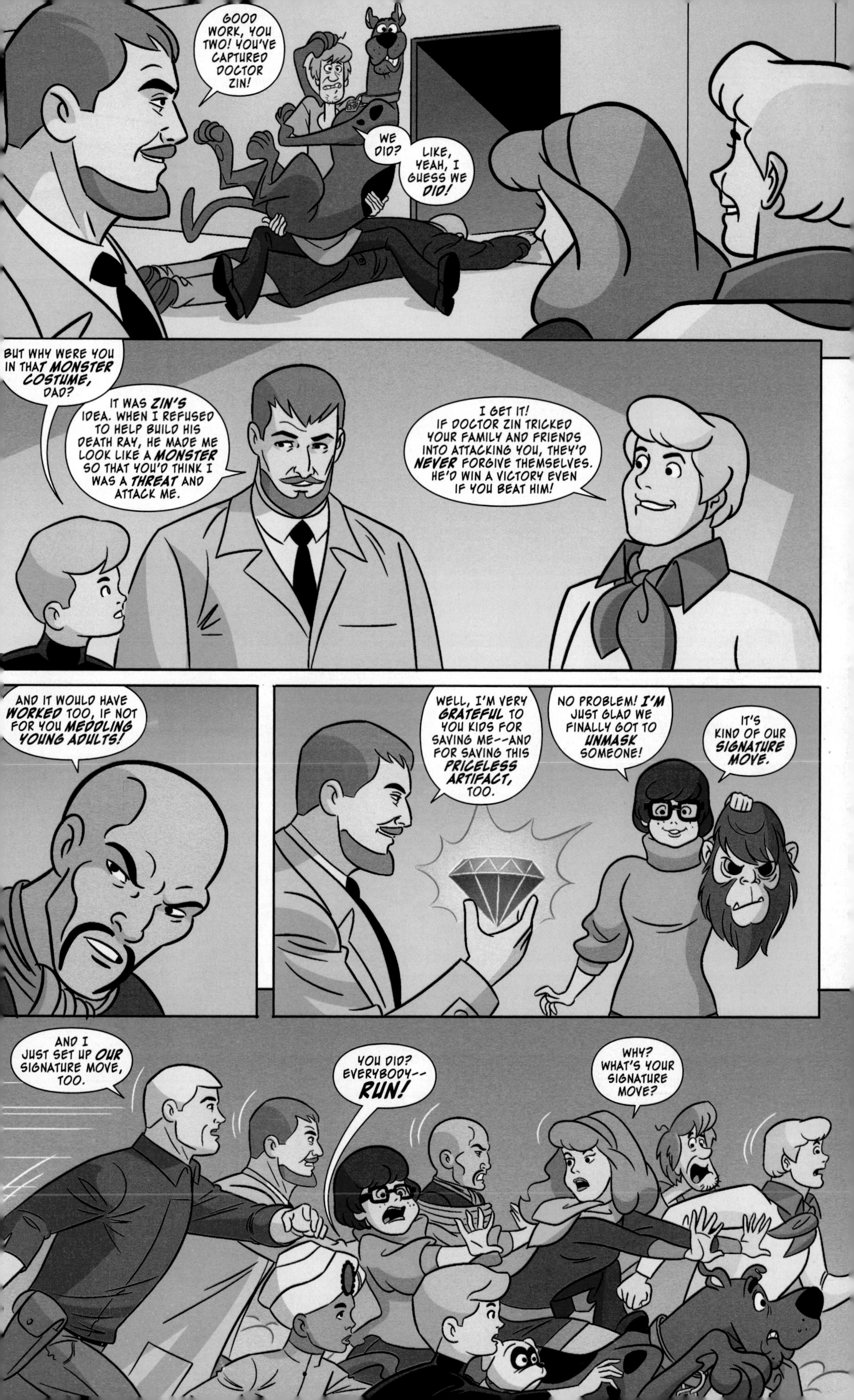
GOOD WORK, YOU TWO! YOU'VE CAPTURED DOCTOR ZIN!
WE DID?
LIKE, YEAH, I GUESS WE DID!
BUT WHY WERE YOU IN THAT MONSTER COSTUME, DAD?
IT WAS ZIN'S IDEA. WHEN I REFUSED TO HELP BUILD HIS DEATH RAY, HE MADE ME LOOK LIKE A MONSTER SO THAT YOU'D THINK I WAS A THREAT AND ATTACK ME.
I GET IT! IF DOCTOR ZIN TRICKED YOUR FAMILY AND FRIENDS INTO ATTACKING YOU, THEY'D NEVER FORGIVE THEMSELVES. HE'D WIN A VICTORY EVEN IF YOU BEAT HIM!
AND IT WOULD HAVE WORKED TOO, IF NOT FOR YOU MEDDLING YOUNG ADULTS!
WELL, I'M VERY GRATEFUL TO YOU KIDS FOR SAVING ME--AND FOR SAVING THIS PRICELESS ARTIFACT, TOO.
NO PROBLEM! I'M JUST GLAD WE FINALLY GOT TO UNMASK SOMEONE!
IT'S KIND OF OUR SIGNATURE MOVE.
AND I JUST SET UP OUR SIGNATURE MOVE, TOO.
YOU DID? EVERYBODY-- RUN!
WHY? WHAT'S YOUR SIGNATURE MOVE?

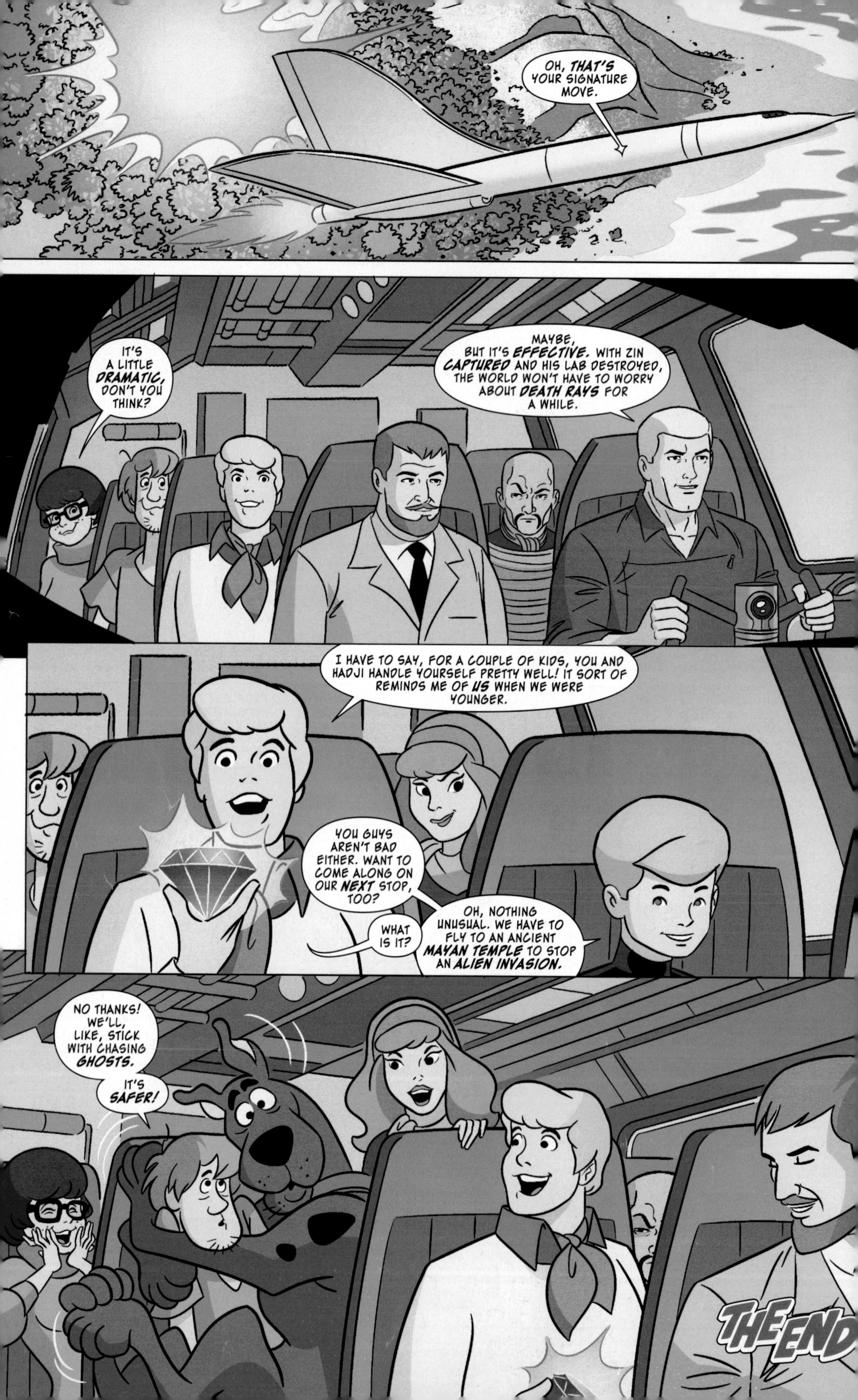

OH, THAT'S YOUR SIGNATURE MOVE.
IT'S A LITTLE DRAMATIC, DON'T YOU THINK?
MAYBE, BUT IT'S EFFECTIVE. WITH ZIN CAPTURED AND HIS LAB DESTROYED, THE WORLD WON'T HAVE TO WORRY ABOUT DEATH RAYS FOR A WHILE.
I HAVE TO SAY, FOR A COUPLE OF KIDS, YOU AND HADJI HANDLE YOURSELF PRETTY WELL! IT SORT OF REMINDS ME OF US WHEN WE WERE YOUNGER.
YOU GUYS AREN'T BAD EITHER. WANT TO COME ALONG ON OUR NEXT STOP, TOO?
WHAT IS IT?
OH, NOTHING UNUSUAL. WE HAVE TO FLY TO AN ANCIENT MAYAN TEMPLE TO STOP AN ALIEN INVASION.
NO THANKS! WE'LL, LIKE, STICK WITH CHASING GHOSTS.
IT'S SAFER!
THE END

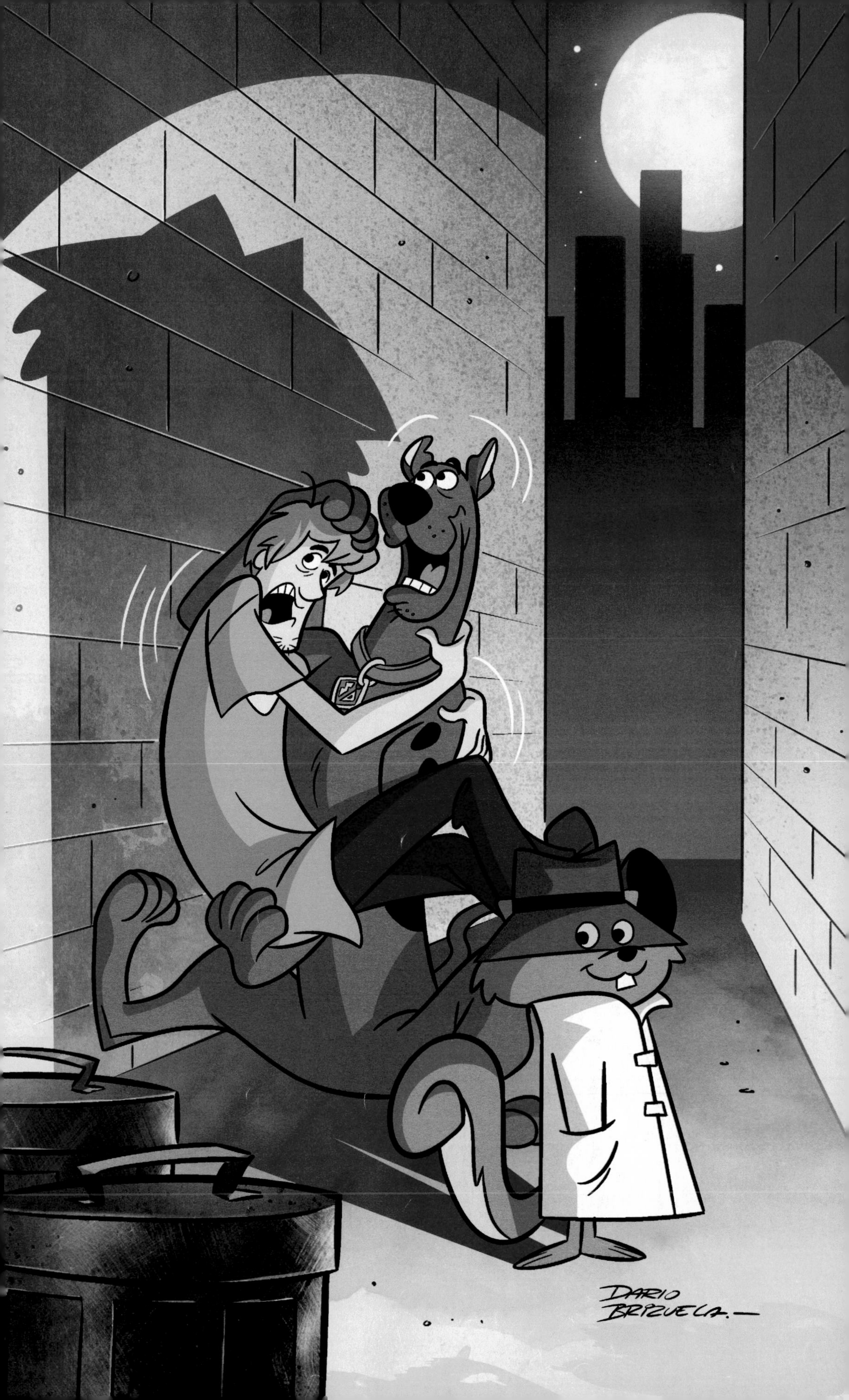

DARIO
BRIZUELA

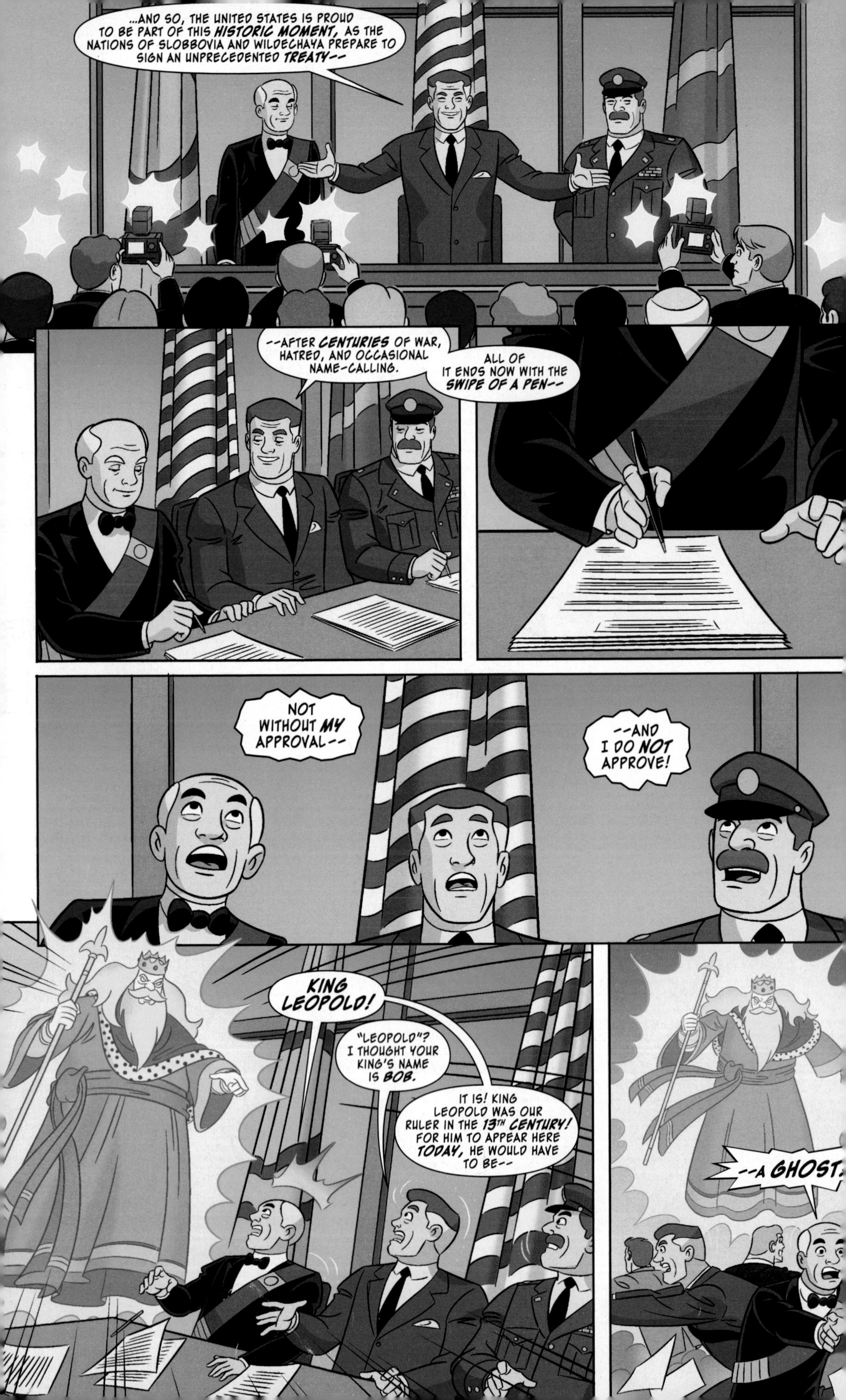
...AND SO, THE UNITED STATES IS PROUD TO BE PART OF THIS HISTORIC MOMENT, AS THE NATIONS OF SLOBBOVIA AND WILDECHAYA PREPARE TO SIGN AN UNPRECEDENTED TREATY--
--AFTER CENTURIES OF WAR, HATRED, AND OCCASIONAL NAME-CALLING.
ALL OF IT ENDS NOW WITH THE SWIPE OF A PEN--
NOT WITHOUT MY APPROVAL--
--AND I DO NOT APPROVE!
KING LEOPOLD!
"LEOPOLD"? I THOUGHT YOUR KING'S NAME IS BOB.
IT IS! KING LEOPOLD WAS OUR RULER IN THE 13TH CENTURY! FOR HIM TO APPEAR HERE TODAY, HE WOULD HAVE TO BE--
--A GHOST!

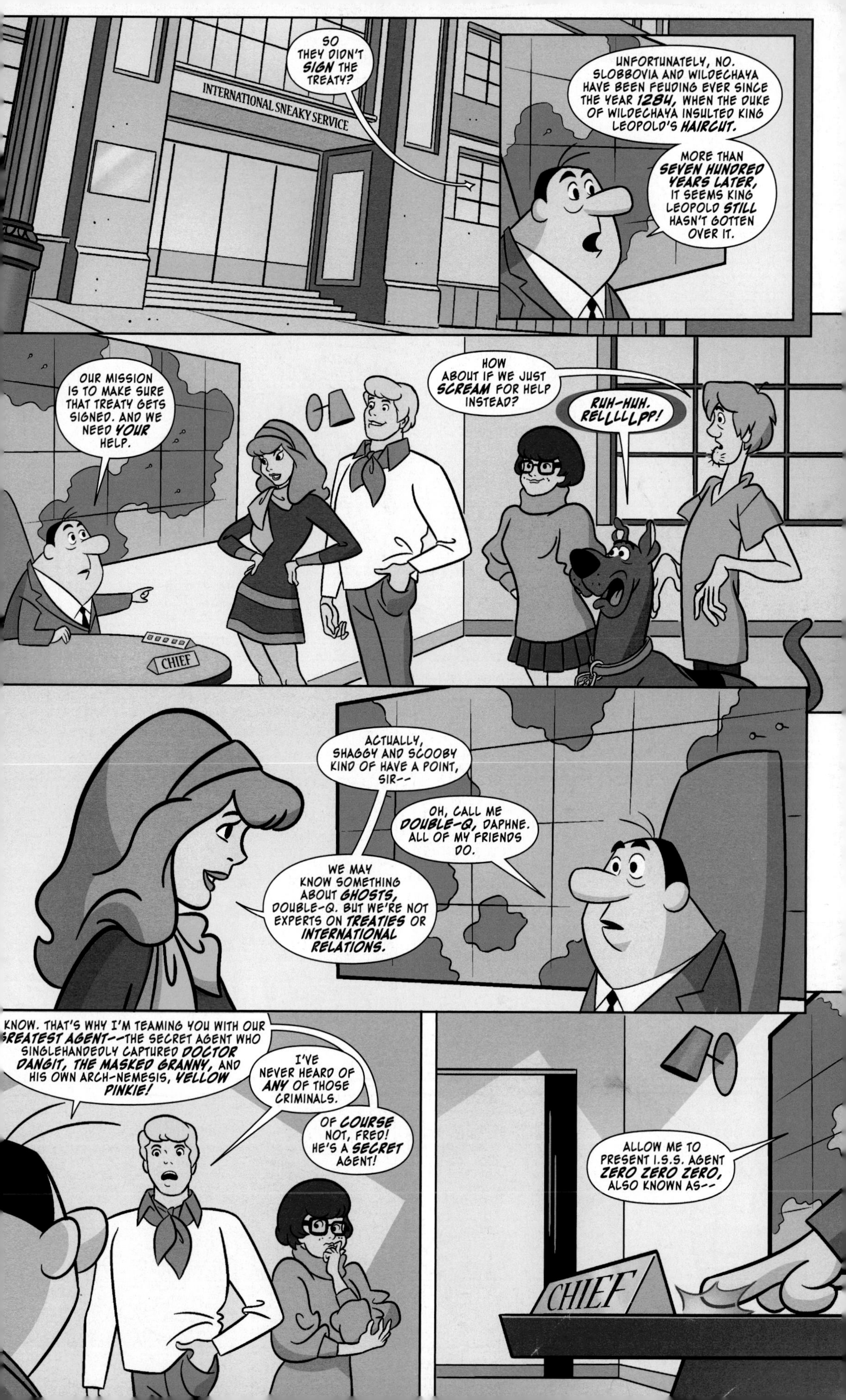
INTERNATIONAL SNEAKY SERVICE
SO THEY DIDN'T SIGN THE TREATY?
UNFORTUNATELY, NO. SLOBBOVIA AND WILDECHAYA HAVE BEEN FEUDING EVER SINCE THE YEAR 1284, WHEN THE DUKE OF WILDECHAYA INSULTED KING LEOPOLD'S HAIRCUT.
MORE THAN SEVEN HUNDRED YEARS LATER, IT SEEMS KING LEOPOLD STILL HASN'T GOTTEN OVER IT.
OUR MISSION IS TO MAKE SURE THAT TREATY GETS SIGNED. AND WE NEED YOUR HELP.
HOW ABOUT IF WE JUST SCREAM FOR HELP INSTEAD?
RUH-HUH. RELLLLLPP!
CHIEF
ACTUALLY, SHAGGY AND SCOOBY KIND OF HAVE A POINT, SIR--
OH, CALL ME DOUBLE-Q, DAPHNE. ALL OF MY FRIENDS DO.
WE MAY KNOW SOMETHING ABOUT GHOSTS, DOUBLE-Q. BUT WE'RE NOT EXPERTS ON TREATIES OR INTERNATIONAL RELATIONS.
KNOW. THAT'S WHY I'M TEAMING YOU WITH OUR GREATEST AGENT--THE SECRET AGENT WHO SINGLEHANDEDLY CAPTURED DOCTOR DANGIT, THE MASKED GRANNY, AND HIS OWN ARCH-NEMESIS, YELLOW PINKIE!
I'VE NEVER HEARD OF ANY OF THOSE CRIMINALS.
OF COURSE NOT, FRED! HE'S A SECRET AGENT!
ALLOW ME TO PRESENT I.S.S. AGENT ZERO ZERO ZERO, ALSO KNOWN AS--
CHIEF

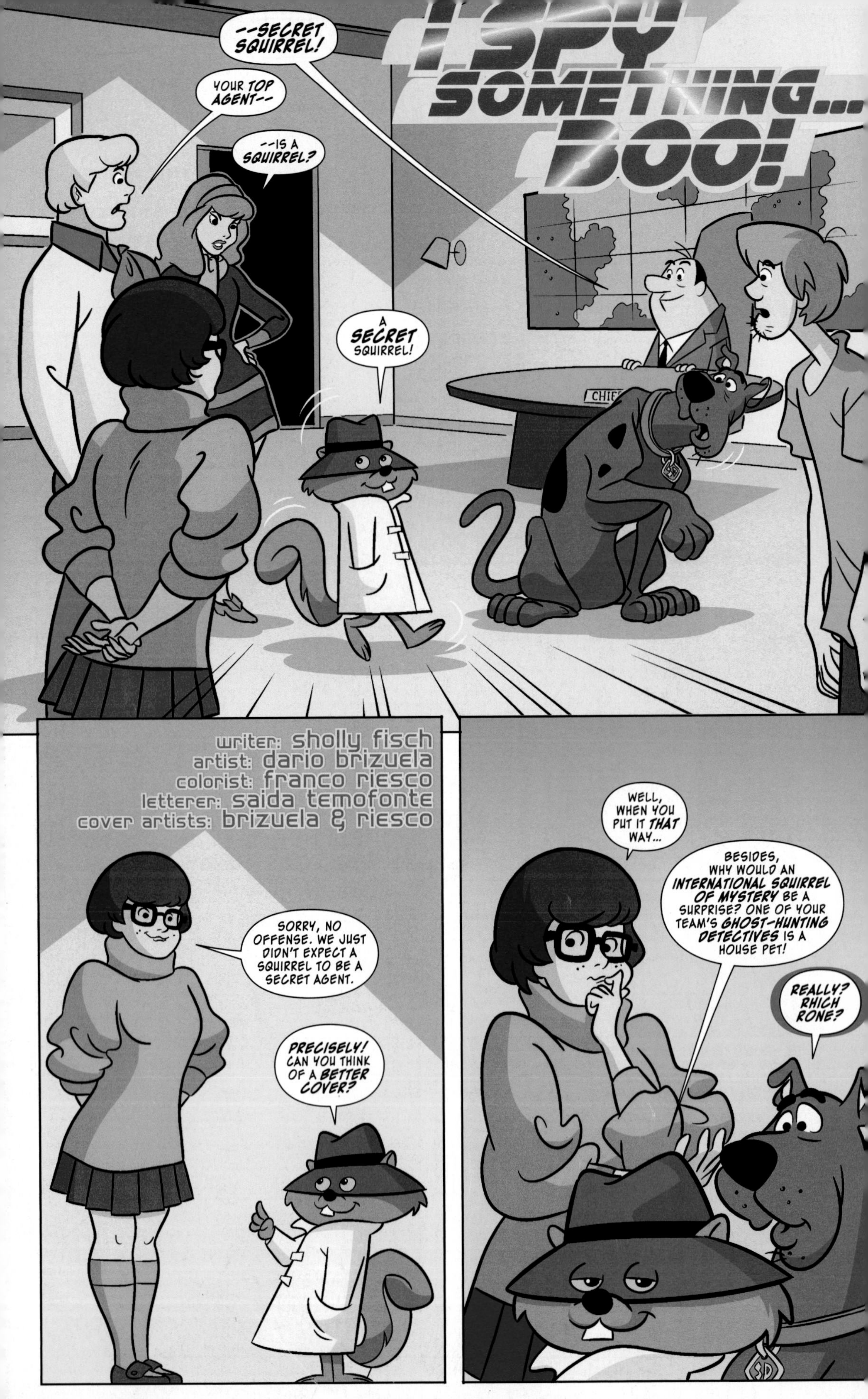
I SPY SOMETHING... BOO!
YOUR TOP AGENT--
--IS A SQUIRREL?
--SECRET SQUIRREL!
A SECRET SQUIRREL!
CHIEF
writer: sholly fisch
artist: dario brizuela
colorist: franco riesco
letterer: saida temofonte
cover artists: brizuela & riesco
SORRY, NO OFFENSE. WE JUST DIDN'T EXPECT A SQUIRREL TO BE A SECRET AGENT.
PRECISELY! CAN YOU THINK OF A BETTER COVER?
WELL, WHEN YOU PUT IT THAT WAY...
BESIDES, WHY WOULD AN INTERNATIONAL SQUIRREL OF MYSTERY BE A SURPRISE? ONE OF YOUR TEAM'S GHOST-HUNTING DETECTIVES IS A HOUSE PET!
REALLY? RHICH RONE?

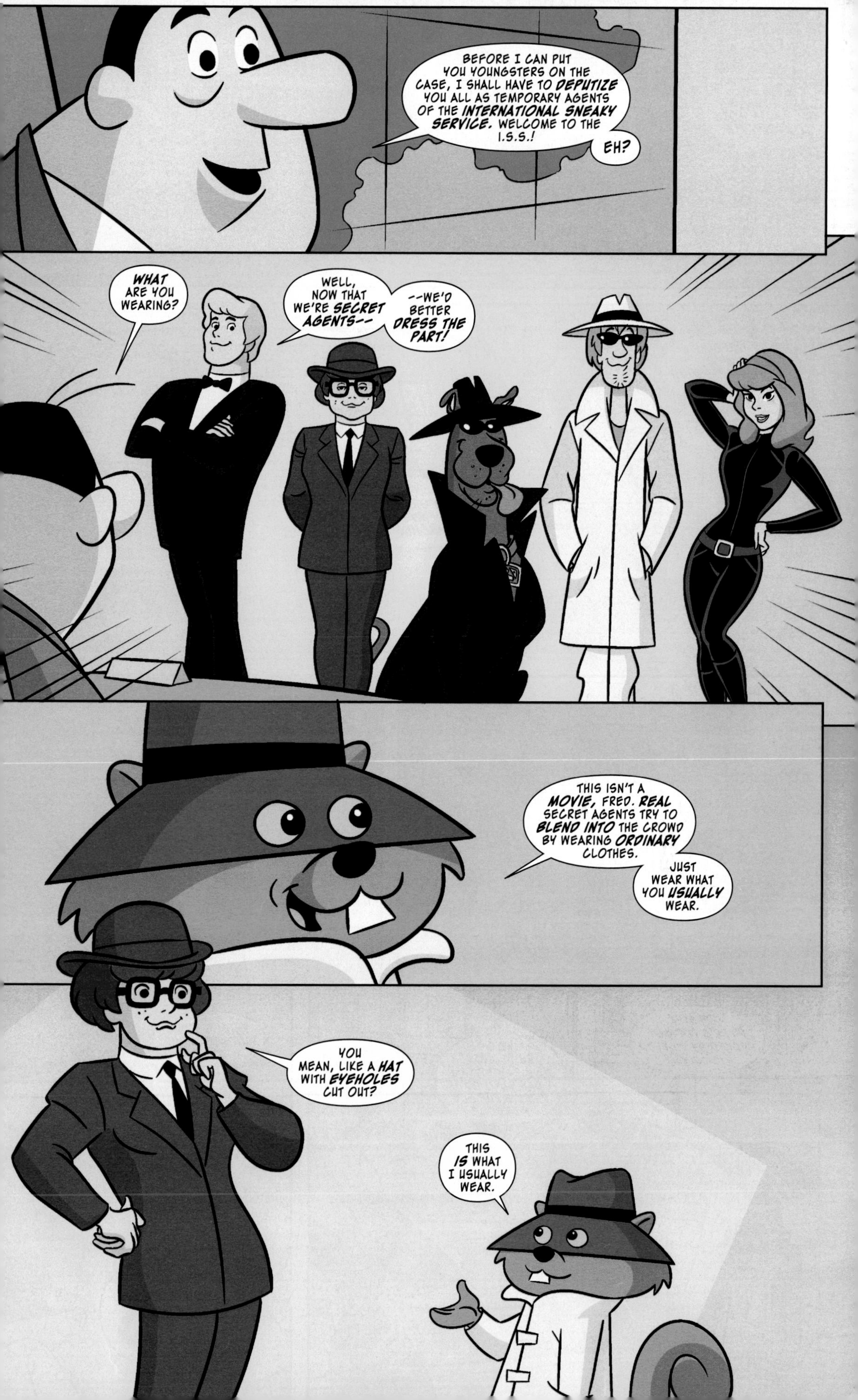
BEFORE I CAN PUT YOU YOUNGSTERS ON THE CASE, I SHALL HAVE TO DEPUTIZE YOU ALL AS TEMPORARY AGENTS OF THE INTERNATIONAL SNEAKY SERVICE. WELCOME TO THE I.S.S.!
EH?
WHAT ARE YOU WEARING?
WELL, NOW THAT WE'RE SECRET AGENTS--
--WE'D BETTER DRESS THE PART!
THIS ISN'T A MOVIE, FRED. REAL SECRET AGENTS TRY TO BLEND INTO THE CROWD BY WEARING ORDINARY CLOTHES.
JUST WEAR WHAT YOU USUALLY WEAR.
YOU MEAN, LIKE A HAT WITH EYEHOLES CUT OUT?
THIS IS WHAT I USUALLY WEAR.

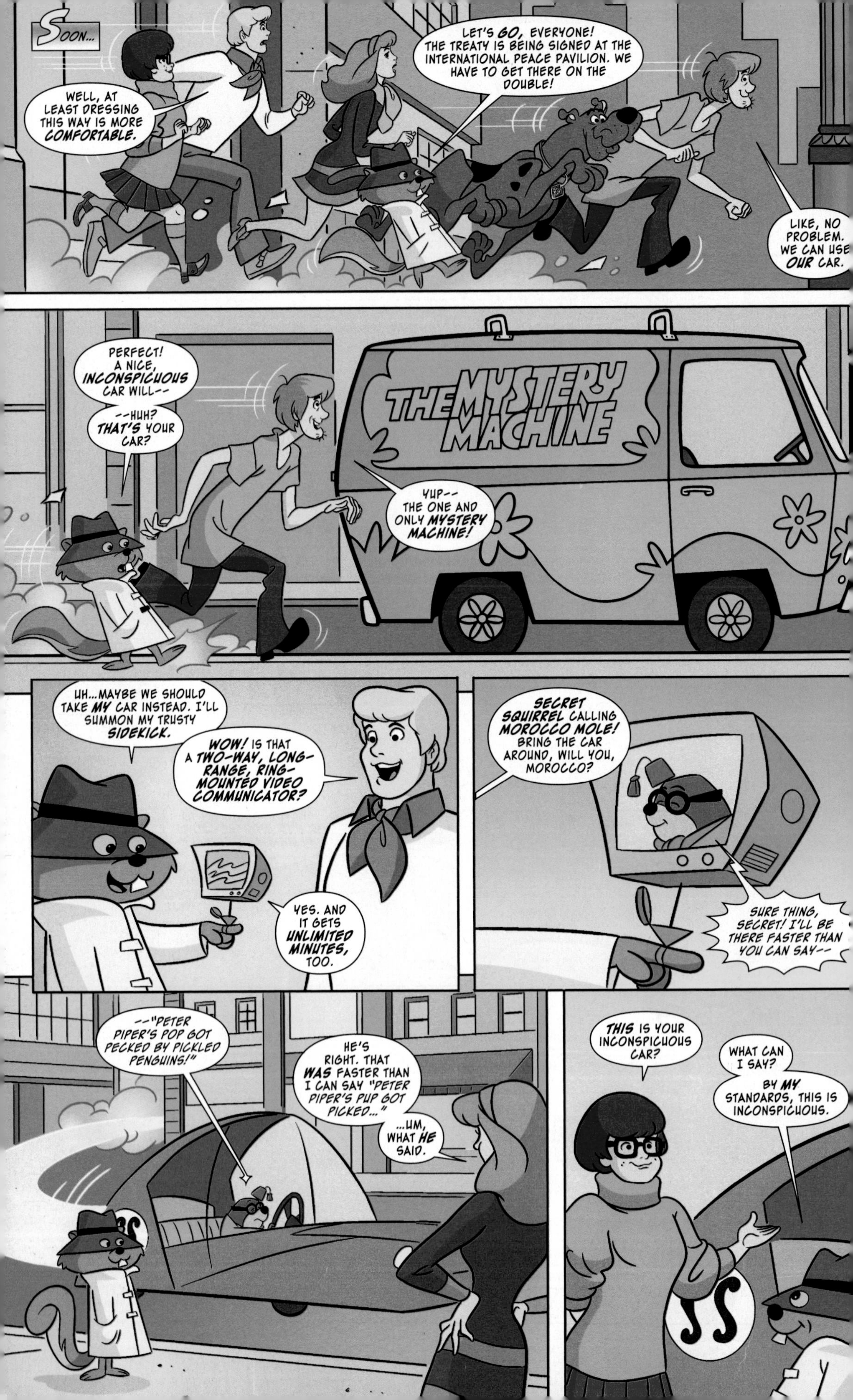
SOON...
WELL, AT LEAST DRESSING THIS WAY IS MORE COMFORTABLE.
LET'S GO, EVERYONE! THE TREATY IS BEING SIGNED AT THE INTERNATIONAL PEACE PAVILION. WE HAVE TO GET THERE ON THE DOUBLE!
LIKE, NO PROBLEM. WE CAN USE OUR CAR.
PERFECT! A NICE, INCONSPICUOUS CAR WILL--
--HUH? THAT'S YOUR CAR?
THE MYSTERY MACHINE
YUP-- THE ONE AND ONLY MYSTERY MACHINE!
UH...MAYBE WE SHOULD TAKE MY CAR INSTEAD. I'LL SUMMON MY TRUSTY SIDEKICK.
WOW! IS THAT A TWO-WAY, LONG-RANGE, RING-MOUNTED VIDEO COMMUNICATOR?
YES. AND IT GETS UNLIMITED MINUTES, TOO.
SECRET SQUIRREL CALLING MOROCCO MOLE! BRING THE CAR AROUND, WILL YOU, MOROCCO?
SURE THING, SECRET! I'LL BE THERE FASTER THAN YOU CAN SAY--
--"PETER PIPER'S POP GOT PECKED BY PICKLED PENGUINS!"
HE'S RIGHT. THAT WAS FASTER THAN I CAN SAY "PETER PIPER'S PUP GOT PICKED..."
...UM, WHAT HE SAID.
THIS IS YOUR INCONSPICUOUS CAR?
WHAT CAN I SAY? BY MY STANDARDS, THIS IS INCONSPICUOUS.

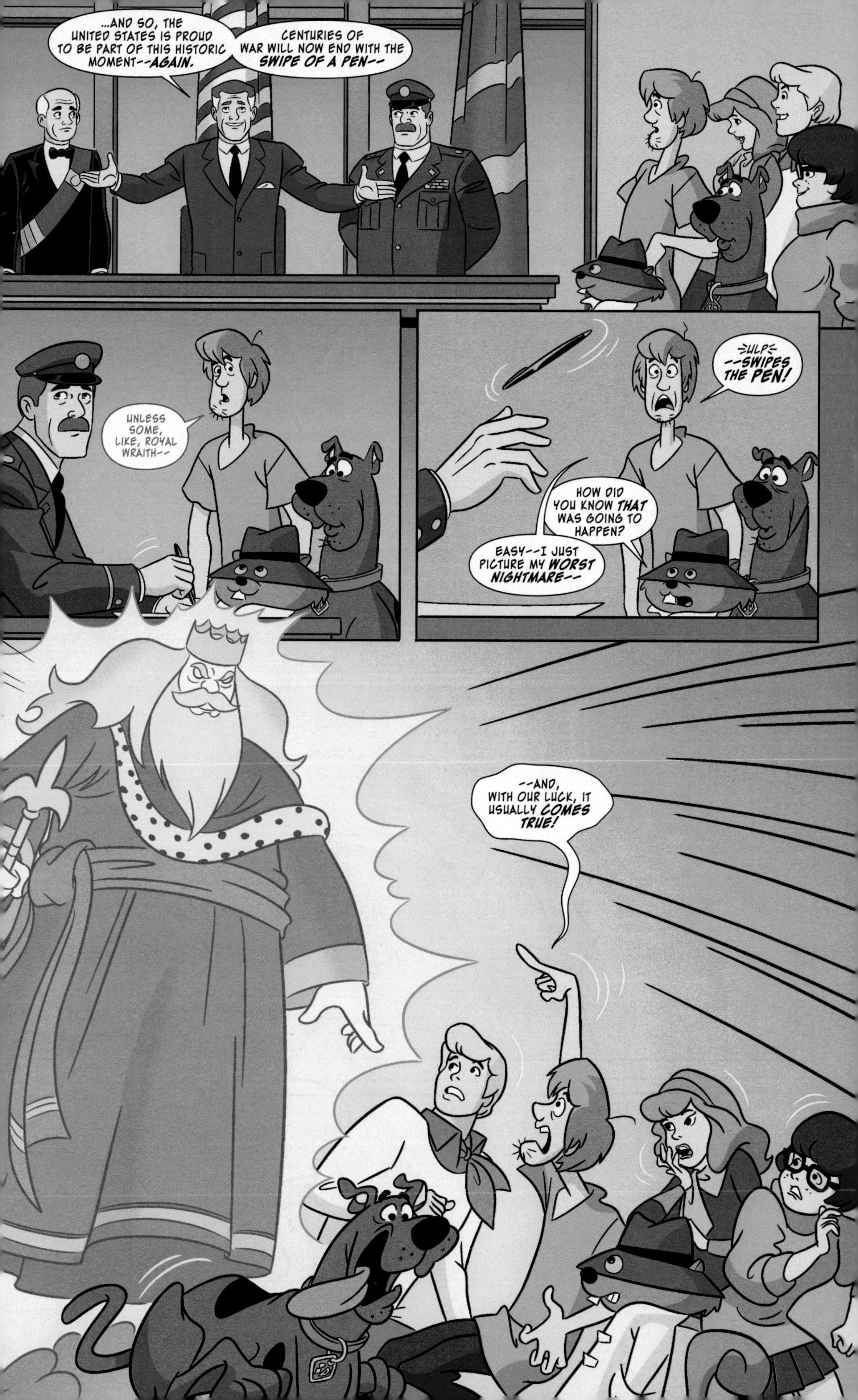
...AND SO, THE UNITED STATES IS PROUD TO BE PART OF THIS HISTORIC MOMENT--AGAIN.
CENTURIES OF WAR WILL NOW END WITH THE SWIPE OF A PEN--
UNLESS SOME, LIKE, ROYAL WRAITH--
=ULP= --SWIPES THE PEN!
HOW DID YOU KNOW THAT WAS GOING TO HAPPEN?
EASY--I JUST PICTURE MY WORST NIGHTMARE--
--AND, WITH OUR LUCK, IT USUALLY COMES TRUE!

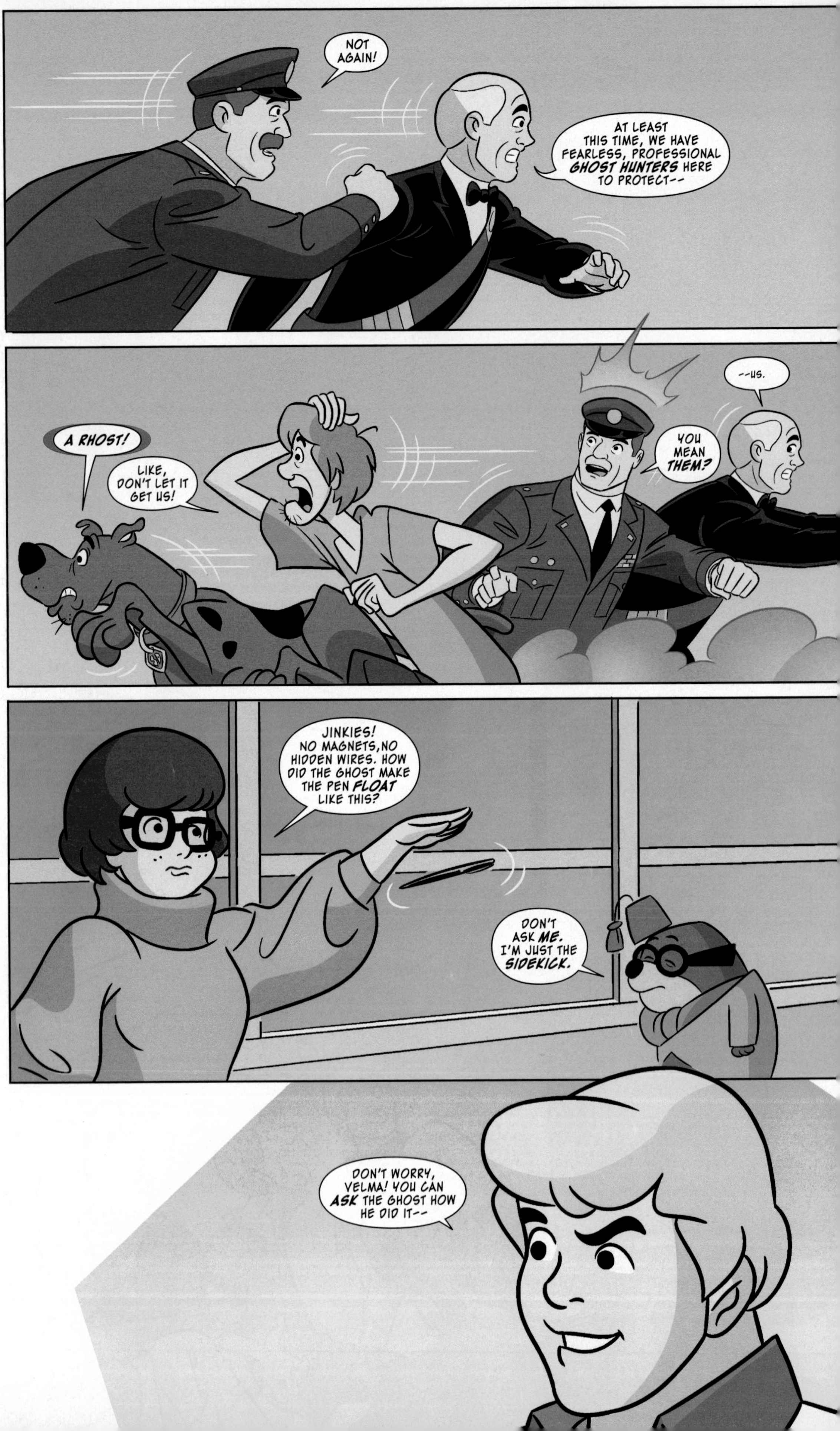
NOT AGAIN!
AT LEAST THIS TIME, WE HAVE FEARLESS, PROFESSIONAL GHOST HUNTERS HERE TO PROTECT--
A RHOST!
LIKE, DON'T LET IT GET US!
YOU MEAN THEM?
--US.
JINKIES! NO MAGNETS,NO HIDDEN WIRES. HOW DID THE GHOST MAKE THE PEN FLOAT LIKE THIS?
DON'T ASK ME. I'M JUST THE SIDEKICK.
DON'T WORRY, VELMA! YOU CAN ASK THE GHOST HOW HE DID IT--

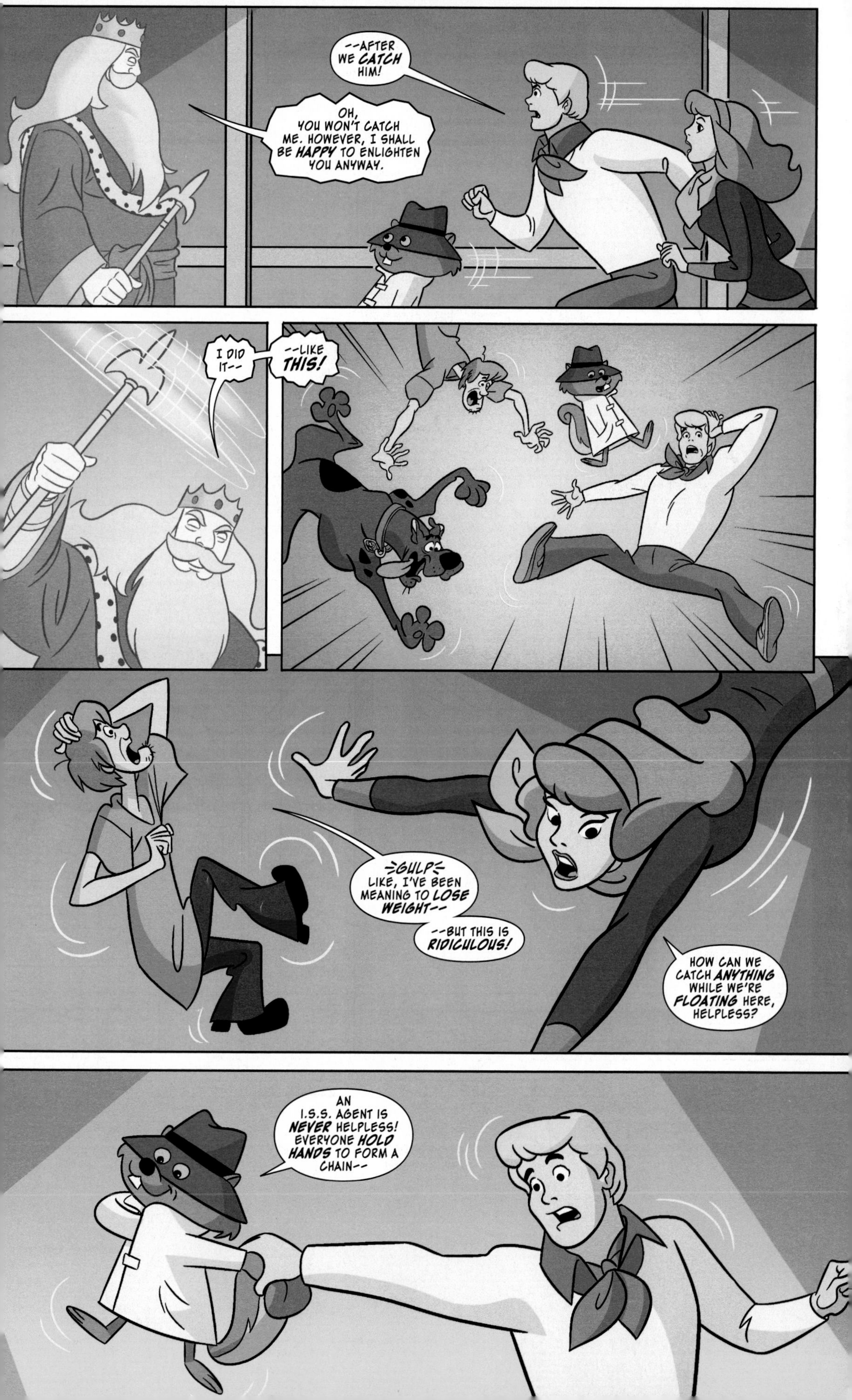
--AFTER WE CATCH HIM!
OH, YOU WON'T CATCH ME. HOWEVER, I SHALL BE HAPPY TO ENLIGHTEN YOU ANYWAY.
I DID IT--
--LIKE THIS!
GULP
LIKE, I'VE BEEN MEANING TO LOSE WEIGHT--
--BUT THIS IS RIDICULOUS!
HOW CAN WE CATCH ANYTHING WHILE WE'RE FLOATING HERE, HELPLESS?
AN I.S.S. AGENT IS NEVER HELPLESS! EVERYONE HOLD HANDS TO FORM A CHAIN--

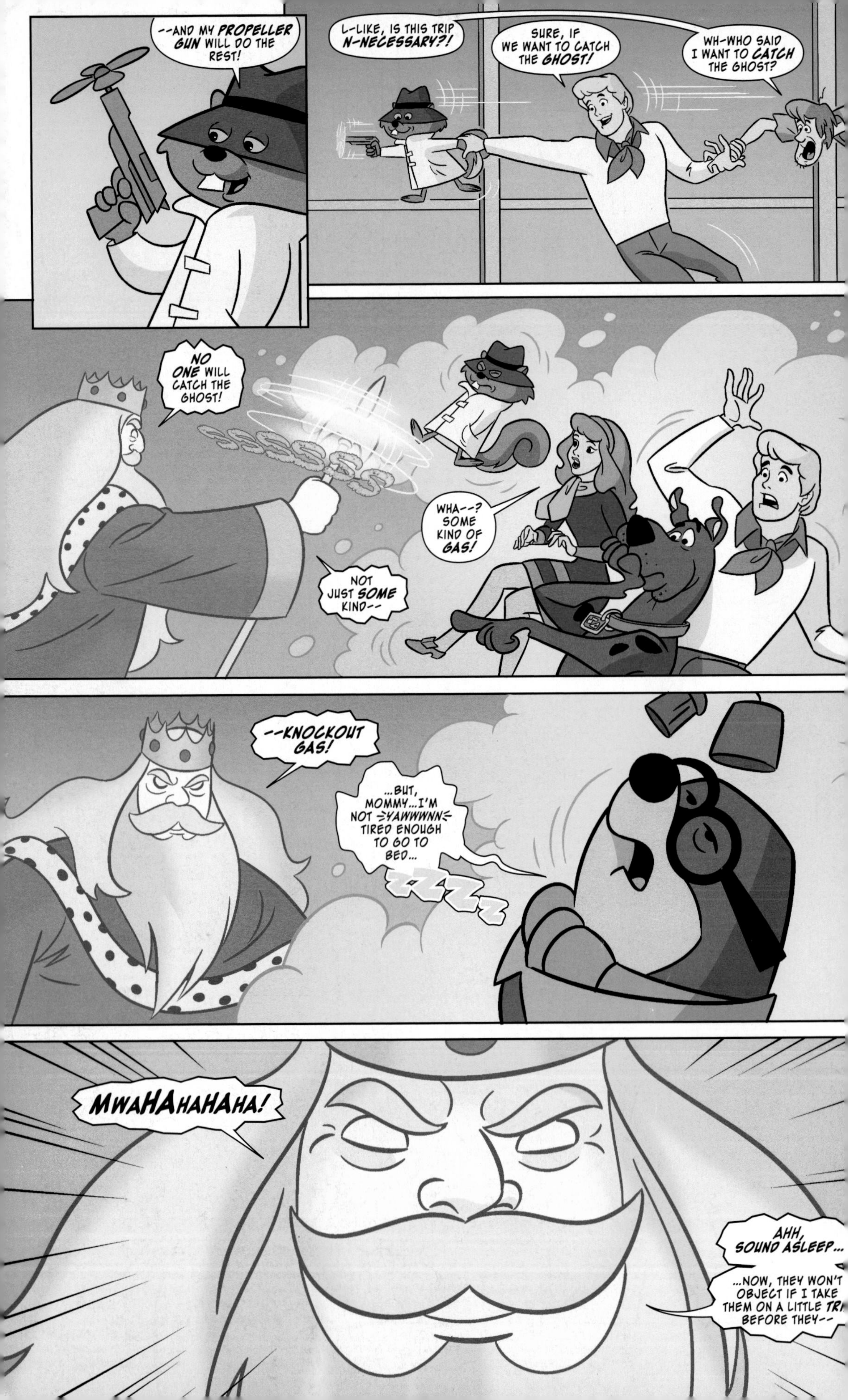
--AND MY PROPELLER GUN WILL DO THE REST!
L-LIKE, IS THIS TRIP N-NECESSARY?!
SURE, IF WE WANT TO CATCH THE GHOST!
WH-WHO SAID I WANT TO CATCH THE GHOST?
NO ONE WILL CATCH THE GHOST!
WHA--? SOME KIND OF GAS!
NOT JUST SOME KIND--
--KNOCKOUT GAS!
...BUT, MOMMY...I'M NOT YAWWWNN TIRED ENOUGH TO GO TO BED...
ZZZZ
MWAHAHAHAHA!
AHH, SOUND ASLEEP...
...NOW, THEY WON'T OBJECT IF I TAKE THEM ON A LITTLE TRI BEFORE THEY--

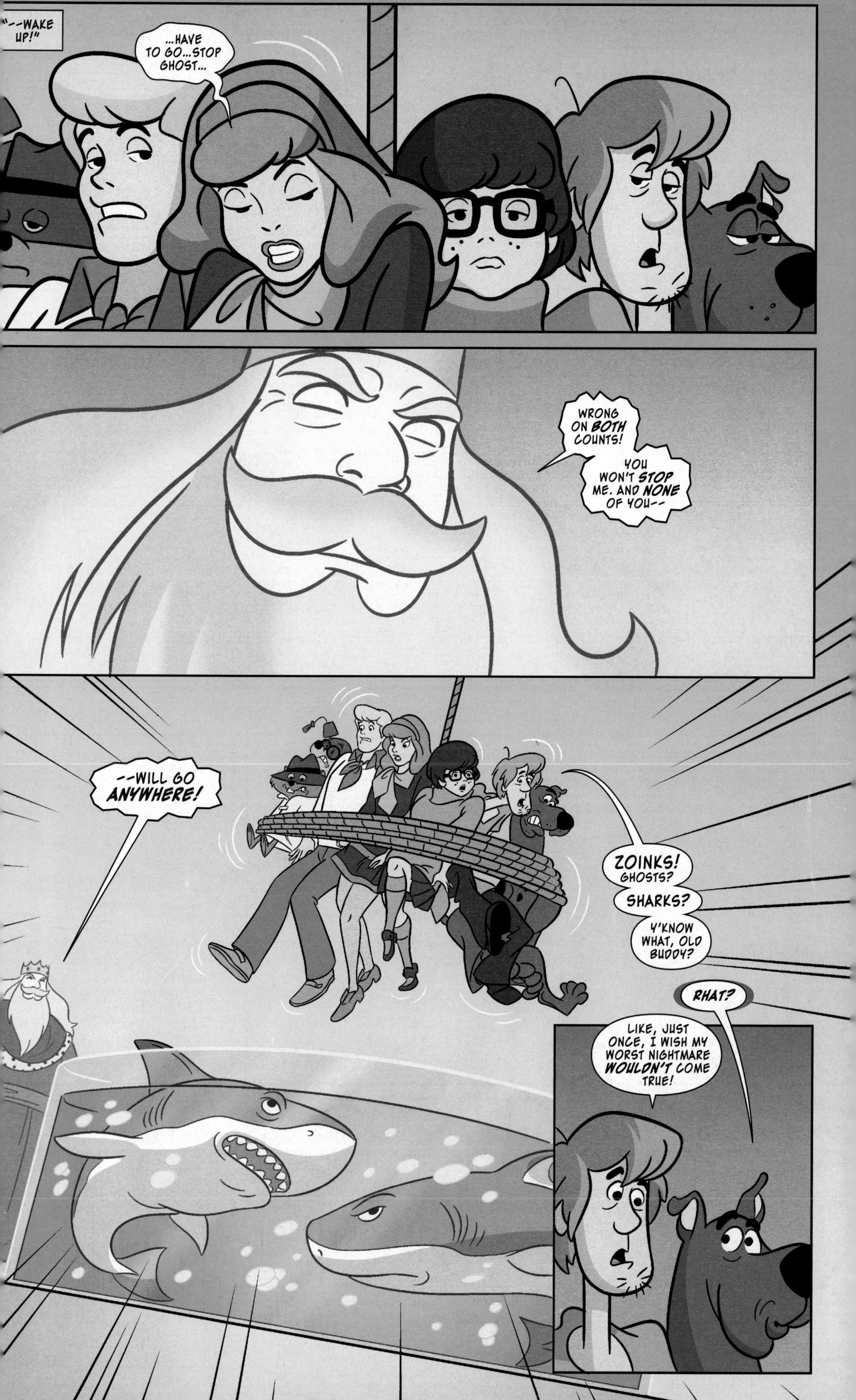
"--WAKE UP!"
...HAVE TO GO...STOP GHOST...
WRONG ON BOTH COUNTS!
YOU WON'T STOP ME. AND NONE OF YOU--
--WILL GO ANYWHERE!
ZOINKS! GHOSTS?
SHARKS?
Y'KNOW WHAT, OLD BUDDY?
RHAT?
LIKE, JUST ONCE, I WISH MY WORST NIGHTMARE WOULDN'T COME TRUE!

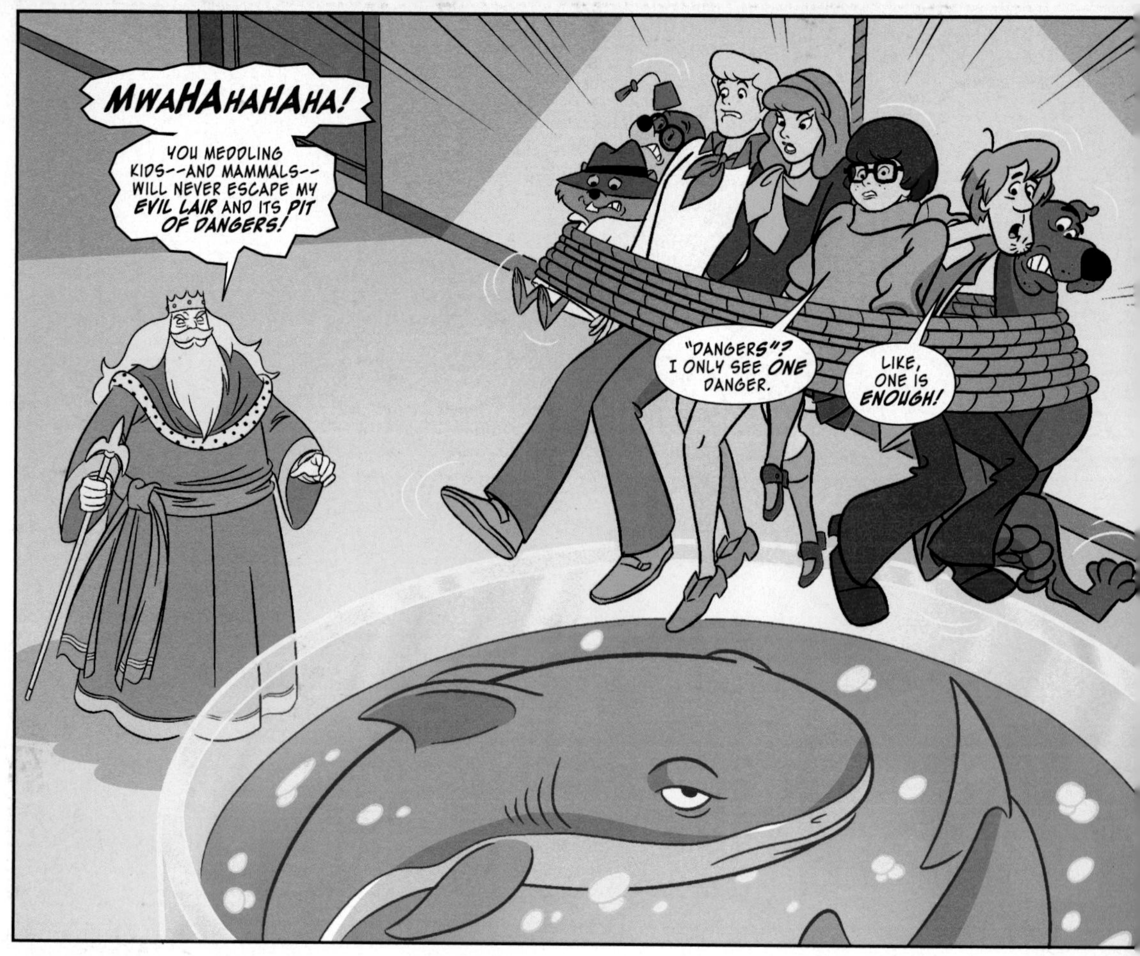
MWAHAHAHAHA!
YOU MEDDLING KIDS--AND MAMMALS--WILL NEVER ESCAPE MY EVIL LAIR AND ITS PIT OF DANGERS!
"DANGERS"? I ONLY SEE ONE DANGER.
LIKE, ONE IS ENOUGH!

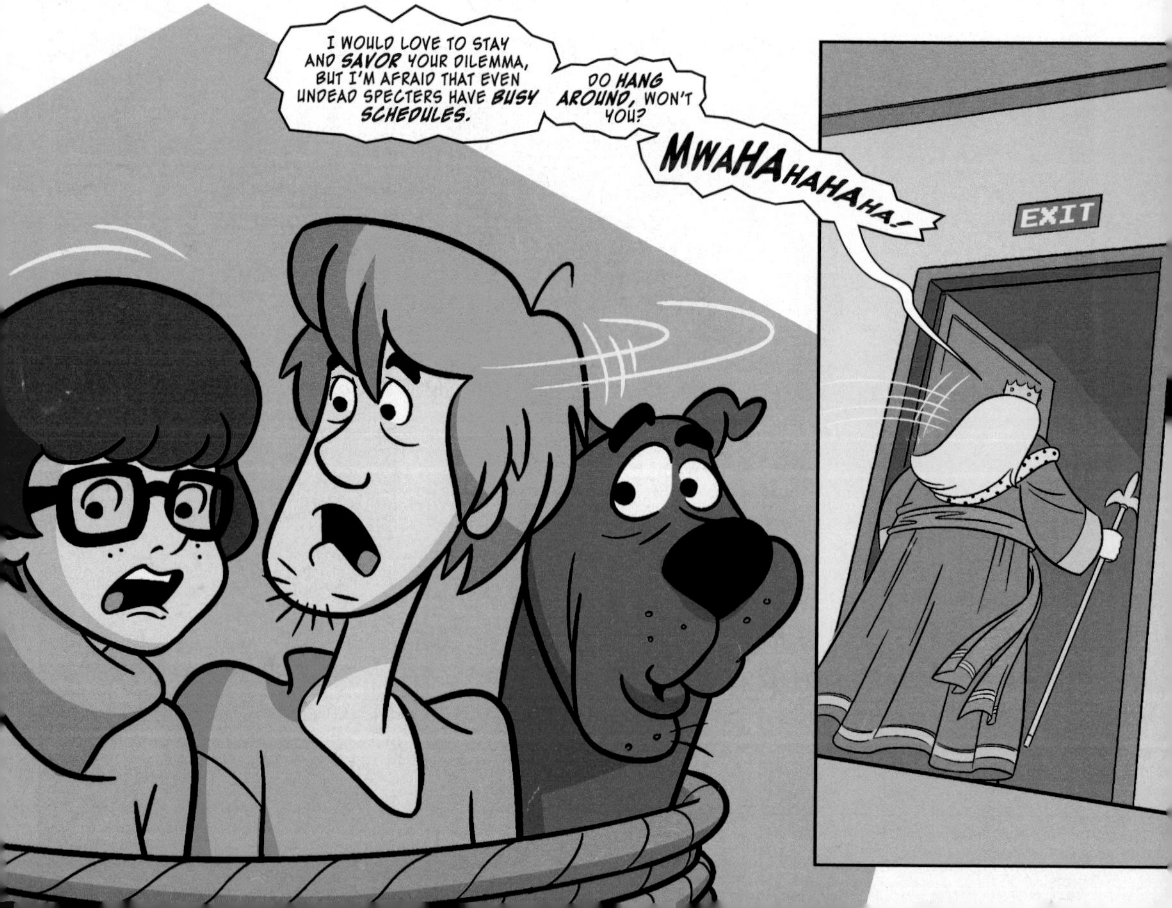
I WOULD LOVE TO STAY AND SAVOR YOUR DILEMMA, BUT I'M AFRAID THAT EVEN UNDEAD SPECTERS HAVE BUSY SCHEDULES.
DO HANG AROUND, WON'T YOU?
MWAHAHAHAHA!
EXIT

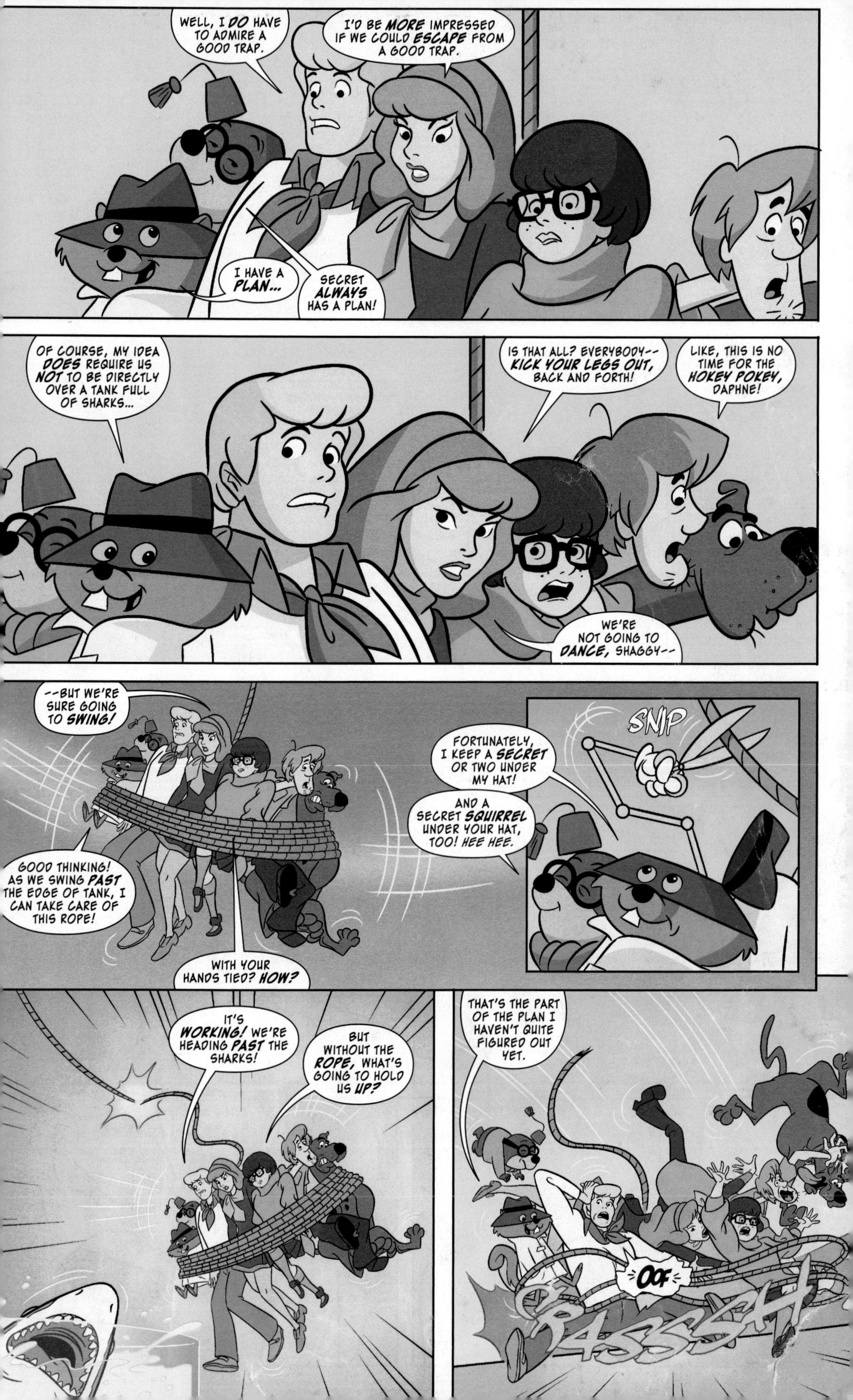
WELL, I DO HAVE TO ADMIRE A GOOD TRAP.
I'D BE MORE IMPRESSED IF WE COULD ESCAPE FROM A GOOD TRAP.
I HAVE A PLAN...
SECRET ALWAYS HAS A PLAN!
OF COURSE, MY IDEA DOES REQUIRE US NOT TO BE DIRECTLY OVER A TANK FULL OF SHARKS...
IS THAT ALL? EVERYBODY-- KICK YOUR LEGS OUT, BACK AND FORTH!
LIKE, THIS IS NO TIME FOR THE HOKEY POKEY, DAPHNE!
WE'RE NOT GOING TO DANCE, SHAGGY--
--BUT WE'RE SURE GOING TO SWING!
GOOD THINKING! AS WE SWING PAST THE EDGE OF TANK, I CAN TAKE CARE OF THIS ROPE!
WITH YOUR HANDS TIED? HOW?
SNIP
FORTUNATELY, I KEEP A SECRET OR TWO UNDER MY HAT!
AND A SECRET SQUIRREL UNDER YOUR HAT, TOO! HEE HEE.
IT'S WORKING! WE'RE HEADING PAST THE SHARKS!
BUT WITHOUT THE ROPE, WHAT'S GOING TO HOLD US UP?
THAT'S THE PART OF THE PLAN I HAVEN'T QUITE FIGURED OUT YET.
OOF
BASSSH

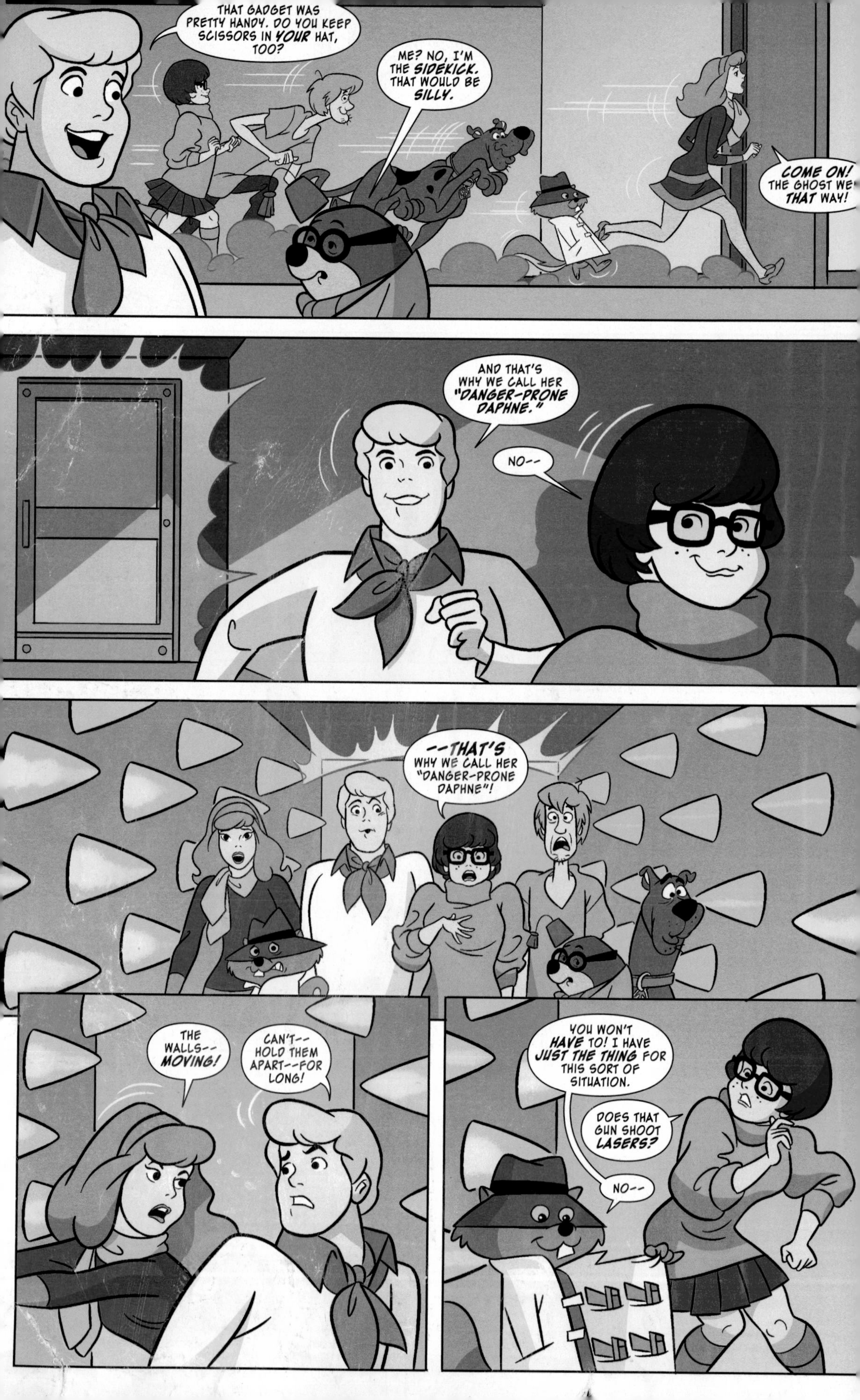
THAT GADGET WAS PRETTY HANDY. DO YOU KEEP SCISSORS IN YOUR HAT, TOO?
ME? NO, I'M THE SIDEKICK. THAT WOULD BE SILLY.
COME ON! THE GHOST WE THAT WAY!
AND THAT'S WHY WE CALL HER "DANGER-PRONE DAPHNE."
NO--
--THAT'S WHY WE CALL HER "DANGER-PRONE DAPHNE"!
THE WALLS-- MOVING!
CAN'T-- HOLD THEM APART--FOR LONG!
YOU WON'T HAVE TO! I HAVE JUST THE THING FOR THIS SORT OF SITUATION.
DOES THAT GUN SHOOT LASERS?
NO--

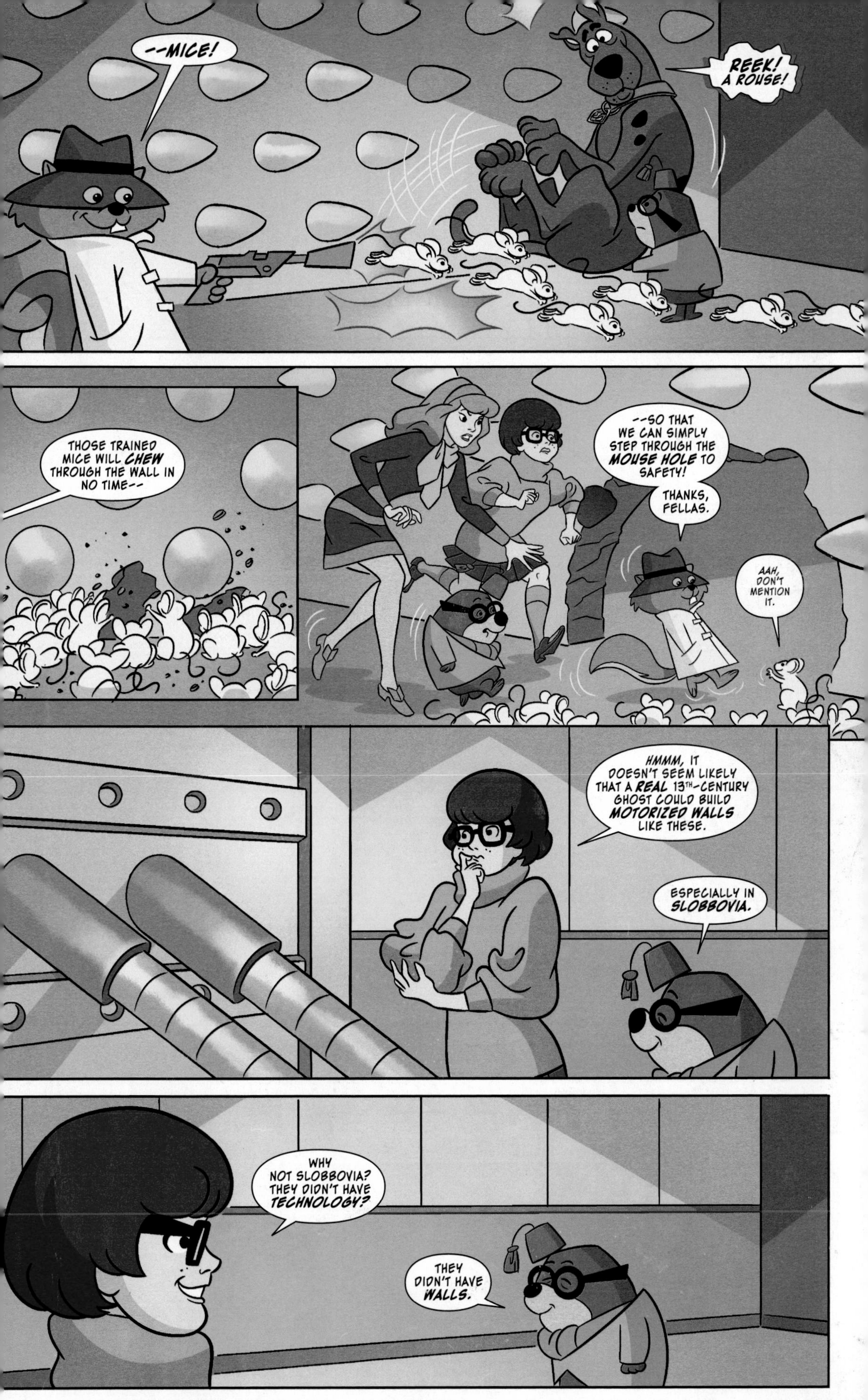
--MICE!
REEK! A ROUSE!
THOSE TRAINED MICE WILL CHEW THROUGH THE WALL IN NO TIME--
--SO THAT WE CAN SIMPLY STEP THROUGH THE MOUSE HOLE TO SAFETY!
THANKS, FELLAS.
AAH, DON'T MENTION IT.
HMMM, IT DOESN'T SEEM LIKELY THAT A REAL 13TH-CENTURY GHOST COULD BUILD MOTORIZED WALLS LIKE THESE.
ESPECIALLY IN SLOBBOVIA.
WHY NOT SLOBBOVIA? THEY DIDN'T HAVE TECHNOLOGY?
THEY DIDN'T HAVE WALLS.

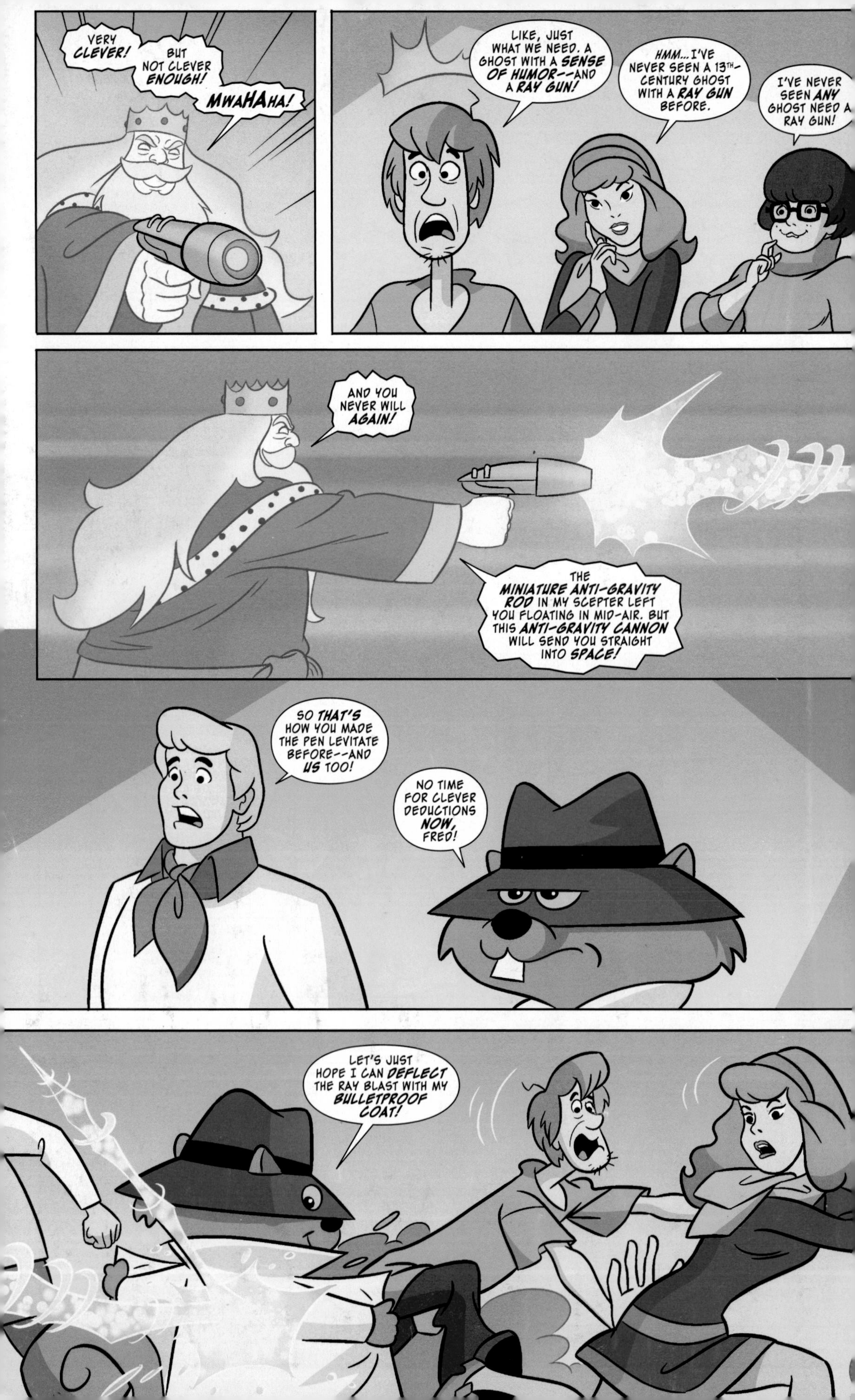
VERY CLEVER!
BUT NOT CLEVER ENOUGH!
MWAHAHA!
LIKE, JUST WHAT WE NEED. A GHOST WITH A SENSE OF HUMOR--AND A RAY GUN!
HMM... I'VE NEVER SEEN A 13TH-CENTURY GHOST WITH A RAY GUN BEFORE.
I'VE NEVER SEEN ANY GHOST NEED A RAY GUN!
AND YOU NEVER WILL AGAIN!
THE MINIATURE ANTI-GRAVITY ROD IN MY SCEPTER LEFT YOU FLOATING IN MID-AIR. BUT THIS ANTI-GRAVITY CANNON WILL SEND YOU STRAIGHT INTO SPACE!
SO THAT'S HOW YOU MADE THE PEN LEVITATE BEFORE--AND US TOO!
NO TIME FOR CLEVER DEDUCTIONS NOW, FRED!
LET'S JUST HOPE I CAN DEFLECT THE RAY BLAST WITH MY BULLETPROOF COAT!

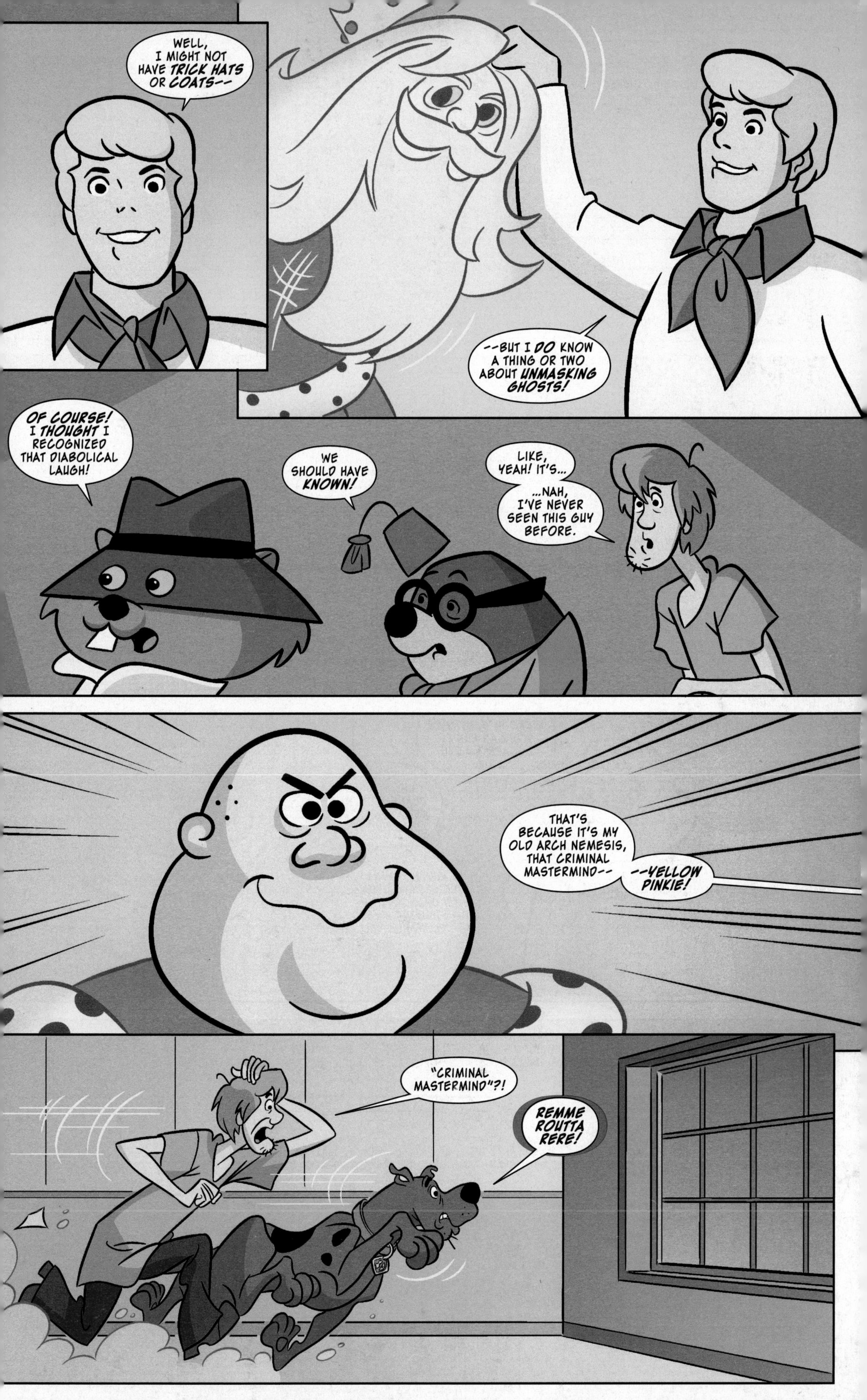
WELL, I MIGHT NOT HAVE TRICK HATS OR COATS--
--BUT I DO KNOW A THING OR TWO ABOUT UNMASKING GHOSTS!
OF COURSE! I THOUGHT I RECOGNIZED THAT DIABOLICAL LAUGH!
WE SHOULD HAVE KNOWN!
LIKE, YEAH! IT'S...
...NAH, I'VE NEVER SEEN THIS GUY BEFORE.
THAT'S BECAUSE IT'S MY OLD ARCH NEMESIS, THAT CRIMINAL MASTERMIND--
--YELLOW PINKIE!
"CRIMINAL MASTERMIND"?!
REMME ROUTTA RERE!

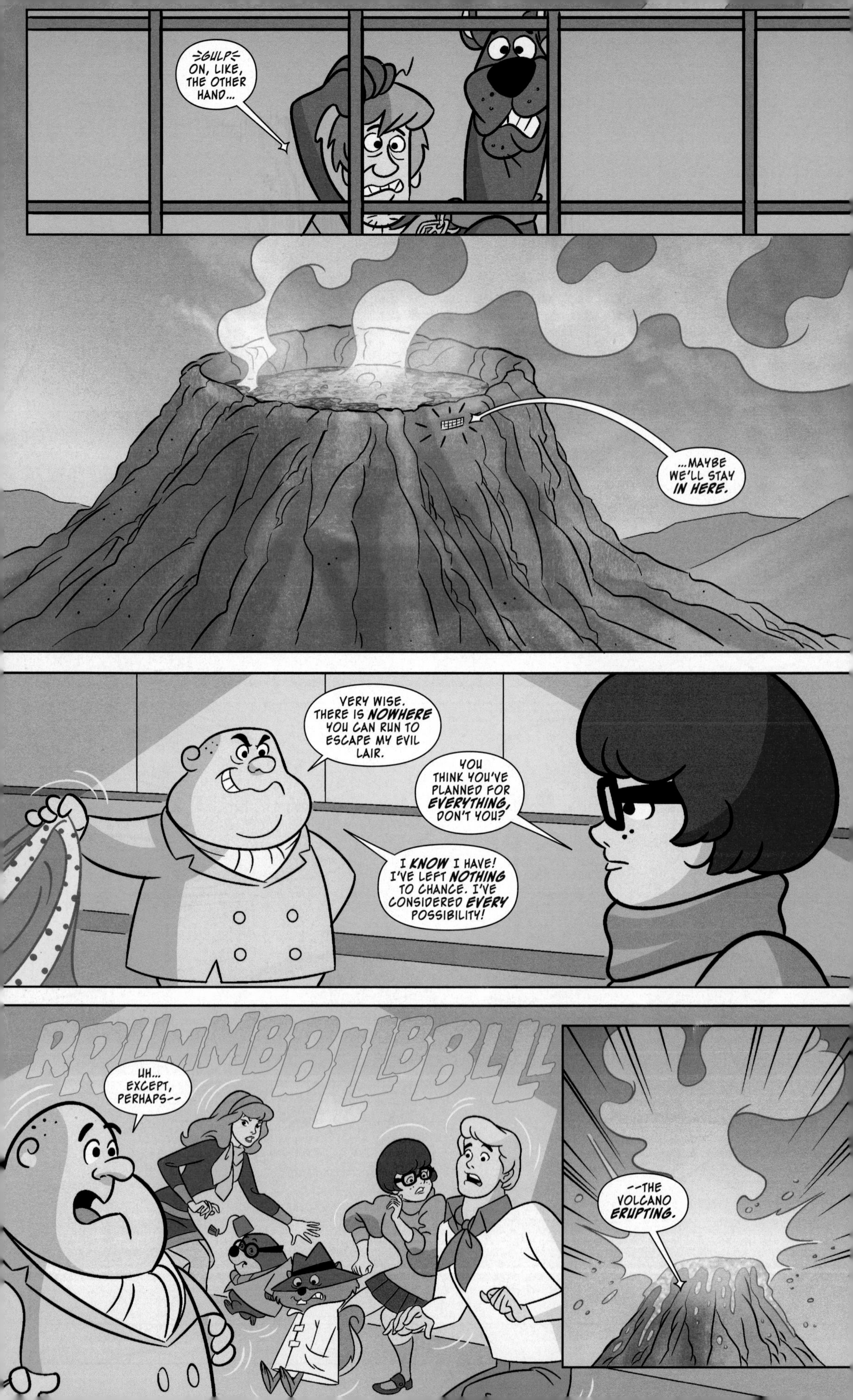

GULP
ON, LIKE, THE OTHER HAND...
...MAYBE WE'LL STAY IN HERE.
VERY WISE. THERE IS NOWHERE YOU CAN RUN TO ESCAPE MY EVIL LAIR.
YOU THINK YOU'VE PLANNED FOR EVERYTHING, DON'T YOU?
I KNOW I HAVE! I'VE LEFT NOTHING TO CHANCE. I'VE CONSIDERED EVERY POSSIBILITY!
RRUMMBBLLBBLL
UH... EXCEPT, PERHAPS--
--THE VOLCANO ERUPTING.

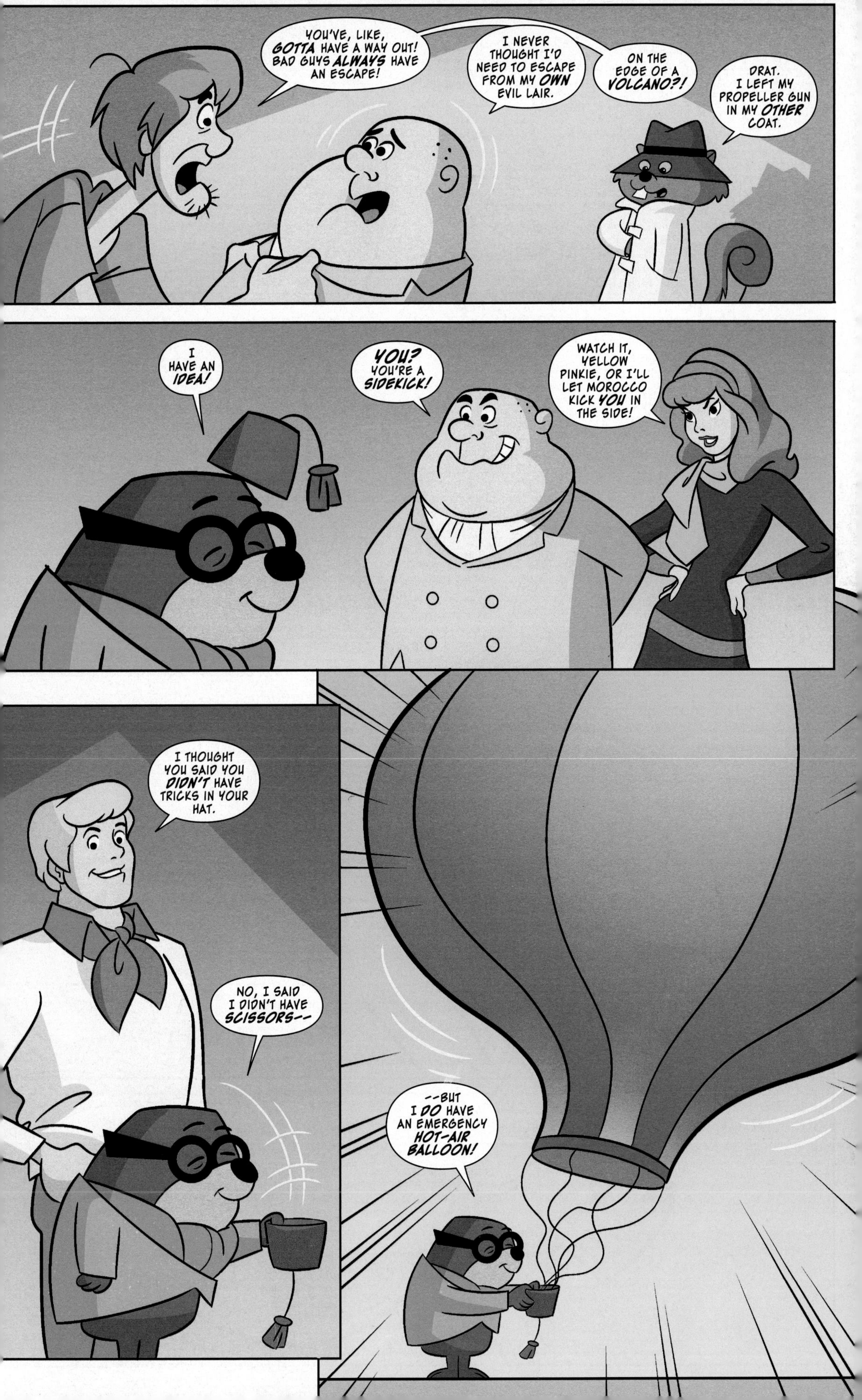
YOU'VE, LIKE, GOTTA HAVE A WAY OUT! BAD GUYS ALWAYS HAVE AN ESCAPE!
I NEVER THOUGHT I'D NEED TO ESCAPE FROM MY OWN EVIL LAIR.
ON THE EDGE OF A VOLCANO?!
DRAT. I LEFT MY PROPELLER GUN IN MY OTHER COAT.
I HAVE AN IDEA!
YOU? YOU'RE A SIDEKICK!
WATCH IT, YELLOW PINKIE, OR I'LL LET MOROCCO KICK YOU IN THE SIDE!
I THOUGHT YOU SAID YOU DIDN'T HAVE TRICKS IN YOUR HAT.
NO, I SAID I DIDN'T HAVE SCISSORS--
--BUT I DO HAVE AN EMERGENCY HOT-AIR BALLOON!

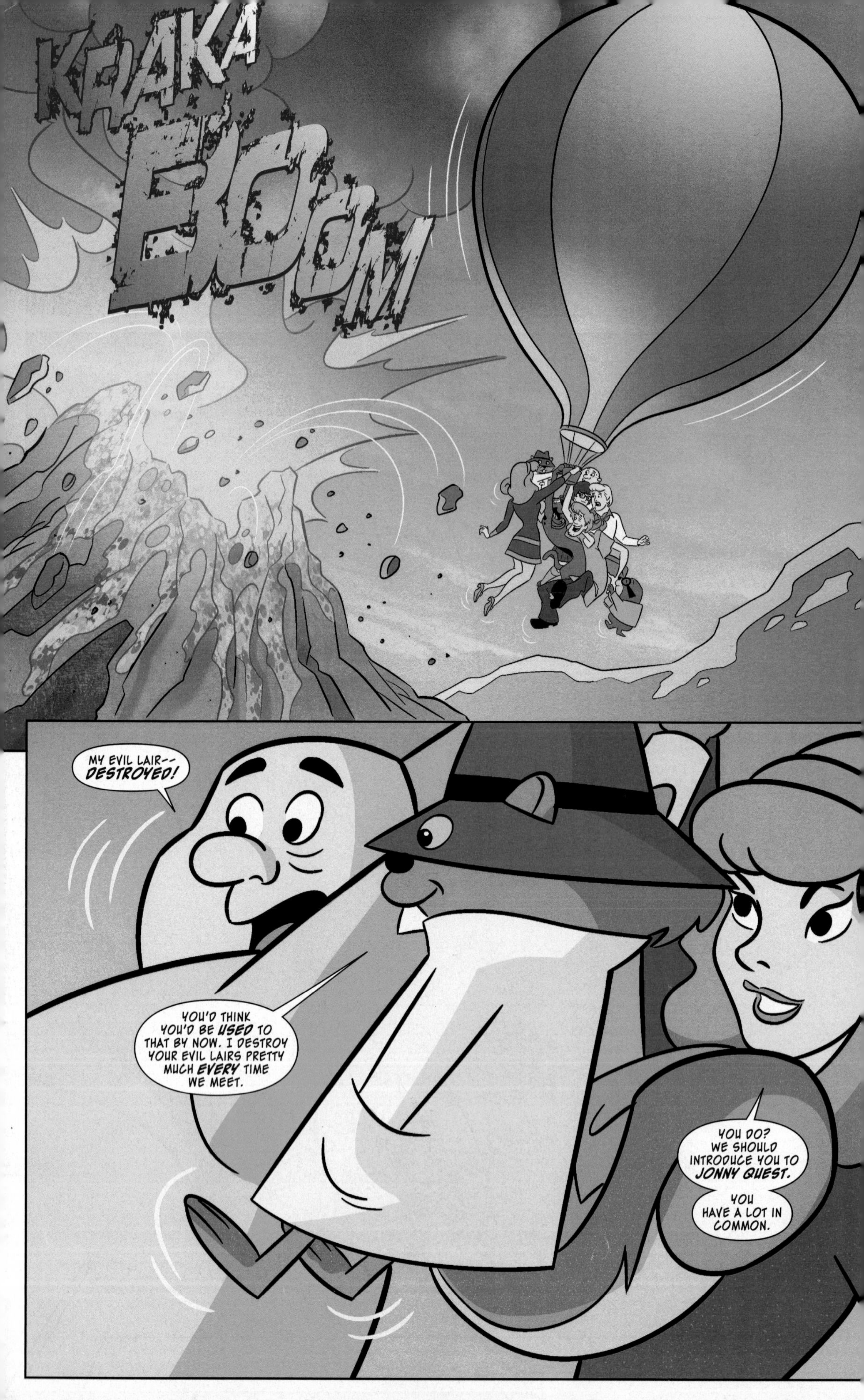
KRAKA
BOOM
MY EVIL LAIR-- DESTROYED!
YOU'D THINK YOU'D BE USED TO THAT BY NOW. I DESTROY YOUR EVIL LAIRS PRETTY MUCH EVERY TIME WE MEET.
YOU DO? WE SHOULD INTRODUCE YOU TO JONNY QUEST.
YOU HAVE A LOT IN COMMON.

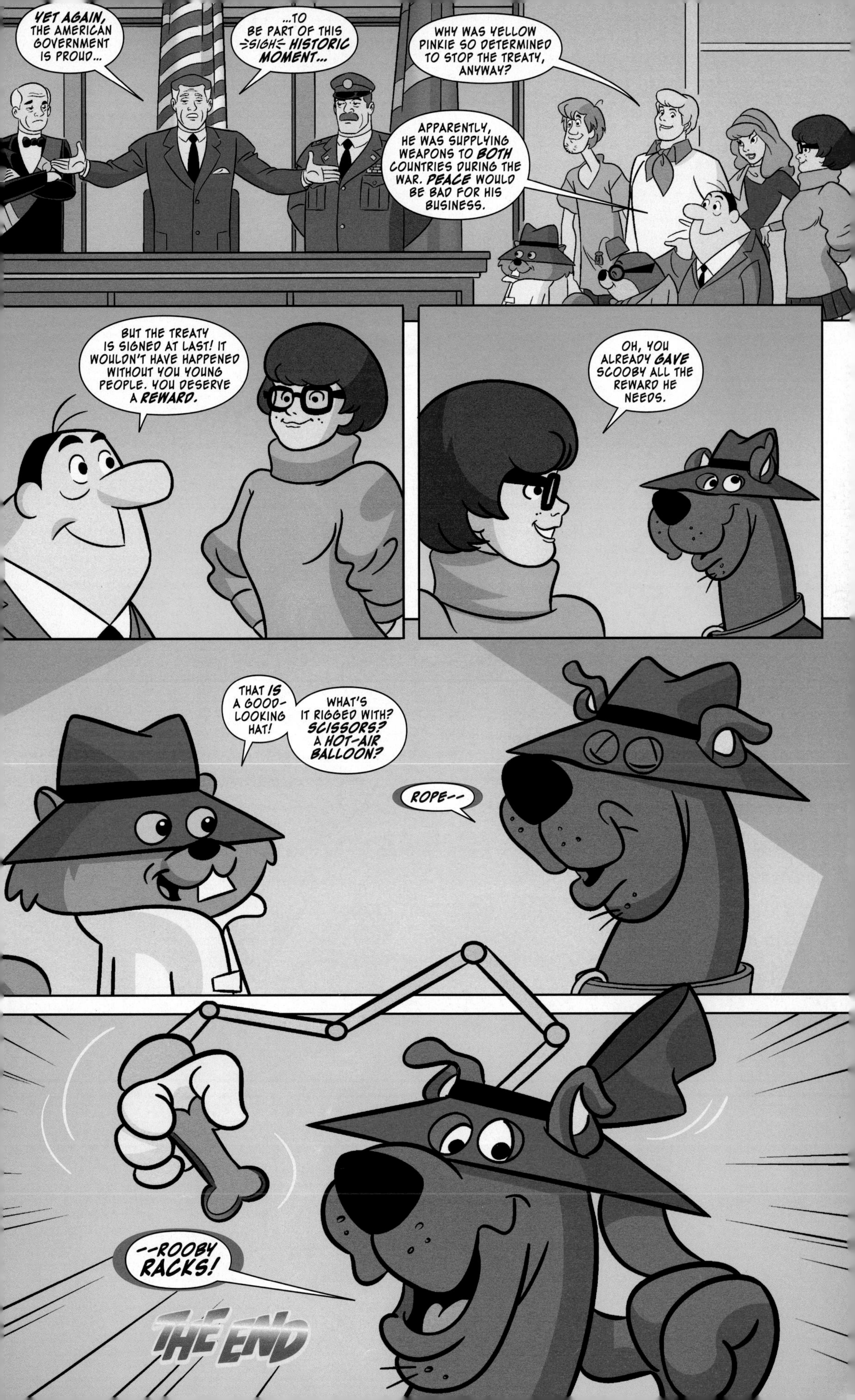
YET AGAIN, THE AMERICAN GOVERNMENT IS PROUD...
...TO BE PART OF THIS =SIGH= HISTORIC MOMENT...
WHY WAS YELLOW PINKIE SO DETERMINED TO STOP THE TREATY, ANYWAY?
APPARENTLY, HE WAS SUPPLYING WEAPONS TO BOTH COUNTRIES DURING THE WAR. PEACE WOULD BE BAD FOR HIS BUSINESS.
BUT THE TREATY IS SIGNED AT LAST! IT WOULDN'T HAVE HAPPENED WITHOUT YOU YOUNG PEOPLE. YOU DESERVE A REWARD.
OH, YOU ALREADY GAVE SCOOBY ALL THE REWARD HE NEEDS.
THAT IS A GOOD-LOOKING HAT!
WHAT'S IT RIGGED WITH? SCISSORS? A HOT-AIR BALLOON?
ROPE--
--ROOBY RACKS!
THE END

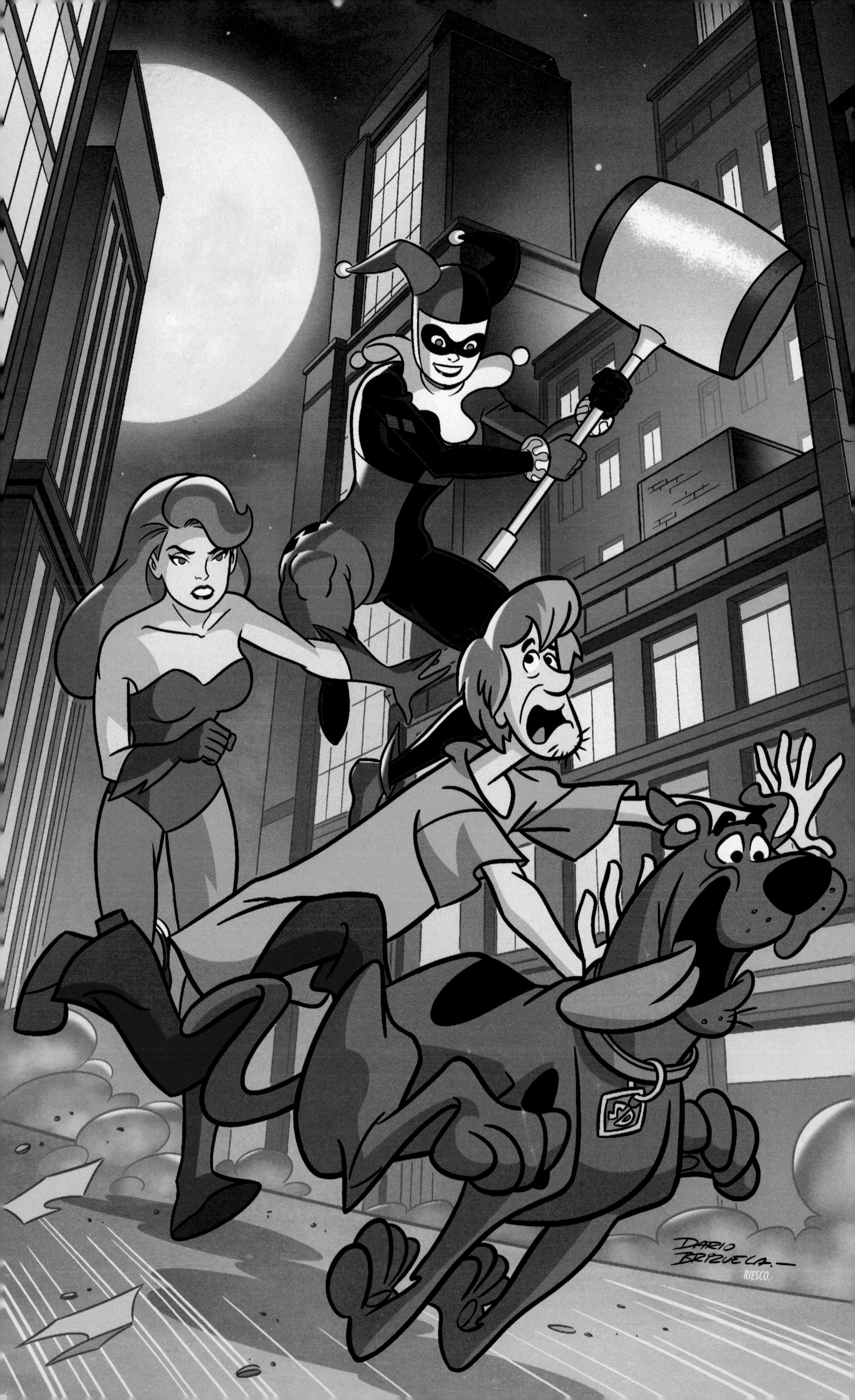
DARIO BRIZUELA
RIESCO.

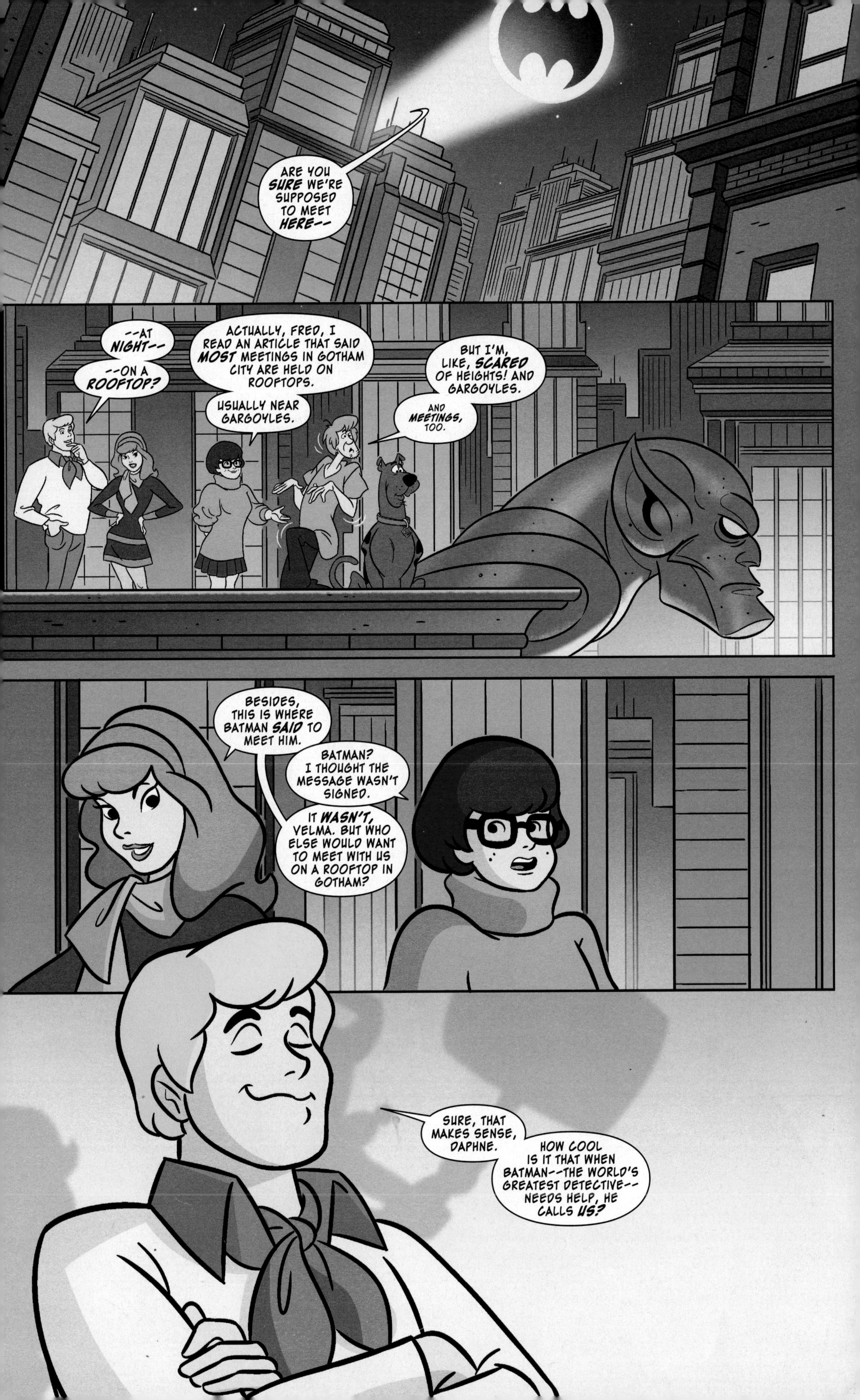
ARE YOU SURE WE'RE SUPPOSED TO MEET HERE--
--AT NIGHT--
--ON A ROOFTOP?
ACTUALLY, FRED, I READ AN ARTICLE THAT SAID MOST MEETINGS IN GOTHAM CITY ARE HELD ON ROOFTOPS.
USUALLY NEAR GARGOYLES.
BUT I'M, LIKE, SCARED OF HEIGHTS! AND GARGOYLES.
AND MEETINGS, TOO.
BESIDES, THIS IS WHERE BATMAN SAID TO MEET HIM.
BATMAN? I THOUGHT THE MESSAGE WASN'T SIGNED.
IT WASN'T, VELMA. BUT WHO ELSE WOULD WANT TO MEET WITH US ON A ROOFTOP IN GOTHAM?
SURE, THAT MAKES SENSE, DAPHNE.
HOW COOL IS IT THAT WHEN BATMAN--THE WORLD'S GREATEST DETECTIVE--NEEDS HELP, HE CALLS US?

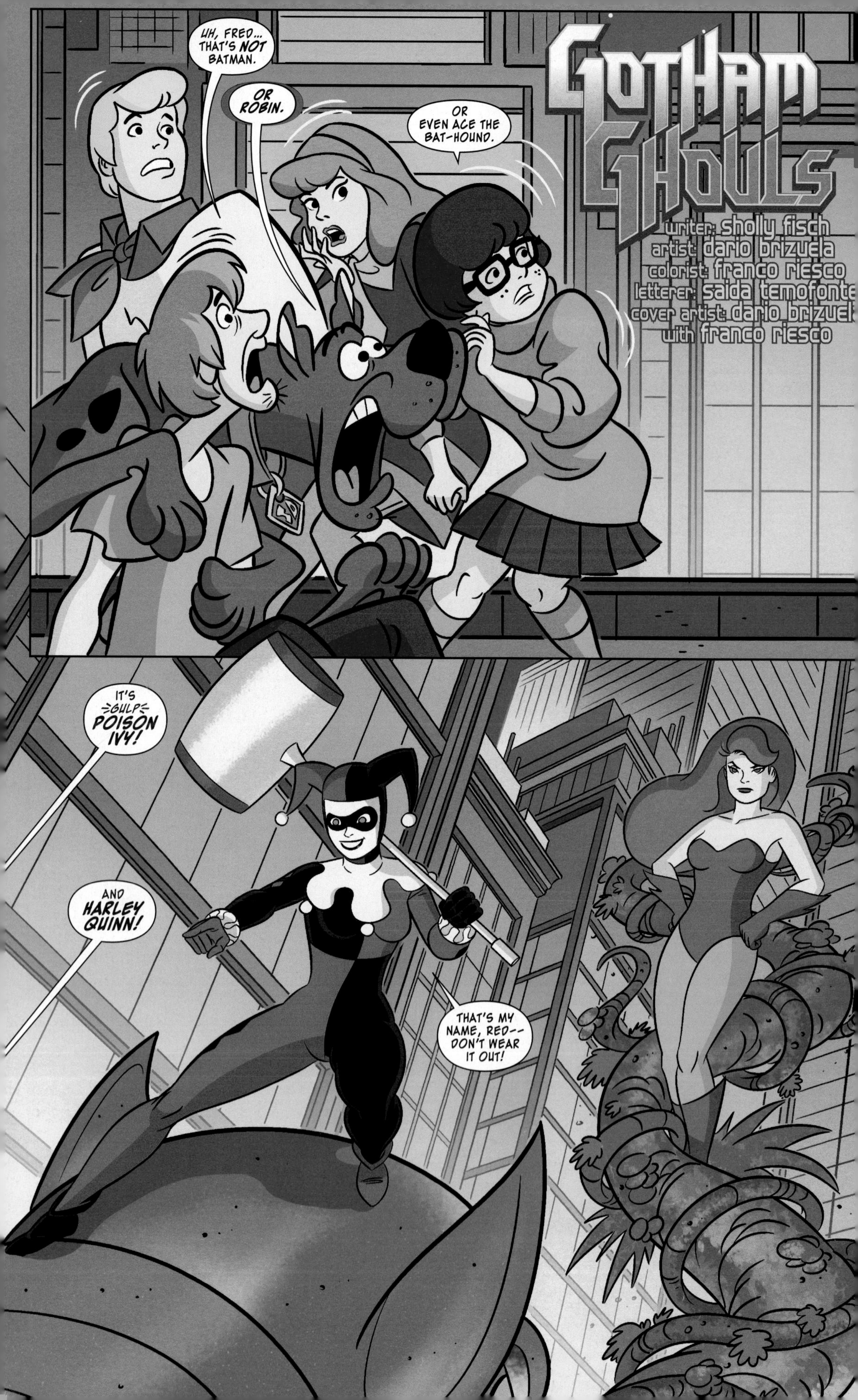

UH, FRED... THAT'S NOT BATMAN.
OR ROBIN.
OR EVEN ACE THE BAT-HOUND.
GOTHAM GHOULS
writer: sholly fisch
artist: dario brizuela
colorist: franco riesco
letterer: saida temofonte
cover artist: dario brizuela with franco riesco
IT'S =GULP= POISON IVY!
AND HARLEY QUINN!
THAT'S MY NAME, RED-- DON'T WEAR IT OUT!

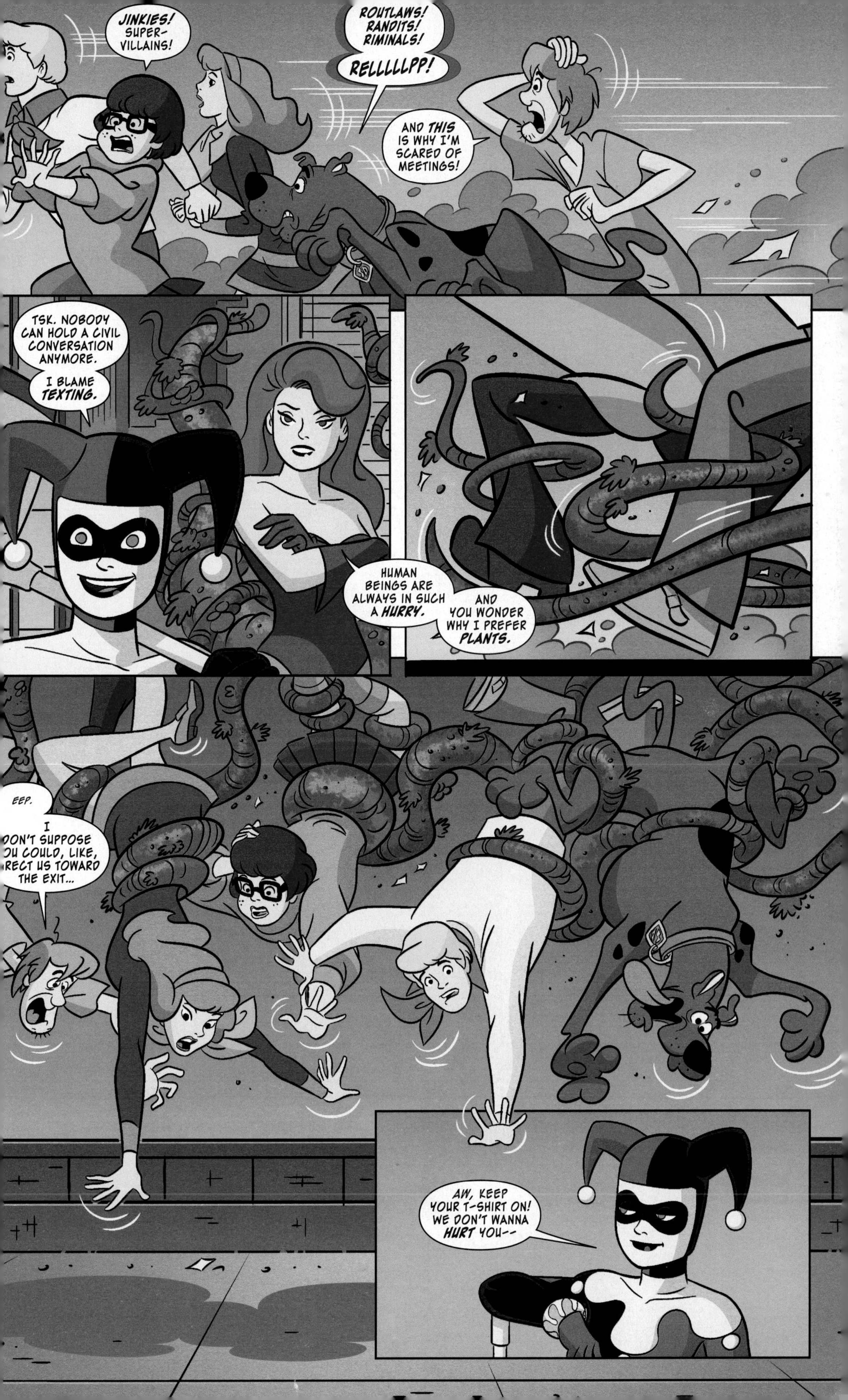
JINKIES! SUPER-VILLAINS!
ROUTLAWS! RANDITS! RIMINALS!
RELLLLLPP!
AND THIS IS WHY I'M SCARED OF MEETINGS!
TSK. NOBODY CAN HOLD A CIVIL CONVERSATION ANYMORE.
I BLAME TEXTING.
HUMAN BEINGS ARE ALWAYS IN SUCH A HURRY.
AND YOU WONDER WHY I PREFER PLANTS.
EEP.
I DON'T SUPPOSE YOU COULD, LIKE, DIRECT US TOWARD THE EXIT...
AW, KEEP YOUR T-SHIRT ON! WE DON'T WANNA HURT YOU--

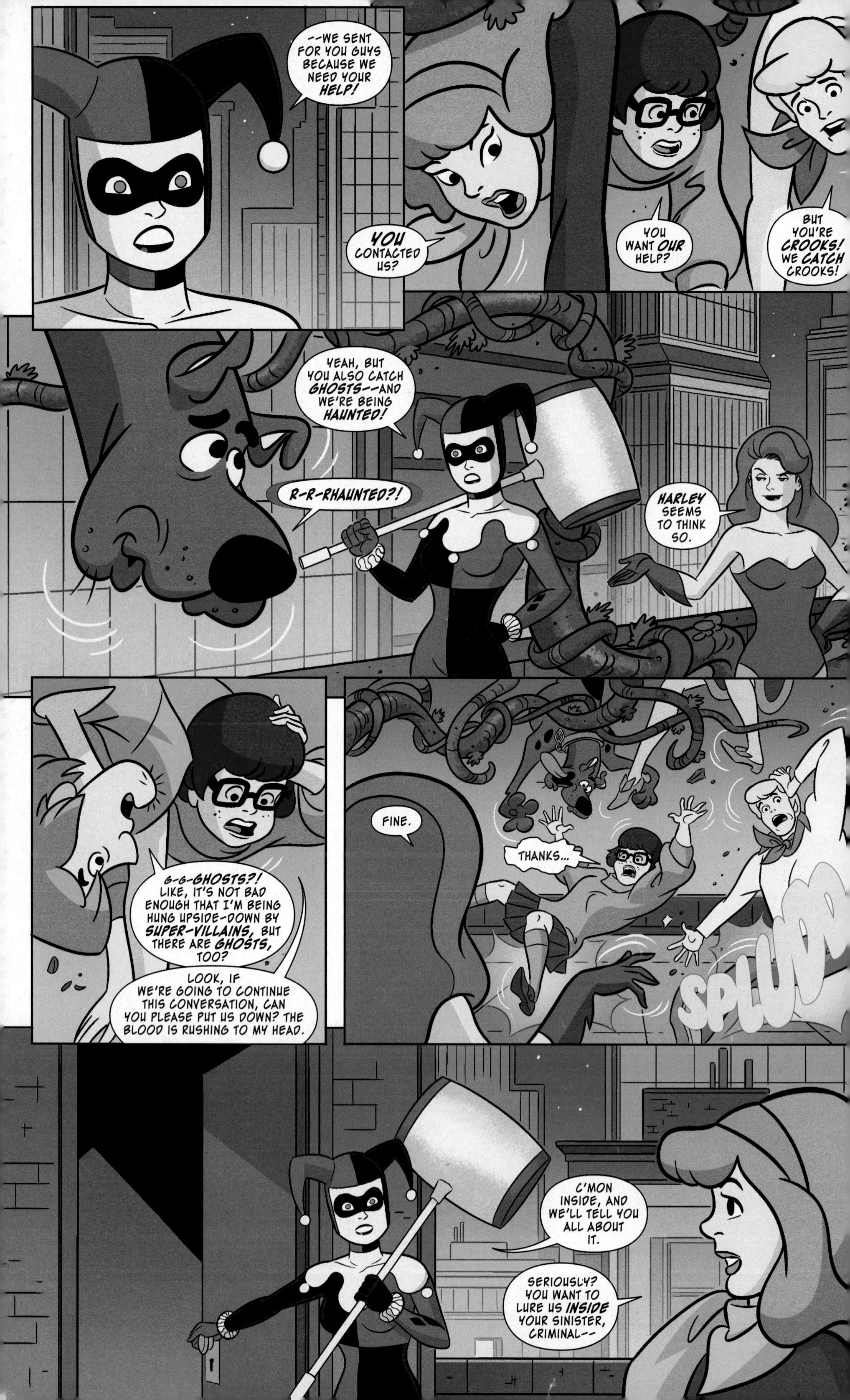
--WE SENT FOR YOU GUYS BECAUSE WE NEED YOUR HELP!
YOU CONTACTED US?
YOU WANT OUR HELP?
BUT YOU'RE CROOKS! WE CATCH CROOKS!
YEAH, BUT YOU ALSO CATCH GHOSTS--AND WE'RE BEING HAUNTED!
R-R-RHAUNTED?!
HARLEY SEEMS TO THINK SO.
G-G-GHOSTS?! LIKE, IT'S NOT BAD ENOUGH THAT I'M BEING HUNG UPSIDE-DOWN BY SUPER-VILLAINS, BUT THERE ARE GHOSTS, TOO?
LOOK, IF WE'RE GOING TO CONTINUE THIS CONVERSATION, CAN YOU PLEASE PUT US DOWN? THE BLOOD IS RUSHING TO MY HEAD.
FINE.
THANKS...
SPLUDD
C'MON INSIDE, AND WE'LL TELL YOU ALL ABOUT IT.
SERIOUSLY? YOU WANT TO LURE US INSIDE YOUR SINISTER, CRIMINAL--

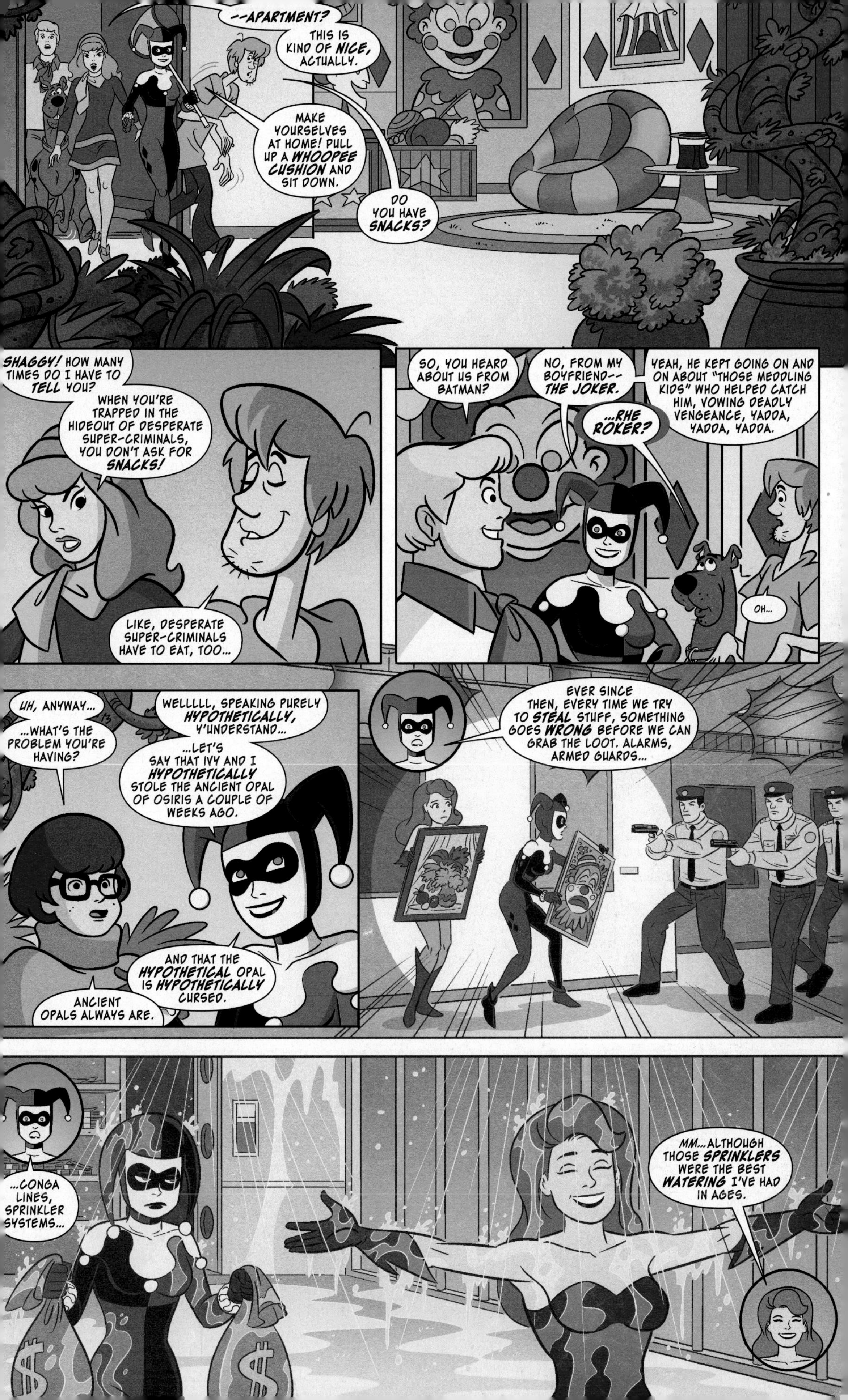
--APARTMENT?
THIS IS KIND OF NICE, ACTUALLY.
MAKE YOURSELVES AT HOME! PULL UP A WHOOPEE CUSHION AND SIT DOWN.
DO YOU HAVE SNACKS?
SHAGGY! HOW MANY TIMES DO I HAVE TO TELL YOU?
WHEN YOU'RE TRAPPED IN THE HIDEOUT OF DESPERATE SUPER-CRIMINALS, YOU DON'T ASK FOR SNACKS!
LIKE, DESPERATE SUPER-CRIMINALS HAVE TO EAT, TOO...
SO, YOU HEARD ABOUT US FROM BATMAN?
NO, FROM MY BOYFRIEND-- THE JOKER.
...RHE ROKER?
YEAH, HE KEPT GOING ON AND ON ABOUT "THOSE MEDDLING KIDS" WHO HELPED CATCH HIM, VOWING DEADLY VENGEANCE, YADDA, YADDA, YADDA.
OH...
UH, ANYWAY...
...WHAT'S THE PROBLEM YOU'RE HAVING?
WELLLLL, SPEAKING PURELY HYPOTHETICALLY, Y'UNDERSTAND...
...LET'S SAY THAT IVY AND I HYPOTHETICALLY STOLE THE ANCIENT OPAL OF OSIRIS A COUPLE OF WEEKS AGO.
AND THAT THE HYPOTHETICAL OPAL IS HYPOTHETICALLY CURSED.
ANCIENT OPALS ALWAYS ARE.
EVER SINCE THEN, EVERY TIME WE TRY TO STEAL STUFF, SOMETHING GOES WRONG BEFORE WE CAN GRAB THE LOOT. ALARMS, ARMED GUARDS...
...CONGA LINES, SPRINKLER SYSTEMS...
MM...ALTHOUGH THOSE SPRINKLERS WERE THE BEST WATERING I'VE HAD IN AGES.

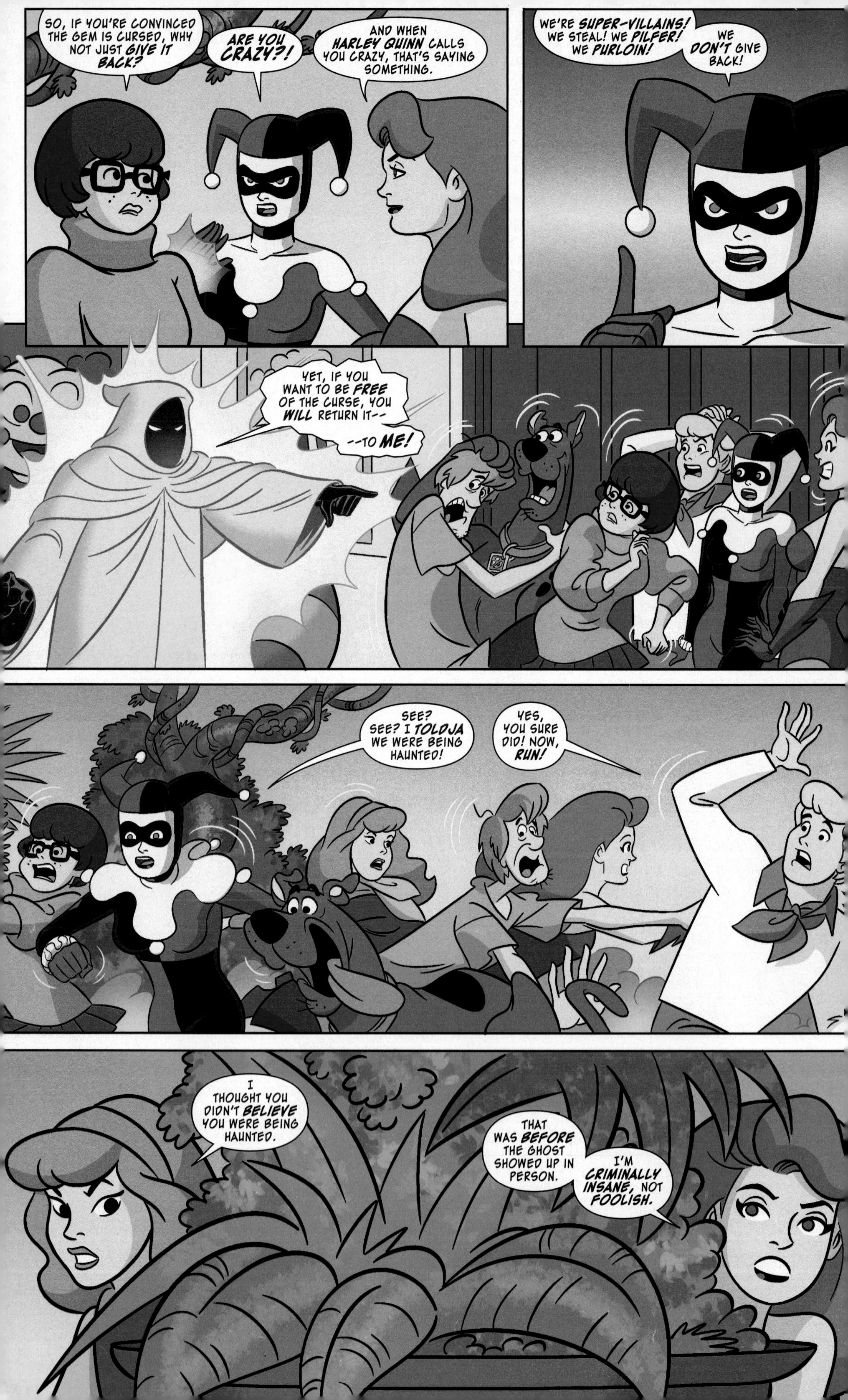
SO, IF YOU'RE CONVINCED THE GEM IS CURSED, WHY NOT JUST GIVE IT BACK?
ARE YOU CRAZY?!
AND WHEN HARLEY QUINN CALLS YOU CRAZY, THAT'S SAYING SOMETHING.
WE'RE SUPER-VILLAINS! WE STEAL! WE PILFER! WE PURLOIN!
WE DON'T GIVE BACK!
YET, IF YOU WANT TO BE FREE OF THE CURSE, YOU WILL RETURN IT--
--TO ME!
SEE? SEE? I TOLDJA WE WERE BEING HAUNTED!
YES, YOU SURE DID! NOW, RUN!
I THOUGHT YOU DIDN'T BELIEVE YOU WERE BEING HAUNTED.
THAT WAS BEFORE THE GHOST SHOWED UP IN PERSON.
I'M CRIMINALLY INSANE, NOT FOOLISH.

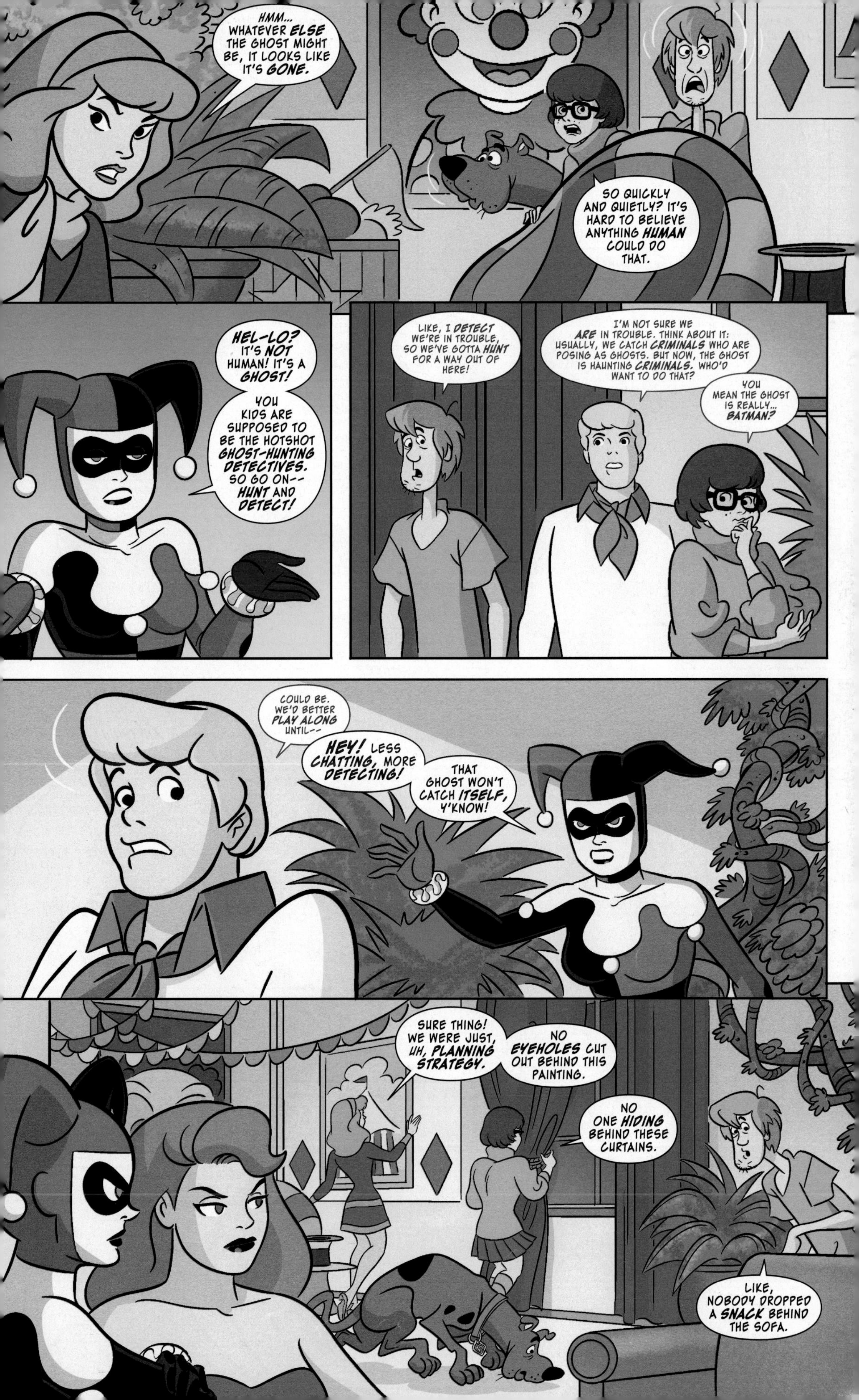

HMM... WHATEVER ELSE THE GHOST MIGHT BE, IT LOOKS LIKE IT'S GONE.
SO QUICKLY AND QUIETLY? IT'S HARD TO BELIEVE ANYTHING HUMAN COULD DO THAT.
HEL-LO? IT'S NOT HUMAN! IT'S A GHOST!
YOU KIDS ARE SUPPOSED TO BE THE HOTSHOT GHOST-HUNTING DETECTIVES. SO GO ON-- HUNT AND DETECT!
LIKE, I DETECT WE'RE IN TROUBLE, SO WE'VE GOTTA HUNT FOR A WAY OUT OF HERE!
I'M NOT SURE WE ARE IN TROUBLE. THINK ABOUT IT: USUALLY, WE CATCH CRIMINALS WHO ARE POSING AS GHOSTS. BUT NOW, THE GHOST IS HAUNTING CRIMINALS. WHO'D WANT TO DO THAT?
YOU MEAN THE GHOST IS REALLY... BATMAN?
COULD BE. WE'D BETTER PLAY ALONG UNTIL--
HEY! LESS CHATTING, MORE DETECTING!
THAT GHOST WON'T CATCH ITSELF, Y'KNOW!
SURE THING! WE WERE JUST, UH, PLANNING STRATEGY.
NO EYEHOLES CUT OUT BEHIND THIS PAINTING.
NO ONE HIDING BEHIND THESE CURTAINS.
LIKE, NOBODY DROPPED A SNACK BEHIND THE SOFA.

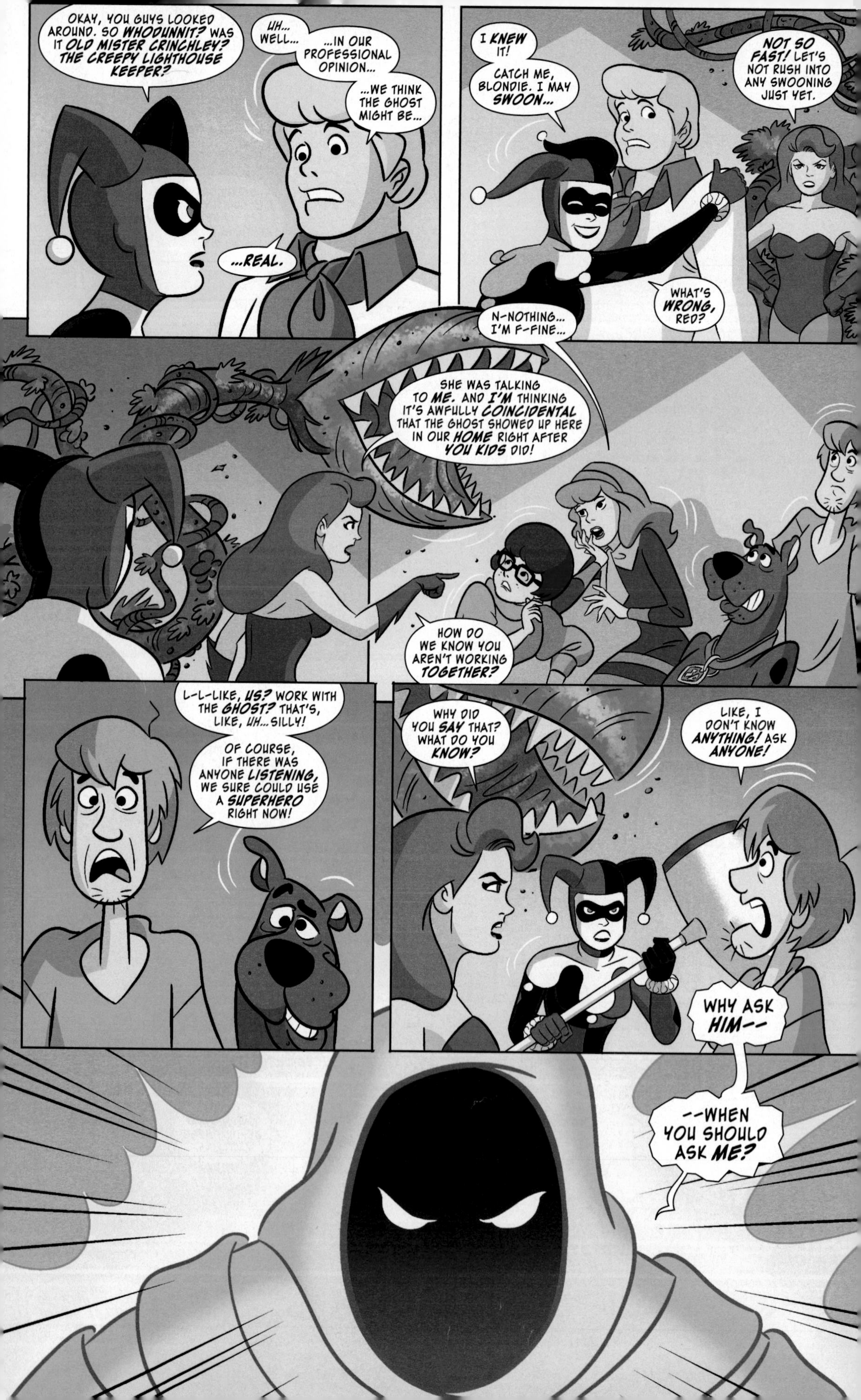
OKAY, YOU GUYS LOOKED AROUND. SO WHODUNNIT? WAS IT OLD MISTER CRINCHLEY? THE CREEPY LIGHTHOUSE KEEPER?
UH... WELL...
...IN OUR PROFESSIONAL OPINION...
...WE THINK THE GHOST MIGHT BE...
...REAL.
I KNEW IT!
CATCH ME, BLONDIE. I MAY SWOON...
NOT SO FAST! LET'S NOT RUSH INTO ANY SWOONING JUST YET.
WHAT'S WRONG, RED?
N-NOTHING... I'M F-FINE...
SHE WAS TALKING TO ME. AND I'M THINKING IT'S AWFULLY COINCIDENTAL THAT THE GHOST SHOWED UP HERE IN OUR HOME RIGHT AFTER YOU KIDS DID!
HOW DO WE KNOW YOU AREN'T WORKING TOGETHER?
L-L-LIKE, US? WORK WITH THE GHOST? THAT'S, LIKE, UH... SILLY!
OF COURSE, IF THERE WAS ANYONE LISTENING, WE SURE COULD USE A SUPERHERO RIGHT NOW!
WHY DID YOU SAY THAT? WHAT DO YOU KNOW?
LIKE, I DON'T KNOW ANYTHING! ASK ANYONE!
WHY ASK HIM--
--WHEN YOU SHOULD ASK ME?

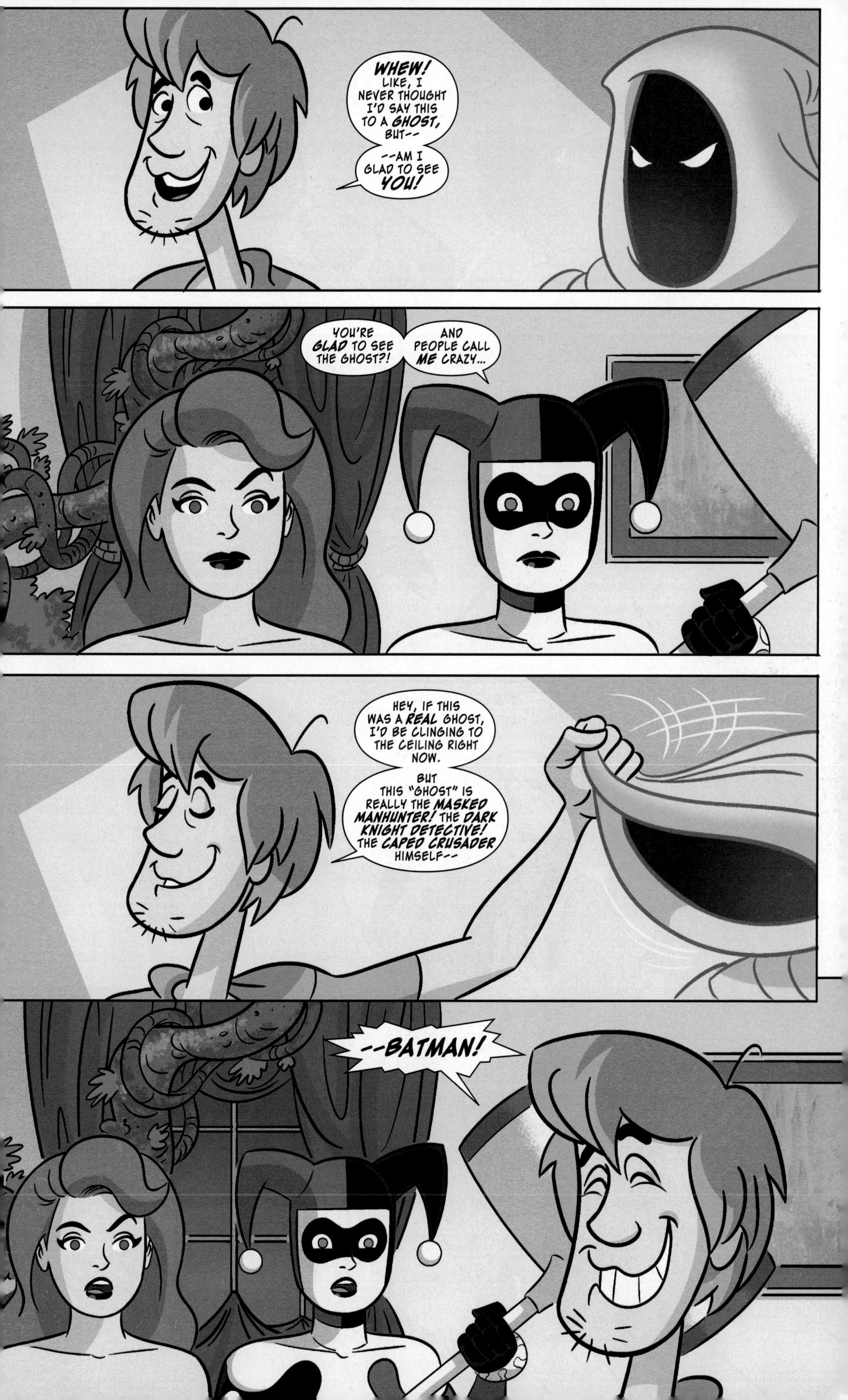
WHEW! LIKE, I NEVER THOUGHT I'D SAY THIS TO A GHOST, BUT--
--AM I GLAD TO SEE YOU!
YOU'RE GLAD TO SEE THE GHOST?!
AND PEOPLE CALL ME CRAZY...
HEY, IF THIS WAS A REAL GHOST, I'D BE CLINGING TO THE CEILING RIGHT NOW.
BUT THIS "GHOST" IS REALLY THE MASKED MANHUNTER! THE DARK KNIGHT DETECTIVE! THE CAPED CRUSADER HIMSELF--
--BATMAN!

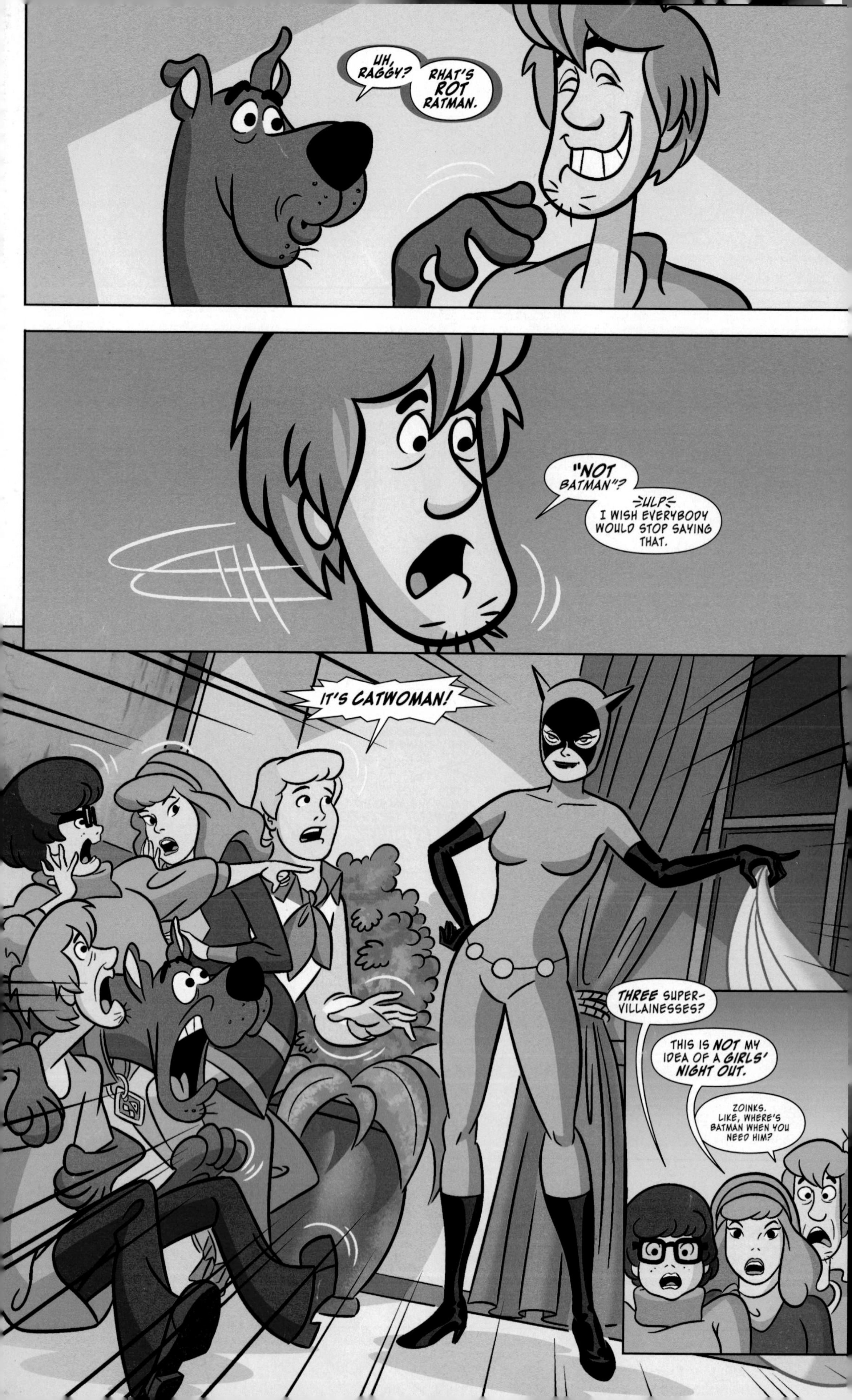
UH, RAGGY?
RHAT'S ROT RATMAN.
"NOT BATMAN"?
ULP
I WISH EVERYBODY WOULD STOP SAYING THAT.
IT'S CATWOMAN!
THREE SUPER-VILLAINESSES?
THIS IS NOT MY IDEA OF A GIRLS' NIGHT OUT.
ZOINKS. LIKE, WHERE'S BATMAN WHEN YOU NEED HIM?

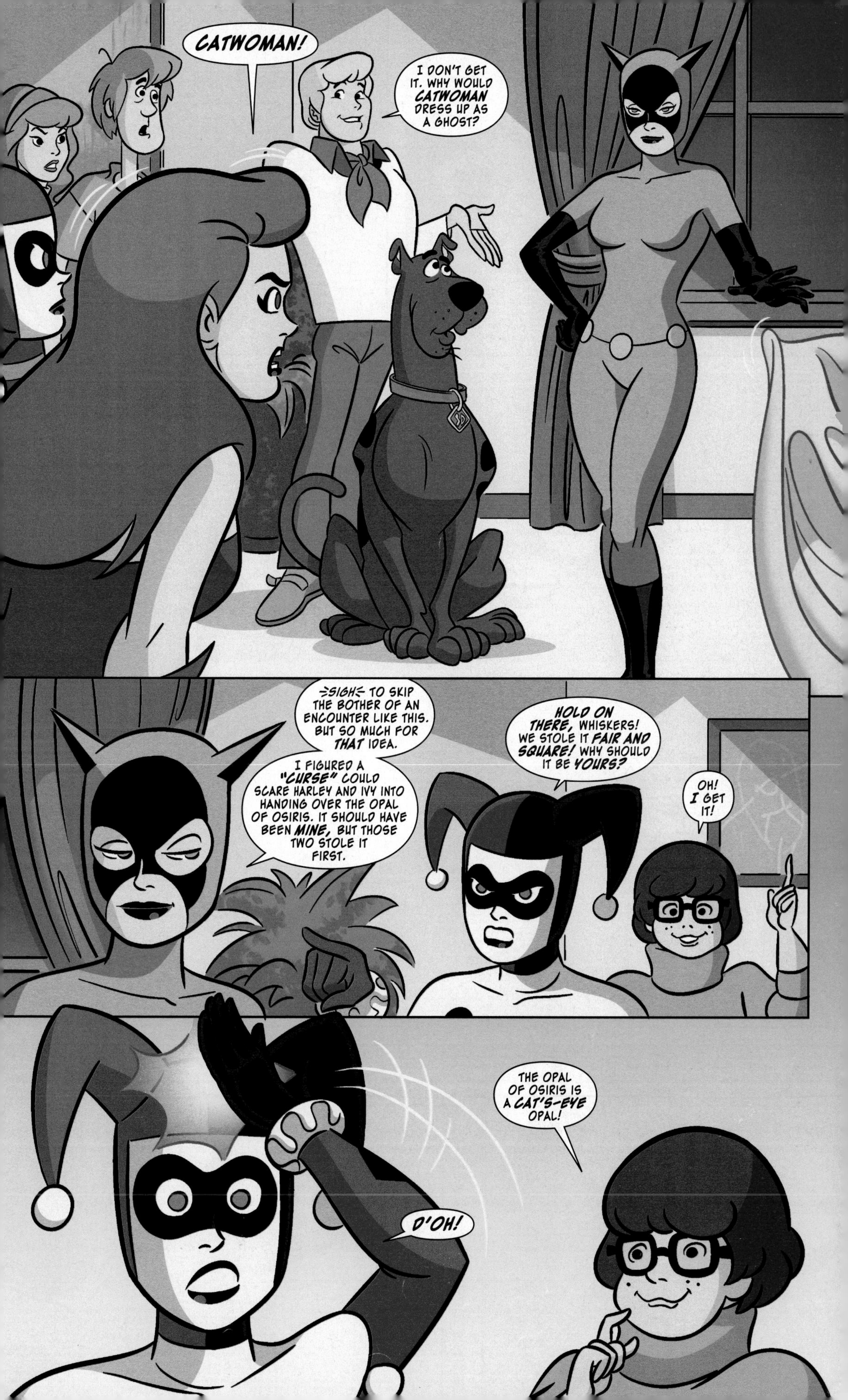
CATWOMAN!
I DON'T GET IT. WHY WOULD CATWOMAN DRESS UP AS A GHOST?
I FIGURED A "CURSE" COULD SCARE HARLEY AND IVY INTO HANDING OVER THE OPAL OF OSIRIS. IT SHOULD HAVE BEEN MINE, BUT THOSE TWO STOLE IT FIRST.
=SIGH= TO SKIP THE BOTHER OF AN ENCOUNTER LIKE THIS. BUT SO MUCH FOR THAT IDEA.
HOLD ON THERE, WHISKERS! WE STOLE IT FAIR AND SQUARE! WHY SHOULD IT BE YOURS?
OH! I GET IT!
THE OPAL OF OSIRIS IS A CAT'S-EYE OPAL!
D'OH!

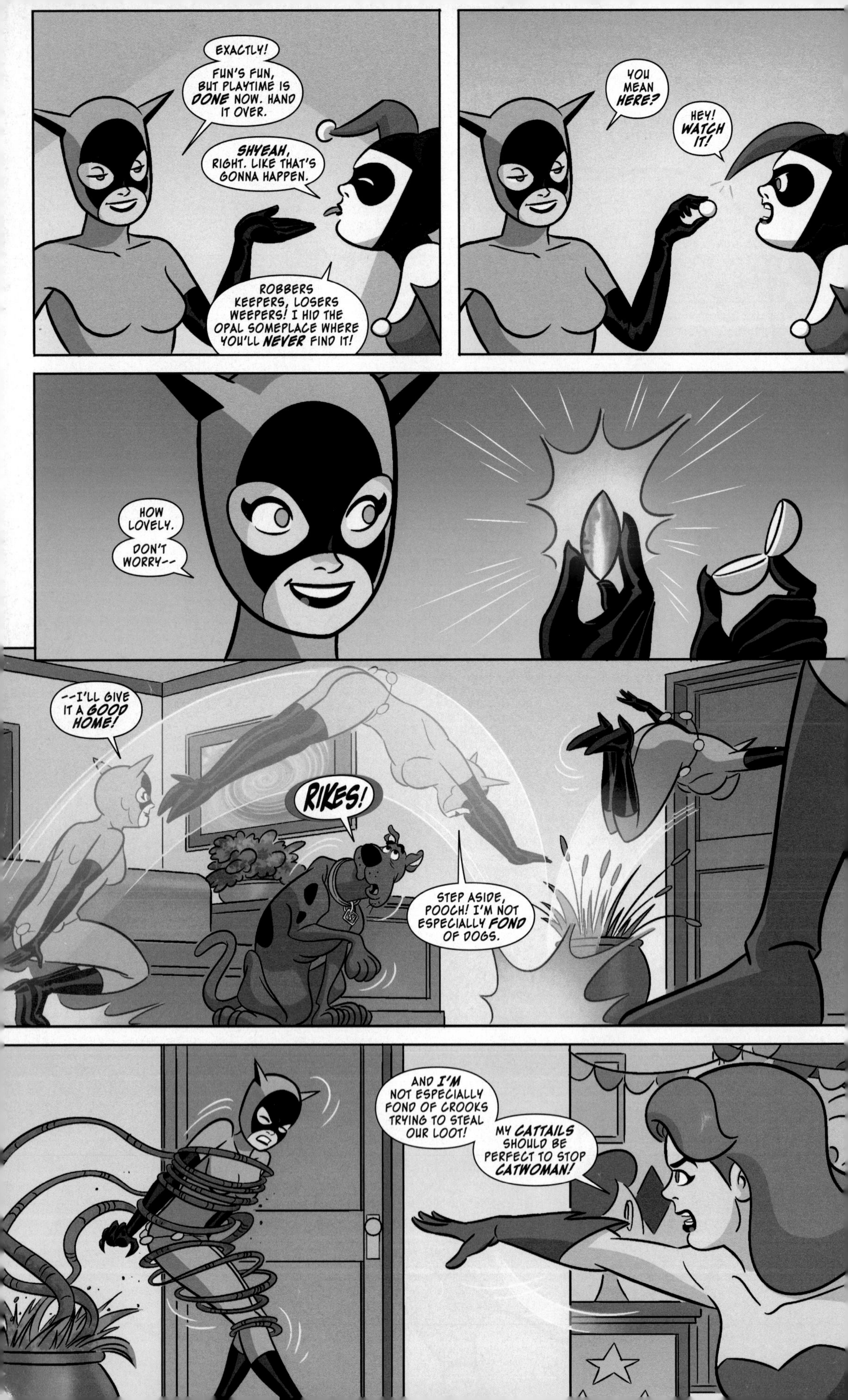
EXACTLY!
FUN'S FUN, BUT PLAYTIME IS DONE NOW. HAND IT OVER.
SHYEAH, RIGHT. LIKE THAT'S GONNA HAPPEN.
ROBBERS KEEPERS, LOSERS WEEPERS! I HID THE OPAL SOMEPLACE WHERE YOU'LL NEVER FIND IT!
YOU MEAN HERE?
HEY! WATCH IT!
HOW LOVELY.
DON'T WORRY--
--I'LL GIVE IT A GOOD HOME!
RIKES!
STEP ASIDE, POOCH! I'M NOT ESPECIALLY FOND OF DOGS.
AND I'M NOT ESPECIALLY FOND OF CROOKS TRYING TO STEAL OUR LOOT!
MY CATTAILS SHOULD BE PERFECT TO STOP CATWOMAN!

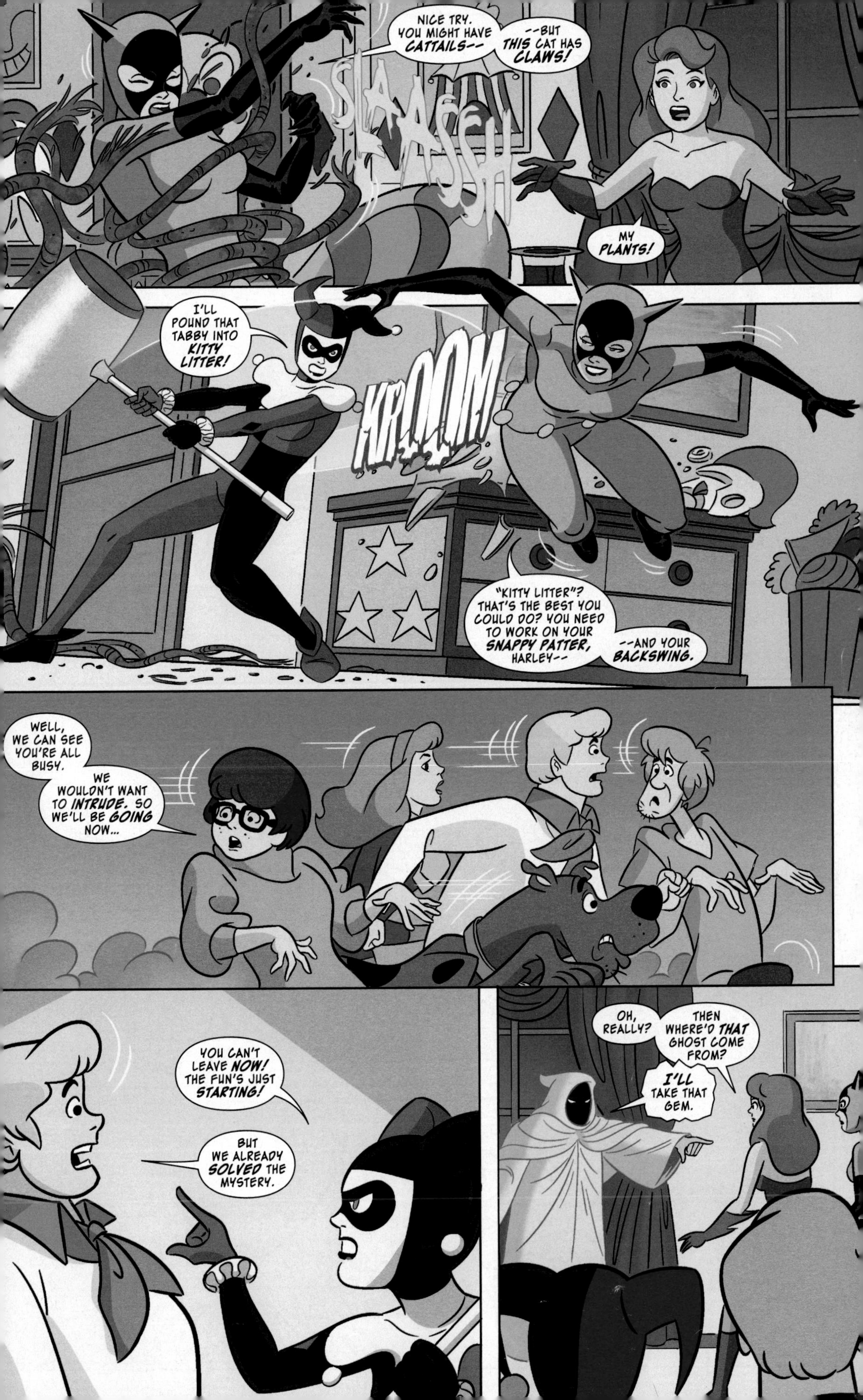
NICE TRY. YOU MIGHT HAVE CATTAILS--
--BUT THIS CAT HAS CLAWS!
SLAASSH
MY PLANTS!
I'LL POUND THAT TABBY INTO KITTY LITTER!
KROOM
"KITTY LITTER"? THAT'S THE BEST YOU COULD DO? YOU NEED TO WORK ON YOUR SNAPPY PATTER, HARLEY--
--AND YOUR BACKSWING.
WELL, WE CAN SEE YOU'RE ALL BUSY.
WE WOULDN'T WANT TO INTRUDE. SO WE'LL BE GOING NOW...
YOU CAN'T LEAVE NOW! THE FUN'S JUST STARTING!
BUT WE ALREADY SOLVED THE MYSTERY.
OH, REALLY?
THEN WHERE'D THAT GHOST COME FROM?
I'LL TAKE THAT GEM.

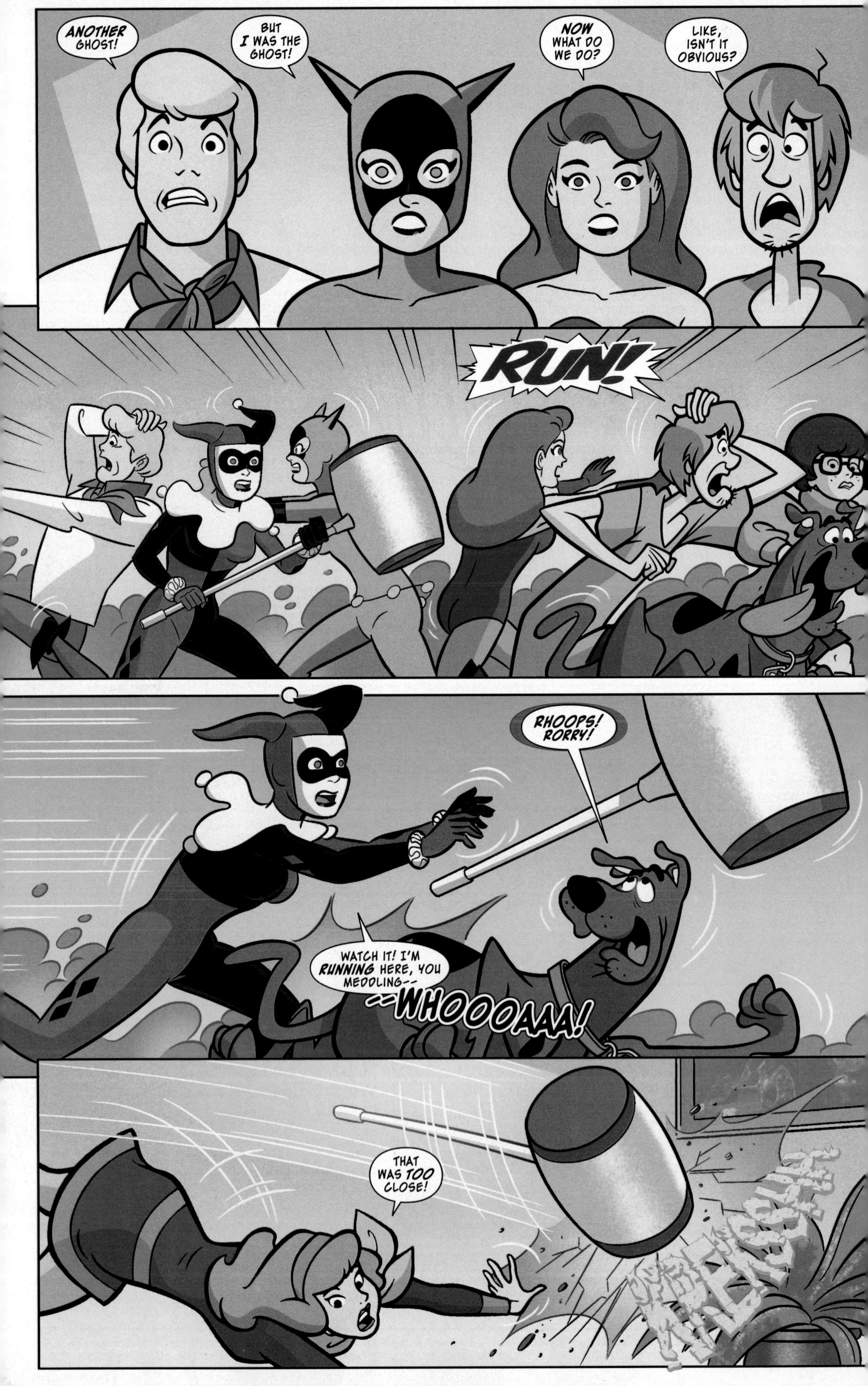
ANOTHER GHOST!
BUT I WAS THE GHOST!
NOW WHAT DO WE DO?
LIKE, ISN'T IT OBVIOUS?
RUN!
RHOOPS! RORRY!
WATCH IT! I'M RUNNING HERE, YOU MEDDLING--
--WHOOOAAA!
THAT WAS TOO CLOSE!

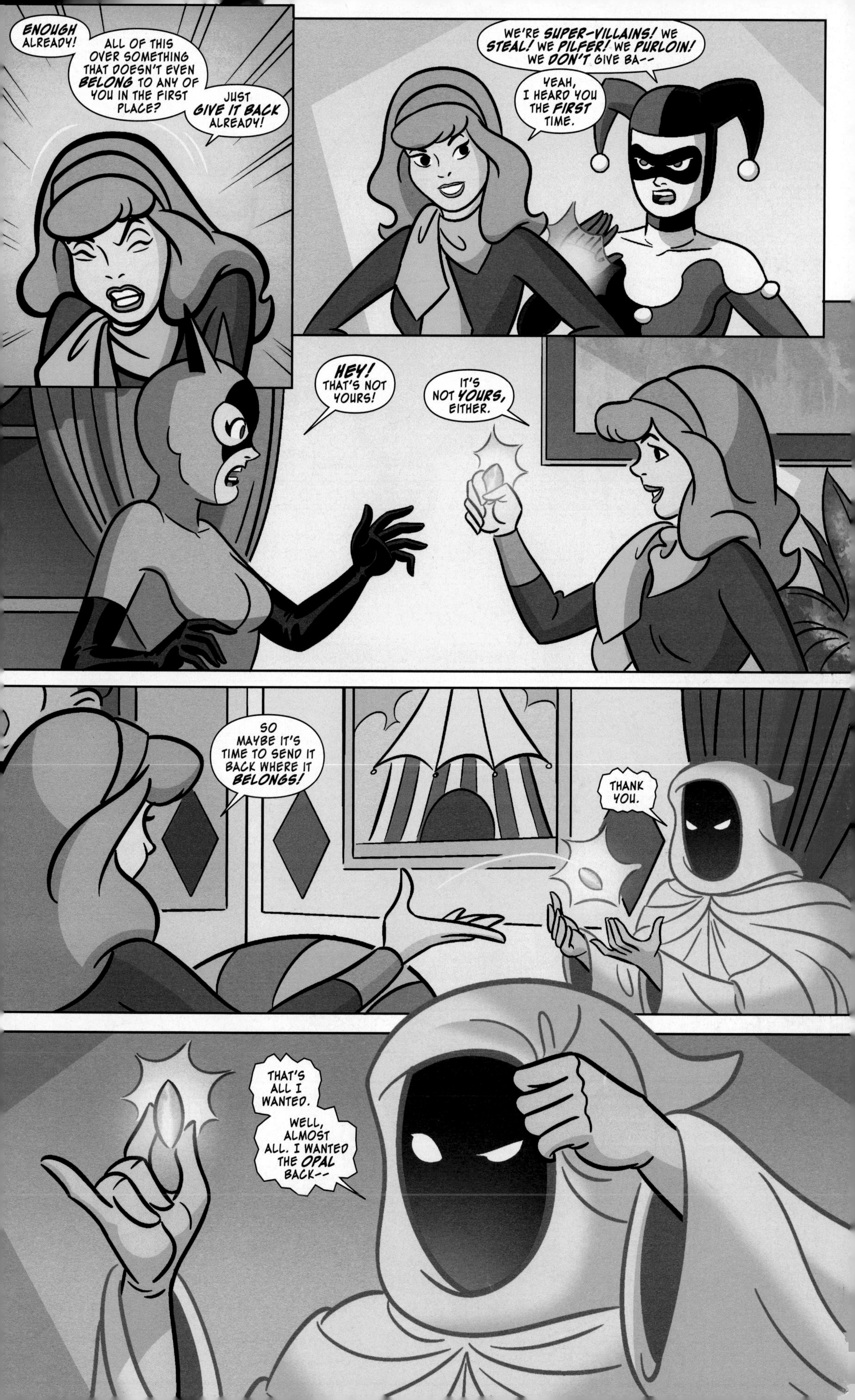
ENOUGH ALREADY!
ALL OF THIS OVER SOMETHING THAT DOESN'T EVEN BELONG TO ANY OF YOU IN THE FIRST PLACE?
JUST GIVE IT BACK ALREADY!
WE'RE SUPER-VILLAINS! WE STEAL! WE PILFER! WE PURLOIN! WE DON'T GIVE BA--
YEAH, I HEARD YOU THE FIRST TIME.
HEY! THAT'S NOT YOURS!
IT'S NOT YOURS, EITHER.
SO MAYBE IT'S TIME TO SEND IT BACK WHERE IT BELONGS!
THANK YOU.
THAT'S ALL I WANTED.
WELL, ALMOST ALL. I WANTED THE OPAL BACK--

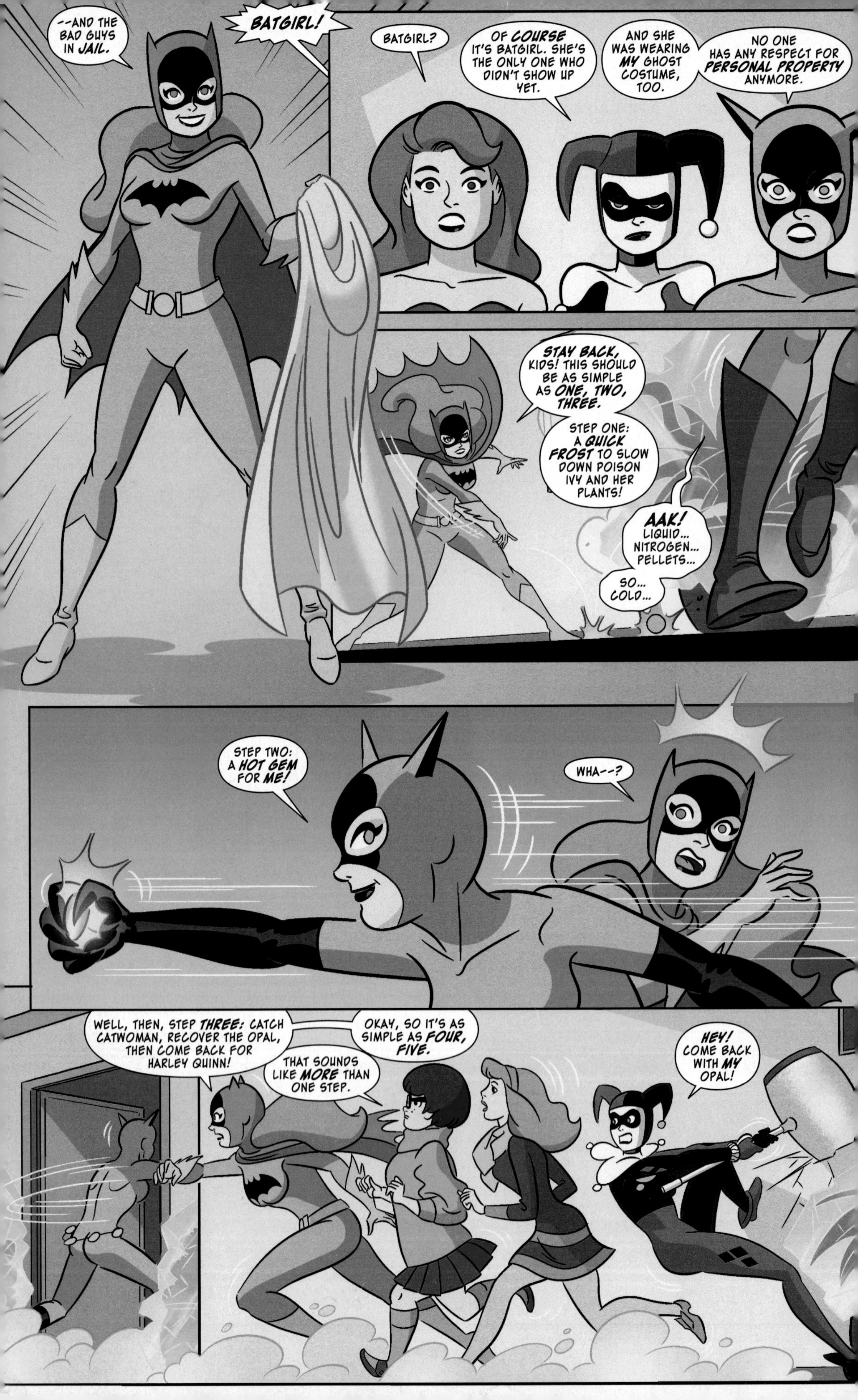
--AND THE BAD GUYS IN JAIL.
BATGIRL!
BATGIRL?
OF COURSE IT'S BATGIRL. SHE'S THE ONLY ONE WHO DIDN'T SHOW UP YET.
AND SHE WAS WEARING MY GHOST COSTUME, TOO.
NO ONE HAS ANY RESPECT FOR PERSONAL PROPERTY ANYMORE.
STAY BACK, KIDS! THIS SHOULD BE AS SIMPLE AS ONE, TWO, THREE.
STEP ONE: A QUICK FROST TO SLOW DOWN POISON IVY AND HER PLANTS!
AAK! LIQUID... NITROGEN... PELLETS...
SO... COLD...
STEP TWO: A HOT GEM FOR ME!
WHA--?
WELL, THEN, STEP THREE: CATCH CATWOMAN, RECOVER THE OPAL, THEN COME BACK FOR HARLEY QUINN!
OKAY, SO IT'S AS SIMPLE AS FOUR, FIVE.
THAT SOUNDS LIKE MORE THAN ONE STEP.
HEY! COME BACK WITH MY OPAL!

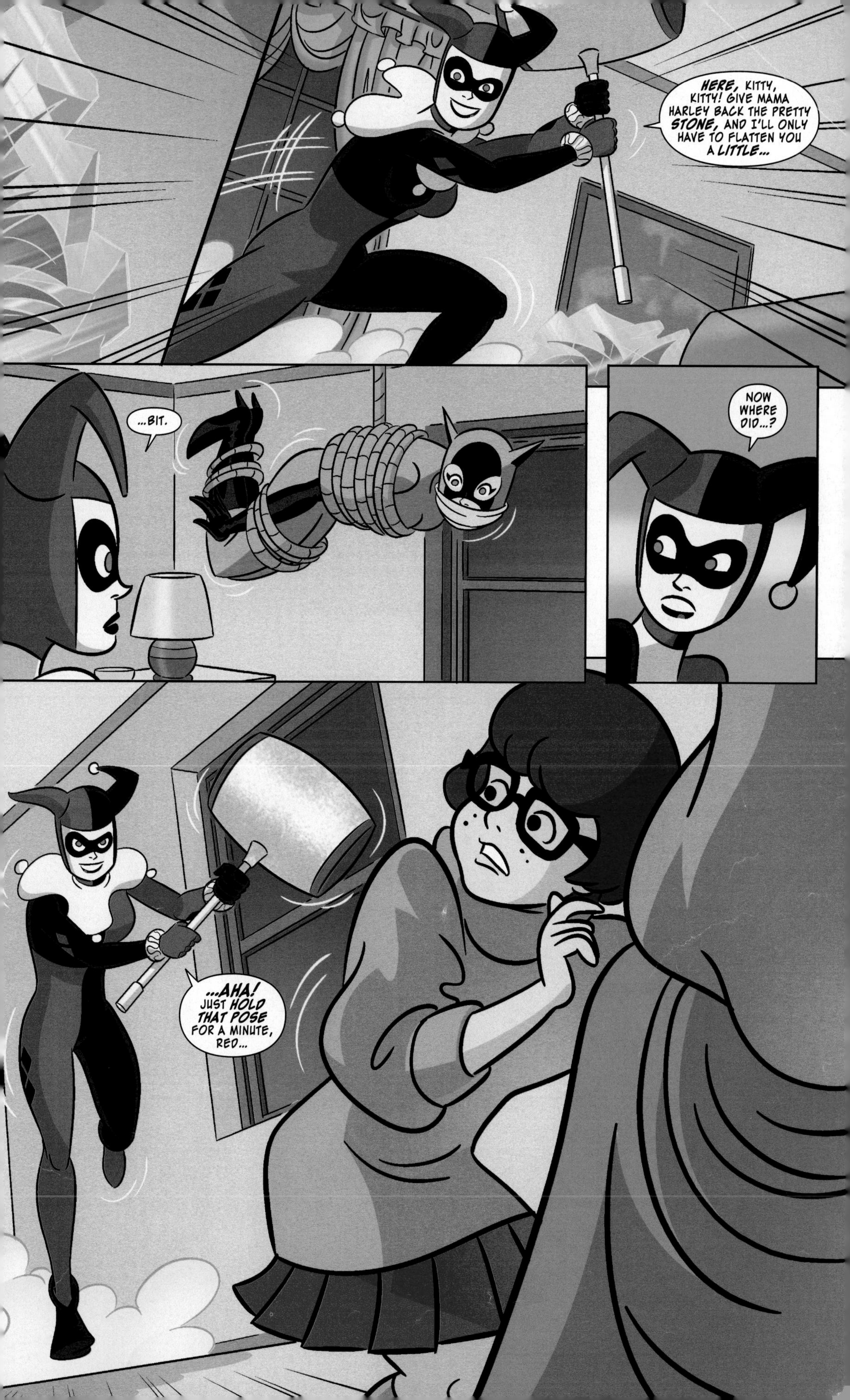
HERE, KITTY, KITTY! GIVE MAMA HARLEY BACK THE PRETTY STONE, AND I'LL ONLY HAVE TO FLATTEN YOU A LITTLE...
...BIT.
NOW WHERE DID...?
...AHA! JUST HOLD THAT POSE FOR A MINUTE, RED...

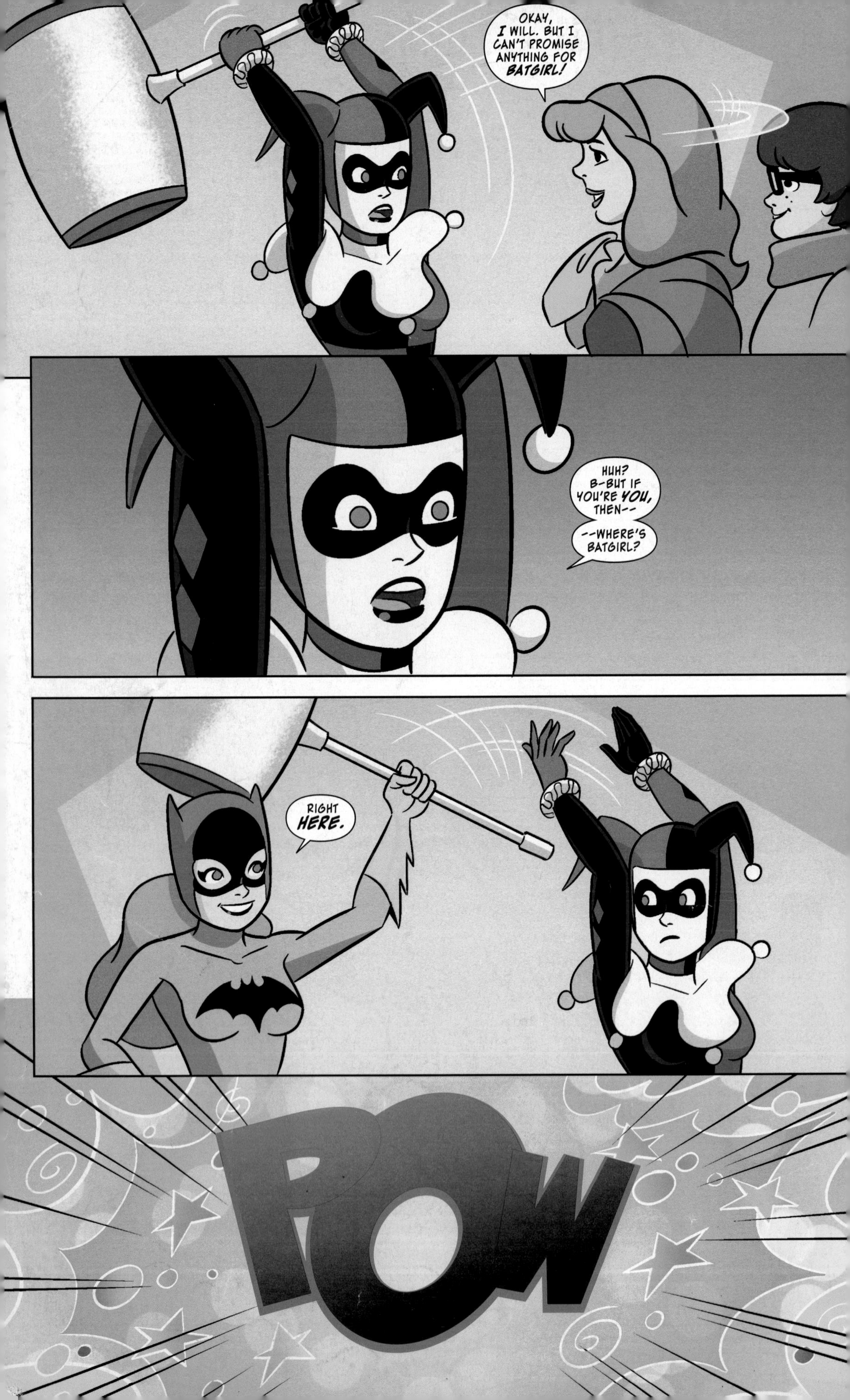
OKAY, I WILL. BUT I CAN'T PROMISE ANYTHING FOR BATGIRL!
HUH? B-BUT IF YOU'RE YOU, THEN--
--WHERE'S BATGIRL?
RIGHT HERE.
POW

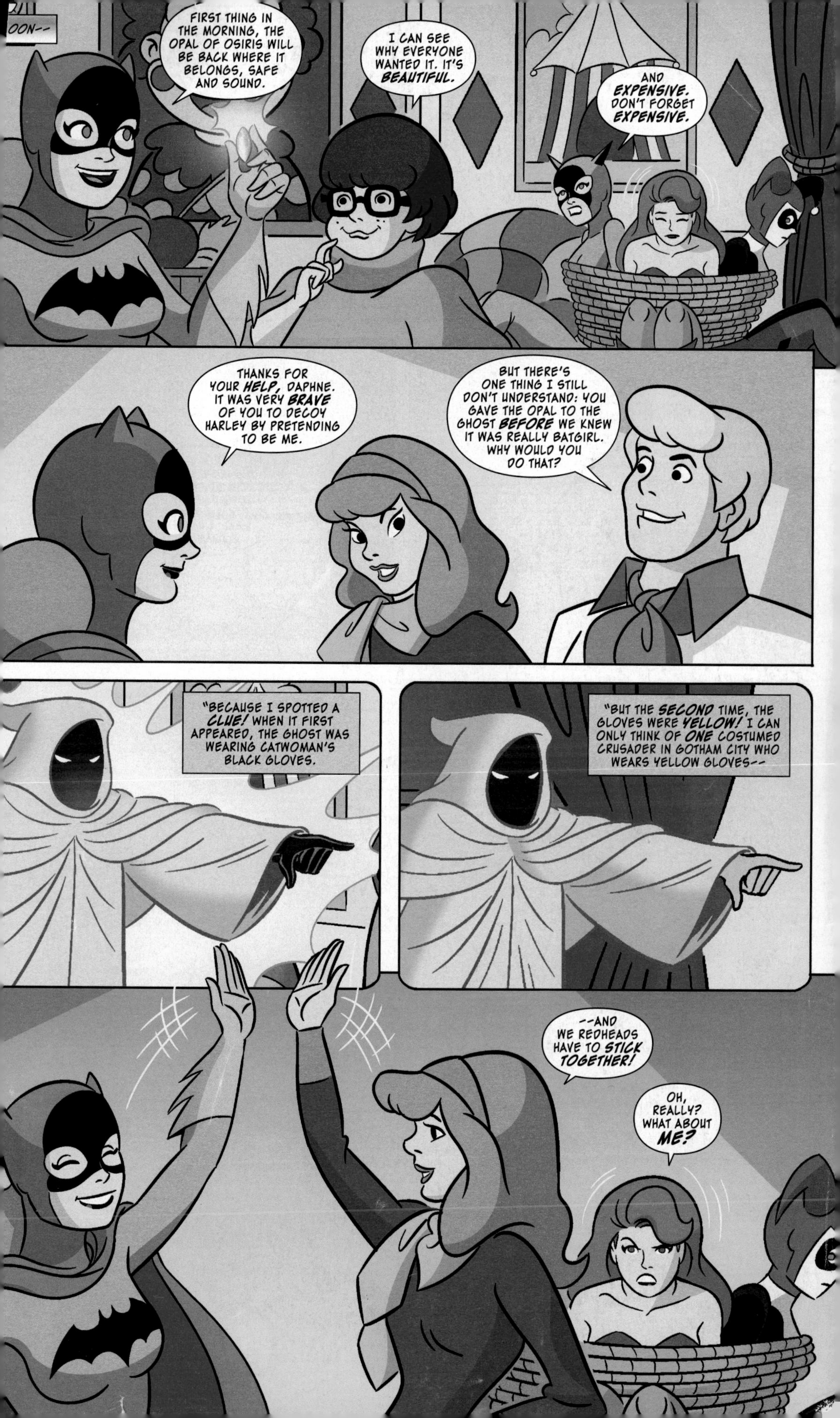

OON--
FIRST THING IN THE MORNING, THE OPAL OF OSIRIS WILL BE BACK WHERE IT BELONGS, SAFE AND SOUND.
I CAN SEE WHY EVERYONE WANTED IT. IT'S BEAUTIFUL.
AND EXPENSIVE. DON'T FORGET EXPENSIVE.
THANKS FOR YOUR HELP, DAPHNE. IT WAS VERY BRAVE OF YOU TO DECOY HARLEY BY PRETENDING TO BE ME.
BUT THERE'S ONE THING I STILL DON'T UNDERSTAND: YOU GAVE THE OPAL TO THE GHOST BEFORE WE KNEW IT WAS REALLY BATGIRL. WHY WOULD YOU DO THAT?
"BECAUSE I SPOTTED A CLUE! WHEN IT FIRST APPEARED, THE GHOST WAS WEARING CATWOMAN'S BLACK GLOVES.
"BUT THE SECOND TIME, THE GLOVES WERE YELLOW! I CAN ONLY THINK OF ONE COSTUMED CRUSADER IN GOTHAM CITY WHO WEARS YELLOW GLOVES--
--AND WE REDHEADS HAVE TO STICK TOGETHER!
OH, REALLY? WHAT ABOUT ME?

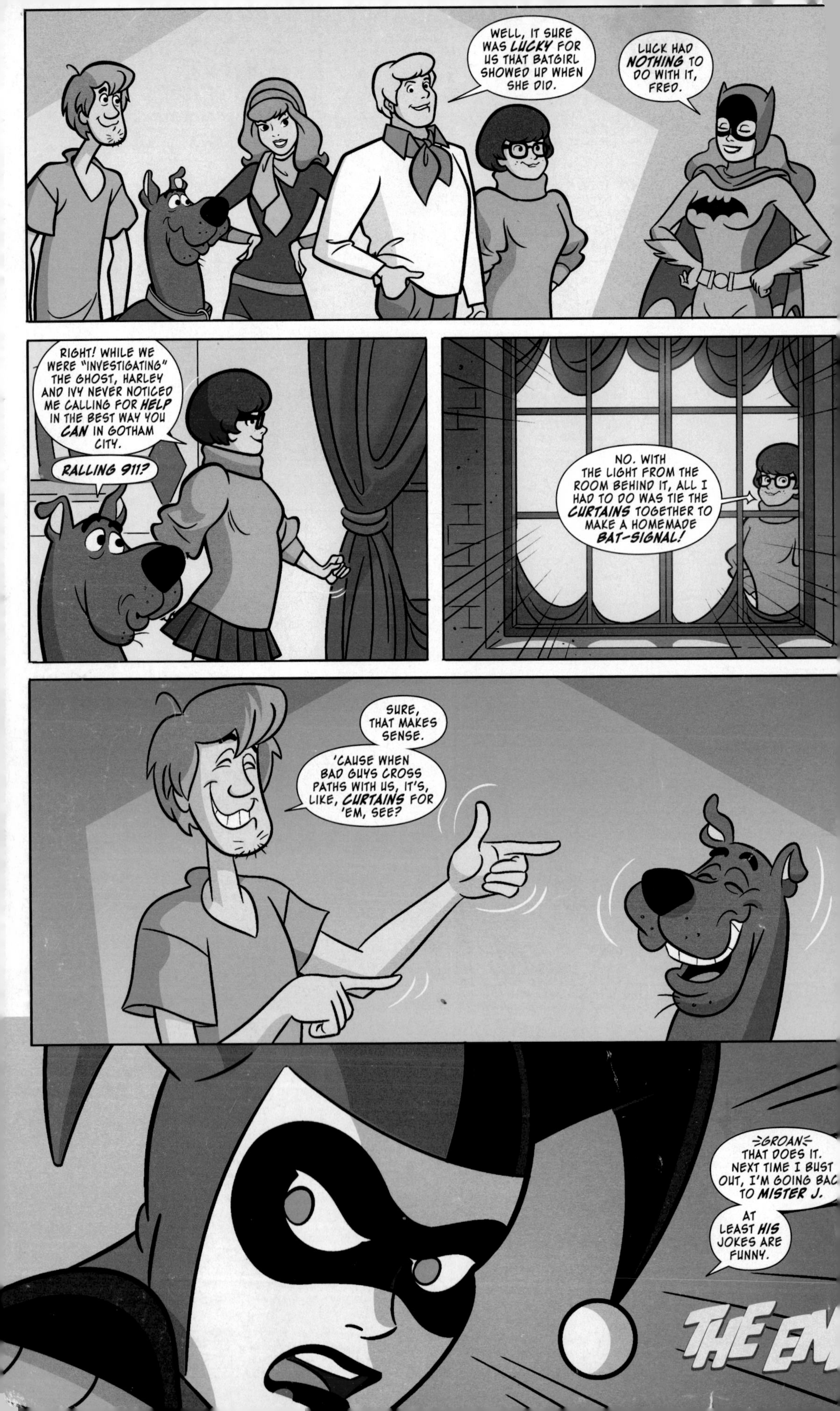

WELL, IT SURE WAS LUCKY FOR US THAT BATGIRL SHOWED UP WHEN SHE DID.
LUCK HAD NOTHING TO DO WITH IT, FRED.
RIGHT! WHILE WE WERE "INVESTIGATING" THE GHOST, HARLEY AND IVY NEVER NOTICED ME CALLING FOR HELP IN THE BEST WAY YOU CAN IN GOTHAM CITY.
RALLING 911?
NO. WITH THE LIGHT FROM THE ROOM BEHIND IT, ALL I HAD TO DO WAS TIE THE CURTAINS TOGETHER TO MAKE A HOMEMADE BAT-SIGNAL!
SURE, THAT MAKES SENSE.
'CAUSE WHEN BAD GUYS CROSS PATHS WITH US, IT'S, LIKE, CURTAINS FOR 'EM, SEE?
=GROAN= THAT DOES IT. NEXT TIME I BUST OUT, I'M GOING BAC TO MISTER J.
AT LEAST HIS JOKES ARE FUNNY.
THE EN